BONANZA BELLE

A NOVEL

ELAINE ULNESS SWENSON

BONANZA BELLE
First Printing, October 1999

All rights reserved.
Copyright© 1999, Elaine Ulness Swenson

All rights reserved internationally. No part of this publication may be reproduced, stored in a retrieval system, or transmitted in any form or by any means, electronic, mechanical photo-copying, recording, or otherwise, without the prior written permission of the author or publisher, except by a reviewer who may quote brief passages in a review.

Interational Standard Book Number 0-9642510-6-X

Printed in the United States of America

Bonanza farms were a phenomena of the Red River Valley of the North in the late 1800's and early 1900's. They came about when wealthy financiers from the East, who owned securities from the financially troubled Northern Pacific Railroad, made good on their holdings by obtaining cheap land from the railroad's large land grant.

Many of these huge farms, which were planted almost entirely in wheat, were very successful for a time. The demise of these farms came about because of a variety of reasons, some of which were taxation, land and wheat prices, and labor troubles, to name a few.

Nevertheless, it was an exciting and colorful time in the history of American agriculture.

The main characters in this story are entirely fictitious, but all references to the Ulness family are true, as far as the author could ascertain.

Other works by Elaine Swenson:

FIRST THE DREAM

DEDICATED TO THE MEMORY
OF MY PARENTS

CARL ULNESS
(1904-1997)
BEATRICE HEGLIE ULNESS
(1905-1970)

CHAPTER 1

Spring Grove, Minnesota - 1908

Hot tears stung Carrie's eyes as she tried to keep her face averted from the gaze of other family members in the wagon. It was a fine April morning, with nary a cloud to blemish the bright, azure sky. The Amundson family was returning from church to their farm home, which was about a three-mile drive from town. Carrie couldn't wait to get home to run and hide someplace and digest the startling news that she had just heard. Her impatience grew as they neared their farm, which was nestled in a grove of large, old cottonwoods.

As Papa drove up the narrow driveway and stopped in front of the white, two-story house, Carrie was the first to jump out, followed by her brothers, Amund and Martin, and her two sisters, Sylvia and Rosina.

Papa helped Mama down, taking her hand and bowing over it. He kissed it, and said, "Just like the aristocrats!" This gesture always brought squeals of laughter from the children and Mama would just smile sweetly.

Seventeen-year-old Carrie was already on her way to find some privacy. She knew she would not find any in their small house so she took off in the direction of the outhouse. No one would follow her there. She went around back of the little structure and headed for her favorite cottonwood tree. She plunked down on the north side of it so she would not be visible from the house. Now she could let the tears flow freely.

"How could he? How could he do this to me?" she cried aloud. A cow by the fence nearby turned his head slowly and looked at her. She buried her head in her hands and sobbed.

That morning, after church services, members of the congregation were standing in clusters of conversation outside the church. Carrie had heard the pastor's wife tell some other ladies that Ted, the woman's son, was engaged to a girl from back East and would be getting married in the summer. Carrie had stood frozen in shock and disbelief.

She, Carrie, was supposed to be marrying Teddy someday! Hadn't he just asked her late last summer, before he went away to school again, if she would be his sweetheart? It was at the church ice cream social. He had taken her hand and led her behind the church and asked her that question and she had said, 'yes', and then he had asked if he could kiss her and she nodded her head. Then he took her in his arms and gave Carrie her first kiss. She thought that she had never felt anything so thrilling.

Remembering all this now brought shame and humiliation and her cheeks burned. To think that all this time she had thought that she was his girl and she had been writing to him every week. She even dreamed of the day that they would be married, although he had never said anything about marriage thus far. He had answered her letters occasionally and told her that he would see her at Christmas time. Then he had written and said that he was too busy to come then but would come for sure at Easter time. Next week was Easter Sunday! This thought brought a fresh batch of tears and she didn't hear her older sister, Sylvia, calling her.

"Carrie! Carrie, where are you?" her sister called. "Ma wants you to come help with dinner."

Carrie tried unsuccessfully to wipe her face with her hankie before Sylvia could see her.

"Carrie, what's the matter?" Sylvia asked, surprised to find her younger sister in such a state.

Knowing that she would have to explain things sooner or later, Carrie got up and started back to the house with her sister.

"Didn't you hear what Mrs. Gunderson was telling everyone this morning?" she asked Sylvia.

"No. What?" Sylvia answered, stopping in her tracks and taking Carrie's arm.

"She said that Teddy is engaged to a girl from back East and that he is getting married soon!" said Carrie, sniffling again.

"What!" Sylvia almost shouted. "I thought you and he had sort of an understanding."

"I thought so, too, but apparently he saw it differently. I wonder how many other girls he has, wondering the same thing."

"Oh, Sylvia," she went on, "I could just die! I thought Teddy and I would be married someday and I've been writing to him every week. Oh, what a fool I've been."

"You had every right to expect that he felt the same about you." Sylvia tried to comfort her sister. "Didn't you notice anything different about his letters as time passed?"

"Not really. They didn't come very often but I thought it was because he was busy with school and work."

"Carrie! Sylvia!" It was their mother calling. "Dinner is ready."

The girls hurried toward the house. Carrie tried to remove the evidence of her tears, but was not too successful. The rest of the family was settling in at their places at the table so the girls slid quickly into their usual spots on the long bench.

Papa waited patiently for everyone to settle in and then he folded his hands and bowed his head. Everyone followed suit.

"Our Heavenly Father, we thank you for this food that we are about to eat and for these loved ones gathered around this table today. May this food nourish our bodies and enable us to do Thy will on this earth." Then the whole family joined in saying the Norwegian table prayer together.

"Where were you, Carrie?" asked Rosina, as the food was being passed around the large, oval table.

Sylvia came to Carrie's rescue by saying that they were using the outhouse and then got to talking. Carrie gave her older sister a look of gratitude but she could see her mother's gaze upon her.

I'll have to tell Mama about this, Carrie thought to herself. She can always tell if something is wrong.

Carrie was silent throughout the meal and was the first one to jump up and start getting the dishwater ready for doing up the dishes.

"My, Carrie is really anxious to do dishes today, isn't she?" Amund teased her. "Usually she takes off for outside with some other chore on her mind."

The rest of the family got up and Papa went to lie down and have his Sunday nap and the children took over clearing the table. Mama also went and sat in a chair to rest awhile. Papa insisted that this was how it would be on Sundays. Mama should rest and the children would clean up.

Carrie starting washing and by the way that she was slinging the dishes around, everyone was aware that something was wrong. The atmosphere was tense in the kitchen. The boys hurried outdoors and Rosina and Sylvia each grabbed a dishtowel and started drying.

"What's wrong, Carrie?" Rosina whispered.

When Carrie didn't answer, Sylvia said, "We'll tell you later, outside." This had to satisfy Rosina for the time being.

With the cleaning up done, the three sisters left the house quietly and started for their favorite place. There was a little clearing amongst the cottonwoods a short distance from the barn. The grass was tall and soft. This area was their playhouse as little girls and they still came here often and sat on the stumps that Papa had moved there for them.

"Ok, what's wrong, Carrie?" demanded fourteen-year-old Rosina, standing with hands on her hips. The other two had sat down, one on the grass and one on a stump.

Carrie sighed and began to tell her younger sister just what she had told Sylvia earlier. Tears pricked her eyes but she was determined not to cry again. At least not until later, when she was alone.

When she had finished explaining to Rosina what was the matter, they saw their mother walking towards them. They fell silent and watched her approach. Their mother, who was in her early forties, was still an attractive woman, even after having six children and working so hard all her life. She was of medium height and build but had a long neck, which made her look taller and almost regal. Her hair was blonde, but now was beginning to show streaks of gray.

All three daughters very much resembled their mother and the boys took after their father, who was darker and had brownish, curly hair. The girls always complained that the boys got the curly hair and theirs was "straight as a stick," as Mama would say.

Mama sat down on a stump and looked from one daughter to the next. How dear these girls are, she thought, and how lovely, all three of them. Sylvia stood and pulled Rosina by the sleeve.

"Come on, Rosy, let's go see what the boys are up to today," she said, wanting to leave Carrie and Mama alone.

Rosina got up and the two girls walked towards the barn.

Mama moved closer to Carrie and looked at her and said, "Can you tell me what's bothering you today, Carrie?"

"Didn't you hear what Mrs. Gunderson was telling everybody after church?"

"No, I was talking with Mattie over by our wagon. What did Mrs. Gunderson say?"

Carrie told her mother everything, all the while keeping her vow not to start crying again.

"I know how hurt you must feel, and how betrayed," her mother said. She put her arm around her daughter and they were both silent for some time.

"Carrie, you probably don't want to hear this right now, but maybe Ted wasn't the right one for you."

As Carrie started to protest, her mother continued. "Maybe he isn't the one you're supposed to marry."

Carrie hesitated. "I just thought that Teddy and I would be so happy together. I had even planned our wedding in my mind. Oh, Mama, I feel so foolish!"

"You needn't feel that way, Carrie. Just hold your head up and pray about it and God will show you the way to get through this. Maybe He has someone really wonderful in mind for you."

With this, Mama got up to leave. "I'll let you sit here alone for awhile. Remember, this trouble will pass and things will look brighter, very soon, I promise you."

Carrie sat and pondered these things for quite some time. She decided that she would not let this get her down. She would hold her head high, as her mother said, and not let others know the pain in her heart.

Later, when Carrie returned to the house, she saw her oldest brother, Olaf, and his wife, Mattie, coming up the road in their wagon. They usually drove over every Sunday afternoon and had supper with the family. They lived about three miles away in a little house that had been vacated several years ago. It was in poor shape but they were making the best of it. They had been married about a year now and Mattie was expecting a baby in a few months.

Around the supper table, the conversation went from spring planting, to house repairs, to the new baby coming, and to the new people who had moved in up the road.

The new neighbors were from Norway and could barely speak any English. "I feel sorry for them, " Mama said, "for I remember how hard it was for us when we first came to this country."

The Amundson family, consisting then of only Papa, Mama and baby Olaf, had come to America back in 1885 from the Hallingdal region of Norway. They were young and full of hope and enthusiasm for a better future. They spent one year in Wisconsin near a settlement of other Norwegians who had come earlier. Papa had worked on a farm there and then they decided to move farther west and get a little farm of their own.

They came to Spring Grove, in Minnesota, because they knew there were others from their homeland living there. They were able to buy a small farm from a fellow who decided to return to Norway. His wife couldn't take it here any longer, he told them. She found it so different and the language barrier too great a problem. They were an older couple and it was hard for them to adapt.

Carrie's parents, Knut and Oline, were determined that they would not let that happen to them. They set about learning the ways and language of their new country. This came easier for Knut, as he was out and about with people more often than his wife was. She was home alone more, with their small children, which now included a new baby, Sylvia. Then came Amund, Carrie, Rosina and Martin.

Over the years, Oline did manage to speak English fairly well but had more difficulty writing it. She and Knut were determined that their children get a good education and they all went to the school which was built about a mile from their farm. Only Rosina and Martin were still attending it.

After supper, Amund told about the letter he had just received. It was from his good friend, Peter Larson, who had gone to the Dakotas about a year ago. He was now working on a large, bonanza farm in North Dakota, in the Red River Valley. This farm, he wrote, was unbelievably big. It was owned by the Daud family from back East, and they farmed over 9,000 acres! Almost all of it in wheat!

He had been told that there were other bonanza farms even bigger than this in the Valley. 'Imagine that, Amund,' he had written. He had started working on the Daud farm a year ago and was still there. They had asked him to stay over the winter and help care for all the horses and mules. There were over 200 of them!

Amund read the last paragraph aloud to the family:

> Why don't you come out here, Amund, and join me in North Dakota? I talked to the foreman and he said he would have work for you. I told him you were good at fixing things. Let me know as soon as possible if you are interested in coming. It would really be great to have you here.
>
> If any of your sisters want to come, too, there is always a need for another hired girl.
>
> Your friend,
> Peter

The men discussed this phenomenon of bonanza farming while the women washed up the dishes once again and talked about babies and housekeeping.

After Olaf and Mattie left, Rosina and Martin went off to bed as they had school the next day. Papa sat down to read a newspaper that Olaf had brought over and Mama sat in the rocker and took up her mending.

Carrie sat at the kitchen table and her eye fell on Peter's letter. She picked it up and read it. She laid it down and stared off into space, thinking.

Her parents went off to bed as Amund came in from the barn. He joined her at the table after pouring himself a cup of coffee from the stove.

"Did you read Peter's letter?" asked Amund, excitement in his voice.

"Yes, I did." She looked at him sharply. "Mannie," that was her nickname for her brother, "are you actually thinking of going out there, like Peter suggested?"

With a quick glance in the direction of their parents' room, Amund leaned across the table and almost whispered, "Well, I have been giving it some thought."

When Carrie looked at him in surprise, he went on. "I'm almost 20 years old and I don't really want to spend the rest of my life on this farm. You know I've never liked farming very much."

"But Pa needs your help, doesn't he?"

"He and Olaf can handle this quarter that we farm and Marty seems like he really loves farming. He'll be a big help in just a couple more years."

"That's true, but what would Pa say if you tell him you're planning to leave here now?"

Amund ran his hand through his hair and said quietly, "I'm not sure, but I guess I'll soon find out. I was thinking I better discuss this with him tomorrow. I need to let Peter know soon. Spring planting season will be starting there shortly."

"It's soon going to start here, too, Mannie," said Carrie. "Pa would really miss you." Then she added, "I'd really miss you, too."

Amund was quiet for awhile, deep in thought. Without saying more, he got up, folded the letter and put it in his pocket. He headed for the stairs. He stopped and turned to Carrie. "I'm sorry about Teddy. I know you really liked him."

"Thanks, Mannie."

"Good night, then," he said. "We'll talk more in the morning."

Carrie cleared the two coffee cups from the table and went to sit in the rocker. She knew she wouldn't sleep well this night so she tried to read but found she had trouble concentrating. She finally laid the book in her lap and thought about the things that had happened that day.

She closed her eyes and began to pray. "Dear Heavenly Father," she half whispered. "I'm going to need help getting over the shock and humiliation of losing Teddy. Please help me to be strong. Help Amund to make this important decision about leaving home." She started feeling very weary so she hastily finished her prayer and retired to her room upstairs, which she shared with her sisters.

"I was wondering when you were coming to bed," Sylvia said quietly.

Carrie blew out the lamp and crawled under the covers next to her sister. "I didn't think that I'd be able to sleep tonight but all of a sudden I felt so tired," she whispered so as not to wake Rosina, who was asleep in the cot next to their bed.

She rolled over and sighed, signaling that she didn't want to discuss anything further. I'll think about things tomorrow, she thought to herself, as she drifted quickly off to sleep.

It was actually Sylvia who had trouble sleeping that night. She felt sorry for her younger sister. How will this turn out, she wondered?

The next morning, as Carrie was helping put breakfast on the table, she wondered how it was going between Papa and Amund out in the barn. Will he actually tell Papa that he is leaving the farm?

She heard the two men come in the back door and wash up in the wash basin. Amund appeared in the kitchen first and Carrie looked at him questioningly. He averted her gaze. Papa came and sat down at the table and Mama poured him a cup of coffee. Rosina and Martin came running down the stairs, ready for school and Sylvia came in from picking eggs. Amund was the last one to sit down.

After the table prayer, Papa helped himself to pancakes and eggs and took a few bites before looking over at Amund. "Oline," he said to his wife, "our son here has it in his head to go join his friend on this bonanza farm." Everyone stopped eating and waited. "What do you think about that?"

Their mother laid her fork down and looked at Amund. "Well, I was a little afraid of this happening. Do you really think that this is a wise thing to do?"

Amund explained to her what he had told Carrie the night before and what he had told his father just that morning. "I would like to try it, Ma. If I don't like it, I can come home again after the harvest season is over."

"Well, if you don't want to stay here and farm, why would you want to go there and farm?" asked Martin.

"It would be a great adventure, to go someplace far away and to see this big farming operation that Peter speaks of," Amund explained to his younger brother.

"Maybe I can come and join you when I get older," exclaimed Martin, excitement growing in his voice.

"You will need to stay and help Pa for many years yet, Marty, before we talk about your leaving, too!" said Sylvia.

Mama stood up and said, "Rosina. Martin. You better hurry now or you will be late for school."

She went and fetched their lunch pails and gave them each a hug. "Do good in school now, children," she told them.

The men were finishing their second cup of coffee when Olaf rode up on his horse. He came into the house and his mother poured him a cup, too. He sat at the table and took a cookie to have with his coffee.

"So, are we going to start planting the wheat today or do you think it's too wet yet?" he asked.

His father was silent and so was Amund. Olaf looked from one to another and asked, "What's the matter?" Before anyone could answer he felt he knew what had happened. He and his wife had discussed it on the way home last night. Mattie had said that she bet anything that Amund would go to North Dakota. Olaf was not so sure.

"Your brother thinks he should go and try his hand at big-time farming," Papa told Olaf. Amund was silent.

"What do you think about that, Pa?" asked Olaf.

"Well, I could sure use him here, all right. Especially now with spring planting about to start."

"Pa, I know this isn't a good time to leave you, but you and Olaf can handle it, I'm sure," Amund said, trying to sound convincing. "Marty can help after school and on weekends."

Papa sighed and stood up and said, "Well, we better get busy. We can't sit around here all day when there's work to do. We'll talk about it later."

It was not discussed again by anyone the rest of the day. The men decided it was dry enough to get started with the planting so they were very busy. Martin helped when he got home and the girls did some of the barn chores. Everyone was very tired at suppertime and no one brought up the subject of Amund's leaving.

One by one, the members of the family went off to bed. When Oline slid into bed beside her husband she could tell that he was still awake. She put her hand on his shoulder and said, "Well, Knut, what do you think about Amund leaving, then?"

Knut gave a big sigh and rolled over to face his wife. "I don't want him to leave but I suppose he is a grown man now, and will have to do as he sees fit."

"I don't want him to go, either," said Oline, "but I can understand his wanting to get away from here and see other parts of the country. He never has cared much for farming. I'm sure you could see that."

"Yes, I guess I always knew he wouldn't be a farmer if he could help it."

"We were about his age when we left Norway for the biggest adventure of our lives and I know our parents didn't approve of our going, did they?" Oline commented, as she snuggled down into the quilts on this cool, spring evening.

"I was thinking about that today and that's why I can't tell him that he can't go. He'll have to do what he wants to do," Knut said.

"I guess that's right. Our family is growing up and some will be leaving us." Oline thought for awhile and then said, "It's too bad what happened to Carrie, too, but I'm sure she'll get over that in time." When Knut made no comment, she realized he was already asleep and snoring lightly.

She lay there thinking about each of her children. I won't always have all of them nearby, she thought. They grow up and leave home. That's the way life is supposed to go. She thought also about the upcoming birth of their first grandchild. This would bring great joy to the family. At least Olaf and Mattie live close by, she consoled herself.

CHAPTER 2

The next two days were very busy around the farm. Amund was quiet and preoccupied but did not mention leaving. Carrie wanted to talk to him about it again but the time never seemed right to get him alone.

On Wednesday evening, Sylvia's beau came calling. His name was Rudy Lokken and he lived and worked in town. He tried to come out once or twice a week to see Sylvia. He was kept pretty busy this time of the year at the livery stable and lumber yard to have much time left over for courtin'. He was a hard worker and was trying to save up enough money so he could ask Sylvia to marry him.

"Good to see you again, Rudy," Pa said, as he came in from finishing up the evening chores. "Missed you last Sunday."

"Yah, that Mr. Folstad, he's a slave driver, he is," answered Rudy. "He had me working on a pair of horses that had to be shoed that day and that was that!" Rudy was tall and lean but had very broad shoulders for someone so young. It came from years of hard, physical labor, he would say.

Everyone in the family liked Rudy and flocked around him when he came. In order for he and Sylvia to have some privacy, they took a walk on this balmy, spring evening. Papa settled down with the paper and the girls finished cleaning up the supper dishes. Mama was setting bread dough to rise for tomorrow. Marty was doing homework and Amund had disappeared up in the boys' room.

"It looks like we'll maybe get a fair price for our wheat this year," said Papa, putting down the paper. "Hope we get a good yield."

"I certainly hope we don't get hail like last year," remarked Mama.

"Yah, you can say that again. I never saw anything like that storm we had." He was thoughtful for sometime.

"I think we should buy some more land and plant more wheat and maybe try some corn," Papa went on. "Olaf thinks we should rather put that money into a larger dairy herd."

He got up and went to get a drink of water from the pail in the pantry. He drank a big dipperful. "I think I'll be heading to bed. You coming, Ollie?" he asked his wife.

"I have some overalls to patch first," she answered. Turning to Marty and Rosina she said, "You children be off to bed now."

"Oh, I can't wait till school is over," wailed Rosina. "Only a couple of weeks left."

"I'll be happier about that than you, Rosy," said Martin. "Then I can help Pa from early morning till night."

A short while later, Sylvia and Rudy came back from their walk and sat out on the porch. Only Carrie was left in the kitchen. She was sitting by the table looking at the dress pattern in the paper. She thought that maybe she should send for this one. It had a new look, which she liked.

Through the screen door, Carrie saw Rudy stand and prepare to leave. She couldn't help but watch when he took Sylvia in his arms and kissed her goodbye. This made her heart ache anew, remembering the one and only kiss she had received from Teddy. Tears threatened to reach the surface, so she hurriedly put away the newspaper and was heading for the stairway when Sylvia came in and closed the door. Sylvia had a dreamy look on her face.

"Did you have a nice time with Rudy?" Carrie asked, a lump forming in her throat at the look of happiness on her sister's face.

"Oh, yes, we always enjoy being together."

She and Carrie ascended the steep, narrow stairs. Sylvia had noticed the tears in Carrie's eyes. When they reached their room, she whispered, "How are you doing, Carrie? Does it still hurt just as much?"

"When I see you and Rudy together, and how happy you both seem, that makes me think of how it could have been, should have been, with me and Teddy."

"Oh, Carrie, I don't know what to tell you. I feel so bad for you."

The girls undressed quietly in the dark and crawled under the covers at the same time.

"When I stop to really think about it, I feel anger and humiliation at the same time."

"Do you think he will write to you and tell you the news himself?" asked Sylvia.

"Well, that would be the right thing to do, but I really don't expect to hear from him. He never wrote very often and he was always so evasive," Carrie said, sitting up and plumping up her pillow.

"Maybe that should have been a clue that he wasn't thinking along the same lines as you were," Sylvia volunteered.

"Maybe, but it really never entered my head that he didn't feel the same way about me as I did about him."

Rosina tossed in her sleep and the two older girls settled down and soon drifted off to sleep themselves.

Only three days left till Easter, Carrie thought to herself the next morning. Oh, I just can't bear the thought of seeing Teddy again. What am I going to do, she asked herself as she hurried downstairs to help prepare breakfast. Mama was already stirring up some pancake batter and the bacon was sizzling in the pan.

"You girls slept late this morning," Mama remarked to Carrie, and to Sylvia who also entered the kitchen just then.

Carrie looked at the clock on the mantle. "I guess we did, at that."

The men came in then and washed and sat down to eat. The girls joined them after everything was set on the table. Mama poured coffee for everyone. The two younger children hadn't come down yet.

Sylvia was eating in a hurry, as this was the day that she usually went into town to help out at Mrs. Narveson's dress shop. She went one or two days a week and then brought work home with her to sew on.

"I'll get the wagon and horses ready for you as soon as I finish eating," Papa said to Sylvia.

"Mange takk, Pa. I slept a little late this morning, it seems."

Amund cleared his throat and blurted out an announcement. He patted his shirt pocket and said, "I've written to Peter, telling him that I am coming." He stopped and waited for everyone's reaction. There was silence for awhile. He looked at Papa, waiting for some argument.

"Well, Amund, I was afraid that this was going to happen but you will get no further argument from me. You will have to do as you see fit."

"When will you be leaving?" asked Mama, an ache forming in her throat.

"I thought I'd better get going in about two weeks. I'll wait till I hear back from Peter."

"Well, I'll have to get all the work out of you that I can before you leave then," Pa remarked dryly, as he left for the barn. "You can help Olaf clean out the stalls this morning."

"Sylvia, I thought I'd send this letter along with you to mail at the post office," Amund said, "and here's money for a stamp."

"I'd better be going now." Sylvia left the rest of her breakfast and hurried to get her things. Carrie helped her carry a finished dress and hat out to the wagon.

"And who is the lucky one to get that beautiful dress and hat, I wonder?" asked Carrie, as she covered them with a sheet to keep them clean during the trip to town.

"I don't know for sure, but Mrs. Folstad said that it was for a lady from over by Mabel. It's always fun to see the garments and hats that I've worked on being worn by someone later."

"I wish I could go into town with you, Sylvia," said Carrie longingly, "but I can't be away all day like that. Ma will need me to help clean and bake today."

"Yah, I suppose I won't be back until almost suppertime." Sylvia climbed up into the wagon seat and took the reins.

"Have a good day," Carrie called after her. Amund came out and headed for the barn. "You have a good day, too, Mannie, doing your favorite job," Carrie teased. She knew that cleaning out the barn stalls was one of the things that her brother hated most. He made a face at her but kept walking. I'm sure going to miss him, thought Carrie. I hope he doesn't like it there and then he'll be back.

Sylvia always enjoyed her ride into town by herself. It felt good to be getting away from the farm and all the chores once in awhile. She met several other wagons going the other way and everyone greeted her with a cheerful, "Good dag." On her way to Mrs. Narveson's, she always drove the street that took her past the livery barn to see if she could get a glimpse of Rudy, but this morning she was disappointed.

Her employer's house was right off the main street so it was a good place for a business. When Mr. Narveson had passed away unexpectedly at quite a young age, his wife decided to start up a little business in her home. She turned the front parlor into a room where she would meet her customers and show them her selection of fabrics and such. A back bedroom was used for the sewing. Sylvia and another woman shared the one sewing machine and much of the work was also done by hand. Sylvia especially enjoyed fashioning the hats and was getting quite good at it.

During the noon hour, Rudy stopped by to see her as he often did if his work allowed. They would eat their sandwiches together on the back porch. Mrs. Narveson brought them coffee.

"This morning," Rudy began, "I heard a couple of men talking and they mentioned that Ted Gunderson would be coming home tomorrow and bringing his 'fancy lady' from back East along with him to meet the family. How is that for a bit of news?"

Sylvia's eyes grew big and she stopped eating. "You don't say! Wait till I tell Carrie."

"You know, I shouldn't say this, but I never did care much for that Ted. He always seemed a little arrogant to me. Like he thought he was so much better than the rest of us fellows just because he was a preacher's son."

"I guess I didn't know him very well, but Carrie seemed to think he was wonderful," Sylvia said. "She sure isn't looking forward to having to face him on Sunday at church, I tell you!"

Finishing his sandwich, Rudy rose and said, "I have to hurry back now. I'll see you on Sunday afternoon, I hope." After looking around in all directions, he leaned over and gave Sylvia a quick peck on the cheek.

"Goodbye," she said, smiling brightly at his retreating back. "Don't work too hard," she called after him as he waved from the street. I sure do love that man, she thought, with a skip in her step as she went back to work herself.

Carrie and Mama were busy all day, cleaning and getting everyone's clothes ready for Easter Sunday. Carrie worked with a growing dread in her heart. I can't face him and everybody else on Sunday, she said over and over to herself. What shall I do?

"You certainly are quiet today, Carrie," remarked Mama, while they were peeling the potatoes for supper.

"Ma, I just don't know how I can face Teddy. I won't know how to act."

"Remember what I told you. Just hold your head high and act as if nothing is the matter."

"That's easy advice to give, Ma, but not easy to do," Carrie complained.

"Have you been praying about this, Carrie?" Mama asked.

"Of course!" answered her daughter. "Every night and sometimes all day long!"

"Well, then, God will take care of everything," Mama said matter-of-factly.

Carrie had no answer for this but was mulling something over in her mind.

That evening after the supper dishes were done, Sylvia suggested to Carrie that the two of them take a walk. Carrie was only too willing to get out of the house for awhile.

"Ma and I sure turned that house upside down today. I'm all in!"

The two automatically went around back of the house and headed for the clearing in the cottonwoods. The evening was cool almost to the point of being chilly.

"We should have grabbed our shawls," said Sylvia, crossing her arms and hugging them close for warmth.

"Oh, I'm so warm from working so hard all day, I don't think I'll cool off till morning," laughed Carrie.

They each sat down on a stump and Sylvia said, "Carrie, I have something to tell you that I found out today and I could hardly wait to get you alone."

"What is it?" asked Carrie, facing her sister.

"Well, Rudy said he heard some men talking and they said that Ted is coming home tomorrow and he's bringing his 'fancy lady', as they called her, home with him!"

Carrie was stunned. "You mean she will be in church with him on Sunday?"

"It would appear so," answered Sylvia.

"Oh, I just can't face them both. I don't want to see either one of them," Carrie wailed.

"How can you avoid it?" inquired Sylvia.

"Maybe I just won't go to church that day," said Carrie resolutely.

"But, Carrie, that's Easter Sunday! How could you stay home that day?"

"I don't know, but I've been thinking some about it and now, for sure, I absolutely will not go."

Without a word, the girls got up and started walking. "Maybe, on Sunday morning, I will tell Ma that I'm sick," said Carrie.

"She'll see through that excuse, Carrie."

"Probably so, but maybe she'll also understand how hard it would be for me to go."

The girls continued walking and Sylvia just kept shaking her head, like there wasn't going to be any easy solution to this dilemma.

Carrie stopped and touched her sister's arm to stop her. "Sylvia, can you keep a secret?"

"Of course, I can. What is it?"

"Well, I've been giving some thought to going along with Mannie out to North Dakota."

"What? Carrie, are you crazy?"

"Maybe I am, but it will be awfully hard for me to stay here, especially if Teddy stays here after he's married. I'll want to get far away."

"You don't know that Teddy will settle here. Surely he will go back East," said Sylvia.

"He hinted that he might be starting at the bank in Spring Grove after he graduates."

"Well, when does he graduate?" asked Sylvia.

"Not until next spring. Do you think they will really get married this summer? Why wouldn't they wait until he's finished with school?" wondered Carrie.

"It does sound a bit strange," Sylvia agreed. "Oh, I'm getting so cold, Carrie! Let's go back to the house." They started walking fast and before long they were racing, just like when they were children.

Out of breath, they reached the house at the very same time and came bursting through the back door. Mama nearly jumped up from her rocker, she was so startled.

"My goodness, what is going on?" She looked at her two grown daughters and had to smile at them.

"Were you racing again or was something chasing you?" teased Papa.

The girls were too out of breath to answer. They both went to the water pail for a drink before sitting down at the kitchen table. Carrie gave Sylvia a look that said, don't say anything about what I just told you about my leaving. Sylvia nodded in return.

When they had rested enough, Sylvia took out her sewing and showed Carrie and Rosina the hat that she had to get finished by the next week.

"You're lucky that whoever ordered it doesn't need it for Easter Sunday," Mama said from her corner. "Bring it here so I can see it."

She fingered the fabric and ribbon lovingly. "I wish I could have had a new one this spring," she sighed. Papa looked up from his newspaper at his wife.

"You could have had Sylvia make you one if you needed to, Oline," he told her.

Mama answered, "Oh, I can get along another year with my old one."

"Maybe if there's some ribbon left from this one, I could change the bow on yours, Ma, and then it would look almost like a new one," volunteered Sylvia.

"Well, we'll just have to see. It doesn't really matter, dear." Mama got up and stretched and announced, "I think I'll be off to bed then. It has been a busy day."

When she was out of hearing distance, Sylvia said, "It's always a busy day for Ma. She works too hard."

"I tell her that, too," Pa agreed, "but she has to have everything just so."

"You work too hard, too, Pa," said Carrie. "This farm life isn't an easy life."

"Well, I never heard that hard work ever killed anyone," remarked Papa, as he, too, headed for the stairway. "Good night, girls." Stopping, he turned around and asked, "Where's Martin, by the way?"

"I think he's still out in the barn with Amund," Sylvia said.

"You better go out and tell him to get to bed soon."

"Ok. Good night, Pa."

"I'll go tell him," Carrie said, jumping up and reaching for a wrap by the back door.

"I'll be off to bed then," said Sylvia. "Come on, Rosina, you, too."

Carrie found Amund and Martin sitting in the straw in one of the stalls. Martin's horse, Jack, was lying down beside them. They looked up as Carrie came quietly in and stood looking down at the threesome.

She raised her eyebrows and said, 'My, my, what do we have here?"

Martin stood up. "Jack doesn't seem to be feeling good. He won't eat and he just lays there."

"That's not like him to lie down in the first place," added Amund.

"Well, Marty, Pa said that you should get to bed now. School tomorrow, you know," Carrie reminded her brother. When he hesitated, she said, "You go on in. I'll stay here awhile longer. Perhaps we'll have to call for the vet tomorrow."

Martin reluctantly left the two to keep watch over his horse. "Good night then," he said, patting his horse lightly on the hind side.

Carrie sat down in the straw beside Amund and pulled her shawl around her a little tighter. "It's really cooling off this evening," she remarked.

The horse gave a low whinny and Amund stroked him repeatedly on his neck. "Marty would really feel bad if something happened to his favorite horse."

"Mannie, I've got something to tell you," Carrie blurted out.

Amund stopped what he was doing and looked at his sister. "What is it?"

"I'm thinking about going with you out to North Dakota," she announced and then held her breath, anticipating a negative reaction from her brother.

Amund resumed stroking the animal gently and didn't say anything for a few seconds. Then he said, "Are you sure you really want to do something like that?"

"Now you sound just like Ma and Pa when you told them that you were thinking of going!" she replied hotly.

"Well, this is a real surprise," Amund said. "What made you decide this?"

"I want to get away from here for obvious reasons, and," said Carrie, "like you, I think it would be a real adventure."

"Well, it would be nice to have you come along. Too bad I already sent the letter to Peter just this morning." Amund stood and ran his hand through his hair. "Have you mentioned this to anyone else yet?"

"Only to Sylvia."

"Have you decided for sure then, or are you just thinking about it?" asked Amund.

"Well, let's just say that I'm thinking very seriously about it. I won't mention it to the folks until I'm sure."

"Whew! I wonder what they'll say to that?" questioned Amund. "They'll think I talked you into it."

"No, they won't blame you, Mannie. I'll see to that. I just can't see myself staying around here with.... the way things turned out with Teddy."

The two left the barn and walked slowly back to the house. "What do you think of Ted, Mannie?"

"I sure don't think much of him now, after the way he's treated you, but before that, well, I guess he was an all-right fellow."

"Sylvia said that Rudy didn't care for him. He thought Ted seemed rather arrogant," Carrie informed him.

"Oh, I wouldn't go so far as to say that, but then, I didn't know him too well."

Amund held the screen door open for his sister and then closed things up for the night.

CHAPTER 3

Carrie awoke early on Easter Sunday and looked out her upstairs window to a gray and drizzly morning. That's kind of how I feel myself, she thought. What am I going to do? Ma and Pa expect me to go to church with them, but I just can't. She crawled back into her bed quietly, trying not to wake Sylvia.

She was dozing when Mama came into the girls' room to rouse them and said, "Time to get up now, girls. We'll have a special breakfast and then we need to hurry and get ready for church."

Carrie groaned and turned toward the wall. Her two sisters got up a few minutes later and put on their everyday dresses. "Carrie, get up. Didn't you hear Ma?" asked Rosina.

"I heard her, but I...ah... don't feel well this morning. I'll just stay in bed awhile longer."

Sylvia and Rosina both gave her a long look and then hurried downstairs.

"Ma," Rosina said right away, "Carrie says she doesn't feel well this morning so she's not coming down."

Mama didn't answer right away, then said, "I'll go and check on her after a bit."

The girls set the table and Mama put out the hard-boiled eggs and a platter of thinly sliced cold meats. She opened a jar of cherry sauce and three different kinds of jams and jellies. She cut thick slices of dark bread and arranged them on a plate.

The men came in from doing the chores and Martin came down from upstairs.

"Carrie is still in bed," he announced. "Is she sick or something?"

"She says she doesn't feel well. I'll go check on her," Mama said. "Why don't you all start eating."

Mama hurried up the stairs and into the bedroom where Carrie lay, looking up miserably at her mother.

"Are you sick today, Carrie?" asked her mother.

Carrie didn't know just how to answer, but only turned her head away.

"Oh, so that's how it is," said Mama kindly, sitting gently down on the bed. "You don't want to go to church today because you don't want to see Ted. Is that it?"

Carrie only looked at her with pleading eyes, tears beginning to form in them. "Mama, I just can't bear to see him. Not yet."

Mama took her daughter's hand in hers and squeezed it gently, all the while wondering how she should handle this situation. She knew that she should insist that Carrie get herself out of bed and go to church with the family. But as she looked into her daughter's face, she felt compassion for her and simply said, "Carrie, you'll have to do as you see fit."

She got up and said, "I need to get back downstairs. I'll leave it up to you."

When Mama arrived back downstairs, the family all turned to her with questioning eyes. She didn't know exactly what to say to them. "Carrie, ah...doesn't know for sure yet if she...ah...feels good enough to go with us to church," she stammered.

She quickly turned to the stove and started getting the ham ready to put into the oven. The rest of the family finished eating and the girls started clearing the table. Sylvia heated water to do up the dishes while Papa went to hitch the horses up to the buggy before changing into his Sunday clothes.

"It looks like it's going to clear off soon so maybe we'll have a nice day after all," he said, after coming back in. The women hurried upstairs to change their dresses.

When Mama passed by the bedroom and saw Carrie's form still lying in bed, she knew what Carrie had decided to do. I can't say that I entirely blame her, Mama thought.

Rosina whispered to Carrie, "Are you really sick, Carrie?"

Carrie pulled the covers over her head and said, "I just can't go today, that's all!"

Rosina and Sylvia finished changing in silence and after smoothing down their hair and putting on their bonnets, they left the room without saying more.

Carried waited to hear the horses leaving the yard and then she jumped out of bed and quickly dressed. As she looked out the window, she could see that the skies had cleared and there was a glimmer of sun starting to peek out from the clouds.

Once downstairs, she rummaged around for some leftover breakfast and then settled herself into the rocker. She guiltily reached for the Bible and searched for the Easter story in the Gospel of John and read it over twice. She asked God to forgive her for what she had just done.

Carrie put on an old coat and walked out to the barn. She stopped by the stall where Martin's horse stood. They hadn't had to call the vet, as the horse seemed to improve daily. I wonder what was the matter with him that night, she mused.

Carrie always felt a sense of peace descend on her when she was in the barn with the animals. As a child she had often taken refuge here when she was feeling troubled about something or when she was afraid of being reprimanded for some wrong she had committed. Like the time when she had pulled the head off Sylvia's only doll and thrown it down the well! She had been so mad at her sister but now she couldn't even remember why. Sylvia was devastated and Carrie had never seen Mama so angry with her. She hid in the barn for several hours until Papa had found her upstairs, covered up with hay. She was spanked soundly and sent off to bed without supper. She had to give Sylvia her very own doll and had to do without one until the next Christmas.

After about an hour, she hurried back into the house before the family returned. She went upstairs, took off her shoes, and lay down on her bed. Lying there, she looked up at the cracks in the ceiling. When the girls were younger, they would pick out different shapes that the cracks formed, like the 'big bad bear' and one that looked like a pig's snout. There were some new cracks now, Carrie noticed.

She heard the horses and buggy come in the yard so she put the quilt over her and pulled it up to her neck so as to cover her dress. She heard the front door slam several times and waited for footsteps on the stairs. She heard none for quite sometime; just kitchen noises as the girls helped Mama finish getting dinner ready. There would be potatoes to boil and the vegetables to heat up.

Soon, though, Rosina popped her head through the doorway and said, "Carrie, are you feeling any better?"

"Ah.. yes.. I think I feel better now."

Rosina plunked down on the bed beside her older sister. She looks the most like Mama, Carrie thought, as she looked at her younger sister. Lucky her!

"We saw Ted with his lady friend!" Rosina blurted out in almost a taunting way.

Carrie buried her head in her pillow.

"She was rather pretty, too," the young girl went on. When there was no response from Carrie, Rosina finally got the hint and quickly changed out of her good dress and went downstairs.

Sylvia came in the room quietly and peered down at her sister. She noticed Carrie's shoes by the bed and they had a little bit of fresh mud on them.

"So you have been up and about, I see," she said to Carrie.

Carrie rolled on her back and flung the quilt back. "I guess I can't fool you, can I?"

"Do you think you'll be able to join us for dinner?"

"I sure would like to. I'm awfully hungry and the ham sure smells good!" answered Carrie. "But I suppose after the trick I just played, I better not. I don't deserve anything to eat for a whole week!" she lamented.

"Well, I'll see what Ma says," Sylvia said as she, too, quickly changed her dress. "I have so much to tell you but it will have to wait till later. I have to help with dinner now." She left the room and Carrie turned miserably on her side and looked out the window. The sun was shining brightly now and she longed to get up and resume her normal activities.

Mama stopped by her room a short while later and saw her lying there, fully clothed.

"Seeing as how you are not feeling well today, I suggest you not eat anything. It may not agree with you." Mama said this kindly but with a firmness that said that Carrie may get by with not going to church but she would pay for her little deception by not eating dinner with them.

Carrie was more miserable than ever now. Maybe I just should have gone and seen Ted and gotten it over with. Well, it's too late now. I did what I did and now I must suffer for it.

It was a couple hours later before anyone came up the stairs again. Carrie's stomach was growling with hunger. Sylvia came in and closed the door. She reached into her pocket and pulled out a napkin with some morsels of food on it. There were several small pieces of ham and a piece of bread.

Carrie sat up and ate the food eagerly. "Thank you, Sylvia. Did Ma see you smuggle this out of the kitchen?"

"I think that she did suspect, but she didn't say anything." Then Sylvia added, "You know, Ma is really a very understanding person, isn't she?"

"She certainly had me figured out from the very start. She knew how I felt about going with you today but she let me make my own decision. But, she also knew that she had to give me some form of punishment." Carrie patted the bed and said, "Sit down now and tell me everything!"

Sylvia removed her shoes and sat fully on the bed next to Carrie. "Well, our family had only been seated for a few minutes when I saw from the corner of my eye the Reverend's wife come up the aisle. Following right behind her was Ted and his fiancée. He walked slowly, as if he was trying to show her off. He glanced at our pew and looked at us all quickly. I think I saw a slight look of relief on his face when he didn't see you."

Carrie sighed heavily and put her hands up to her face. "Did you speak to him afterwards?"

"I was so upset with him all during the service that I think that if I would have talked to him, I would have given him a piece of my mind, I tell you!"

"On the way out, he tipped his head in Ma's direction but she wouldn't look at him," Sylvia went on. "His fiancée--oh, by the way, I found out that her name is Birdie McBride. Birdie McBride! Have you ever heard of such a name?" Both girls almost burst out laughing.

"Rosina said that she was pretty. Was she?" asked Carrie, hesitantly.

"I guess you could say that she was pretty, in a fashionable way," Sylvia commented. "Her dress was really something! She was almost overdressed, at least for our little church."

"Now for the best part, Carrie," said Sylvia, sitting up now. "When we were all heading for our buggy, Ted stopped Marty and asked him where his 'other sister' was today!"

Carrie sat straight up in anger. "You mean he couldn't even say my name?"

"Apparently not," said Sylvia, getting up and standing beside the bed.

Carrie got up, too, and she was standing, with her fists clenched in the air just as Mama opened the door. She looked from one girl to the next. "Sylvia, Rudy just came. Didn't you hear him drive up?"

Sylvia hurried to put her shoes on and left mother and daughter alone. Mama sat on the bed but Carrie was too worked up to sit down or even to pretend that she wasn't felling well.

"Mama, did you hear that? He asked Marty where his 'other sister' was today!"

"By 'he,' I assume you mean Ted. No, I didn't hear that." Mama paused for awhile to let Carrie calm down. "I know you're very upset, Carrie, but you will just have to accept the fact that he is marrying someone else and learn how to live with it."

"I know, Mama," wailed Carrie, almost crying again, "but I'm so angry now. I hate that man. I know that we're not supposed to hate anyone, but I can't help it right now."

"Carrie, you must not hate anyone. You'll have to find it in your heart to forgive him. Even if he has wronged you."

"Oh, I can't, Mama," said Carrie, "I just can't!"

"You will in time, dear," Mama said gently. "You must." She rose to leave the room and then turned to add, "You better come downstairs now. It's turned out to be a beautiful day."

"I'll be down shortly, Mama," answered Carrie. She changed into a different dress and was combing her hair when Rosina came into the room.

"Oh, good! You're feeling better, I see. Rudy is here and Olaf and Mattie will be over soon, I'm sure." Rosina skipped out of the room and down the stairs.

Carrie soon followed and while going down the stairs, she thought that 'playing sick' was not much fun and it would be good to join the family again. Papa was sleeping in his chair and Mama was fussing in the kitchen with something. Sylvia and Rudy were out on the porch. Carrie brought out a kitchen chair and joined them.

"It's good to have you up and around again, Carrie," exclaimed Sylvia, with a wink.

"Yes, I hear you weren't feeling well this morning," said Rudy, with a knowing glance at Sylvia.

"I'm all right now," she said. "And how are you, Rudy?" she asked, to change the subject. "Did you make it to church this morning or did your task master make you work again?"

"Oh, I made it all right. If he had made me work on Easter Sunday morning, I think I would have told him to find another man." He shook his head. "I'd like to find another job, that's for sure."

They heard someone coming up the driveway and it was Olaf and Mattie in their buggy. Olaf dropped his wife off by the front of the house and he went to unhitch the horses.

"Hello, Mattie," they all chorused. They hadn't seen her for a week and it looked like she had really 'popped out' in front. Her dress was stretched to the limit. She seemed conscious of this as Rudy jumped up to go and fetch her a chair from the kitchen.

"You're really starting to show a lot, Mattie," Sylvia murmured under her breath, before Rudy came back.

"Yes, I've been sewing some bigger dresses this past week but hadn't finished any of them yet," she said. "Oh, thank you, Rudy," she added, as she sat down in the chair he had retrieved.

Mama came out onto the porch. "Oh, hello, dear," she said to Mattie. "Where's Marty? I want him to get some ice from the ice house for the lemonade."

"Oh, goodie! Lemonade!" exclaimed Rosina, joining the rest of them. "I'll go find him. He's probably in the barn, where he always is."

"It's turning out to be such a warm afternoon, I thought I'd fix some cold drink for us all as a special treat this Easter Sunday," Mama explained, before returning to the kitchen.

"When Marty comes with the ice, Ma, I'll help you serve it," volunteered Carrie.

Papa joined them at this time and Olaf came from the barn. More chairs were brought outside.

Marty came with the ice and Carrie jumped up to go help her mother. The two women soon brought out enough glasses of lemonade for everyone. They all found seats and sat drinking the cold beverage with satisfaction.

"This tastes mighty fine, Ollie," Papa said to Mama. "It's warming up right well, after a cool start this morning."

The women started talking about the church service and what some of the women were wearing and the men launched into one of their favorite topics nowadays, the gas-engine automobiles.

"Mr. Amundson, did you read in the newspaper yesterday about that Mr. Ford from Michigan?" asked Rudy. "He's introduced a new vehicle, the Model T Ford. He thinks it will revolutionize the way Americans get around."

Olaf shook his head. "I don't think it looks too dependable. I wouldn't be in any hurry to try one."

Papa agreed. "Look what happened to the electric car idea. That didn't last very long. I think it's just a craze."

"I think its more than a craze," Amund chimed in, just coming up to the house. Mama handed him a glass. He took a couple of long swallows and sat down on the top porch step. "I think it's the coming thing. The automobile makers will just keep making them better and better until we all are driving one someday."

"We won't be using horses anymore then?" asked Marty.

"Maybe just for farming," Olaf stated.

"Huh, maybe one day we won't be using horses anymore for farming either," said Amund. "Maybe they'll come up with gas-driven machinery."

Everyone laughed at this absurd idea. All except Amund. He was thinking ahead.

"So, Amund, tell me about this trip to the Dakotas that you're planning to take," suggested Rudy.

"Well, I'll be going in another week or two. I'm waiting to hear from my friend Peter. You remember him, don't you?"

"Yah, I have seen him around. Didn't he go out there last year?"

"He's put in one year's work there already and seems to like it all right," answered Amund.

"I was reading about these bonanza farms," continued Rudy, "and they sound fascinating. So huge! My uncle, Ole, who still lives in Norway, wrote and was asking about them. They have been talking about them in the papers there, too. They call that valley of the Red River the 'New Canaan', and he was wondering if that was true, and if so, how come we all haven't moved there!" The men chuckled at this.

"Well, we can't all move there, I guess," said Papa. "I'm sure all the land is taken by now anyway." He had kind of a wistful look in his eyes as he looked beyond his own farmland.

"You know, when I first thought about coming to America," said Papa, looking over at Mama, "that was my dream, to own a huge farm and grow many acres of wheat, just like the papers bragged about." He sighed and continued, "This is all that I could afford but I guess we're better off here than we would have been back in the old country."

"We're doing all right," Mama said, putting her hand on Papa's arm. "We've never regretted coming here, have we, Knut?"

"No, I surely haven't. I had four older brothers so what was there for me there?"

"Don't you ever get lonesome for your family and where you grew up?" asked Mattie. "My parents talk about Norway all the time and how they miss it still."

"I miss my family but not where we grew up," Mama said simply. "It was a very hard life for my parents. They could hardly make a living on that small place. My only regret is that I never got to see them again before they died."

Papa patted her hand gently in understanding. His parents, too, were now deceased.

"I'd like to go back someday and visit my brothers before its too late. They aren't getting any younger!" Papa stated.

The family sat and visited for quite sometime before Mama stood up and said, "I'll go in and fix some supper for us. That ham will make good sandwiches. Rosina, you can come and help me."

CHAPTER 4

The Friday after Easter Sunday, Amund received a reply from his friend, Peter. He said he was excited about having Amund join him. He had talked to the foreman and everything was all set. He gave him advice on the best way to get there and hoped to see him soon.

"After you get your train ticket, drop me a line to let me know what day and time you will be arriving and I'll be there to pick you up," the letter continued.

"I'll drive into town in the morning," Amund told his family at the supper table, "and see what I can arrange and then send off a letter to Peter at the same time." Amund was excited about the prospect of finally leaving and was anxious to get going.

Carrie thought that this was about as good a time as ever to inform everyone of her decision so she worked up her courage and during a lull in the conversation, she blurted out her news.

"I've been giving some serious thought to going along with Mannie out to North Dakota," she told everyone.

There was a collective gasp from all. Mama was the only one to find her voice. "Oh, no, Carrie! Not you, too!" Tears started forming in her eyes but she didn't wipe them away.

"What makes you think you want to go all the way out there, young lady?" asked Papa.

"Yah, why do you want to leave us, too?" chimed in Rosina.

Carrie cleared her throat and spoke. "I just want to get away for a short while. I'll go with Mannie for a few months and see how I like it. I....I just can't stay around here right now."

"It sounds like you have made up your mind for sure. Is that right?" Papa asked

"Yes, I guess so. Mannie can tell Peter in his letter tomorrow." Turning to Mannie, she added, "I'll go with you into town in the morning. We can check out the tickets and everything together."

"Whew! Won't Peter be surprised!" said Amund.

"Well, he said earlier that if any of your sisters wanted to come along, we could," Carrie stated hotly.

"That's true, he did," agreed Amund. "Well, it will be nice having company on the trip out there."

"I wish I were going someplace," wailed Rosina. "There won't be many of us left here."

Mama didn't like this turn of events and she was looking very distressed. The lump in her throat was too big for her to try speaking. She rose and busied herself with clearing up the table. The others were reluctant to move. They didn't want to miss out on any discussion of the forthcoming trip.

Carrie finally rose and started to help her mother and then the others followed, each going their own way.

"Ma, I'm sorry to spring this on you so unexpectedly but I didn't know how else to do it. And with Mannie saying he was going into town tomorrow to get his ticket, well, I had to finally tell all of you what's been on my mind lately."

"I never for one minute thought something like this would happen," said Mama, shaking her head back and forth.

"Well, Ma, I'm past seventeen now and being I won't be planning a wedding soon, I need to get on with my life and find something to do. I don't want to stay around here, the way things turned out."

Mama didn't say anything for awhile, but she kept herself busy washing the dishes. She brushed a tear away now and then. How she loved this middle, strong-willed daughter of hers! How she loved all of her children and it was hard to think of two of them leaving home at the same time.

"Ollie, why don't you come sit out on the porch with me for awhile," suggested Papa. "It's a lovely evening." As he said this, he carried an extra chair out the door.

Mama started to protest but then suddenly took off her apron and left the rest of the dishes to Carrie and joined her husband. Without a word, she took her husband's hand and indicated that he should follow her.

"Let's take a walk, shall we?" She barely got this out before she burst into tears. She was glad that she was out of sight of the house.

Papa put his arm on her shoulder, but words wouldn't come for him either. There was a lump in his throat, too, now. They continued to walk in silence.

After Mama had a good cry and when she had control of herself, she said, "Is this how it's going to be, Knut? Our children grow up and leave us, one by one? I didn't know it was going to hurt so much."

"Well, you know, when Olaf got married, he only moved a few miles down the road so that wasn't so bad, but this," he said, shaking his head, "going all the way out to the Dakotas, that's something else."

"I know now how my mother felt when I left Norway with you and little Olaf," Mama said. "Just think how much that must have hurt! We don't realize these things until we are parents ourselves," she mused.

"We'll just have to accept this turn of events and be happy for them. They're young and eager to see some of life. Let's not make it difficult for them to leave. We have to keep in mind that we did the same thing many years ago," Knut told his wife.

"Remember how excited we were those days before we boarded the ship?" he went on. Mama nodded but didn't answer.

"No one could have changed our minds. We were determined to head for America and that was that! I remember how hard my mother took it, too, but my father didn't have much to say. I guess he knew it was inevitable that at least one of his sons would get 'America fever'." Mama was silent.

"I suggested that he come along," Papa continued, as they turned around at the end of the driveway and headed back to the house. "All he said was, maybe if he had been younger. I always thought of him as sort of the adventurous kind." Mama nodded in agreement.

"So, Ollie, let's get rid of our tears and be happy for our children," Papa said, as he took her arm and urged her to walk a little faster.

"You always make me feel better, Knut," Mama said. "I just was so shocked with Carrie's news. I wasn't prepared for it. She hadn't given any sign as to what she was thinking. Maybe this will be good for her. She will get over Ted sooner, maybe, if she goes away for awhile."

The two of them stepped up onto the porch and Carrie came out just then. She looked from one to the other, a question in her eyes.

Papa indicated that she and Mama were to sit on the two chairs on the porch. "Carrie, you have our blessing on this idea of yours," he said. "We will try to be happy for you and will not stand in your way." He paced back and forth. "You are almost a grown woman now and you will have to do what you see fit."

"Thank you, Pa," Carrie said. "And how do you feel about it, Ma?" she asked, turning to look at her mother.

"The same, Carrie, the same," she replied. "You go and have this little adventure and then maybe you will be ready to come back to us."

"Perhaps that's how it will turn out," Carrie said. "Maybe I'll get so lonesome, I'll come right back before you know it!"

"I'm going in to read the Posten before I turn in," Pa said. "How about you, Ollie?"

Mama rose as she said, "Yah, I have some things to do before bedtime," and she followed her husband into the house.

Carrie got up and wandered over to the barn. Amund and Marty were in there, finishing up the evening chores.

"Well, you sure dropped a bombshell, didn't you, Carrie?" said her older brother.

"I guess I did. I figured I might as well just come out with it. It's been on my mind for days, just how I was going to break the news."

Martin finished giving his horse a pail of oats and then he left the barn.

"Ma and Pa talked it over and they gave me their blessing, so that's a relief," Carrie went on.

"Well, tomorrow we'll go and get our tickets then," said Amund. He blew out the lantern and they headed for the house.

CHAPTER 5

The rhythm of the moving train and the warm sun in the window had lulled Carrie to sleep shortly past noon. Amund was reading a newspaper. They had both risen early that morning to take care of last-minute preparations for their trip. Their father had driven them to Spring Grove, where they boarded the train. They had to transfer in Austin and again in Minneapolis, where they were allowed enough time to walk around a bit. They ate the sack lunch that Ma had packed and they purchased some hot coffee to go with it.

Amund looked over at his sister in the next seat. She was resting peacefully. He leaned his head back and closed his eyes. He was tired, too. He had worked very hard the last few days, trying to help his Pa as much as possible before leaving. Just as he was about to fall asleep, Carrie started to say something, then stopped.

"Oh, Mannie, I'm sorry! I didn't know you were trying to sleep."

"That's all right," he said, sitting up straight. "I'll sleep better tonight if I stay awake all day. I'm not used to napping in the daytime anyway."

"I was so tired," Carrie said, still drowsy. "I didn't sleep very well last night. I was too excited, I guess. And then I'd been trying to help Ma as much as I could, plus trying to finish sewing that black skirt......."

Her voice trailed off into a sigh and they were both silent for awhile. Each was thinking of what lie ahead. Carrie turned in her seat and looked at Manny. "Do you think we made the right decision to leave home and go so far away?"

"Well, I believe that I did and North Dakota isn't so very far away, but I don't know about you, Carrie, if you made the right decision or not."

Carrie raised her chin in determination, glaring at her brother. "Well, if it's right for you then it's right for me, too."

"It's not the same, Carrie," Amund replied. "It's different with men; it's easier for us to leave home and move around and find jobs and things."

When she didn't say anything in reply, he went on. "It might be harder for you out there, in a strange place and all, on that big farm with all those men."

Carrie sighed and Amund noticed a doubtful look on her face. "You aren't having second thoughts now, are you?" he asked her.

"Well, the way you're talking, you don't think I should be going, do you?" she asked pointedly.

"I didn't say that! I guess I just want to prepare you for a big disappointment. Maybe you won't like it and you'll want to go home right away."

"Oh, Mannie, I don't know," she said, putting her hands up to her face. "I hope I did the right thing. I will always see Ma's face, tears running down her cheeks, but trying to look happy for us." Mannie didn't know what else to say, so he leaned back again and closed his eyes. Carrie did the same.

The next thing they knew, the conductor was calling out, "St. Cloud, next stop."

Amund took a small map from his suit pocket. "Let's see now, next will be Sauk Centre, Fergus Falls and then Breckenridge. We'll be staying there for the night." Looking at his packet watch, he estimated that they would get there about eight o'clock.

"I'm glad we don't have to change trains anymore today," said Carrie.

"I think when we get to Fergus Falls, we'll be able to get out and stretch for a few minutes."

Carrie took a bit of handwork out of her traveling bag and settled back as the train stopped for a short time. Her thoughts started to wander and she thought about Teddy and then about that woman he was going to marry. What was her name again? Oh, yes, it was Birdie. Birdie McBride. She smiled to herself then and soon a burst of laughter escaped from her lips.

Amund looked sharply at his sister to see what was the matter. Then he saw that she was laughing. "What's the joke, may I ask?"

"Oh, I was just thinking about Teddy."

"And that made you laugh?" he questioned.

"Well, then I thought about Birdie, the woman he's going to marry. I think that's such a funny name!" she exclaimed.

"Don't you know you shouldn't laugh at someone's name, Carrie?" He was trying to sound stern and then he burst out laughing, too.

An old lady across from them gave the pair a dirty look. This made Carrie laugh all the harder.

"She looks like her name should be Birdie," Carrie whispered, nodding in the woman's direction. Amund nodded his head and laughed some more, too.

"I'm glad you can laugh about this, Carrie," Amund said a short while later. "Maybe you're starting to get over it."

"Maybe so, Mannie," she answered. "Maybe so."

Silently, to herself, she wasn't so sure. The hurt and humiliation were still there. They had replaced any feelings of love, however. Maybe she hadn't really loved him in the first place. What is love anyway, she wondered? She picked up her handwork once more and stitched the miles away until she grew tired again.

"Next stop, Fergus Falls, ladies and gentlemen," the conductor called out.

"Oh, my," said Carrie, sitting up and gathering her things together. "I must have dozed off again."

At this stop the two of them got off the train and walked around a bit. "This looks like such a pretty little town," remarked Carrie. "So many big trees!"

They walked for about two blocks and then retraced their steps and went into the station. They each used the rest room and then boarded the train again for the last leg of the journey for the day.

Breckenridge was the next stop and the place where they would spend the night. When they got off the train there, they inquired about a place to stay. The depot agent nodded to his left and said, "Hotel down the block that way."

Amund carried their valises and they headed for the hotel. They each got settled in their rooms and agreed to meet later and take a little walk around the town. After they had walked for about a half an hour, they came back to a cafe that they had seen earlier and went in and had some pie and coffee.

"Well, do you think we'll be able to sleep now then, Carrie?" asked Amund, as they approached their rooms, which were side by side.

"Oh, I sure hope so!" exclaimed Carrie. "If only I can keep from thinking about tomorrow. I'm a little nervous about everything."

"I'll see you about 7 o'clock then. We'll just have time for breakfast before we have to board the train at 8."

"Good night, Mannie," Carrie called from the doorway of her room. She undressed quickly and lay down on the bed. The thought struck her that she had never slept in any other bed but her own before. My, it's about time I got out into the world a little bit, she thought to herself. She pulled the blanket up to her neck and fell asleep almost instantly.

It was suddenly morning and Amund was knocking on her door, telling her to hurry or they would miss breakfast.

An hour later, as the train pulled out of Breckenridge, Carrie could feel her stomach starting to tie up in knots. Like she had told her brother the night before, she was nervous about what this move would bring.

"Tell me again, Mannie, about this big farm that we're going to."

"Well, to give you an idea of how big it is," he started, "Pa and Olaf farm about 120 acres in all. This Daud farm is 9,000 acres. Many times bigger!"

"Oh, my, I can't even imagine it. I'll have to see it to believe it," said Carrie.

They were both silent for quite sometime, passing through some small towns. Carrie read their names on the small depots----Dwight, Galchutt, Pitcairn. They stopped briefly in Colfax where a passenger got on and then they stopped again in Walcott for a few minutes.

"It shouldn't be too much longer now," remarked Amund. Peter said we would get into Davenport before noon."

The next stop was not even a real town but the sign by the water tower where they had to fill on water said 'Ulness'.

"We have some relatives by that name," remarked Amund. "I remember Ma mentioning that. They lived over in Lansing."

It took awhile to fill on water but finally they were on their way again. Carrie was getting more anxious by the mile. The train had barely gotten underway before they made another stop in Kindred. Several people boarded here.

"Next stop, Davenport," the conductor announced, as he did for every stop.

Carrie sat up straight and gathered her things together. "I wonder if Peter will be there waiting for us," she wondered aloud.

"I surely hope so," said Amund, not knowing quite what he would do if his friend wasn't there.

They got off the train, each carrying their bag, and began looking earnestly for Peter. He spotted the pair first and came running up to them.

"I can hardly believe my eyes, Amund! It's so good to see you!" said Peter, shaking his friend's hand vigorously. Turning to Carrie, he shook her hand, too, and said, "And it's good to have you here too, Carrie. You know, its going to be nice having two of my friends out here. It won't seem so lonesome now." He took Carrie's bag from her and led them both to the buggy he had taken into town.

"We'll leave your things in the buggy here," Peter said. "And then, being it's so close to noon, I thought we would go over to the cafe and I'll buy my dear friends some dinner!" He gave each of the two horses an affectionate pat on their foreheads and then he led Carrie and Amund down the street towards the cafe.

"My, you have quite a bustling little town here, don't you?" remarked Carrie, looking around at all the business places.

"Yes, it is rather a busy town. With two different railroads coming in here, it's expected to grow even more."

They passed by the Tuskind General Store and Carrie looked in the window. "That's a nice-looking store," she appraised. "I hope to go in there sometime."

"Mrs. Daud likes to shop there sometimes so maybe you'll be lucky enough to go with her," commented Peter.

Before Carrie could ask more about Mrs. Daud, Peter stopped in front of a cafe and he opened the door for the pair and they stepped into a small room with tables and chairs and the wonderful smell of home cooking. They were early so they had their pick of tables.

"Here, let's sit by the window so you can look out, Carrie," he said, holding a chair for her to be seated.

Mary Carr, the owner herself, came out and took their order. She said that the special of the day was roast beef so they all ordered that.

"This was the first building built in Davenport," Peter informed them.

"How old is this town?" asked Amund.

"Well, I think it was started back in 1882 or so," Peter said.

"That really isn't all that long ago, you know." said Amund.

"Well, North Dakota isn't nearly as old as Minnesota. It only became a state in 1889. That's not even ten years ago."

Mrs. Carr hurried from the kitchen, bringing a plate of homemade dinner rolls and a pitcher of water. Shortly after, she came with three heaping plates of steaming roast beef, mashed potatoes, and string beans. The three dug into their food with gusto.

"This is the first good meal we've had in a couple days," remarked Amund.

Between bites, Peter inquired about their trip and about everyone back home.

After finishing their meal, they leaned back to catch their breath, and then Mrs. Carr brought them each a piece of apple pie and some coffee. Amund and Carrie groaned. They were already so full!

"You'll get used to big meals like this everyday at the Daud farm," said Peter.

"I can see that you have put on some weight, Peter, since you left Spring Grove!" joked Amund.

"Are you sure that it was all right that I came along, Peter?" asked Carrie. "Does Mrs. Daud really need more help?"

"Oh, yes, she sure does," Peter assured her. "Every spring it's a struggle to find enough help for the busy season. Both in the kitchen and on the farm. Many of the girls that come there to work stay for one season and then they get married and leave. The men move around, too," Peter continued. "We keep only so many over the winter and then every spring, Mr. Daud has to advertise in the papers for help again."

In spite of claims of being so full, the three of them ate every last crumb of the wonderful pie and accepted refills on their coffee.

"That was great pie, as usual, Mrs. Carr," Peter said. "You can always expect good food here," he said to the newcomers.

Shortly after, Peter pushed back his chair reluctantly and announced that they had best be moving on. He paid for the meals and left a tip on the table.

"Mr. Thompson, the foreman, gave me the morning off to come and get you," he said as they walked back to the depot where the buggy was sitting. "Mrs. Daud insisted I take the buggy instead of the wagon because you were along, Carrie. She thought the wagon would be so dusty and hot."

"It is warming up pretty good today, isn't it?" remarked Amund.

"Yah, it's rather warm for early May here," said Peter. He helped Carrie up into the buggy and Amund sat behind her. Peter got behind the reins and they headed north out of town.

They passed by a small farmstead nestled in some trees. The lady of the house was out hanging clothes on the line. She favored the passing buggy with a friendly wave. After that, Carrie could see no more farms. In fact, she could see no more trees. Just endless fields.

She leaned toward Peter and said, "So tell me more about these bonanza farms. What exactly are they?"

"Well, the way I've heard it told is this: the Northern Pacific Railroad owned large tracts of land here and sometime in the early 1870's they faced bankruptcy. The wealthy people back east who owned stock in the company exchanged their depreciated bonds for portions of land owned by the railroad. When these people realized what great farmland they had purchased, they came out and set up big farming operations. The wheat crops were excellent and the price for wheat was high, so huge profits were made."

"So did this Daud family come from back East someplace?" asked Amund, leaning forward to hear every word.

"Mr. Daud, John is his name, came here with his brother, C.J., back in 1880. John came from Chicago. He was in the manufacturing business, a family-owned business of some kind, and his brother came from Ohio and he was in banking. Anyway, they had bought the land from someone else who had gotten it through the railroad deal.

"They bought up some more adjoining land," Peter continued, "and now it totals about 9000 acres."

"So what made this land so special, that it became so productive?" asked Amund.

"Well, it's flat, as you can see," explained Peter, extending his arm in several directions. "It has few trees and rocks, and the soil is rich and fertile. And the weather is favorable here for growing wheat."

"Do they raise anything else except wheat?" asked Amund.

"Well, I guess they didn't at first but now they do grow other crops."

"I just can't imagine a farm that big," said Amund, shaking his head in wonder.

"There are bonanza farms around here a lot bigger than this one!"

exclaimed Peter. Amund leaned back in his seat to digest this fact.

"We'll soon be there," said Peter, as he turned a corner to the right. "There, you can see the buildings way down the road." He pointed straight ahead.

As they neared the buildings, Carrie was not at all prepared for what she saw. Her heart sank. Where are the trees? It looks like a little town in the middle of nowhere, she thought to herself.

CHAPTER 6

Both Carrie and Amund were silent as Peter pulled into the yard. He stopped in front of the big house and stepped out of the buggy. He went around and reached up to help Carrie down. She was sitting there with a dumbfounded expression on her face.

"Well, friends, here it is. Home sweet home!" he exclaimed, not noticing their astonished silence.

Carrie allowed herself to be helped down from the vehicle and stood looking in all directions. "My, this isn't at all what I expected," she said to Peter.

"What do you think, Amund?" he inquired of his friend as he slapped him on the back. "Pretty big spread, huh?"

"It looks like a town in itself," Carrie said, finally finding her voice.

Peter grabbed her bag and led the way up to the side porch. "This is where you'll stay, Carrie. The family lives here and the cooks and hired girls stay here, too."

Hilde, one of the cooks, saw Peter standing in the doorway with the two newcomers. "This must be my new helper," she declared warmly, as she looked at Carrie. She reached for the bag and said she would show Carrie to her room. Peter and Amund left, saying they would see Carrie later.

"Have you eaten anything?" asked Hilde, panting as she slowly ascended the stairs.

"Yes, Peter treated us to dinner in the cafe in Davenport."

Hilde opened the door to a small room with two beds and a dresser and one chair. There was a dormer window that looked out into the yard.

"You'll be sharing a room with Pauline, another dining-room girl. You'll like her," Hilde declared. "I'll just let you get settled a little bit and then you can come down to the kitchen and someone will show you around."

"Which bed is mine?" asked Carrie.

"Well, I'm not so sure. You'll have to wait and ask Pauline later." With that, she turned and hurried downstairs to get to work.

Carrie stood in the middle of the small room and then she opened the closet and found some hangers. She opened her bag and took out what little clothing she had brought along. There were two black skirts, three white blouses and one good dress. She hung them on the hangers, shaking out the folds and wrinkles somewhat. She put her underthings in one of the dresser drawers. With that done, she took a peek out the window once more and then hurried down the stairs.

She found her way to the kitchen where Hilde and another older woman were obviously making cookies. Some were already cooling on racks and the smell was unmistakably molasses. Hilde looked up and smiled at Carrie and introduced her to the other cook whose name was Cora. Just then, a young and pretty girl hurried into the room.

"This is Pauline," said Hilde, "and this is Carrie, your new helper." The two girls smiled at each other. "Pauline, you show Carrie around and then see if you can find Mrs. Daud. She wants to meet Carrie."

Pauline motioned for Carrie to follow her into the big dining hall. "This is where all the men eat," she said. There were four long tables with benches. "There's room for about 20 men at each table," she explained. "During our busiest times, like during harvest, these tables are filled with hungry men."

Carrie looked about her, amazed at the large room with such big tables.

"This is where you and I will do most of our work. We have to set the tables, serve the meal, clear the tables and bring all the dirty dishes to the kitchen, clean up after the men have left and sweep the floor. Then we help with washing the dishes. Three times a day!" Pauline exclaimed.

"Oh, my, it sounds like a lot of work. Aren't you just played out by the end of the day?" asked Carrie.

"Oh, you bet I am," said Pauline, laughing, "but you get used to it."

Pauline led Carrie into a room with several sofas, chairs and a beautiful piano.

"This is the front parlor and we're allowed to use this room whenever we have some free time, like in the evenings or on Sundays. There's a desk over there with writing paper that we can use for letters and such."

"This is very nice," declared Carrie, looking around.

"The rooms along the other side of the house are the Daud's private living quarters," Pauline indicated, as they entered the front hall. Carrie was just about to comment on the beautiful open staircase when she saw someone coming down the stairs.

It was Mrs. Daud and when she saw the two girls, she exclaimed, "Well, well, this must be our new helper!" Coming toward Carrie and taking her hand, she said, "I'm Clareen Daud and I understand you are Carrie Amundson. Welcome to our farm!"

"Pleased to meet you, ma'am," said Carrie, already impressed with her new employer.

"Pauline, why don't you get us each a cup of coffee and bring it into the front parlor. Miss Amundson and I will have a little visit and get acquainted."

She led Carrie back to the front room and they seated themselves on one of the horsehair sofas. It was a rich brown and the accent chairs were a deep burgundy. There were doilies on all of the armrests, Carrie noticed. Two large ferns on tall plant stands stood on either side of the bay window.

"This is a very pretty room," commented Carrie, looking around with interest.

Mrs. Daud looked at Carrie kindly and said, "Tell me a little about yourself. I understand you and your brother are friends of Peter Larson."

"Yes, he is Amund's best friend and their family's farm is not far from ours."

"We sure like Peter," Mrs. Daud said. "He is a nice young man and Mr. Daud was glad when he was able to persuade Peter to stay the winter here. He's very good with the horses."

"Oh, yes," chuckled Carrie, "that was always his favorite thing back home. His father told him once that he could just as well move to the barn, for all the time he spent out there!"

Pauline arrived with a tray and set it on the coffee table. She poured a cup for Mrs. Daud and one for Carrie, and with a wink at Carrie, she excused herself.

"So tell me about you, Miss Amundson," said the elder woman.

"Well, I'm seventeen years old, soon to be eighteen," Carrie started. "I've just been helping my mother at home since I finished school. I can cook and sew and houseclean."

"And what made you decide to come out here with your brother, my dear?" asked Mrs. Daud with genuine interest.

Carrie paused here before answering. "In Peter's letters to my brother, he said that you could use some girls to help out here. I thought that maybe it would be...ah...good for me to get out into the world a little bit." Carrie shrugged and said, "So here I am. I hope that I will be able to do a good job for you."

"I'm sure you will," said Mrs. Daud, "and I think I'm going to start calling you Carrie, if I may. We're very informal here and I'm sure you will work out just fine." She passed a plate of the newly baked cookies to Carrie and then took one herself.

"We're like a big family here and we want you to feel at home in this house," she continued. "Did Pauline tell you that you can use this room anytime you want, just as if it was your own? Mr. Daud and I have the quarters on the whole north side. There's a dining room, parlor and library. Our bedroom and private guest rooms are upstairs."

Mrs. Daud rose and went to the piano and took a picture and brought it back to show Carrie. "This is our family," she explained. "We have three children. Two sons, Walter and Charles, standing there in the back, and our daughter, Eunice, seated between Mr. Daud and myself. It was taken in Chicago a number of years ago. The children are all grown and on their own now, of course."

"You have a very nice-looking family, Mrs. Daud," Carrie commented politely.

"Thank you, my dear, and tell me about your family."

"Well, besides Amund, I have a brother, Olaf; he's the oldest, and an older sister, Sylvia, and a younger sister and brother, Rosina and Martin. We farm just outside of Spring Grove, Minnesota. Just a little farm," Carrie laughed, "with some dairy cattle, horses and a few pigs."

"So where did your family come from?" inquired Mrs. Daud.

"My parents came from Norway back in 1885 when Olaf was just a baby. They lived in Wisconsin for a little while before coming to Spring Grove. They knew several other families who lived there. My father bought some land and started farming." Carrie felt a feeling of homesickness as she spoke of her family. I'll have to get used to this, she thought.

Mrs. Daud finished her coffee and stood up. "This has been very interesting visiting with you and I hope to get to know you very well before the season is over. The girls and the cooks are all fine people and I think you all will get along splendidly."

Carrie followed Mrs. Daud back to the kitchen. Mrs. Daud was a tall, rather large woman with graying hair and a kind face. Kind of motherly looking, thought Carrie.

"I'll leave you here then, Carrie. The girls can explain everything to you and show you around some more." With that she left the room and retreated to the family quarters.

The women in the kitchen were just finishing their afternoon cup of coffee. "We're having a little rest after making that big batch of cookies," said Hilde with a sigh. "Soon we'll have to start thinking about supper."

A middle-aged woman whom Carrie hadn't met yet was also sitting at the kitchen table.

"Hello, Carrie," she said, extending her hand, "I'm Stella Iverson, and I'm the Daud's housekeeper and personal maid."

"Nice to meet you," replied Carrie.

With that, Stella got up and headed out the kitchen door. The others were silent until she was out of earshot.

"She's nice enough but she kind of thinks she is a little better than the rest of us because she only has to take care of the Daud's quarters," commented Cora.

"Oh, she's all right," said Hilde, "she's just a very private person and a little hard to get to know."

Pauline rose and said to Carrie, "We have some time yet. I'll show you around some more."

She led Carrie outside toward the back of the house. "Here we have a small garden. Mrs. Daud enjoys fresh tomatoes and onions, so they will be planted soon. The rest of the vegetables they buy in bulk. Either canned or dried."

"That looks like lilac bushes over there," commented Carrie.

"Yes, they'll be blooming in a few weeks. We'll fill the house with them. Mrs. Daud just loves them."

The mid-afternoon sun felt warm on this side of the house. The two girls sat down on a small bench near the flower garden.

"The daffodils and tulips are starting to bloom now. It was rather cold here the first part of April but has warmed up nicely now," commented Pauline.

"How long have you been here?" asked Carrie, shading her eyes as she turned to look at her newfound friend.

"Well, this year I came the first of April but I worked here all last season, too."

"Where did you come from?" asked Carrie.

"I came from over in Minnesota, up by a town named Crookston. I answered an ad in our local paper for help wanted here at the Daud farm. I liked it so I came back."

"So how long did you stay last year?" Carrie wanted to know.

"I stayed until the first of November. By that time most of the men had left and they didn't really need me anymore," explained Pauline. "They only keep about six or eight men over the winter."

"Oh, there's Ida over there!" exclaimed Pauline, jumping up and heading toward the woman. "She's the foreman's wife and they live in that house over there."

"Hey, Ida!" she hailed the woman. "I want you to meet someone new here."

As they neared the foreman's house, Carrie saw a short, plump woman with braids piled on top of her head. She walked toward the two girls with a big smile.

"I heard that a new girl was coming soon," she said. She extended her hand to Carrie and said, "I'm Ida Thompson. My husband is the foreman here and we live in this house."

"Nice meeting you, ma'am," said Carrie, "and my name is Carrie Amundson."

"Oh, don't 'ma'am' me," she said, laughing. "Just call me Ida."

"I thought I'd show Carrie the store," said Pauline.

"Oh, my, yes!" exclaimed Ida. "We have our own little store right on the farm. Isn't that something?" She led the way to the back of their house and opened the door for the two young girls to enter. The 'store' was a small room with shelves on two walls and a counter in the middle.

Carrie looked around her with interest.

"We have many things here that the men can buy as they don't get to town real often," Ida told Carrie enthusiastically. "There's cigars, chewing tobacco, candy, peanuts," she said, pointing to things on a glass counter. Turning to the wall, she said, "there's overalls, caps, shirts, even some underwear. We don't carry shoes, though. For those they have to go to town if they need some."

"This must be real handy for the men," offered Carrie.

"Oh, my, yes!" said Ida. "They really appreciate it. It was my husband's idea and Mr. Daud went along with it and it has worked out very well. I tend the store myself," Ida stated proudly. "We even have writing paper and postage stamps. If you need to mail anything, just leave it here on the counter and I'll get it to the mailbox. You will pick up any incoming mail, here, too," Ida went on.

"Well, we better get going and start helping Hilde with supper," stated Pauline.

"Nice meeting you, Carrie, and I hope you get along well here," said Ida.

"Oh, I'm sure I will, Mrs. Thompson, and it was nice meeting you, too."

"Just call me Ida, everybody else around here does," she laughed.

When Carrie and Pauline were outside, Carrie said, "Ida seems like quite a jolly person!"

"Oh, yes, she is. Everyone loves her!" exclaimed Pauline.

As they were walking over to the main house, they saw two young boys coming up the driveway.

"There are the two Thompson boys, just coming home from school. They have to walk about a mile and a half to the east of here," explained Pauline.

""Hi, Billy! Hi, Joey!" she called to them and waved. They waved back and came running up to the two girls.

"Boys, I want you to meet Carrie Amundson. She'll be working with me in the kitchen."

The two politely removed their caps and greeted the newcomer. "We better be getting to our chores," said Billy. "We had to stay a little late and help teacher with something." With that the two boys raced to their house.

"They seem like two nice young boys," commented Carrie.

"Yes, they are. Billy is about thirteen now and I think Joey is a year younger. They do chores around here after school and all during the summer.

They fill the wood boxes and do many errands for Hilde."

"Speaking of Hilde," added Pauline, hurrying her steps, "we better get moving."

When the two girls entered the kitchen, Hilde said good-naturedly, "I thought you two were playing hooky on this nice day!"

"Ummm, what is that good smell?" asked Carrie, turning her nose towards the stove.

"I'm cooking up a big kettle of chicken soup. We had lots of chicken left over from dinner yesterday." Hilde opened the lid to check on its progress.

"You can get Carrie started on slicing the bread, Pauline, and then put it on plates and cover them with dish towels. When Joey or Billy get here," she went on, "have them bring in some more butter."

The girls did as they were told and then they went to the dining hall to set the tables.

"How many men are here now?" asked Carrie.

"There are about twenty-five in all, right now, with more coming every week, it seems," Pauline explained. "We'll set two tables tonight, with ten at one and fifteen at the other.

"What time do we feed them?" asked Carrie, setting a cup by each plate.

"This time of the year we eat by 6:30," said Pauline. "During the busy times it gets a little later."

Shortly before 6:30, men began to file into the dining hall and take their places at the two tables set up for them. Carrie watched for Amund and Peter to come in. They were almost the last to enter and take their places. Amund caught her eye and gave her a wave.

Carrie and Pauline carried the big soup tureens in and set two at each table. They dished up the soup into bowls and passed them down the rows until each man had one. Crackers, bread and cheese were passed while the girls poured coffee or water. The men, accustomed to eating fast, were ready for refills before the girls could get back from the kitchen with more of the delicious soup. Then it was to hurry and get more bread and crackers and cheese.

"My, how these men can eat!" exclaimed Carrie to Pauline, as they passed each other going from the kitchen to the dining room.

Plates of the frosted molasses cookies and more coffee rounded out the meal. Each man had at least three of the big cookies, Carrie observed.

"They are really starving by the time they get here for supper," explained Pauline. "They aren't given lunches out in the field like at some farms. Mrs. Daud put a stop to that when she came out here. She said it was too much work for the cooks to haul lunches out to the field."

"Back home, Ma made both forenoon and afternoon lunches for our men," said Carrie. "We kids would have to walk out in the field where they were working and bring them lunch and coffee. We'd carry the coffee in a big enamel coffee pot."

"Yah, that's the way it was at our house, too," agreed Pauline. "Sometimes, though, Pa and my brothers would come to the yard and eat if they weren't real busy."

After the men started leaving, Amund came up to Carrie to see how she was faring.

"Oh, it's going all right," she said. "How about you? What have you been doing?"

"Peter has been showing me around the farm. This is really quite the place, isn't it?" he asked his sister. "The folks back home just wouldn't believe it, would they?"

Peter came up to them just then. "I noticed the new girl was getting many second looks from the men!" he joked.

"What do you mean?" asked Carrie.

"Didn't you notice? The men were stealing glances at you the whole meal," Peter went on.

Carrie just scoffed at such an idea. "Why would they look at me when Pauline is around?"

"Because you're someone new, that's why!" laughed Peter. "And the men always like to see a pretty face around here."

"I need to go and help Pauline clear the dishes," Carrie said, as she hurried off. "See you tomorrow."

After the dishes were washed, dried and put away and the dining hall was swept clean, Carrie was feeling very tired. She told Pauline that she thought she would go up to her room and rest. "Which bed is mine?" she asked as she removed her apron and headed for the back stairs.

"The one closest to the door," answered Pauline.

When Carrie got herself settled in her room, she thought she would just lie down on her bed for awhile. I am so tired; I'll just rest a little, she thought.

When Pauline came up about an hour later, Carrie was sleeping so soundly that she didn't have the heart to wake her and tell her to get undressed. She covered the girl with a quilt from another room and then went to bed herself. If she's tired after just a half day here, she hasn't seen anything yet, chuckled Pauline to herself before drifting off to sleep.

CHAPTER 7

Carrie was awakened early the next morning by sounds of someone moving around in their room. Pauline was already dressing and when she noticed that Carrie was awake, she announced cheerfully, "Time to get up now!"

Carrie sat up and swung her feet onto the floor and sat awhile on the edge of the bed. She just then realized that she still had her clothes on. She jumped up and exclaimed, horrified, "Oh, my, did I sleep in my clothes last night?"

"You were fast asleep by the time I came up here. I didn't have the heart to wake you to undress." Pauline reached over and pushed a button on the wall and the room flooded with light.

"Oh, my!" exclaimed Carrie, shielding her sleepy eyes. "I've read about houses in the city that have electric lights in the ceiling. I can't believe that they have the same thing here!"

"The farm has its own light plant," explained Pauline. "It was put in the year before I came. It sure is nice, isn't it."

"Oh, I am really a wrinkled mess!" moaned Carrie, looking down at her skirt. "I've never done anything like that before," exclaimed Carrie.

"Well, I'm sure you were all played out after a day-and-a-half of traveling and then we put you to work right away," Pauline commented, as she twisted her auburn-color hair into a bun at the back of her neck. She then took up a small compact and powdered her face a bit, trying to cover the band of freckles that spread across her nose.

As Carrie headed for the bathroom, Pauline said, "I'll be going down now. You just come when you get ready."

In less than ten minutes, Carrie had joined the other women in the kitchen. The coffee smelled so good, thought Carrie, as she was told to help herself to a cup.

"Have a doughnut with your coffee," suggested Cora. "It will tide you over until you have time to eat breakfast.

Carrie did just that, looking over the kitchen to try and see what the cooks were making. She could smell bacon frying, and saw a huge bowl of eggs waiting by the range.

"Umm, bacon and eggs! One of my favorite breakfasts," she exclaimed to no one in particular.

Finishing her doughnut and coffee, Carrie stood up and inquired, "What do you want me to do now?"

Pauline jumped up, too, and said, "We'll set the tables first and then we'll start cracking the eggs."

The men starting coming in about six o'clock. There was much joking and bantering back and forth among them as they found their places. The two girls served the bacon and eggs and poured coffee, went back to the kitchen for refills and poured more coffee.

She caught Amund's eye and he gave her a wink. Then he raised his eyebrows and gave her a questioning look. I suppose he's wondering how it's going for me, thought Carrie.

An older man came into the dining room from the private quarters so she assumed that this must be Mr. Daud, whom she hadn't seen last night. He sat down at the end of a table full of men and Pauline hurried to serve him breakfast.

When she and Pauline were both back in the kitchen, Carrie asked if that was Mr. Daud.

"Oh, I forgot that you probably hadn't met him yet. He was gone until late last night. Yes, that's him. Sometimes he has breakfast with Mrs. Daud in their own quarters but often he comes out here and joins the men. In the busy times, he always eats out here."

Pauline picked up the coffeepot and before heading back to the dining hall, she said, "He'll probably want to talk with you this morning."

In about a half an hour, the men were done eating and out the door. Mr. Daud lingered with his second cup of coffee and had opened up the newspaper that he had brought with him. Pauline and Carrie gathered up all the dirty dishes and started wiping off the long tables.

"Don't let us disturb you, Mr. Daud," Pauline told him, as she left his half of the table until later.

He looked up and then looked at Carrie and said, "So, this must be our newest helper! I'll want to have a few words with you before I go out."

"Yes, sir," was all Carrie could get out.

The girls finished all they could in the dining hall and went to help in the kitchen. They would have to sweep later.

"You don't have to be afraid of Mr. Daud," said Pauline, suspecting that Carrie was a little nervous about talking with her new employer. "He's very kind."

"Thank you for telling me that," responded Carrie, as she peeked into the dining hall. "Will he send for me?"

"Oh, he'll let you know when he's ready for that talk," smiled Pauline.

"You girls sit down now and eat your breakfast before it gets too cold," suggested Hilde. She and Cora joined them at the kitchen table.

"Mrs. Daud said that two new men would be joining us sometime today," Hilde informed them. "There'll be new ones coming regularly now."

"Where do they all come from?" asked Carrie, helping herself to a big spoonful of the eggs. She was feeling mighty hungry.

"A few come from around here but most come from far off. Like you and your brother, Carrie, many come from Minnesota," explained Cora. "Some come from the lumber camps in Minnesota and Wisconsin. Mr. Daud advertises in several papers."

"Do they all just show up here, without him ever seeing them?" asked Carrie.

"They write him after seeing his ad or maybe they hear about the job from someone who has worked here before," said Hilde.

"And, of course," volunteered Cora, "some come back year after year."

Just then, Mr. Daud entered the kitchen, bringing his coffee cup with him. "And how are my favorite cooks this morning?" he asked them as he set his cup by the stack of dirty dishes.

"Just fine!" Hilde was the first to exclaim.

He looked at Carrie. "Miss Amundson, I believe?"

When she nodded, he said, "Would you like to follow me into my study for a few minutes? I'll have her back in time to help with that stack of dishes," he joked.

Carrie rose and followed him down the hall into what Pauline had said was the library. She had not been in this room before. It had shelves on two walls and they were filled with books almost to the ceiling. A large desk sat in the middle of the floor. Mr. Daud pulled up a small chair for Carrie and he sat behind the desk.

"Well, now. Mrs. Daud tells me you came with your brother from over in Minnesota."

"Yes, sir. From Spring Grove," Carrie answered.

"And I understand that you are friends of Peter Larson."

"Yes, we're friends as well as neighbors."

After some more small talk, Mr. Daud got down to business. "Your pay will be $20 a month except during the harvest months, then we pay you $25 because it's a lot of work for you women to keep all those men fed!"

"And," he continued, "if you stick it out through November, we will give you a bonus. I'm afraid some of our young ladies haven't had the stamina to stay the full course and they just up and leave. Sometimes in the middle of harvest!"

"Oh, I wouldn't do that, sir," responded Carrie.

"I'm sure you won't," said Mr. Daud, standing up now and indicating that the interview was over. "By the way, we tell all our men to treat you ladies with respect so if you ever have any trouble with any one of them, you report it to Mrs. Daud and we will take care of the problem."

He walked her to the door and reached out to shake her hand. "Welcome to the Daud farm. I hope you will like it here."

"I'm sure I will, sir," Carrie said, and left the room to return to her duties.

"Well, that wasn't so bad now, was it?" said Pauline, making room for Carrie by the sink.

"No. He's really a very nice man, isn't he?" Carrie answered.

While the girls were doing the dishes, they could see the men leaving the yard with the machinery. "I guess they are going to finish seeding the wheat today," said Pauline.

Carrie looked out and counted eleven seeders go by, one after the other, each pulled by three horses. There were three wagons following the seeders, hauling the wheat for seed, Pauline informed her. She noticed that Mr. Daud was riding on the last wagon with his foreman, Mr. Thompson.

"Oh my, that looks like a real parade, doesn't it?" she remarked. "Things are sure done on a large scale around here!"

When the dishes were done and the dining hall put to rights, the two girls took a little breather. Pauline suggested they walk outside for a few minutes. It was a fine spring morning. The sun shone brightly and it felt good to walk and let it beam down on their backs.

"Let's go over to the store and see Ida," suggested Pauline. "It's too early for the mail yet, though. We'll go over later for that."

Pauline opened the door and a little bell rang out, announcing their entrance. "Hello there, Ida," she called out, and the woman came from the kitchen, wiping her hands on her apron.

"Well, well, I have some early customers today!" she exclaimed.

"We're just taking a little break on this nice, sunny morning," explained Pauline.

"So, how is it going for you, Carrie?" Ida asked.

"Well, it's going fine. I just hope I can keep up when it gets really busy. Pauline has been warning me that during harvest we will really be hustling around here!"

"Oh, that you will be, that you will be," Ida nodded her head in agreement. Then she smiled and said, "You will do just fine, I'm sure. Don't let Pauline scare you."

After visiting a short while, Pauline said, "We better be going back. There's always another meal to get ready!"

As the girls headed for the main house Pauline said, "I haven't shown you the laundry yet, have I?" She steered Carrie to the back of the house.

"We'll go in the back way. The laundry is in the back room here." She opened the door and led Carrie into a large room with a washing machine and wash tubs and clotheslines and ironing boards filling up the whole space.

"Oh, my!" Carrie said in awe as she just stared.

"There's a lady from Davenport who comes over one day a week and she washes all the clothes from the main house here. Some other time I'll show you the laundry where all the men's dirty clothes are washed!"

"Does this lady do those, too?" asked Carrie.

"No. There's actually a man who does that. Mrs. Daud decided that that job was just too much work for a woman. Do you remember that man at the table this morning who asked me if you had just arrived?" Without waiting for an answer, Pauline continued, "Well, that's Corky, the man who washes the men's clothes. He's quite a guy. Everybody likes him. Besides washing clothes, he does other odd jobs, too. I'll have to show you around more later."

As they headed down the hall, they heard gales of laughter coming from the kitchen.

"What's so funny in here?" Pauline asked as sternly as she could. Cora and Hilde turned to look at them, wiping tears from their eyes.

"Have you been peeling onions or was the joke really that funny?" asked Pauline.

When Hilde could get herself composed, she said, "Oh, Cora was just telling me about the time when she got chased by a pig and she fell into the slop pail. You've probably heard it before but I laugh just as good every time I hear it."

"Cora will have to tell Carrie that story sometime," said Hilde. I don't think I could take it, hearing it again so soon." Here Hilde started laughing again.

"What are we serving the men at noon, Hilde?" asked Pauline.

"We're going to have corned beef and cabbage. Gingerbread for dessert. I'm stirring that up now."

"Pauline, why don't you take a peek in the oven and see if the bread looks ready yet," suggested Cora.

Pauline did as she was bid and after looking into the big, cavernous oven, she declared them to be done. "Carrie, come and help me take all these loaves out, will you?"

The girls lined up 12 loaves of bread on the counter. Carrie was in awe once more.

"I can't believe all this bread!" she exclaimed. "Is this for just one day?"

"This will be gone by tonight," Cora said. "During harvest, we bake about 30 to 40 loaves every day!"

"Oh, my," Carrie said, shaking her head. "This all amazes me so." She watched as Pauline used a small piece of cloth to spread butter on the tops of each warm loaf.

"You girls can put this cake batter in pans and start baking them," Hilde said, as she found two oversized cake pans for them. "Grease them first. You can use your same rag, Pauline."

Cora was getting the beef ready for the other oven. There were two wood-burning stoves in the kitchen with two large ovens in each. Carrie had never seen ones so large. Each stove had six burners. A huge wood box stood on each side. I bet these take an awful lot of wood, Carrie thought to herself.

"Carrie, you can squeeze those lemons over there for the lemon sauce. The juicer is in that drawer there," said Hilde, pointing.

"Do you put the lemon sauce on the gingerbread cake?" asked Carrie.

Hilde nodded in the affirmative.

"We always put applesauce on our gingerbread," remarked Carrie. "Mama made gingerbread often. With lots of whipped cream, too."

"We use cream, too. We'll give you the job of whipping that later," said Hilde.

The next couple hours were busy for all four women. Carrie was just wondering about Mrs. Daud when she appeared in the kitchen door.

"How is everything going in here, ladies?" asked Mrs. Daud pleasantly.

"We're just humming right along," laughed Hilde. It seemed to Carrie that Hilde laughed a lot. But this was good. It made working here fun, Carrie thought.

"Have the eggs been delivered yet?" asked Mrs. Daud.

"No, but they should be coming sometime today," answered Cora. "We're soon out."

Pauline explained to Carrie that eggs were delivered a couple times a week by various neighbors. "We use many dozens a day!"

"Cora, will you be ready to go with me this afternoon to town?" asked Mrs. Daud.

"Oh, for sure, for sure!" exclaimed Cora.

"We'll leave about half past one then," Mrs. Daud said as she left the busy room.

Carrie looked at Pauline and raised her eyebrow in a question.

Pauline explained, "About once a week or so, Mrs. Daud gets the itch to take the buggy and go to one town or another and shop. She's very good about taking one of us along every time. You'll get your turn, too, sometime. She takes Ida along quite often."

"That sounds fun. Where is she going today?" Carrie inquired.

"We're just going into Davenport today," answered Cora. "I have to start thinking of things I need to purchase. I know I need to get some blue thread for one thing."

"Test the potatoes there, Pauline, and see if they are soon done," Hilde ordered. "The men will be here soon. Did you get the butter out, Cora?"

"Yah, I did and the cream, too. Carrie can soon start whipping that," Cora said, as she stirred the lemon sauce.

"The potatoes will be done in a jiffy," reported Pauline.

"Are the tables all set?" Hilde asked, hearing someone coming in the dining room. "Are they already coming?" She hurried to get the large serving bowls ready to fill.

Two hours later, it was all over. The men ate and went back to work; the girls cleaned up and did the dishes and sat down for a break with Hilde. Mrs. Daud, who wanted to get an early start for town, had rescued Cora from some of the clean up.

"Well, I suppose Cora and Mrs. Daud are in Davenport by now, going up and down the aisles of Tuskind's," said Hilde pleasantly, as she sipped carefully from her coffee cup. She liked her coffee hot and strong and it was definitely both of those, thought Carrie.

"It will be fun to see what she comes home with," remarked Pauline wistfully. "My turn comes next week and my list is getting longer and longer!"

"Does she go every week?" asked Carrie.

"She usually tries to go once a week," answered Hilde. "She grew up in Chicago and was used to going shopping any time she liked. Her family had money so that was no problem."

"She's kind enough to take one of us with her every time. She says that we all work so hard and it does a body good to get away from the hard work and routine once in awhile," Pauline stated.

"So she drives the buggy herself?" asked Carrie.

"Yes, usually, unless the roads are a little tricky. If Mr. Daud can spare a man, then Corky will drive her," Hilde answered her.

"Hilde, you should take your turn and go with her more often," Pauline scolded the older woman. Then to Carrie, she said, "Hilde says she never has anything to buy, so she lets someone else go."

"That's true!" exclaimed Hilde. "What does an old lady like me need anyway?"

"You need to get off this farm once in awhile, that's what you need," said Pauline with conviction.

"Well, I do go before Christmas," conceded Hilde. "I like to buy gifts for several people. That I do like to do," she uttered as she got up and refilled her cup.

"What are we making for supper?" asked Pauline, changing the subject.

"Tonight it will be simple," stated Hilde. "It will be milk mush with cinnamon and sugar and bread with jam. Then you'll see all that bread disappear in a hurry, Carrie!"

"Yes, that will be simple," agreed Pauline. "Carrie, we could go up to our room and rest for awhile if you'd like. I'm going to, anyway." She stood and started for the door.

"That sounds like a good idea," said Carrie. "I don't want to be as tired tonight as I was last night!"

The girls went down the hall, passing Hilde's bedroom. Hers was the only one on the main floor, Pauline told Carrie. "She has trouble doing stairs," she said.

"I don't see much of Stella around here," remarked Carrie as they ascended the steps.

"No, she keeps pretty much to the Daud's private quarters. She brings their meals from the kitchen and eats with them. She and Cora each have a bedroom at the end of the hall there," Pauline said, nodding in that direction.

Pauline stretched out on her bed and Carrie did likewise. "Oh, this feels good," she sighed tiredly.

They both were silent for sometime. Then Carrie asked, "Where does Hilde come from and does she have a family?"

Pauline raised herself on her elbow and said, "Hilde comes from over by Chaffee. That's a small town west of here."

"She never married?" asked Carrie.

"No, she always says, 'who would marry someone with a face like this.' Then she laughs."

"You know," Carrie confessed, "when I first met Hilde, I thought that she was one of the most unattractive woman I'd ever met! But now," Carrie went on, "I don't even think about that. She has such a kind heart and is so pleasant."

"Yes, we all love her dearly. She kind of mothers all of us."

"How long has she worked here?" asked Carrie.

"Well, I think she's been here almost fifteen years now," Pauline reflected. "When Mr. and Mrs. Daud decided to come out here and actually live here and manage the farm themselves, they hired her as a helper and then she took over as cook soon after."

While Carrie reflected on this, Pauline went on, "Many of the bonanza farmers don't actually manage their farms themselves. They hire farm managers. The Daud's had one of these, too, in the early years, but he died suddenly one winter so then Mr. Daud and his brother came out to get things in order for the next planting season. His brother, C. J., and his wife disliked it here so they didn't want to stay."

"Did the Daud children grow up here then?" asked Carrie.

"The two boys weren't here much as they were attending boarding schools back East by then. The daughter, Eunice, however, spent a lot of time on this farm. She would go back to Chicago in the fall to attend school. Her mother always went with her. They spent the summers here, though. Eunice ended up marrying a fellow from up at Casselton, a banker, so she lives there," Pauline went on.

"That's not very far away so Eunice comes back to the farm here often. She has two children now."

"How did you find out all this?" asked Carrie.

"Oh, Hilde told me lots of things the first year I was here. She likes to talk once she gets going!" Pauline laughed. "You'll notice, too, that she likes to tell the same things over and over."

The girls were silent again and Carrie almost fell asleep. Then she heard horses come galloping into the yard, past the house. The girls both sat up to look out the window.

"Oh, that's the wagon from the Powers farm at Helendale. That's southwest of here. They deliver meat to us from their farm. They come twice a month, usually," Pauline went on to explain. "But during harvest, they deliver one hog and one beef a week!"

"Where do you keep all that meat?" asked Carrie, wide-eyed.

"They have a big ice house here. I need to show you that." Pauline jumped off the bed and said, "C'mon, I'll show you now, when they're putting the meat in it."

The girls slipped on their shoes and hurried down the stairs. Pauline led the way outside and over to the other side of the foreman's house. There stood a small wood structure and the wagon from Helendale was out front. Two burly young men were unloading big slabs of meat from an ice trunk in the back of the vehicle. The two girls stood outside and watched.

When the men finished, Pauline told them to leave the door open as she was going in. The light hanging from the ceiling was turned on, as there were no windows. Pauline quickly closed the door after Carrie.

"Oh, it sure feels chilly in here!" exclaimed Carrie.

The little building was divided into two small rooms. The first was the cooler. The meat was left to hang here.

"It looks so much smaller inside," observed Carrie.

"Yes, well, the walls have about a foot of sawdust insulation all around," explained Pauline.

"Oh, my! They think of everything around here, don't they?"

"We also keep milk, cream and butter in this first room," said Pauline. She opened a small, upper portion of a door and Carrie could see that the next room was filled almost to the ceiling with huge chunks of ice and lots of straw.

"Oh, this is really something!" exclaimed Carrie. "Our ice house back home is actually just a little closet in one of our sheds. We bury the ice deep into some straw."

"On our farm," Pauline said, "we had to put things down in our well to keep things cool. And like I told you," Pauline went on, "this meat will last us about two weeks."

On their way back to the house, the girls stopped in at the store. "Any mail for me, Ida?" asked Pauline.

"Not today, I'm afraid," she answered from the other side of the wall.

"OK," said Pauline. "Just wishful thinking."

That evening after the supper clean-up, Pauline suggested that the two of them go into the parlor and sit a spell. They were the only ones in there. She sat down at the piano and played a simple little song very softly.

"I wish I could play the piano," lamented Carrie. "Did you have one at home?"

"No, my aunt had one and she lived in town but we girls could go there and play any time we wanted. She gave us all lessons. I'm not very good at it, though."

"Does Mrs. Daud play?" asked Carrie.

"No, she doesn't, but Eunice does. She took lessons in Chicago during the school year so she plays quite beautifully." Pauline rose and took a place on the sofa next to Carrie.

"Eunice and her family come here often on Sundays and Eunice plays for all of us. We all look forward to her visits. We have some real songfests then."

"How many children does she have, did you say?" asked Carrie.

"She has two. A boy and a girl. Real darling children. Hilde just loves them to death when they come. You'd think they were her very own grandchildren!"

Pauline picked up a newspaper, *The Fargo Argus,* which was a couple days old. Carrie stifled a yawn and finally said, "I guess I'll go up and turn in now. I can hardly keep my eyes open."

"You go on up. I'll join you soon," said Pauline.

Carrie got undressed this time and after a trip to the bathroom she sat on the bed and took her small Bible out of her drawer. She was paging through it when her roommate came in.

"Maybe we can have devotions together each evening," suggested Pauline. "You choose something while I get undressed."

After the girls had read Psalm 23 together and talked about it some, they took turns saying a short prayer. Carrie reached up and pushed in the light button.

"It isn't even totally dark outside yet, is it?" Carrie remarked. "It seems to get dark later here than where I come from."

Carrie stared out the window awhile and then she asked Pauline, "Do you have a special fellow back home?"

"No, I don't," she answered, "do you?"

"No, not anymore," Carrie said sadly. After some encouragement from Pauline, Carrie told her the whole story.

"Well, it sounds like he wasn't the one for you, Carrie."

"That's what Ma told me. I guess you both are right." With that the two lay silent until they each fell into an exhausted sleep.

CHAPTER 8

When Carrie and Pauline came into the kitchen the next morning, Hilde and Cora were already busy rolling out pie dough.

"Pie today, girls!" exclaimed Hilde.

Carrie could see apple slices in a colander nearby. "Where did you get the apples?" she inquired.

"We get dried apples by the bulk from our wholesaler," Hilde answered. "I set them to soaking last night."

When Carrie looked skeptical, Cora said, "They will taste just like fresh apple pies, you'll see."

"Hilde doesn't trust us to roll out the crusts," Pauline teased.

"I never liked rolling crusts at home but I can do it if I have to," remarked Carrie.

"We're having corn fritters for breakfast today," announced Hilde. "Pauline, you can open up those cans of corn and start stirring up the batter. Carrie, you can put the apples into these bottom crusts. Just divide them up evenly."

"Yah, that's a good girl," Hilde told Carrie when the girl had finished her task. "Now you can go and set the tables. Cora, is the coffee ready?"

After breakfast was over and the girls were helping with the dishes, Pauline looked out the kitchen window at the sound of horses coming into the yard.

"Here comes Mrs. Schmit," she announced. Turning to Carrie, she explained, "That's our washerwoman I told you about."

A few minutes later, a short and stout woman came in the back door and greeted them all. "Good morning, girls," she said.

"Well, good morning, Berta," they chorused.

"Berta, meet out newest helper, Carrie Amundson from Minnesota," Pauline said.

"Good to meet you," she acknowledged the new girl.

"Have you time for a cup of coffee before you start?" asked Cora.

"Well, I'll have to go and see if Corky has everything ready for me or not." With that, the woman lumbered down the hallway to the laundry room.

"I'll have to take you back there after awhile, Carrie, when she gets things going," stated Pauline.

Cora opened the oven door to check on the pies and the kitchen was filled with the aroma of apples baking.

"No one makes pies like these two women," said Pauline. "The men will be happy today when we bring in pie for their dessert!"

"What else are we having?" asked Carrie.

"Just pie!" laughed Hilde.

"The men would probably like that!" exclaimed Pauline.

"We'll be having roast pork today, potatoes, gravy and a vegetable," Hilde informed them, more seriously this time.

"Oh, that sounds so good," Carrie said, smacking her lips.

A short while later, Pauline said to Carrie, "Let's go back and see how Berta is doing with the washing."

The room was already getting steamy. Berta was putting another load into the washing machine. Stella was there, helping her.

"How did she get the water hot so fast?" asked Carrie.

"Corky comes over early and starts a fire in that big boiler outside and that heats up the water, which is piped through it, and then it comes into the house here," she pointed to a faucet over the washing machine. "There's another faucet over the rinse tubs. One for hot water and one for cold."

Carrie listened and watched in amazement. "Well, how does the water get here?" she questioned. There was a cold-water faucet in the kitchen but she had never asked about it before.

"A couple years ago, the men put pipes in the ground to bring water to the buildings. There's a big holding tank upstairs in one of the barns. That's all I know," laughed Pauline. "You'll have to ask Peter to explain it to you."

"It's all pretty modern around here, if you ask me," said Carrie, shaking her head. "And how does that washing machine work?"

"It's run by a gas engine down here," Berta said, pointing to the little motor near the bottom of the machine. Carrie was surprised to see the wringers turning by themselves.

Corky came in from outside just then with an empty clothesbasket. "I got the first load hung up already," he announced. Seeing the girls, he said, "Mornin' to you, young ladies."

"Good morning, Corky," they said in unison.

"By golly, that wind outside will dry them clothes fast today," he said.

Stella was sending a batch of clothes from the final rinse water through a wringer so Corky set his basket down on the floor to catch them.

"In the winter time," explained Pauline, "we have to hang the clothes on these lines here," and she spread her arm to indicate the lines strung from one wall to the next.

"O course, we don't have as many clothes then," Stella added.

Corky headed out the door with another basket of heavy, wet clothes. The girls went back to the kitchen and resumed their work.

The next couple days sped by quickly for Carrie and soon it was Sunday morning. Peter had told her and Amund the night before that he would get a buggy and the three of them could drive into Davenport for church services.

After helping the cooks fix a breakfast of pancakes and eggs, Carrie and Pauline were given the rest of the day off. How great that will be, thought Carrie!

Mrs. Daud insisted that the women should have a day of rest on Sunday, just like the men. There would be no big Sunday dinner. Many of the men would eat elsewhere. Some went home for the day if they lived close enough and others would go into Davenport or Kindred for a meal. Many went to church services somewhere, as Mr. Daud encouraged his workers to do so.

Peter and Amund stopped the buggy in front of the house and Carrie, who was watching for them from the parlor window, came hurrying out the front door.

"Good morning, boys," she called as she neared the rig.

Amund got out and helped his sister step up into the buggy. Peter flicked the reins and off they went.

"I saw the Dauds leaving the yard a short time ago," said Amund. "Where do they go to church?"

"They often go over to the Moravian church which is west of here a few miles. Sometimes they go to Davenport to the German Lutheran church," answered Peter.

"Where are we going to church today?" Carrie asked Peter.

"We'll go to the Norwegian Lutheran one in Davenport. Then," Peter added, "we'll stop in the cafe there and have dinner again. What do you think of that?"

"That will be fine," said Amund, and Carrie agreed.

"It will be so nice to eat somewhere where I don't have to serve it!" exclaimed Carrie. "Or do the dishes!"

"How has the week been going for you then?" asked Peter. "Do you think it's going to be too much work?"

"Well, it is taking a bit getting used to. We hardly have a free moment but I think I'll make it. Everything is made and served in such big amounts here!"

"Just wait until harvest time. Then we have about twice as many men," said Peter. "But by then you should be used to it."

As they neared the town of Davenport, Carrie said to her brother, "I need to write a letter sometime today to Ma and Pa. I bet they are surely wondering about us! I've just been too tired in the evenings to do it."

Amund agreed. "Write for me, too. You know I'm not much at letter writing."

"Yah, I found that out," teased Peter. I was here for a year and I only got about two letters from my very best friend!"

They tied the horses at the hitching post in front of the church and joined the other latecomers as they filed into the building. They sat near the back as the congregation was just starting the opening hymn.

The sermon that day was about new beginnings. That is very fitting, Carrie thought. My life here now is very different than just a week ago, but the good Lord remains the same. I must never forget that, she mused.

Pastor Lium greeted them as they left the church and welcomed them to worship with them regularly. "It was good to be here," Amund said, after Peter introduced his two friends.

"We'll just leave the buggy here and walk down to the cafe," said Peter, and they had a pleasant walk past many nice little homes.

"You know," Carrie said, "it seems strange that exactly a week ago we were in our own little church back home and now, one week later, we are in such a different place!"

"Yah, out at the farm, it's different all right," agreed Peter, "but this little town here isn't much different than any other little town in Minnesota."

"I guess you're right there," said Carrie. "The people certainly are nice and friendly."

As they were enjoying a dinner of chicken and mashed potatoes, Carrie asked Amund to tell her all about what he had been doing since they arrived.

"I'll have to show you all around the farm today, Carrie," he told her. "There is so much to see. Truly amazing things!"

"The folks back home just won't believe some of the things I tell them," Carrie said. "Imagine, hot running water to do the laundry! And did you see that icehouse, Mannie? And all that big machinery that leaves the yard every day!"

The meal was topped off with bread pudding and coffee. As Carrie looked around, she noticed some of the men from the farm having their dinner there, too.

"What was your friend, Pauline, doing today?" Peter asked Carrie. "She could have come with us."

"I asked her if she wanted to join us, but she was going home with Cora for the day. She lives out west here someplace. Near a town called Leonard."

On the drive back to the farm, Peter told them more about the Daud family. "Mr. Daud's family in Chicago was into manufacturing. Buggies and carriages, I think. Mr. Daud considers himself kind of an inventor so that's why all the new-fangled things here on the farm.

"Whenever he's been to Chicago," Peter went on, "he comes back with some new ideas. Things that they do in the city. Like that running water, for instance.

"Another thing, he likes to keep up with the other Bonanza farms around here."

"So how many other big farms are there and where are they?" asked Amund.

"Well," said Peter, thinking, "there's the Dalrymple farm up by Casselton. Then there's the farms run by the Chaffees. All those are really big. You couldn't even imagine!

"There's one about the size of ours, the Downing farm, down by Wahpeton or Mooreton. There's a smaller one in Comstock, about straight east of here, just across the river into Minnesota. And then, of course, there's the Power farm at Helendale."

The buggy turned into the driveway to the Daud farm. "There are many large farms up and down the Valley, on either side of the border," Peter added.

He stopped the buggy in front of the house so Carrie could get off.

"Shall I take you on a little trip around the farm then, Carrie?" asked her brother.

"I'd like that, but I'll want to change my shoes and maybe my dress first."

"I'll come by in about fifteen minutes. Do you want to go along, Peter?"

"No, I think I'll take a little nap this afternoon. See you later, Carrie." With that the two men drove further on to the barns to unhitch the horses.

Carrie changed her clothes and was waiting down in the parlor for Amund a short while later. Hilde was sitting on the sofa, resting and reading a newspaper.

"I've never seen you out of the kitchen before," remarked Carrie, laughing. "I thought perhaps you lived in there!"

"Oh, yah, I sometimes think that myself." Hilde chuckled. "It's nice sitting here in the sun in the afternoon. On Sundays I have to get caught up on reading the *Davenport News* and such. Who are you waiting for?" she asked, noticing that Carrie was looking out the window every few minutes.

"My brother is coming back and we're going to take a tour of the farm. I haven't seen much besides this house, you know."

"Did you go into Davenport for church this morning?" asked Hilde.

"Yes, we did and then we had dinner at the cafe afterwards. We had some wonderful chicken. How about you? What did you do?"

"Well, I went to the Moravian church with the Dauds. Then I came back here and just found myself something to eat in the kitchen."

"Did you have to make something for the Dauds?"

"No, they were invited over to the Murphy's for Sunday dinner so they just dropped me off."

"Who are the Murphys?" asked Carrie, noticing Amund coming up the porch steps.

"They have a big farm east of here someplace. They are good friends of the Dauds."

Carrie opened the door for Amund and motioned for him to step inside. "Amund, have you met Hilde? The best cook in these here parts? This is my brother, Amund."

He removed his cap and stepped forward to shake her hand. "No, I guess I haven't had the pleasure to meet the person who cooks those big, wonderful meals!"

"I don't know how wonderful they are, but you men will eat anything if you're hungry enough," Hilde said, and laughed her deep, rich laugh.

"Well, I'm ready for the tour, Mannie," said Carrie, taking his arm and leading him out the door. "See you later, Hilde."

Brother and sister headed in the direction of the barns. Walking past the foreman's house, Amund said, "I suppose you've been there before. In the store in the back."

"Oh, yes, several times. Have you met Ida? The foreman's wife?"

"Yah, for sure. She's a jolly one, all right," he answered.

"And I've been in the ice house. Have you seen it?" Carrie asked her brother.

"Peter has taken me around to every building on this place!" he exclaimed. "I've seen every square inch, and I tell you, there are many of them!"

They walked past a building with the doors wide open and they looked inside. "This is the blacksmith shop," said Amund. "It looks like Hogie is in there, too."

He entered the darkened building and called, "Hey, Hogie! Aren't you supposed to be taking a day of rest?"

A large, muscular man with dark, curly hair stepped into the light and Carrie could see that the man was considerably older than his physique portrayed.

"Carrie, this is Hogan Henke, but everyone calls him Hogie. This is my sister, Carrie. You've seen her up at the big house."

"Yah, I certainly have and she's always working so hard that she doesn't have time to give me a second look!" With this he threw back his head and laughed. "Of course, she'd rather look at something younger than me!"

"What are you working on today?" Amund asked him.

"Oh, I was just in here looking for something that I couldn't find yesterday. It makes me so gol-derned mad when I can't find something."

"I'm just showing my sister around the place. Hope you find whatever it is you're looking for."

They left the shop, both squinting in the bright sunlight. "He's a colorful character," remarked Carrie. "He reminds me of the blacksmith in the poem we had to learn in school, 'The Village Blacksmith.'"

They both looked at each other and began reciting, "'Under a spreading chestnut tree the village smithy stands; The smith, a mighty man is he, With large and sinewy hands; And the muscles of his brawny arms are strong as iron bands.'"

Here they both stopped and laughed. "Old Miss Sorlie would be proud of us, that we remembered so much of it," said Amund. "Was that by Longfellow?"

"Yes, and I think I could say more if I had a little prompting. I remember that it was a long poem and we had to know the whole thing. It was kind of a sad poem, too, if I remember right."

"Well, I wasn't really interested in poetry and all that stuff," said Amund.

They stopped in front of a long, narrow building. Amund led the way inside. "This is one of the machine sheds." It had wide double doors on each end and also on the sides. "And these are the seeders that they just finished using. Yesterday we had to clean them all out and put them away till next year. Except for a couple that need repair. They're over in the building where I do all of my work. We'll see that next."

"I can't hardly believe it each day when I see all that machinery leave the yard!" exclaimed Carrie. "Wouldn't Pa and Olaf love to see all this?"

"Yah, that they would, for sure, for sure," he agreed.

"How wide are these seeders here anyway?" Carrie asked. "They sure make the one we have at home look like a toy!"

"These are ten footers, I think Peter told me. And see, there's a place to sit on each one of them. At home we had to walk behind."

At the far end of this same building were rows of harrows, which were used before the seeding.

"Let's be moving along, then, or it will take all day," said Amund. They left by a side door. "This next building is where I practically live!" he told her. "This is the repair shed. I'm glad it's not too far from the blacksmith because sometimes I need Hogie to weld something for me."

He pulled a string and a light came on overhead. She could see the workbench with numerous familiar tools and such.

"Have you been real busy repairing things?" she inquired.

"Oh, my, yes! Several things break each day, it seems."

The next stop was one of two big horse barns. "How many horses are on this farm anyway?" asked Carrie.

"There are close to 150 horses and about 30 mules."

"My, that takes a lot of hay and feed, doesn't it?" she remarked. "I suppose this is where Peter spends most of his time."

"Yah, here and in the next barn. I have to take you upstairs there and show you something."

They climbed the narrow stairway of the next barn and Amund pointed out a huge, round tank. "That's the holding tank for the water which is piped into the house and the barns and the bunkhouse, too."

Carrie moved closer to it and she just couldn't get over how large it was.

"It's fifteen feet in diameter, Peter told me. I asked him how in the world they got it up here! He said they had done this the year before he came here and that they had to cut out part of the front wall to get it in. It took many horses to pull the ropes that hoisted it up here. The floor had to be reinforced, too."

They both shook their heads in wonder as they headed back down the stairs.

Beyond the barns was the elevator, a tall building that made this farm look almost like a little town. Behind it Amund showed her a set of railroad tracks that came right up to the building.

"You mean they have their own railroad track and train coming in here?" She was incredulous.

"This is a railroad spur that comes from a little town named Addison, just west of here. During harvest or at other times when needed, a short train with some grain cars comes right up here and loads up with grain!"

"Oh, I can't wait to tell the folks back home about this. It's going to be a long letter!"

"Next I'll show you the food storage shed," said Amund. This building was also on the railroad spur.

Amund pushed open a big sliding door and helped Carrie up.

"The Dauds get all their bulk food supplies by rail car," Amund told her. "It comes from a wholesaler in St. Paul."

Carrie stood in the middle of the room, in a spot just big enough to turn around, and looked at all the shelves of foodstuffs.

"There's the wooden crates of dried apples that we made apple pie out of the other day. There's dried tomatoes, too."

"Here's crates of canned vegetables, like green beans, corn, and carrots." Amund was reading the labels. "These big sacks here are beans. And here's coffee beans in these wood barrels," he went on.

"How often does a shipment come here?" asked Carrie.

"Peter didn't exactly say, but I think maybe twice a year, or more if needed. Peter says that Mr. Daud has a telephone in his office, which is at the back of the foreman's house. You know, the room right next to the little store."

"Yes, I guess I saw an office there," said Carrie. "I didn't know that it was Mr. Daud's."

"He and Mr. Thompson spend many a late night poring over the books in there. Well, anyway, that telephone can be used to call St. Paul for supplies. They use the telephone to call the other big farms in the area, too.

"Sometimes even Mrs. Daud comes and uses it to call the wives of the other big farmers who have telephones," Peter went on. "And, of course, their daughter has a telephone where she lives, in Casselton."

"They should have one in the house, too," remarked Carrie.

"Well, I think that Peter said that this summer they plan to have one installed in the study."

There were several sacks of flour with the words "Queen of the Valley" written on them.

"Peter said that some of the wheat grown here is taken down to the mill south of Kindred and ground into flour there. The mill is called the Sheyenne River Rollers Mill. Isn't that quite some name?"

After spending some time looking at all the crates, barrels and sacks, the pair jumped down from the building and Amund pushed the door shut.

"I wonder if they have a mice problem in there, in those sacks," said Carrie.

"They have traps set all around," Amund informed her.

"Oh, good thing we didn't step on one!"

"Now, are you ready to see where I sleep?" asked Amund, taking Carrie's hand and leading her quickly to the next building. It was a wooden, two-story structure with many windows.

Amund said, "I'll stick my head in the door first and make sure everyone is decent!" Then he motioned for her to enter. The first room was a lounge area with several leather sofas and about half a dozen wood chairs. A pot-bellied stove sat in the middle with a full wood box next to it.

Carrie could see a barber chair way back in the corner. "Do you have someone who cuts your hair here?"

"Yah, that would be Big Swede. He's been doing it for years. He charges ten cents for a haircut and a shave. I guess he gets pretty busy on some Saturday nights!"

Peter nodded at the door that separated the two downstairs rooms. "That's where we sleep. There are rows of bunk beds, some shelves and pegs for our clothes, and that's about all. On each end of the room, there's a sink with piped-in water. It's cold, though."

Amund nodded toward a stairway. "Up these stairs are more bunks. They're used when there is a full crew here."

Then he led her toward the back of the building. "There are several bathtubs in there," he pointed out. "If Corky fires up the boilers, then we get hot water for a bath once in awhile. In the summertime, there are shower stalls outside with tanks up above. The sun warms the water and by evening, the men can take a quick shower, Peter tells me."

"This is all so interesting!" exclaimed Carrie.

"Also in the back there, is the laundry where Corky does all the washing for the men. Right now, he's doing it alone but later he'll get help, I understand."

As they were heading for the house, Peter came hurrying up to them. "Well, hello there! Did you have a good tour of the farm then?" he inquired of Carrie.

"Oh, yes! This is quite the place. I'm going to write home about it tonight. I was telling Mannie that it will be a long, long letter!"

"Greet your folks from me, " Peter requested. "I don't write home much myself but I guess it's about time I did."

Changing the subject, Peter turned to Amund. "Say, some of the fellows are going to get a game of baseball going after a bit. Would you like to play?"

"I've hardly played it but I would like to learn," Amund answered. He said to Carrie, "I'll see you later then," and he turned and went with his friend.

CHAPTER 9

Carrie was glad she had sat up late and finished a long letter to her family back home because the next few days just flew by. She was totally exhausted each evening when she went to bed. I should be getting used to this constant work pretty soon, she thought.

Several times, besides the usual kitchen work, she was asked to help with the ironing. Stella ironed the clothes and linens for the Daud family, but the kitchen helpers were to do the other items, such as all the aprons, dishtowels, bedding, etc. Each person was responsible for doing their own clothes, though, but sometimes Carrie and Pauline would do Hilde's, too.

Carrie was surprised the first time she tried ironing. She was accustomed to using flat irons, which were heated on the kitchen stove and replaced when one cooled off. The irons in the Daud laundry each had an apparatus fueled by kerosene to heat the appliance. This was hard for Carrie to get used to at first but as she had no choice, she soon became adept at using them. They were rather clumsy but it was nice not to have to keep changing them.

The month of May remained dry and Mr. Thompson mentioned to Peter and Amund concerns about the newly planted wheat lying in dry dirt. Early one morning, though, Carrie was awakened by big drops of rain pelting the window of her room.

The tone was almost jovial at breakfast that morning, as all the men had shared the same concern. This also meant a day of rest, at least until the rain stopped. Then Mr. Thompson would find work for them to do, like cleaning out stalls and other unsavory jobs.

It rained off and on all that day but the next morning the sun shone brightly. By afternoon, the men were put to work painting outbuildings and chopping wood for the insatiable appetite of the kitchen stoves!

One morning, as Carrie was taking freshly baked loaves of bread out of the oven, Ida came in the kitchen door and cheerfully announced that a letter had come for Carrie.

"I thought I'd run over here with it as I know how you have been waiting for a letter!" announced Ida cheerfully.

Hilde convinced Ida to have a cup of coffee with them, at the same time shooing Carrie out of the kitchen so she could go someplace by herself and read her letter. Carrie reluctantly did so. She ran up to her room and sat in the chair by the window and opened the letter with excitement.

It was in her mother's handwriting, but as she quickly looked down the two pages, she could see that Sylvia had added something toward the end. She started to read, savoring each word as if it was a tasty morsel of her favorite food.

Her mother first commented on how happy they were to finally hear from Carrie that she and Amund had made it there all right. Here Carrie felt guilty for not writing sooner, at least to let them know of their safe arrival. Reading on, her mother filled her in on day to day things. Olaf's wife, Mattie, was feeling pretty good but the baby wasn't due until July. She and Rosina had found the time to sew some baby garments and she was now knitting a blanket.

Carrie's mother went on to say that Martin and Rosina were through with school now for the year and Martin was so excited to be able to help his pa from morning till night. He was going to be the farmer that Amund never was.

Carrie had to put the letter down for a few moments as her eyes blurred with unshed tears as she read about the things going on at home. She felt a wave of homesickness overwhelm her. Composing herself, she read on. Pa had gotten his way and he and Olaf rented another eighty from a neighbor and they planted it all in wheat. They had just received a much-needed rain.

Sylvia had a long paragraph at the end of the letter with her exciting news. Rudy had finally proposed and they would be getting married in December. Oh, good, thought Carrie, I'll be home for the wedding. Rudy had started a new job with his uncle in the hardware store. His cousin had died unexpectedly so his uncle needed his help.

Carrie quickly folded the letter and put it in her apron pocket. She would have to give it to Amund to read. She would reread it again tonight. She hurried back down to the kitchen.

Ida had left already and Carrie remembered that she had not even thanked the woman for bringing the letter to her.

"So did you have news from home?" Hilde inquired.

"Yes, it was from my mother and also my sister. They were so happy to finally hear from me." Here the tears threatened to appear again so Carrie couldn't say anything for awhile.

"Yah, and I suppose you have been feeling a little homesick from time to time, haven't you, child?" Hilde asked kindly.

Carrie could only nod and Hilde understood and didn't probe further.

Carrie busied herself with peeling potatoes and when she could talk again, she announced, "My older sister, Sylvia, is getting married so there'll be a wedding in December. Also, my brother and his wife will be having their first baby in July."

Hilde seemed genuinely interested in Carrie's family and asked many questions. In the long run, this made Carrie feel better, being able to talk to someone about each of her family members.

At noon, after the men had finished eating, Carrie went over to Amund and told him she had received a letter and she gave it to him to read. He went out on the porch and sat down over in the far corner on a bench and began reading. He read it over again and then came back into the dining hall and returned it to Carrie.

"It sounds like things are going well at home then, don't you think?" he asked his sister.

She nodded. "I'm so happy for Sylvia," she said. "And I can just imagine how happy Marty is, like a calf let out to pasture!"

The two laughed and shared some more comments about their family and then Amund said he had to hurry back to work. There were harnesses to repair. Carrie had to help with the dishes, another never-ending job.

Then there was ironing to do. She really hated ironing, but usually she and Pauline or Stella would both be ironing at the same time as there were two ironing boards and two irons. The time passed more quickly with someone to talk to.

Hilde and Cora were making doughnuts in the kitchen and it wasn't long before Carrie could smell the aroma back in the laundry. Her mouth began to water just thinking about them. The back door banged open and startled

Carrie and Stella.

"By golly, I smelled them doughnuts way across the yard and I had to think of some excuse for coming in the house and maybe Hilde would give me a doughnut and a cup of coffee." It was Corky, with an armload of firewood, and he laughed heartily as he wiped his shoes off on the rug and headed down the hall to the kitchen.

Stella and Carrie looked at each other and Stella said, "That sounds like a good idea to me, too! How about it, are you soon finished?"

Carrie said that she just wanted to finish the shirtwaist she was doing and then she would join her in the kitchen. When Carrie finished her job, she followed the inviting aroma and the sound of laughter met her.

As she entered the room, Hilde was pretending to whack Corky's knuckles as he reached for yet another doughnut. When he sprang out of her way, he knocked several of them right onto the floor. He got down on his hands and knees and was crawling around under the table because they had rolled every which way.

The women laughed until tears rolled down their checks as he made such a funny sight. He retrieved all the doughnuts and rose and held them out to Hilde.

"Oh, you can have them now, after they've been on the floor!" she told him, trying to sound stern.

He took out his handkerchief and wrapped them up and put them in his big overall pocket. "Gee, Moses, I've got to get outta here before I really get into trouble!" he exclaimed, and he made a dash for the door.

The women's laughter followed him way out into the yard. "He had already eaten three of them," explained Hilde to Carrie, "and he was reaching for more!" She shook her head, chuckling out loud. "I think he loves doughnuts more than anybody I know."

Carrie helped herself to one and poured a cup of coffee. "I can see why he loves yours so much, Hilde. These are better than my mother's, even."

Pretty soon there was a timid knock on the side door. It was the Thompson boys. They had smelled the familiar aroma, too, and it had led them to the 'big house,' as it was called. Hilde motioned them to come in and she told them to sit down and help themselves. She reached into the icebox and pulled out a jar of milk and poured them each a full glass.

"When you finish eating, boys, you can run out to the ice house and get some more ice for the kitchen here," Cora said, nodding towards the icebox where the milk had just come from.

"We sure will, Cora," they said agreeably, helping themselves to one more doughnut each.

"Now that school is out, we're going to keep you boys really busy with all kinds of chores," teased Hilde. They just grinned and gulped their milk, making moustaches on their upper lip.

"Don't eat anymore, now, boys, or you'll spoil your supper and then your ma will be mad at us!" warned Cora.

They ran off for the ice and the girls helped clean up the mess from the doughnut making. They poured the hot lard into a pail and put it aside for next time. It would be kept in the cooler in the icehouse.

Supper that night was leftover roast beef in gravy and served on slices of bread. A simple meal, topped off with rice pudding and fresh doughnuts. The men helped themselves to at least three each!

That night, up in their bedroom, Carrie and Pauline finished their evening devotions and then Carrie took out the crumpled letter from home. Pauline settled down to sleep and Carrie propped herself up with her pillow and began to read.

When she finished, she thought she heard music. She turned off the light and went to the window, which they had opened slightly to let in a little of the fresh, spring air. It sounded like harmonica music, coming from the bunkhouse. It was a haunting melody, and she listened for a long while. The plaintive strains stirred up feelings of homesickness in Carrie, which were already close to the surface. She went back to her bed and buried her face in her pillow and let the tears flow freely but silently.

The next morning, Carrie awoke feeling tired but then she perked up when she remembered that this was the day when she would get to go to town with Mrs. Daud. She hurried and got dressed and actually beat Pauline down to the kitchen.

She grabbed an apron from the hook and as she was tying it, Hilde said, "So, you get to go shopping today, do you?"

"Yes, and I'm really excited. I wonder where we will go?"

"I haven't heard where she plans to go today," remarked Hilde. "The weather and roads should be fine."

The women served a breakfast of soda biscuits and eggs. "I hope the Jorgensons get the eggs here before long," said Cora, as they were cleaning up. "We need them for the custard we planned for dessert at noon."

They heard a wagon coming in the yard but it was not the Jorgensons with the eggs. It was the Schultz' hired man with the milk. He drove up to the icehouse and left six pails full of milk in the cooler and he also left cream and butter.

"I'm surprised the Dauds don't have milk cows to provide all the milk they need here," remarked Carrie. " And chickens, too, for all the eggs we go through."

"Mrs. Daud hates chickens and Mr. Daud didn't want to bother with milk cows. It would take several men to take care of them," explained Hilde. "He said it's just easier to buy from the neighbors. Heaven knows, they've got the money," she sighed.

A few minutes later, Mrs. Daud appeared in the kitchen and Hilde hoped that she hadn't heard her last remark. She didn't give any indication of doing so.

"Well, Carrie, did you remember you're going to town with me today?" she asked.

"Oh, yes! I couldn't forget a thing like that. It will be so much fun!"

"Well, you need a day off, that's for sure," said the older woman. She turned to leave the room.

"We'll depart about one o'clock. We're going to go to Horace today," she said. "I read in the paper that the Thue store has a new shipment of fine kid gloves and I certainly am in need of some."

When she left, Pauline turned to Carrie and said, "Oh, you'll love the Thue store. It has so many things."

"It maybe has many things, but I don't have the money to buy them!" said Carrie good-naturedly.

They heard another wagon enter the yard and it was the eggs this time. They were unloaded at the icehouse so Pauline went to bring back a basketful so the cooks could get the custard started.

Carrie was watching the clock in the dining hall as she was sweeping up after dinner. She would just have time to run up to her room and make a quick change and do a little something to her hair.

She came down at precisely one o'clock. Mrs. Daud entered the kitchen a few moments later. "Shall we go then, Carrie?" she asked as she headed for the door. "I told Corky to have the carriage outside and ready for us."

And indeed it was. The two women got in and Mrs. Daud deftly handled the horses like she had been doing it all her life. "Driving the buggy so much is certainly hard on my gloves," she told Carrie. That's what I plan to buy at the store. What do you need today?"

"I guess I'll just look first. Maybe I'll find a nice shirtwaist. I should have some more for everyday. I don't have time to sew myself one."

"Oh, I'm sure you will find just what you need there. It is a very nice store for a small town."

"I suppose it's very different shopping in Chicago than it is around here," said Carrie conversationally.

"It certainly is, but I enjoy going to these little towns. Mainly, I like to get off the farm once in awhile," she laughed. "When we're in Chicago in the wintertime, I try to buy up things that I know that I'll probably not find here."

"It certainly is a beautiful day for a drive," exclaimed Carrie. "How long will it take to get there?"

"It takes almost an hour. I suppose you have never been there before. It's almost straight east of us. It's a nice drive."

Carrie noticed that the wheat had come up since Sunday when they drove to church. The fields for miles around were green with the new shoots.

"It looks so pretty, with the fields so green now and the soil so dark. The soil is different than back home. It's not so black as it is here."

"Yes, this is my favorite time of the year to go driving. It's also mighty pretty when the wheat is ripe and ready for harvest," Mrs. Daud reflected.

The pair found many things to talk about and soon they saw the town of Horace a short distance away. The horses seemed to speed up and soon they were stopped beside a hitching post at one end of the boardwalk.

"We'll leave the horses here as this is where we'll end up." She led

Carrie to the other side of the street and they headed for the Thue Mercantile Store.

Upon entering, Carrie was amazed at how large it was. She began walking up and down each aisle, picking up everything and looking at it. "You just take your time now," Mrs. Daud told her. "We have no need to hurry."

They must have spent almost an hour in there, Carrie figured. She had found a nice shirtwaist and purchased it and also some other little things she needed. Mrs. Daud bought several pairs of the kid gloves that she wanted and the two walked out quite satisfied with themselves.

"Oh, that was so much fun to see all their nice merchandise!" exclaimed Carrie. "Thank you for bringing me."

"Well, we aren't done yet," said Mrs. Daud. "I always like to stop off for a little treat before we head for home. There is the Union Hotel where we could go for coffee and maybe a piece of pie or we could go to the drug store where they have an ice cream parlor. I'll let you decide." She looked at Carrie for an answer.

"Oh, perhaps the ice cream parlor would be fun."

"The ice cream parlor it is," said Mrs. Daud, as she took Carrie's arm and they strode off expectantly for the drug store.

"This is where I often want to go, too," said Mrs. Daud. "I have a weakness for ice cream, don't you?"

"I haven't had it very many times except when we made it at home in the winter time. And, oh, it tasted so good."

"Have you ever tried an ice cream soda?" asked the older woman.

"Only once, when we went to Lansing a few years ago."

"I'll think that's what I'll have today. A cherry soda," said Mrs. Daud.

"Me too," said Carrie, excited as a child.

"This is a nice store," commented Carrie after they had ordered.

"It's owned by the town's doctor, Dr.Chagnon," Mrs. Daud explained.

A short while later, they were slurping the remains of the delicious ice cream concoction from the tall glasses. They laughed at the noise that it made and looked around them. Then they got down from the high stools, retrieved all their packages and headed for the buggy.

"This has been such a fun day!" said Carrie with delight, as they were leaving town. "Almost like a holiday!"

"We'll do this often then!" laughed Mrs. Daud.

Carrie thought the older woman looked almost like a young girl herself when she laughed.

"There are several other towns I'll want to show you. Have you been to the Tuskind Store in Davenport yet?"

"Not yet. I only get to town there on Sunday mornings and of course the store isn't open then."

"We'll have to go there next time. And we must go to Kindred, too. They have two nice department stores. And an ice cream parlor," she added with a laugh.

The bright, late afternoon sun shone in their eyes all the way home but the trip went fast and Carrie was soon in the kitchen, putting on an apron and telling everyone about her exciting day.

"Show us your purchases," Pauline suggested. Carrie pulled out her new shirtwaist and held it up to her. She also took out the other little items for the women to see. There was a pretty comb to wear in her hair, a nail buffer, a pair of stockings and a small box of face powder.

"You did right well for yourself," said Hilde, after looking at the new items.

"That store had a good selection of ready-mades," said Carrie. "I only wish I had the money to buy some of them. I saw a beautiful dress that I would love to have to wear on Sundays." She sighed and put her things back in the brown paper that they were wrapped in and set it aside to bring up to her room later.

"Now, what do you want me to do first, Hilde?" she asked, eager to get to work after her wonderful afternoon off.

"We're going to have soup and bread and cheese. Cookies for dessert. You can set the tables first, girls, and then slice the cheese. It takes a lot of cheese to full up those men."

"What kind of soup is it tonight?" inquired Carrie.

"Chicken with dumplings," answered Cora. "I let Hilde make the dumplings, though. She makes the best ones!"

"Another new man showed up today, girls," Hilde called to them as they headed for the dining hall, "so set another place."

Pauline and Carrie set the tables and hurried back to start on the cheese and the bread. Hilde was mixing up the dumplings. "What do you put in your dumplings to make them so special, Hilde?" asked Carrie.

"Oh, the usual, but I add some leftover mashed potatoes. Then I drop them into the broth, cover tightly and steam for about twelve minutes. The secret is not to peek!"

"I'll be anxious to taste them, if the men leave us some!" remarked Carrie.

"I'll put some aside for you girls. I've made plenty."

Hilde was true to her word and Carrie thought her dumplings were the best she'd ever tasted, "I'll have to get your recipe and give it to my mother," she told Hilde. "These cookies are delicious, too. What kind are they?"

"They're banana oatmeal. I thought Corky and the Thompson boys were going to eat them all up before supper!" exclaimed Cora. "Bet they weren't very hungry for their supper."

"You two are just such good cooks and everyone around here knows it," Pauline told them.

After supper clean-up, Carrie and Pauline took a walk around the farm and then down the driveway and back. "It's such a lovely spring evening," commented Pauline.

"Yes, and to think tomorrow is the first day of June! Time is really going fast."

"Did you take much notice of the new man who arrived today?" Pauline asked Carrie.

"Not really," shrugged Carrie. "Why?"

"Well, I thought he was rather good looking. He kept looking at us, like he was interested."

"Tomorrow at breakfast I'll take a good look at him and give you my opinion," laughed Carrie. The girls went in the house and stopped by the kitchen. Hilde was still in there.

"Hilde, what are you still busy with?" asked Carrie.

"Oh, I'm just putting the beans in water to soak overnight. Baked beans tomorrow for dinner."

They bid her good night after she assured them that she didn't need any help and they went up to their room to get ready for bed.

A half-hour later, as Carrie pulled the covers up to her neck, they heard the music start up again through the open window. "Who is it that plays the harmonica so nicely?" asked Carrie. "I heard it one other night, too."

"That's probably Karl, the man who came last month. He was here last year, too, and I remember that he played the harmonica."

The girls went to sleep to the tune of "In the Gloaming."

CHAPTER 10

Carrie thought that her birthday, June 3, would be just like any other day. She had received a letter the day before from her family wishing her a happy birthday. She was almost feeling a little bit sorry for herself, not having any family around on her special day. Except Amund, of course, but knowing him, she grumbled to herself, he would be too busy to think of it.

After breakfast, Ida popped in the kitchen door and came up to Carrie and wished her a happy birthday and then she invited all the ladies to come to her house in the afternoon for cake and coffee. "We'll have a little party!" she said.

This lifted Carrie's spirits and put a little skip into her step as she went about her work. I'm sure glad there is no ironing today, she thought. She was busy peeling potatoes and had just taken the loaves of bread out of the oven when she heard a knock on the side door. It was Amund. He looked a little sheepish as he admitted that he had forgotten that it was her birthday but had just thought of it now.

"Somebody had mentioned the date, June 3, and then it rang a bell!" her brother said. "I'll talk to you later. I have to get to work now."

"Oh, thank you for stopping by, Mannie. You don't know how much this means to me!"

Mrs. Daud stopped by next. "I hear there is going to be a party for the birthday girl," she remarked, looking at Carrie. Carrie didn't know quite what to say, as she didn't know if Mrs. Daud was invited or not. Then her employer started discussing something with Hilde and the awkward moment passed.

Dinner was served and the women hurried to clean up and do dishes. Cora said, "Carrie shouldn't have to do dishes today. I'll take over. You run upstairs and take a little rest and freshen up a bit," she ordered.

Hilde and Pauline were nodding their heads in agreement so Carrie did as she was told. An hour later they were all sitting in Ida's kitchen, around her round oak table. She had put on a lacy tablecloth and in the middle was a pretty vase full of lilacs from the bushes out back. They gave off a wonderful fragrance and, mingled with the aroma of freshly brewed coffee, it made for a pleasant atmosphere.

There were six places set around the table but so far it was Carrie, Hilde, Cora and Pauline and Ida, of course. Then Ida mentioned that they would wait a few more minutes before she served the cake, as Mrs. Daud should be coming over in a short while.

When Carrie looked surprised at this, Ida said, "Oh, Mrs. Daud won't miss a party if she can help it! There's nothing uppity about her. She likes to mingle with the women who work here."

Her voice trailed off as she saw the woman she was talking about coming up the walk. She went to the door and welcomed her in. Mrs. Daud, out of breath and flushed from rushing, sat down and began to explain the reason why she was late.

"I was about to go out the door and that new telephone that we just installed in the house last week rang and it was for me. It was Mrs. Dalrymple, inviting me to a tea party next Friday. How fun that will be!" she exclaimed. "She gives the best parties!"

Ida served the coffee and pieces of cake to each and then sat down herself.

"Oh, my!" exclaimed Carrie, "this cake tastes just heavenly. What kind is it?"

"It's a Lady Baltimore cake. I make this for special occasions. It's my family's favorite."

"This filling is what makes it so good," commented Pauline. "I just love nuts!"

Ida tried to push seconds on the ladies and they finally relented and said they would each have just a half piece more.

"After all, we may not taste this cake again for a long time," laughed Hilde.

After a lot of talking, laughing and eating, Mrs. Daud remembered that she had brought a little gift for Carrie. She pulled it out of her pocket. It was wrapped in brown paper with the Thue Store name on it.

Carrie opened it, saying all along that Mrs. Daud shouldn't have gone to the bother of giving her a present. When she saw what it was, she gave out a little gasp. It was a pair of kid gloves, like the ones Mrs. Daud had purchased when the two of them had gone to Horace together a short while back.

"I hope you like that color, dear," the older woman said. "They call it 'fawn' and I know they will fit. Remember I had you try on some pairs at the store?"

Carrie laughed and said, "Yes, but I sure didn't know that they would be for me!"

She put them on and everyone said how nice they were and how well they looked on her. They all had to take turns trying them on.

"Oh, thank you so much," said Carrie, "and thank you, too, Ida, for this lovely party. It made the day so special for me. I have to admit that I was feeling a little blue this morning, thinking about my family and birthdays past. Ma always made cakes for each of us and cooked our favorite meal."

Joey and Billy came in the house and asked if they could have some birthday cake. After Billy finished his, he left again, but Joey lingered. He looked at Carrie and asked. "Carrie, how old are you today?"

When she told him that she was eighteen now, he was silent for awhile, figuring something in his head. "Only five years older," he announced.

"What do you mean by that, Joey?" asked Carrie.

"Well, Billy wants to marry you when he grows up and I was just wondering how much older you are." With this, he jumped off his chair and hurried out the door after his older brother.

Everyone looked after him in astonishment and then they all burst out laughing.

Ida shook her head, "Oh, that Billy! I don't know how he got that idea into his head."

"Well, he's growing up, you know," said Mrs. Daud with a merry twinkle in her eye.

The women reluctantly left the warmth and coziness of Ida's kitchen and returned to their work. "It's a good thing I planned a simple supper tonight so that we could stay later at Ida's," Hilde remarked, as they made their way back to the big house.

That evening after supper, Amund caught Carrie's eye and said that he and Peter would come by later and have a little visit. Carrie and Pauline were sitting in the parlor when the two men arrived.

"It's such a nice evening, why don't we go out on the porch and sit?" suggested Amund.

The girls sat on the bench and the men sat on the railing. It was a very peaceful evening. There was a warm breeze, and when they were quiet enough, they could hear crickets chirping.

Carrie told them about the birthday party and Amund said that he didn't have a gift, but he had a surprise for her instead. It would 'arrive' soon. She was curious but he wouldn't say anything more.

Peter told Pauline that the young man who had been sweet on her last summer was coming again and that he would be here in a few days.

"Now who would that be, for heaven's sake!" she said, blushing in the semi-darkness.

"As if you didn't know!" teased Peter.

Carrie looked at them both questioningly. Amund appeared interested, too.

"Don't you remember the man who took you for a buggy ride or two? Do I have to refresh your memory?" Peter turned to Carrie and then to Amund. "His name is Emory Strom." He let the name roll off his tongue like he was announcing royalty. "He's from Wisconsin and he wrote Mr. Thompson a few days ago and said that he would be coming to work here again this summer."

Carrie looked again at Pauline. "He was just a friend," she started to explain. "Several of us went to some dances together and he was among the group. I didn't know that he was sweet on me," she said, glaring at Peter until they all laughed.

Just then they heard music coming up the path toward them. It was that harmonica player, Carrie could see, and he wasn't alone. There were several other men with him.

"Here comes your surprise!" exclaimed Amund as he jumped off the railing and walked toward the group of men. He ushered them right up onto the porch and they gathered around Carrie and began to sing to her. First they honored her with the birthday song and then they sang some of Carrie's favorites. Amund had told them what to sing.

They sang "K-K-K Katy," but the second time through they substituted Carrie's name. They sang "Oh! Susanna" and "Jeanie With the Light Brown

Hair," again using Carrie's name; and "Blest Be the Tie that Binds."

Then the men sat down and Karl played the harmonica and they all listened until dark. Carrie saw Hilde and Cora sitting in the parlor, listening, and she could imagine that probably the Dauds could hear the music upstairs.

The musicians left and Carrie thanked them graciously. Then she thanked Amund for thinking of such a great gift.

"That bunch of fellows sing many an evening in the bunk house. They really enjoy it and we often sing along," commented Peter.

"I've heard the harmonica playing sometimes from our bedroom window. It has put me to sleep several nights," said Carrie.

About an hour later, Carrie was again lying in her bed, thinking of how wonderful this birthday turned out after all. "That sure was nice of Mrs. Daud to give me those beautiful gloves!" she remarked to Pauline.

"Yes, she loves to give gifts. She's a very kind and generous person."

"I don't even know when your birthday is, Pauline."

"January," she answered. "January 20th. I just turned nineteen this year."

"Tell me about this Emory fellow that Peter was talking about."

"There's nothing to tell," answered Pauline. "Like I said, we all went to some dances together around here." That's all she volunteered.

"What about the buggy rides?" persisted Carrie.

"Well, he did take me on a couple of buggy rides," Pauline admitted. "And then he left."

The next Sunday morning, on the way to Davenport for church, Peter said to his passengers, "After church, we have to wait around for a passenger who is getting off the train about noon and give him a ride to the farm."

The church was very crowded this fine June morning. Carrie looked around and saw a few familiar faces. Some were from the farm and a couple others were people from town that she had gotten to know.

"We'll go to the depot and see if the train will be in on time," Peter announced. "If it is, we'll wait and take our passenger to dinner with us. I'm sure he'll be starved."

"Do you know this man?" Carrie asked.

"It's that fellow I was telling you about. Emory Strom!" Peter exclaimed.

"That's why I asked you to invite Pauline along to church this morning."

"She was going to go with the Dauds to the Moravian church today," said Carrie.

A short while later, they had picked up their passenger and taken him over to the cafe with them for dinner. Carrie thought that he was a nice young man. He was very polite and soft-spoken but he had many interesting things to say. He was from a large family and raised on a farm in Wisconsin. In the winter, he would go and work in northern Minnesota as a lumberjack.

"That's really hard work and some of those fellows are mighty tough characters," he related. "I soon learned to stay out of the way of some of them. They'd rather fight than anything!"

On the way back to the farm, Peter asked Mr. Strom if he remembered a girl named Pauline who worked there last year.

"Oh, yes!" he enthused. "She was a cute one, she was."

"Well, you're in luck, my dear fellow," said Peter. "She's here this year, too, and still cute as ever!"

Carrie was embarrassed at Peter's frank remarks and she poked him in the ribs in reprimand. He looked at her in all innocence and shrugged his shoulders.

Carrie decided not to tell Pauline about Emory being here but let her find out herself. The next morning at breakfast when he entered the dining hall, he caught Pauline's eye and gave her a smile and a wave. She got all flustered and the color rose to her cheeks.

"So, he was nothing special to you, huh?" Carrie whispered to her friend as they passed each other while serving the men. Pauline had nothing to say to that.

That same morning, Hilde informed the girls that there would be a special guest for dinner so they were to set the square table with a tablecloth and set places for three. Mr. Power was coming over from the Helendale farm to talk with Mr. Daud. Mr. Thompson would be joining them for the meal.

They would be serving roast pork, mashed potatoes, stewed turnips, and custard with a caramel sauce. Mrs. Daud was in the kitchen several times to see that everything was just so. She needn't have worried. Hilde always had everything under control. Carrie wondered if anything ever flustered that woman.

Mr. Daud and Mr. Power came into the dining hall before the other men started coming in. Hilde told Pauline to ask if they wanted coffee while they were visiting. She came back in the kitchen and said that they would each like a cup.

Carrie was just finishing up with setting the long tables. She stole some glances at their guest. He was about average height, wore spectacles, had a balding head and a drooping moustache. The men were obviously talking about farming. What else, Carrie thought?

Long after the hired hands had their meal and left the room, the three men sat at their separate table, talking. As far as Carrie could tell, Mr. Power was explaining some new farming technique and Mr. Thompson was skeptical. Mrs. Daud came into the room and inquired about Mrs. Power. The couple had just celebrated their 50th wedding anniversary the year before and the Dauds had been in attendance at the celebration.

That evening as Pauline and Carrie were sitting on the front porch, Amund and Peter came strolling over. Peter started telling the girls about the dinner guest they had today. He said that Mr. Power had been influential in changing the way farmers farmed around the state. He actually was more interested in cattle farming than anything else, but he was also very interested in soil conservation and developing new seed varieties, Peter told them.

"He was even president of the North Dakota Agricultural College in Fargo for a few years. He was also director of their Experiment Station," Peter went on. "He was always promoting North Dakota as a state to be reckoned with."

A week later, Mrs. Daud caught the train at Davenport and went up to Casselton, a short distance further north, to stay with her daughter, Eunice, for a few days. And also to attend the tea party put on out at the Dalrymple farm, which was a few miles east of Casselton.

"I'm surprised that I haven't met the Dauds' daughter yet," Carrie said to Hilde one day. "You said that she often came out here, especially on Sunday afternoons."

"Well, she hasn't been feeling well for a couple months-- female trouble, Mrs. Daud said,-- but she is much better now. Mrs. Daud said the two of them were going to do some shopping in Casselton and then Friday is the big tea party. She'll be home on Saturday evening. She'll have plenty to tell us then!" laughed Hilde.

The men were busy getting ready for the haying season. They would start cutting in a few days. Amund said that he was busy sharpening up the sickles on the hay mowers and Peter had several more horses to have re-shoed. They hoped the weather would remain dry.

Peter told Carrie and Pauline that there was going to be a dance in Davenport on Saturday night. Many of the young men were planning to attend.

"We're going to get a couple wagons-full so why don't you two girls come along?"

"Oh, that might be fun," replied Carrie, and Pauline nodded her head in agreement.

The next few days passed by quickly as the two girls talked about the upcoming dance and what they would wear. Actually Carrie had no choice but to wear her Sunday dress. As she was ironing it in the laundry room that afternoon, Corky came in the back door.

"I hear you girls are going to the big dance tonight with all the fellows," he said to Carrie. "By Jiminy, if I were about twenty years younger, I'd jump in that wagon and go along!"

"Why don't you come, Corky," Carrie suggested. "You can dance with me."

"I used to dance a lot but I guess those days are over for me," he lamented.

"Why do you say that?" Carrie wanted to know.

"Well, the missus and I loved to dance but when she passed on I lost the taste for it. I'll leave it up to you young people."

"You could come and watch," said Carrie.

He didn't answer but walked on toward the kitchen. Carrie thought he looked sad, which was different for him. He was always joking and teasing. Later on, after Corky had left and Carrie was in the kitchen with Hilde, she asked the cook about him.

"Oh, Corky has had rather a tough life," she confided. "When he and his wife were young, they made quite a dashing couple. He was tall and rather handsome, in a rugged sort of way, and she was a real beauty. They had two children."

Hilde sat down at the table with a cup of coffee and a faraway look in her eyes. "There was a fire in their house one night. The two little girls died in that fire and Corky's wife was badly burned. She almost died, too. Her face was burned and left her quite disfigured. He nursed her and took such gentle care of her for several years until she died one winter of pneumonia."

The two women were silent as Carrie took in this tragic story. Pauline came bursting into the room, ready to say something about the dance to Carrie when she saw the two long faces.

"What's the matter?" she asked, almost fearfully.

"Oh, I was just telling Carrie about Corky's family."

Carrie wiped a tear from her eye. "I didn't have any idea. I was telling him just a little while ago that he should come to the dance with us."

"Speaking of the dance," Pauline said, changing the subject, "Emory asked if I was going and he said he wanted to dance many dances with me!"

"Speaking of dancing," Hilde said with mock sternness, "you girls better dance around here and help get supper ready or you will all be late!"

Carrie laughed and said, "Hilde, I think you should come along with us."

"You could be our chaperone!" suggested Pauline.

Hilde threw her head back and laughed at that idea. "If they saw me near you girls, the men would run in the other direction!"

Supper was light that evening and the girls cleaned up in record time. They hurried upstairs to get ready. They had to fix each other's hair and change their dresses. They came down to the parlor for Hilde's inspection.

"Oh, are these the same two girls who just a little while ago were elbow-deep in the dishwater?" Here she laughed. "I hope you put some hand creme on those rough, red hands or the fellows won't want to hold them," she teased.

The girls picked up their shawls and went out on the porch to wait for the wagon. Hilde came out and waited with them. "Too bad Mrs. Daud wasn't here to see how pretty you both look. I like your new hairstyles!"

"I thought Mrs. Daud was getting back tonight," said Carrie.

"Yah, she's coming in on the train, about now I'd say. Mr. Daud went to town to fetch her."

Soon they saw a pair of horses pulling a wagon coming from the barns. It pulled up in front of the house. There must have been eight or ten men sitting in the back. Peter was driving and Amund was sitting along side of him. Amund jumped down and assisted the girls into the wagon.

Hilde waved to the group. "Have a good time now, you young uns!"

There were straw bales around the sides of the wagon. The men scooted over to make room for the girls. Emory suggested that they sit over by him. Carrie let Pauline go first so that she could sit next to Emory. Amund plopped down beside his sister in a protective manner. Karl whipped out his harmonica and the group was singing with gusto when they left the yard.

Hilde watched and listened until she could see them no more. She was turning to go back into the house when she saw Corky come around the corner of the house.

"Evenin', Hilde." He lifted his hat in greeting. "A nice night for the young people's outing, wouldn't you say?" She nodded in agreement.

"I got here just in time to see how pretty the girls looked," he said wistfully.

Hilde suggested that she go and get some coffee and the two of them could sit on the porch awhile. Corky thought that would be a nice idea, as he sat down on the top step.

A couple miles from the farm, the wagon met Mr. and Mrs. Daud in their buggy. The group whooped and hollered and waved to their employers. The older couple waved and laughed at the wagon full of enthusiastic young people.

"They sure have a fancy buggy there," one of the newer men remarked.

"They always have the newest model. Mr. Daud's family is in the carriage-making business in Chicago," explained someone, " so each year he comes back with a new one."

The group had lost some of its steam so they quieted down for awhile. When they came in sight of Davenport, they started up again with renewed vigor. They wanted to make their presence known in town! Peter let them all off in front of the town hall and he drove the horses over to the livery stable.

The dance was well attended. Malchow's Orchestra provided the music. The women were so outnumbered by the men that Carrie and Pauline hardly got to rest at all! Emory monopolized most of Pauline's time but Carrie danced with about every unattached fellow there.

After the dance, Peter suggested that they all go to Teigen's restaurant for lunch. Some of the group had ice cream while others had coffee and doughnuts. Carrie had suspected that some of the men in their party had gone out back of the hall during the dance occasionally for a little snort of something, but all in all, they were a pretty well-behaved bunch.

On the way home, some of the men hunkered down in the straw and slept. Emory made sure he was sitting next to Pauline and Amund sat down by Carrie.

"Well, what did you think of the dance?" Peter called back to them. "I thought it was one of the better ones I've been to. No fights for a change!"

Carrie raised her eyebrows in question. Emory told them that last year he had been to a couple dances in the area and usually fights would break out between the different ethnic groups.

"Later on this summer, when more men come to work around here, then we might see some action," he said.

When the girls got into the house, they could see by the big clock in the parlor that it was almost 2 o'clock in the morning. They were very tired and slept a little late the next morning.

When they came down to the kitchen, Hilde and Cora were already starting to flip pancakes. The bacon was ready on the stove. They hurried and set the tables and some of the men started to come in before they were done.

None of the men from the dance last night were among the early comers, Carrie noticed. On Sunday mornings, the men could eat in two different shifts if they wanted. The first breakfast was served at 7 o'clock and another at 8:30.

As they washed up the dishes, Hilde had to know every detail about the dance. Then everyone hurried up to get changed and ready for the trip to town for church. Pauline was going with Carrie to Davenport. When Peter and Amund pulled up in front for them, they noticed that Emory was also in the buggy.

"Oh, my," Pauline whispered to Carrie, "I didn't know he would be along!"

It was a tight squeeze to get three in the back seat of the buggy but Pauline and Emory didn't seem to mind the crowded condition.

Sunday evening, Mrs. Daud joined Hilde and the two girls in the parlor and told them all about her trip to Casselton. Her daughter had accompanied her out to the Dalrymple farm for the tea party.

"It was a grand affair!" exclaimed Mrs. Daud. "There were about twelve ladies there. Mrs. Chaffee had the most exquisite dress! And, oh, the hats! Simply the very latest. I'm glad I had brought along the newest one I bought in Chicago," she said.

"And Mrs. Dalrymple, she loves hats, and she wears one even in her own home. She is such a gracious hostess and loves to entertain. I love her parties!"

"Don't keep us in suspense any longer. What did you have to eat?" asked Hilde.

Oh, I have never seen so many courses at a tea party. There were tiny sandwiches of all kinds. Sandwich loaves with fillings that I'd never seen before! And little tea cakes, individually frosted and decorated. Small frosted cookies, too. Then a seafood salad served in a pastry. Very tasty! I need to get that recipe for you, Hilde!"

After describing all the food and the women's attire, she then told them about her shopping trip with her daughter in the stores of Casselton. "I bought....." Here she stopped and said, "I think I'll make you wait until it's delivered next week. It will be such a fun surprise for all of you!"

The women protested but Mrs. Daud had made up her mind and she wouldn't tell them. "It should be delivered on Wednesday," she said, with a mischievous look in her eye. They would just have to wait until then.

CHAPTER 11

Come Monday morning the sun was shining brightly which made for good haying weather. The men left the yard with the hay mowers and started cutting a field several miles north of the farm. Since they weren't too far away, they were all brought back to the house at noon for dinner.

During an afternoon break, Carrie hurried over to the store to see if Ida had any mail for her. Sure enough, there was a letter from home. Since she had a few minutes, she went out in the back yard and sat down on a bench near the garden and tore open the letter. She scanned it quickly at first and then read it over again. There was no important news, but just holding the letter in her hand made Carrie feel rather homesick. She had noticed, however, that those feelings were not coming as often anymore. She liked it here and the people on this farm were becoming like family.

She put the letter in her pocket and spent some time looking over the garden. Corky had planted the onions and tomatoes that Mrs. Daud wanted and they were coming up nicely. We could use some rain for the garden, she thought, but the men wouldn't like that for their haying.

That evening, Carrie and Pauline took a walk in the direction of the shed where Amund did his repairs. Just as they thought, he was busy fixing something. "Come in, come in," he said, delighted to see them.

"I'm just finishing up this broken hay mower. They need this as a spare in case one of the others breaks down tomorrow." He stopped his work and motioned them outside. Amund plopped down on the grass and the girls each sat on some stumps by the door.

"Whew, it got kind of hot today, didn't it?" He remarked, wiping his forehead with his big, red hankie. "I spent most of the afternoon over at the blacksmith's."

"The kitchen was heating up pretty good, too, by late afternoon," said Pauline.

"Mannie, I got a letter from home today," said Carrie, as she removed the letter from her pocket and handed it to him. "Ma says that we have some relatives living south of Kindred that we should look up. She had heard from her cousin, Ingeborg, the one from Lansing, Iowa. Do you remember her?"

Amund nodded his head. "She says that their cousin, Engebret Ulness and his family live in that little village of Ulness that we stopped by when our train was putting on water, remember?"

"Yah, I called your attention to that name on the sign by the tracks."

"Well, she thinks that we should go and visit them someday. I would have to write them first though."

"I suppose we could do that some Sunday afternoon," Amund said.

"This Ingeborg said that there is an Ulness family living around Davenport, too, but that they are more distantly related."

"I'll ask Peter about them. He seems to know most everybody who lives around here already."

Amund stood up. "Well, now that you've told me everything in the letter, I won't have to read it," he teased.

Carrie laughed and said, "All right, give it back to me."

"Oh, I better read it and make sure you got everything right!"

"Come on, Pauline, let's continue our walk."

"Be sure to stop by the bunkhouse, maybe Emory is sitting waiting for you." Here Amund threw his head back and laughed.

The bunkhouse is the last place they would stop, they told him in no uncertain terms, and they left him to enjoy his joke.

Finally it was Wednesday, the day that the delivery wagon would be bringing the big surprise. They had all tried to guess what it might be. Every time the women heard a team coming into the yard, they would hurry and look out the kitchen window.

As they were washing up the dinner dishes, they looked out and saw a wagon from The Lewis Furniture Store in Casselton drive up to the front of the house and stop. Two men got out and made their way up the front walk.

"Go and tell Mrs. Daud that her surprise is here," Hilde said to Pauline. The girl hurried to the stairs. Cora and Carrie went to the front porch before the men had a chance to knock. Hilde followed close at their heels.

"Good afternoon, ladies," one of the men said. "We have a delivery for

Mrs. Daud."

"She'll be down in a minute," Cora said. The men went back to the wagon and opened the back doors. Then Mrs. Daud came out on the porch and she hurried down to the wagon.

The men brought out two small trees, which were leafed out, and the roots and soil were wrapped in burlap.

"You can just set those trees in the shade of the house there and the furniture you can carry up onto the porch," she directed.

The women watched in wonder as the men began carrying some wicker furniture pieces up on the porch. There was a white wicker settee and three matching armchairs. They all had soft matching cushions in a bright green floral. The men arranged and then rearranged the pieces of furniture the way Mrs. Daud pointed out. She signed her name on a piece of paper and they headed for the wagon.

Mrs. Daud called after them, "Would you care for a cup of coffee before you start your long drive back again?"

"No thank you, ma'am. We have to make a stop in Davenport first."

Mrs. Daud turned to the women and, clapping her hands in glee, asked them what they thought of her surprise.

"Oh, my! I've never seen anything like it in my life," Carrie was the first to say. They all agreed heartily.

"Well, let's sit down and try them out," Mrs. Daud suggested, plunking herself down into one of the chairs. Hilde and Cora took the other two and Pauline and Carrie took the settee, which could seat three people.

Mrs. Daud beamed. "I saw how much you all are using the porch in the evenings and realized that there wasn't much for sitting on out here."

"Oh, won't this be wonderful?" cried Pauline.

"We'll put these old benches over on the other side," said Mrs. Daud. "Maybe Corky can paint them up and they won't look so bad."

The women sat for a few minutes longer and then Cora said, "The dishes aren't getting done this way!" and she hoisted herself to her feet and the others did likewise.

"Those chairs are just too comfortable!" exclaimed Hilde. "Oh, and what are those trees you got?" she asked.

"Oh, I almost forgot about them. They're apple trees. I'll have the men plant them in the back yard. I thought we needed some more trees around here."

When the women returned to the kitchen, they found that the dishwater had grown cold so they had to heat up some more on the stove. They were busy talking about the nice surprise for the next half-hour and the dishwashing chore went extra fast.

The haying seemed to go on for a long time, Carrie thought, but on the Fourth of July, Mr. Daud gave everybody the day off. After breakfast, nearly everyone was going to drive down to Kindred for the celebration there.

A parade started things out, followed by some political speeches, a free dinner and then a baseball game. Pauline and Carrie got too hot as they sat and watched the game so they decided to walk uptown and find a cool place to wait for the fellows.

They went into Ben Anderson's store where there was a soda fountain. They couldn't resist having a soda. One had strawberry and one had cherry and they lingered over them, enjoying every last drop.

When more people started coming in, they figured that the game was over so they went out to look for the others. The group debated whether to stay for the dance or not, but most of them agreed that it had already been a full day. The men had to continue with the haying the next day and it would take them almost an hour to get back to the farm.

"We are a bunch of party poopers!" Peter said to those riding in his wagon. "When we get all through haying, we'll have to take in the dance in Davenport in two weeks. One last fling before harvest." They all agreed to this and it was a tired bunch on the way home.

Toward the middle of July, there were new men coming almost every day. Someone would take a wagon to Davenport when they knew the trains from the east would be coming and pick up any men who might be arriving that day.

One evening at supper, Carrie was astonished to see a very large man who was so dark, he almost looked like a Negro. He walked in ahead of Amund and he looked around to see where he should sit. The Irishmen at one of the tables moved over to make room for him.

Later, in the kitchen, Pauline told Carrie that this man had come last year, too, and that he was an Irishman. The Norwegians called him 'Svarten' which means someone dark.

"The men never mess with him! He's strong as an ox," Pauline told her.

Later that night, when Amund and Peter had come to sit on the porch with the girls, Peter told more about the new man. "He comes from northern Wisconsin and has been coming for several years now. He can do the work of two men."

"And he can eat like two men, too!" exclaimed Pauline.

Amund told Carrie that the haying would be done in a couple days, so maybe they should plan to make their trip to Ulness on Sunday. "I'll get a buggy and we'll go right after church."

"I better write a letter to them tomorrow, then," said Carrie.

The next day, she posted the letter, and hoped that she would get a reply before Sunday.

On Sunday morning after church, sister and brother, in their borrowed buggy, were sharing a lunch that Carrie had packed for the two of them to eat on their way down to Ulness. The water in the jug had turned quite warm from sitting in the buggy during the services. They drove slowly as they didn't want to get there too early, before their cousins had eaten their dinner.

They turned into Kindred and drove around, looking at all the houses and the businesses on the main street.

"A pleasant little town, isn't it?" remarked Carrie. "It reminds me somewhat of Spring Grove."

Amund checked his pocket watch and said that it was now late enough for them to proceed on their journey. Ulness was only about a mile-and-a-half further south. They crossed the track and noticed the familiar water tower. The flour mill was off to the right, as was the little store owned by their cousin. The family dwelling was to the west a short ways.

As they drove into the yard, they admired the large two-story house with a porch on the front. There were many big, old trees surrounding the yard.

"This must be the place," said Amund. Then they saw a man coming down the porch steps toward them.

"You must be our long-lost cousins," he remarked jovially. He helped

Carrie down from the rig and Amund got down, too. "I'm Engebret and you must be Carrie and Amund." They shook hands cordially.

Carrie saw several children come out of the house and Mr. Ulness called to one of his sons. "Randolph, you take these horses and unhitch them, won't you?"

He led Carrie and Amund up the steps and started to introduce his children. "This is Louis, and Carl," he said, patting two boys on the head. "The tall one there is Alfred. The girls are all in the house helping their mother." He held the screen door open for them.

As they entered, Carrie noticed the beautiful etched glass in the front door. They entered a spacious hallway and the aroma of the family's dinner still lingered in the air. A little girl toddled up to them and held out her arms. "That's Gladys," Engebret told them. "She's two and goes to everybody!"

Two older girls came out of the kitchen, patting at their hair and smoothing their dresses. "This is Gilla and there's Hannah," he continued with the introductions. Then his wife, Lena, appeared, also, and it was very obvious that she was with child again.

She was very pleasant and was so glad to meet them. "It was a surprise to get your letter. It's always fun to see relatives from back home," she told them.

Engebret indicated that they should all move into the parlor and sit down. The children gathered on the floor or on the straight-back chairs.

"My, you have a nice, large family, don't you?" asked Carrie.

"Yah," boomed Engebret proudly, "and one more to come in September."

Then he asked about his cousin, Oline, who was Carrie and Amund's mother. "I remember her when we were both quite young back in Norway. She was born the same year that me and my twin sister, Barbro, were born. Your mother's family came to visit us once in awhile."

"And is Ingeborg, who lives in Lansing, your older sister, then?" asked Carrie.

"Yah, that is right," nodded Engebret. "After the rest of our family immigrated to America, we lived with her for a time. In fact, after my mother died, I lived with her until I was confirmed and then I struck out on my own for this area to join the rest of my family."

"When did your family come to America?" asked Amund.

"Well, my older brother, Elling, and my sister, Ingeborg, came together in 1870. They wanted some adventure and to try their luck in the new country which they had heard so much about. They first went to Lansing and that's where Ingeborg was when the rest of us came over about two years later. I was only seven at the time. How about your family?" he asked.

"Our parents came in '85 with our older brother, Olaf," Amund said. "Carrie and I and three other children were born in this country."

"So, your parents farm over by Spring Grove, is that right?"

Amund nodded. Engebret went on, "I remember that community. In fact, Lena's family lived there for a short time. When they came to America, they settled first in Wisconsin and then on to Spring Grove and then to Leroy, Minnesota. In about '80 or '81 they came to Dakota Territory. Isn't that right, Lena?" he asked his wife.

"Yah, I can only remember Spring Grove a little bit. I was quite young when we lived there," Lena stated. "I remember traveling to this area, though. Papa walked the entire way, herding our cattle. We loaded most of our things in wagons except the kitchen stove. We sent that by train. It didn't arrive until about four months after we got here so I remember Mama cooking over a fire built in a hole in the ground."

Lena picked up little Gladys and held her in her lap until the child nodded off. "Here Hannah, why don't you take her upstairs and lay her down," said their mother.

Some of the children were getting restless, listening to the grown-ups talk, so they left to find something to do.

"When I first got to this area," Engebret said, "I worked with my older brother, Elling, for awhile. He had a store down by Norman, just east of Kindred a few miles. The mill was over there then. I worked in the mill, too, for a time."

Here he held up his hand to show that parts of three fingers were missing. "I have this to show for it. I had a little accident while working there."

Lena shook her head. "I didn't know him yet, then."

"About that time, Elling decided to move his family west of here to La Moure County where he homesteaded. He also had a store there. I went to live with the rest of my family on our farm near Walcott."

"Oh, our train stopped in Walcott on the way to Davenport," remarked

Carrie.

"Lena and I got married in '88," Engebret went on, " and we lived on the farm for awhile and then moved into Walcott. I worked at the store there for a couple years."

Lena interrupted here by suggesting that Engebret take Amund over to see the mill and the store. Alfred and Louis tagged along. Little Carl followed his mother and Carrie out onto the porch.

"We'll sit out here where it's a bit cooler," said Lena.

"You have such a nice, shady yard," remarked Carrie. "And is that the river just over there?"

"Yah, we are pretty close to the river, all right. I sometimes worry about the children falling in."

Engebret led Amund over to the mill first and showed him all around. "When the railroad came through here instead of by Norman," he explained, "the mill was moved to this site."

"How could such a big structure like that be moved?" Amund was curious to know.

"Rollers were put under it, and by using a cable, a pulley and many horses, it was skidded across the frozen ground. They had to go about three miles across country."

Pointing to the dam, he continued, "They used big timbers to build this dam, which provided the power to operate the mill. This water power also provided electricity to the mill--the only place around to have such a luxury back then."

They walked along the riverbank until Engebret stopped and pointed to a footbridge which had been strung across the river. "Many of the men who work at the mill live over on the other side so it made sense to make it easier for them to walk to work."

"How did they do that?" asked Amund, stepping up to the footbridge for a closer look.

"They stretched hog-netting and rope from bank to bank and then planks were laid across the netting. It sways more than a little! Want to try it out?"

Amund started walking across and, indeed, it did sway quite a bit, but he kept going to the other side and then turned around and came back again, stepping carefully.

"That's really something!" he exclaimed. "What will they think of next!"

They headed in the direction of the store. "When did you move here from Walcott?" Amund asked.

"Well, Elling moved back to this area and built this store here. It had a post office and he was the postmaster for a few years. Then he got itchy feet again and decided to move once more so he asked me to come and take over the store and the postmaster's job. That was about seven years ago now."

Engebret unlocked the store and Amund stepped in. It was full of all kinds of things, he could see. Everything that one would expect in a country store. It had a pot-bellied stove in the middle with a couple of old chairs on each side of it. A spittoon stood nearby.

"We no longer have a post office here now, though. When Rural Free Delivery came in, in '05, then this one was closed and I lost that job," Engebret explained. "All the mail comes out of Kindred now."

As the men walked back toward the house, they could see that a game of baseball had started on a grassy lot east of the place. Engebret's boys had joined the group.

"They play baseball there almost every day in the summer," Engebret said, shaking his head. "Never did play, myself, but the boys sure like it. There's enough neighbors around here to make up two teams anytime!"

As they neared the house and spotted the women sitting on the porch, Engebret called to his wife, "Lena, have you got the coffee going?"

"Yah, and it will soon be ready. Sit down and rest awhile," she suggested.

"You probably didn't know yet that my father just passed away," said Engebret. "About four months ago, now. He had been living with us the past couple years. We found him dead in his bed one morning." Here he looked thoughtful for some moments. "He lived to the ripe old age of 81 so I guess you couldn't ask for much more than that."

Lena got up and said she would check on the coffee and would call them when everything was ready. Carrie stood up and followed her into the kitchen to help. The two oldest girls, Gilla and Hannah, came in the back door. They had been watching the ball game.

"Randolph just hit a home run!" exclaimed Hannah.

"Oh, my. Good for him," said his mother. "Will you girls set out the good cups and saucers on the dining-room table?"

"Don't go and fuss now just for my brother and me," pleaded Carrie.

"Oh, no trouble at all. It's so nice to have you here," Lena assured her.

She cut pieces of cake and arranged them on the glass cake plate. "Gilla, you go and call the men in."

The grown-ups sat down around the big table and the two girls joined them. Lena brought the coffee and filled their cups. Cream and sugar lumps were passed.

"Oh, this cake looks delicious!" exclaimed Carrie as she took a piece.

"It's Mama's specialty," said Gilla. "White cake with lemon filling."

"Yah, they can't get enough of it around here," said Lena, laughing. "I save it for special occasions, though."

"Every Sunday is a special occasion, Lena!" boomed Engebret.

They heard a little girl's cry and Hannah ran upstairs to fetch Gladys. The child was fussy and a bit shy when they came back down, but when her mother put a piece of the cake in front of her, she broke out in a smile and began to eat the frosting with her fingers. She would look slyly at everyone and then she'd do it again.

The group lingered over their coffee and second helpings of cake and then Amund announced that perhaps it was time for the two of them to head back to the farm.

"Thank you for the wonderful afternoon," Carrie said to their cousin and his wife. They were on the porch, waiting for Amund to bring the buggy around.

"We loved having you," replied Lena. "Engebret was excited when we got your letter."

After everybody shook hands, Engebret helped Carrie into the buggy and bid them farewell. Brother and sister waved goodbye to the children and waved again as they passed the ball game still in progress.

After they had crossed the tracks, Carrie leaned back with a sigh. "That sure was a pleasant afternoon, wasn't it, Mannie?"

"I enjoyed it very much," he said. "The mill and the store were interesting to see. I even walked across the river on a foot bridge."

"Remind me to send Lena a note, thanking her for the nice time we had."

CHAPTER 12

One evening as the girls were setting the tables for supper, the men started to file in and Carrie remarked, "They're coming in a little earlier than usual, aren't they?"

Amund was among them and he came up to Carrie and she asked them why they were coming early for supper.

"Oh, I guess they want to hurry and eat because we're having a big baseball game tonight. The Norwegian team against the Germans. Of course," he confided, "we have a few Swedes on our team, too, and the Germans have a few Irishmen and some Russians."

Carrie just shook her head as she continued setting the table. How could these grown men get so excited about a game of ball, she wondered. Just then she looked up and there by the door stood the newest arrival, and a most handsome man at that. He was looking right at her. He smiled and took his hat off and then turned to search for a place to sit.

Carrie felt her heart start beating a little fast. Pauline gave her a curious look and Carrie fled to the kitchen.

Pauline followed her. "What's the matter, Carrie? You look all flustered."

"Here, girls, you better start serving now," said Cora, and she handed them each large, steaming bowls of potatoes.

There was a lot of bantering back and forth among the men during the meal. They were excited about their little competition which would come later. Three of the long tables and part of the fourth were now filled with workers. With the harvest soon to begin, most of the expected men had arrived. But Amund had told the girls that morning that about a half dozen fellows from Chicago would be coming in on the next morning's train.

After supper, as the girls washed dishes, they could hear shouts and hollering from the makeshift baseball field over by the machine shed. They could sometimes hear the whack of the bat as it hit the ball squarely and then, after a few seconds, one side or the other was screaming wildly.

"That must be some game going on over there," commented Cora. "I just hope no fighting breaks out afterwards."

Carrie looked at her for an explanation and Cora complied. "Some years the competition gets so stiff that the losing side starts a fist fight with the winners. The German-Russians and the Finns are especially hotheaded. They're usually put on the same team, though, or there would be fighting before the game even got started!"

"How can this game be fun if it brings out fighting and squabbling?" asked Carrie.

"If you can answer that question, then you are smarter than most of us," laughed Hilde. "That's just the way men are, I guess,"

"You girls are finished, now; why don't you go out there and watch the game," suggested Cora.

Carrie and Pauline looked at each other and shrugged their shoulders. They hung up their aprons and started out the back door.

"Should we go over there?" asked Pauline.

"Is it safe?" laughed Carrie. "We might get in the middle of a good fight."

The girls ambled over towards the action. Carrie knew very little about the game so Pauline said she would try and explain it to her as best she could. They were standing off to the side and Carrie saw that the handsome new man was a short distance away, watching the game.

"Pauline, did you notice that new fellow at supper tonight? He must have come just this afternoon."

"How could I help but notice. He sure is good looking, isn't he?"

Just then he looked their way and he tipped his cap to them and then turned his attention back to the game. One of the teams just scored and there was plenty of noise for awhile.

Amund's team was walking off the field and he came over to the girls for a few minutes. "Did you see that play, girls? I think we have the game for sure now."

"What's the score?" asked Pauline.

"It's five to two but, of course, it ain't over yet."

"There isn't going to be any fighting, is there?" asked Pauline.

"I hope not, but Peter says we could expect some squabbling afterwards. There's some bad feelings among some of these fellows." He turned and rejoined his team just in time to see the other team hit the ball far and away. The opposing team was screaming and throwing their caps on the ground.

"This could get interesting," said Pauline. "We'll have to stay and watch to the end."

The game lasted quite late and ran into the tenth inning. The mosquitoes were beginning to bother the girls somewhat but it was too exciting to leave and go indoors. The game had been tied but the Norwegian team hit a homer and that settled the matter. A big, burly Russian came up to one of the Norwegians and started poking him in the chest. He claimed there had been an unfair call.

A big, powerful-looking Swede named Sven stood up close to him and wondered if the two of them should settle the matter behind the shed. The Russian thought that would be a good idea and both sides began cheering on their man. They followed the two oversized fellows behind the building and everyone rolled up their sleeves. They evidently knew that there would soon be a free-for-all.

The girls watched from a distance, hoping no one would get hurt.

"How dumb, to fight over an old game," said Carrie. "I thought games were supposed to be fun."

"Well, I guess when it involves men from all these different nationalities, it goes beyond being played for fun."

The Russian took a swipe at the Swede and the fight was on. There was more cheering now than during the game. It wasn't long before things got out of hand completely. Now all the Russians joined in to protect their man and then the Finns started taking shots at the Russians, their own teammates! The Germans didn't know who they should be defending so they started in on the Irishmen. The Norwegians went for anyone left who looked like they wanted to fight. It was no longer just one team against the other. The old animosities of the different homelands came to light here.

It was a real melee but it came to a quick end when suddenly Mr. Thompson and Mr. Daud were standing in the middle of the small groups, trying to pull them apart. The men backed off and some tried to slink out of sight quickly.

Mr. Daud looked very angry when he shouted at the men, telling them to all go to the bunkhouse and turn in for the night. "And if there is any more ruckus out of you fellows, you'll all be without a job in the morning!"

"Those were some pretty brave words from Mr. Daud, what with harvest about to start," remarked Carrie as the two girls hurried back to the house. "What if he had to fire half his crew?"

"I don't know, but Mr. Daud is a man of principle and keeps his word so he would have to do it."

That night when the girls went to bed, there was no soothing music coming from the bunkhouse. There was, however, a soft breeze coming in their open window and the sound of chirping crickets lulled them to sleep.

The next day, there came a letter for Carrie from home. Actually, it was for both her and Amund but the letters were always addressed to her. She learned that Olaf and Mattie's baby had been born the week before. It was a girl and she was beautiful and healthy, Carrie's mother had written. They named her Manda and Carrie thought that was a very pretty name.

That evening, Carrie walked over to the repair shed to see if she could find Amund. Sure enough, he was working, as usual. He led her out back and there stood the biggest machine she had ever seen close up. It was one of the steam-powered threshing machines that the men would soon be using.

"I'm going over it from top to bottom to make sure everything is in working order," he told Carrie.

"But, Mannie, how do you know anything about a machine like this?" she asked him.

"When the threshing crew would come to our farm each summer, I'd watch the operator and everything he did. Hogie, the blacksmith, was over here this afternoon and helped me some, too."

Carrie shared the news that was in the letter with her brother as he took a little break from his work.

"I suppose Olaf was looking for a boy, to help him with the farm work someday," Amund remarked.

"Well, I guess Mattie gets her helper first this time."

A couple of the fellows walked by and Amund motioned for them to come in. She knew two of them, but the third was the handsome newcomer.

"This is my sister, Carrie," Amund told the man, "and Carrie, this is Alphonse Kastet. He's new here, from Canada."

Mr. Kastet bowed slightly and removed his cap. "Nice to meet you, Miss, but please just call me Alfie. Everyone else does."

Carrie could think of nothing to say. She was dumbstruck. He was so incredibly good looking that it almost took her breath away, she thought. She could only nod and offer a simple smile.

The men visited awhile with Amund and then drifted off to their destination, which was the bunkhouse. They had told him that there would be a card game starting soon.

"Oh, no," cried Carrie, "I hope that this game doesn't end in another fight!"

"No, only a few guys get involved in the card playing and they're all pretty good sports. This Alfie really likes to play poker and he plays for pretty high stakes."

"Now, don't you go and get involved in any gambling, Mannie," she admonished.

"Don't worry about me; I'm trying to save every penny I can, not lose it in a card game."

Carrie walked back to the house and joined Pauline in the parlor. "I got to meet the handsome stranger!" she told her friend. "His name is Alfie something-or-other and he comes from Canada. I was so nervous that I forgot his last name. And I couldn't even think of anything to say to him!"

The next evening, Amund came over to the house to talk to the girls. They were sitting on the front porch, reading some of the weekly papers.

"Do you girls remember that the big dance in Davenport is this Saturday night?"

"Oh, yes," answered Pauline. "We were just reading about it in the Davenport News."

"Almost all the fellows are planning to go," Amund said. "We'll be taking about three wagons."

"That will be so much fun!" exclaimed Carrie. "We haven't danced for quite sometime now."

"Well, I better be moving along," said Amund, as he rose to leave.

"What's your hurry?" asked his sister.

"I'm going to see if I can catch the barber for a hair cut. Peter says that there will be a real lineup on Saturday. Everyone will be wanting cuts and shaves. They'll all want to look nice for you girls," he teased. With this, he went off, whistling an unrecognizable tune.

A short while later, Emory came by and sat down on one of the wicker chairs. He seemed a little nervous about something and he finally spat it out. "Pauline, would you go to the dance with me on Saturday night?"

She was taken aback and didn't know what to say. "Well...I...ah...thought we were all going together," she stammered.

"Well, yes...ah.. we are," he stammered also, "but...well...I just wanted you to be my date for the evening." He was looking very uncomfortable by this time so Pauline took mercy on him.

"Why, yes, Emory, I'd be glad to be your date for the dance," she said clearly.

He swallowed audibly and rose to leave. "Thank you, then. I'll come by here shortly before the wagons come and we can sit together."

"All right, I'll be ready," Pauline answered.

They waited until he was out of earshot before the girls dared look at each other. "Boy, was he ever nervous," remarked Carrie.

"Yes, I've never seen him like that before. I almost felt sorry for him."

"He's really a nice fellow, though, Pauline."

"Yes, but I thought it would be more fun if no one was paired up but I didn't have the heart to tell him that."

"I wonder if Alfie will be going," said Carrie. "I suppose he'll find the prettiest girls to dance with and we won't see much of him. I wish I had a real pretty dress to wear. I'll have to wear the same old thing I always wear when I dress up."

"Me, too," said Pauline. "I wish I had time to sew some clothes for myself but there's just no time for anything."

"Oh, well, let's just go and have a good time and not worry about what we're wearing."

"Can you do my hair up like you did last time?" asked Pauline. "I really liked the way you did it."

"That's how my sister, Sylvia, wears her hair and she has me do it for her sometimes."

Here Carrie drew quiet. Just remembering her sister made her homesick. She hadn't had time for those feelings in a long time.

Saturday was a busy day and everybody was excited about the evening ahead. Carrie and Pauline had barely enough time to iron their dresses before it was time to get ready. They quickly did each other's hair and hurried downstairs to await their chariot, as they called it.

Emory came by and waited on the porch with the girls. Cora and Hilde were there, too, to see the young people off. When the wagon, driven by Peter, stopped by the house, Emory took Pauline's arm possessively and helped her into the back. It was as if he wanted to make a statement to the other fellows that Pauline was taken for the evening.

They waited for the other two wagons and then they all started for town in a noisy fashion. It was almost dark before they entered Davenport. There were buggies and wagons all over the place.

"It looks like a big turnout this evening," remarked Amund. He helped Carrie down and the group started for the hall.

"We'll really fill the place up when we all come in," said Peter. They heard the sounds of a lively polka and a lot of hootin' and hollerin' as they walked up the stairs. "It sounds like a pretty good orchestra tonight, doesn't it?"

Pauline and Carrie never got to sit down until intermission time. "Whew!" laughed Carrie, as she sat heavily down on the bench, "this dancing is almost as hard as working in the kitchen all day!"

Pauline had to agree. Emory offered to go and get punch for the two girls.

Carrie would never have admitted it, but she was hoping that Alfie would ask her to dance. She had seen him dancing with several girls, most of whom she didn't know. They were all attractive girls, with pretty dresses on. She looked down at her frock and felt a little stab of envy. Then she remembered what her mother would always say. "Pretty is as pretty does."

Carrie had just put a smile back on her face when she looked up and saw Alfie coming toward her. She could feel her heart lurch in her chest.

"Miss Amundson, may I have the first dance with you after intermission?" he said with a mock bow.

"Well, I guess you may, Mr...ah...."

"Kastet." he finished the name for her. "Not a familiar name around here, eh?"

Emory returned with cups of punch for the girls and Alfie said he would return as soon as the music started again. Pauline gave Carrie a sly smile behind her punch cup and Carrie blushed slightly.

Alfie was Johnny-on-the-spot when the first strains of a waltz began. Oh, no, a waltz, thought Carrie. I'm not very good at that. He whisked her away and, in his arms, the dance was made easy.

After awhile she said, "You're a very good dancer, Mr. Kastet."

"We grew up dancing at our house so I guess that accounts for it," he said to her compliment. "You must call me Alfie, though, or I will bring you right back to your seat!" he laughed.

Carrie danced with Alfie several more times during the remainder of the evening. During their last dance together, Alfie asked Carrie if he could sit by her on the way home.

"Well, I guess that would be all right," she answered hesitantly but inwardly she was excited.

Two of the wagons left for the farm right after the dance, filled with those who were tired and wanted to get back. Those in Peter's wagon, however, decided they were hungry and went to Teigen's for some lunch. Some had coffee and pie and others had a sandwich.

When they left the cafe and headed for the remaining wagon, someone looked at their timepiece and announced that it was already two o'clock in the morning! Nobody seemed to mind; they were all having so much fun.

The ride home was considerably more subdued than the ride to town had been. Some of the men sprawled out in the hay and fell asleep. Pauline and Carrie sat with Emory and Alfie. Alfie wanted to put his arm around Carrie but Amund was sitting directly across from the pair, keeping a good watch on all of Alfie's moves.

The wagon stopped in front of the big house and let Pauline and Emory and Carrie and Alfie out. The two couples proceeded to the front door. The moment was rather awkward but then Pauline said that she was very tired and, after a hasty good night to Emory, she went in the house. Emory nodded to the remaining couple and left for the bunkhouse. Alfie asked Carrie if she wanted to sit on the settee for awhile but she said that she thought that she should be going in.

"I wish I had had my own buggy tonight to bring you home in," apologized Alfie.

"Oh, that's all right," Carrie hastened to say. "It was fun riding with everyone."

"We could have had more fun by ourselves," Alfie remarked. "I noticed your brother is rather protective of you, eh?"

"I've never thought about it, but I guess he maybe was tonight," laughed Carrie. "Well, I better be going in now. It's awfully late."

It was very difficult to get up the next morning after so few hours of sleep. Carrie and Pauline dressed quickly and hurried down to help Hilde and Cora. Big bowls of pancake batter had been mixed up and were waiting to be ladled onto the griddles. Bacon was sizzling on the stove.

"I love the smell of bacon in the morning," exclaimed Carrie, as she helped herself to a strip.

"We have a few minutes, girls, so why don't you grab a cup of coffee and we'll sit down and you can tell us all about last night," suggested Hilde.

After recounting all the highlights of the past evening, they heard the first of the men coming in for their breakfast. Out in the dining hall, Carrie could see that the ones coming in to eat so early were the ones who had not been at the dance.

Amund and Peter finally came in about an hour later and Amund asked Carrie if she was planning to go to church.

"Of course, aren't you?"

"Yah, I plan to. Peter says he's not going today. I'll pick you up in about a half hour."

Carrie hurried to help with the dishes and then she and Pauline dashed upstairs to change dresses. They were ready and waiting when Amund pulled up in front of the house. Emory was along, too, and he jumped down and helped Pauline into the back and joined her, leaving Carrie to sit up front with her brother. Carrie found herself wishing that Alfie had been along, too.

That afternoon, Mrs. Daud told the ladies that her daughter and family would be driving over from Casselton shortly. Finally, I'll get to meet this daughter, thought Carrie.

About three o'clock, a large buggy was seen coming up the driveway. Carrie had been dozing in a chair on the porch. She was so tired from the night before. Mrs. Daud ran down to meet the buggy and two children came tumbling out and hugged their grandmother.

When the party reached the porch, Mrs. Daud introduced her daughter, Eunice and her husband, Ed Martin to Carrie. As she shook hands with the young woman, she could see a striking resemblance between mother and daughter. Both were tall and had dark, brown hair and the same friendly manner.

The children, a boy about four years old, named Benny, and a little girl, Gena, who was almost two, quickly ran into the house, calling for Auntie Hilde.

"They call Hilde their auntie," laughed Eunice. "They love her so and the feeling is mutual, as you will soon see."

They ran into her big arms and she hugged them to her with an iron clasp. Carrie could see tears form in the older woman's eyes. Why, these children are like her own family, thought Carrie.

Standing up and seeing Carrie watching her closely, Hilde said, "I practically raised their mother so these children are like my own grandchildren. The grandchildren that I'll never have." She wiped her eyes and stood beaming down at the boy and girl as they tugged on her skirt.

"C'mon, Hilde," said Benny, "let's go find some cookies."

"Tookies," echoed the little girl.

Mr. Daud came downstairs to join the noisy group and they all sat down in the parlor. Carrie felt that she was intruding so she went upstairs to see what Pauline was doing. She found her napping so she left the room quietly and went downstairs and out the back door. She went to sit on the garden bench for awhile. Ida came from next door to join her and they had a nice visit.

Later Pauline and Carrie helped Cora fix up a light supper of sandwiches and salad and cake. It was served in the private dining room off the parlor. Hilde was allowed to just sit and enjoy herself, for a change. She played with the children and visited with Eunice and Mrs. Daud.

Some of the men who were not gone for the day, came in the dining hall and had sandwiches and salad, too. When the dishes were all done, Mrs. Daud came into the kitchen and told the women to come and join them in the parlor. Eunice was going to play the piano.

Eunice played old favorites and everyone sang along. Mr. Daud had a beautiful baritone voice which could be heard above everyone else's. Mrs. Daud could hold her own, too, with her rich, contralto voice.

After awhile, Carrie could see out the window that some of the men were drifting up from the bunkhouse to get closer to the music. Some ventured up onto the porch and they could be heard singing along.

Mrs. Daud winked at Carrie and said, "This always happens. They just can't resist joining in."

With the voices finally exhausted, Cora scurried into the kitchen to make some coffee before their guests departed. Carrie and Pauline followed after her and helped get the cups on the table and they filled a large serving plate with cookies.

About eight o'clock, Ed said that it was time to get ready to head back to Casselton. It would take them almost an hour and by then it would be soon dark. There were many hugs and some tears and even Carrie felt an emptiness after the guests left. She had just met them but she felt a warmth and affection for them already.

Hilde sighed and walked slowly to the kitchen. Carrie and Pauline followed her and asked if there was something they should help her with.

"Oh, I was just going to set the beans to soaking. You can get that big kettle from the pantry and I'll find the beans. Corky brought a new bag from the supply shed yesterday but I don't know just where he put it."

"I think I saw it back in the laundry room," said Pauline. "I'll go and get it."

"Well, you may need help carrying it," said Hilde, following along.

After the beans were put into the kettle of water to soak overnight and the few coffee cups were washed and dried, Mrs. Daud came into the kitchen and sat at the table.

"Oh, I always feel so blue after they leave," she sighed, referring to her daughter and family.

Hilde joined her at the table and said, "Me, too. Those little ones are so precious and Eunice brings so much life to the house with her music."

Carrie and Pauline left the two older women sitting together and went upstairs. They needed to retire early after their lack of sleep the night before.

"What do you think of Alfie?" Carrie asked Pauline when the two had undressed and were sitting on their beds.

"Well," answered Pauline slowly, "he certainly is charming and handsome!"

"And can he ever dance!" added Carrie.

"I think he's kind of sweet on you," said Pauline.

"Oh, I don't know about that, but I think Emory really likes you, Pauline."

"I guess he does, but I don't know if I should encourage him or not."

"Why not?" asked Carrie. "Don't you like him?"

"Well, yes I do, and he's very nice and everything, but ...well...I don't know if he's the kind of man I'd want to marry. He's only a farm worker. I...want something better out of life than being a farmwife."

"I guess I do, too, when you mention it," agreed Carrie, "but having some fun with them doesn't mean we're going to marry them!"

"Well, no, but it could lead to getting serious about someone that you don't want to get serious about," Pauline tried to explain.

Carrie started to laugh. "Here we sit talking about marriage and all we've done is have a few dances with those two fellows!" The two girls had a good laugh and then settled down to their evening devotions.

"Maybe we should pray that God leads us to the right man to spend the rest of our lives with," suggested Pauline.

"That might be a good idea," agreed Carrie. "I haven't been very good at making choices thus far, at least when it comes to picking the right man."

The two girls laid awake for awhile, each listening to the night sounds of the farm as, little by little, it quieted down for the night.

CHAPTER 13

The wheat harvest began in earnest the first week of August. The oats and the barley had been cut earlier and were standing in shocks, waiting for the thresher. The large scale upon which the harvesting process was done on this farm fascinated Carrie. In the mornings, she would watch as a long parade of McCormick binders left the yard. Each binder was pulled by three horses.

The work of the women increased ten-fold and then some. Two young girls, sisters, from a neighboring farm were hired to just wash dishes all day. Breakfast was now served at 5:30, and dinner was delivered out to the field starting at 11 o'clock, then an afternoon lunch, and then supper at 7:30.

Dinner and afternoon lunch were brought out to the men in the field in a lunch wagon, a large box-like vehicle, with room for all the food and for storing the plates. When meals were eaten in the field, tin plates and cups were used. The food was packed around heated crocks and put inside trunk-like boxes.

The first day that Carrie went along with Pauline to deliver dinner was an eye-opener for Carrie. Corky, who drove the wagon, explained things to her while they waited for the men to stop their work and come to them.

"Why do they need so many binders?" Carrie asked Corky.

"Well, we have about 8000 acres in wheat and we need five binders for every thousand acres so that makes 40 binders," he explained.

Carrie's jaw dropped. "Forty binders!" she exclaimed. She shook her head. "I just can't believe what I'm seeing out here."

"You'll get used to this big-scale farming after awhile," chuckled Corky.

"The binders cut the wheat and leave it in rows," he went on, "and then men come behind and gather up the bundles. They stand 8 or 10 of these upright, leaning against each other to make a shock. These shocks are left there until it's time to do the threshing."

Wagons carried the hungry men to the lunch wagon and the two girls were kept busy serving them. The men were given an hour off to eat and rest. Also the horses needed the rest. The girls gathered up the tin dishes and loaded the wagon and they headed back to the farm. The whole process took almost two hours.

The two young dishwashers, Sally and Betsy, came running out to help them carry everything into the house. Cora and Hilde were busy frying doughnuts for the afternoon lunch. While the two young girls washed all the dishes, Carrie and Pauline started making sandwiches and stacking them into dishpans. They covered them with dishtowels and set them aside. They then sat down, at Hilde's bidding, for a quick rest.

Corky joined them for a cup of coffee and fresh doughnuts. He then helped the girls load up the wagon again for the trip to the field with the lunch. He carried the heavy coffeepots last and set them down carefully. Rags were stuffed into the spouts to keep the coffee from sloshing around and spilling. This time Sally went with Carrie instead of Pauline.

It was very hot out in the sun and the flies were terribly bothersome. Carrie didn't know how the men could be so hungry already, the way they had eaten at noon.

"Those fellas, they really work up an appetite!" exclaimed Corky. "They'll be just as hungry again at suppertime; just you wait and see."

The sandwiches and doughnuts were devoured quickly and were washed down with the hot coffee.

"How can they drink coffee when it's so hot out here?" Carrie wondered. "You would think they would rather want something cold."

"Sometimes Hilde sends out ice cold lemonade," said Corky, "but, by Jiminy, if those fellas don't seem to prefer the coffee instead!"

On the way back to the farm, they met young Joey, the foreman's youngest son, driving a wagon toward the field.

"That's the water wagon," remarked Corky, after giving Joey a friendly wave. "The big barrel is filled with water and he goes around to the different groups of men and offers water to them. Mr. Daud believes strongly in giving his men and horses plenty of water to avoid heat exhaustion."

"Joey looked pretty proud of himself, sitting in the driver's seat of the wagon," remarked Carrie.

"Oh, yes, he is," said Corky. "This is his first year doing that job. He makes 50 cents a day and that is big money for him!"

"What is Billy helping with then?" asked Carrie.

"Well, you see him carrying loads of wood for the kitchen stove a couple times a day now. He keeps the blacksmith supplied with wood, too, for his forge. It's a hot, tiring job but he's a good worker, that Billy is."

When Carrie returned to the kitchen, the women, plus Mrs. Daud, were busy getting things started for the next meal---supper. Carrie noticed that Mrs. Daud wasn't afraid to roll up her sleeves and pitch in when needed and she was surely needed now, during this busy time.

The once-weekly afternoon shopping trips were discontinued during harvest, of course. Carrie had gone with Mrs. Daud twice earlier and had thoroughly enjoyed herself. She hoped to go again soon, when things slowed down. How long will this fast pace last, anyway, she wondered?

About 6:30 in the evening, the binders and horses began returning to the yard. By the time the horses were unhitched and tended to, and the men got themselves washed up a bit, it was 7:30 before they came into the dining hall for their last meal of the day.

Carrie could tell that they were all bone-tired. The hot temperatures didn't help matters, either. They were a quiet bunch as they slowly ate their supper.

Later that night, Carrie could hardly wait to go up to her room and crawl into bed. It was hot and stuffy in their room so she opened their only window as far as it would go. She heard no music drifting from the bunkhouse this night. She fell asleep almost immediately, as did Pauline.

The next morning, the girls rose at five o'clock with the help of their alarm clock. When they reached the kitchen, Hilde was whistling a tune and rolling out piecrusts. Cora was kneading bread dough.

"We're making green tomato pie today, girls," announced Hilde. "That's the favorite of most of the men."

"I've never tasted green tomato pie!" exclaimed Carrie. "In fact, I've never even heard of it."

"Well, you'll like it for sure, if there's any left for us!" Hilde teased.

"Carrie, you can start cracking eggs," said Cora. "We're having scrambled eggs and ham this morning. Pauline, you cut that ham there into small chunks."

"I've got the soda biscuits ready for the oven," Hilde told them. "We can put them in now."

"What are we serving for dinner today?" asked Carrie.

"We're having roast beef, boiled potatoes, and stewed turnips. And, of course, the pie," answered Hilde.

Carrie and Pauline hurried up with the scrambled eggs and ham and soon had it dished up, ready to serve as the first of the men straggled in. The soda biscuits came out of the oven and were served piping hot with butter and jam.

Carrie had only a few moments to talk with Amund during breakfast. She could also feel the eyes of the handsome Canadian upon her. She tried to keep her mind on what she was doing and didn't look up at him until the serving was all done. When she caught his eye, he winked and she flushed hotly. She whirled on her heel and hurried into the safety of the bustling kitchen.

Sally and Betsy drove into the yard just as the last of the men left the house. They hurried in and started washing up the breakfast dishes. Carrie and Pauline helped cut up the green tomatoes for the pies. It took two cups of tomatoes for each pie, plus 3 tart apples, sliced up. There was white sugar, brown sugar, cinnamon, nutmeg, allspice, flour and lemon juice, too.

"Maybe this won't taste so bad after all!" exclaimed Carrie.

"Oh, you'll love it for sure," said Hilde. "Some cooks put raisins in instead of the apples. We make it both ways here and the men don't seem to care either way."

Cora and Pauline were shaping the bread dough and putting it in pans. Then the pans were put near the stoves to raise.

Carrie counted the loaves. "Forty loaves of bread for one day! Wait till I tell Ma that!"

"You'll see that there won't be much left by tonight," commented Hilde.

The roasts were placed in large roaster pans and put in the ovens. Carrie looked out the window as the parade of binders left the yard once more. Would she ever get used to seeing this spectacle, she wondered?

"Carrie, run out to the ice house and get some butter, will you please?" asked Cora.

Carrie was glad for the respite from the kitchen, which was already getting warm. On her way back with the butter, she stopped in to see if the mailman had left a letter the day before.

"Oh, I certainly would have brought it over if there had been one for you," Ida assured her.

"I figured you would have, but I guess I just wanted an excuse to drop by," said Carrie.

"Yah, you girls are so busy now I almost need an appointment to see you!" Ida laughed.

"Well, there aren't very many spare moments anymore, that's for sure!" exclaimed Carrie as she went out the door.

A wagon came in the yard and Carrie saw that it was the egg man. He came four times a week now. When she entered the kitchen, she saw that Hilde and Pauline were dragging a big sack of potatoes over to the sink. I know what I'll be doing for the next hour, she thought.

She and the two young girls peeled potatoes and put them in big boilers and covered them with water, ready to cook up later.

Another wagon came into the yard and this time it was the neighbor with the milk and cream. He drove right over to the icehouse and put the cans of milk into the cooler.

The roasts had to come out of the ovens for awhile now because the pies had to be baked, all 18 of them! An hour later, the roasts were put back into the ovens and then a little later had to be taken out again while the bread baked.

"It's a wonder that the roasts get done, at this rate," commented Carrie, to no one in particular.

When the bread was all baked, and the roasts back in the ovens, the potatoes were put on to boil. The turnips were heated through and a tomato sauce poured over them. At the last minute, while some of the food was being packed into the boxes, Hilde removed the roasts from the pans and stirred up the gravy. The meat was sliced and soon everything was ready to go.

"It isn't quite so hot today, is it?" Carrie said later to Corky as they waited for the men out in the field again.

"No, and it looks like it's going to cloud up by late afternoon," Corky said as he looked toward the western skies.

The men really dug into the meat and potatoes and were especially pleased when they found out that there was green tomato pie for dessert. For some of the men, though, it was their first taste of it. Some were reluctant to try a piece.

"The name just don't sound too appetizing," commented one of the men.

"That's right, Clem, the pie is no good at all," said another. "Why, I'll be a good fella and offer to eat your piece for you."

Clem, however, tried the pie and liked it just fine. "This sure is good stuff. Got any extras?" he asked the girls.

"Only one piece to a customer," Pauline laughingly told him. She was hoping that there would be some left for her and Carrie when they got back to the house.

They needn't have worried. Hilde was looking out for them and had held back a whole pie for all the women. Carrie and Pauline were starved by the time they got back to the house. They helped themselves to the beef, potatoes and turnips, bread and of course, the pie.

"This is good!" said Carrie after several bites. She slowed down and savored every last morsel.

By suppertime, it had indeed clouded up and it looked very much like it may rain later on. Carrie, tired as she was, heard it thundering sometime during the night.

When she came downstairs the next morning, she heard that it had not rained much but just enough to halt the harvesting for the day. The men came to the house for all their meals, which made things so much easier for the women.

That evening, Carrie and Pauline, along with Sally and Betsy, were sitting on the front porch.

"Oh, the air smells so good and fresh, doesn't it?" Pauline said. "I love it after a rain."

"I don't suppose Mr. Daud was too happy that it rained," commented Carrie. "And after only two days of harvesting."

"Well, it didn't rain much and it looks all clear to the west now," remarked Pauline.

Carrie looked up and saw a familiar figure coming toward the house.

"Here comes Alphie!" she exclaimed, as a shiver of excitement ran through her.

By the time he approached the first step, she managed to look engrossed in a newspaper.

"So, the Bonanza Belles are getting some fresh air tonight, eh?" he said as he reached the top step and leaned on the pillar. He removed his cap and Carrie noticed how brown his face had gotten in the last couple days.

"I imagine you men are enjoying your day off, aren't you?" asked Carrie.

"Yes, and I presume you ladies are enjoying a little lighter load today, too. It can't be easy trying to feed us hungry men so many times a day!"

Carrie appreciated that he even would think of that. "Have a seat, why don't you?" she said.

Pauline rose and suggested to the two younger girls that they come inside with her and help her with something. They were reluctant to do so, but Pauline persisted and they finally went with her.

"That's better," said Alphie, sitting down on the settee alongside Carrie. "Now I can talk with you alone."

Carrie didn't know what to answer.

Alphie did most of the talking. He told her of his home in Canada and how he came down to work on the big farms every summer.

She asked him about his name and what nationality he was.

"Oh, I'm quite a mixture! My mother was English and French. She died when I was only ten. My father is Scotch-Irish and German."

"Oh, my!" exclaimed Carrie. "That is really a mix. I'm only one thing---Norwegian!"

"Ah, yes, and a very pretty one at that!" He moved a little closer to her and said, "And I've always been attracted to the fair good looks of the Scandinavian women."

Carrie stammered as she tried to think of a reply to this. He had put his arm on the back of the settee and his hand brushed against her neck. This sent shivers up and down her spine.

"Too bad we'll be too busy to go to any more dances for awhile," Alphie said. "Maybe we could go for a buggy ride some Sunday. What do you say to that?"

"Ah, well, I--ah-- suppose that would be all right." She stumbled over the words.

Mrs. Daud stepped out onto the porch just then and Alphie jumped up and quickly excused himself, saying he should be getting back to the bunkhouse.

"Everything all right out here?" she asked Carrie.

"Why, yes. Mr. Kastet and I were just talking." Carrie rose and gathered up the newspaper that she had failed to finish.

Mrs. Daud settled herself into one of the wicker chairs and said, "Oh, it sure feels cooler out here. It was getting so stuffy inside."

Carrie bid the older woman a good night and went into the house and upstairs to get ready for bed. Pauline was already there, sitting on her bed in her nightgown.

"It's almost too hot in here to sleep," she commented. "It's so humid!"

"I see you've opened the window as far as it will go. It doesn't help much, does it?"

Carrie undressed and lay down on top of her bedspread. "Is it your turn to read tonight?"

"Yes, I guess it is," Pauline said as she reached for the Bible. She read a passage from the Gospel of John and after they discussed it, Carrie reached up and turned out the light.

As she was praying her evening prayers, she noticed that her mind kept wandering to a certain young man.

After awhile, Pauline asked, "Well, what did Mr. Kastet have to say then?"

"Well, he told me about his family and home back in Canada. He also asked if I would like to go for a buggy ride some Sunday afternoon. Then Mrs. Daud came out on the porch and he hightailed it back to the bunkhouse."

Pauline laughed. "She probably came out there to see if you needed rescuing!"

Carrie lay awake for quite sometime. If I'm not tired enough to sleep, I should get up and write a letter home, she told herself. But she didn't move and soon she heard the haunting strains of a harmonica playing "Annie Laurie."

"That melody is so beautiful, it almost makes me cry," she said in the darkness, but there was no answer from her roommate.

Harvest continued the next day and went uninterrupted for the remainder of the week. Sunday was a day of rest for the men. Mr. Daud was very strict about this. No working on the Sabbath.

Alphie had told Carrie the night before that he would get a buggy the next afternoon and they could go for their ride.

On the way to church that morning, Amund brought up the subject of the Canadian.

"You need to be careful around him, Carrie. I've heard--ah--some things about him and I don't think he is your type of fellow."

"Well, we're just going for a ride, Mannie," she retorted hotly. "And I think he's very nice."

Amund shrugged his shoulders and said, "I'm only telling you what I heard."

When Alphie pulled up in front of the big house that afternoon with the buggy, Carrie was ready and waiting in the parlor. She had put on her best skirt and shirtwaist and borrowed a perky straw hat from Pauline.

"Make him come up to the door for you, Carrie," said Hilde. "Any man who doesn't do that isn't worth bothering with!"

Carrie resisted the urge to peer out the window. Soon a knock sounded on the screen door. Pauline went to answer it but not before shooing Carrie into the kitchen.

"Is Miss Amundson ready?" asked Alphie.

"I don't know," fibbed Pauline. "I'll go and see."

She went into the kitchen and made Carrie keep him waiting a full five minutes before letting her go into the parlor.

While he waited, he was busy charming Hilde. At the sight of Carrie, he rose and extended his hand and tucked it inside his arm and led her out the door, after bidding good day to the other women.

Carrie smiled up at him. This is going to be a fun afternoon, she thought to herself.

They drove to Davenport but none of the stores were open on Sunday so they headed out again, going west of town. Alphie turned the buggy down a narrow field road toward a clump of trees.

"Where are we going?" asked Carrie.

"Oh, just a place where we can get out and walk a little and be alone," he answered.

When he stopped, he helped Carrie down from the vehicle. With one hand he removed her hat and grabbed her around the waist with the other and pulled her to him. This all happened so fast, she wasn't prepared when he tried kissing her. She pulled away after a few seconds.

"Mr. Kastet! What are you doing?" she cried.

"What do you think I'm doing?" he answered, laughing. "I'm just trying to kiss a pretty girl on a beautiful Sunday afternoon."

"Well, I--ah--don't want you to kiss me. I mean, I don't feel I know you well enough for that yet."

"You'll get to know me real quick if you let me kiss you," he said, still laughing playfully.

"I let someone kiss me once before and it became a very--ah--unpleasant...situation. I don't want to be hurt like that again."

"You aren't hardly old enough to have been hurt by anyone yet." He tried grabbing her again. "Here, let a real man kiss you."

She pulled away and he grabbed her arm and twisted it. "I know you really want to," he said.

By now Carrie was getting a little scared and also very furious. "I said 'no!' Don't you understand that?"

He reached out and took her by the shoulders and she pushed him away, but not before he ripped her shirtwaist open, sending several buttons flying and a ripped sleeve dangling down her arm.

Carrie gasped. She tried slapping him across the face, but he clasped her arm tightly in his grip.

"You scoundrel!" she exclaimed. "I can't believe you would do this to me!" She got away and started running towards the road.

"All right, all right," he called after her. He got in the buggy and turned it around and stopped alongside her. "Get in," he ordered. "You can't walk all the way home."

She ignored him and kept walking.

"I should just leave you and let you walk but I won't do that. Get in! I won't touch you again. Please, just get up in this buggy. Now!"

Carrie stopped and considered this. She couldn't walk all the way. She didn't even know the way back to the farm.

"I won't try to touch you again. I promise."

She reluctantly got back into the buggy and he urged the horses on with a flick of the reins. Carrie could hold the tears back no longer.

After some minutes of silence, he looked at her and almost sneered. "You're just a baby, you know that? I need to find me a real woman!"

Carrie cried in deep sobs now and he just looked at her in disgust.

He urged the horses to go faster and after about a half-hour, Carrie felt relief as they turned down the Daud's driveway.

"Now, don't go blabbing to everyone what happened out there," he warned her, with a menacing look on his face. "Just say that you tore your dress on a tree branch."

He stopped in front of the house and she jumped out immediately, without turning back to look at him. She ran around to the back door and slipped into the kitchen, intending to run right upstairs. She ran smack into Mrs. Daud.

Carrie gasped and so did the older woman.

"Carrie, what happened to you?"

Carrie couldn't say anything for a few moments, she was so surprised. And she really didn't know what she was going to say so she just started crying all over again. Mrs. Daud took the girl into her arms and let her cry.

Finally she held the girl out at arm's length. "Carrie, did that Mr. Kastet do something to you?"

Pauline and Hilde came into the kitchen just then and were surprised at the scene unfolding there. They had heard Mrs. Daud's question.

"Carrie! What happened?" asked Pauline, afraid for her friend.

Carrie finally found her voice. "He...he...Alphie tried to k..k..kiss me and I didn't want him to so he got rough and...and..." Here she looked down at her blouse and her disheveled appearance.

"Why, that beast!" exclaimed Pauline.

"And I thought he seemed like such a gentleman!" chimed in Hilde. She put her arms around Carrie and held her close for awhile.

"You go now and get yourself fixed up," Hilde finally told her. "Pauline, you go up with her."

When the two girls were out of earshot, Hilde and Mrs. Daud sat down by the table and just looked at each other.

"Wait until my husband hears about this! He doesn't tolerate any such behavior on this farm. Why, he's warned the men about this sort of thing time and again."

Without another word, she rose and left the room, in search of Mr. Daud.

CHAPTER 14

Before breakfast the next morning, Mr. Alphonse Kastet of Canada was no longer employed on the Daud farm. Mrs. Daud came into the dining hall as Carrie was setting the tables and told her that Mr. Kastet had left that morning in a wagon driven by Mr. Thompson. He was taking the young man to Davenport to catch the train.

"Thank you for telling me," Carrie said in a low voice. At least now she wouldn't have to worry about facing the man again. Her cheeks flushed as she thought about the whole incident. "I wonder if everyone on the farm knows about it by now," she muttered to herself.

During the serving of the meal, she felt that all eyes were upon her and that the men were all blaming her for sending one of their co-workers away, right in the middle of harvest yet! But when she got the nerve to hold her head up high and look out at all the men, no one was looking at her at all. They seemed totally unaware that something had happened. Even Amund didn't come over to her after he finished eating to talk.

Late in the morning when the women had a few moments to take a break, Hilde asked Carrie if she could come out to the garden with her to check on the tomatoes. Hilde took a basket along and Carrie followed her out. Hilde sat down on the garden bench and Carrie did the same.

"So, how are you doing this morning, my dear?" Hilde asked kindly. "Mrs. Daud told me that Mr. Daud had had a talk with Mr. Kastet late last night and dismissed him."

"Yes, Mrs. Daud told me this morning that he was gone already." Here Carrie almost started to cry again. "Do you think I reacted too strongly? Now Alphie has lost his job! I didn't mean for that to happen."

"Mr. Daud will not stand for any misconduct between his men and the female workers here. He tells the men that when they start working here. Alphie knew that."

"I feel bad for what happened. I....just didn't....want him to ....kiss me, that's all. If only he would have just taken no for an answer none of this would have happened. If only Mrs. Daud hadn't seen me in such a state when I came home yesterday afternoon."

"Well, I was there too, remember?" Hilde reminded her. "I probably would have reported it to Mrs. Daud.

"Have there been incidents like this here before?" Carrie asked.

"A few times. Some of the men who have worked here haven't been...shall we say...of the best character and they have not lasted long. There has also been a girl or two who has lost her job, too."

"Really? What happened?" Carrie wanted to know.

"Well, one had a habit of slipping into the bunkhouse during the night to see a certain young man. When Mr. Daud found out about that, he dismissed both of the involved parties!"

Hilde rose and started to look for ripe tomatoes. "Let's see if we can find enough ripe ones to slice for dinner, shall we?"

The subject was closed and Carrie and Hilde picked a basketful.

That evening, Amund and Peter came calling at the front door and Carrie went out on the porch with them.

Amund fixed his gaze on Carrie and said, "We heard some talk today about Alphie's sudden departure. Can you shed some light on the subject?"

Carrie hesitated and Peter chimed in. "It seems strange that you went out for a buggy ride yesterday afternoon with him and then early this morning, the man was gone."

"Sit down," Carrie said, "and I'll tell you the whole story." When she finished relating the incident, Amund stood up and started ranting.

"Carrie, I warned you about that man. I told you I had heard some things about him and I didn't think you should be getting friendly with him."

"Carrie started sobbing again. "I know, but I thought he was nice and that you were wrong about him. I guess I'm not a very good judge of character, am I? First there was Ted and now Alphie."

"I wouldn't put Ted in the same category as this fellow, Carrie. This fellow is...let us say...a little bit more worldly than your preacher's son."

"I don't even want to hear what you've heard about him, Mannie. I just want to forget the whole incident. Do all the men know what happened? That I was involved, I mean?" she asked, standing up herself now.

"No, they were told that he had to leave for a family emergency. Mr. Daud was considerate to protect your reputation," Peter said.

"Mr. Daud is a fine man, isn't he?" Carrie said. "Like a father."

"Well, we better be off," Peter interrupted. "Another busy day tomorrow."

"I just wanted to find out what happened and if you were all right," said Amund. "See you in the morning."

"Thank you for stopping by. It was good to talk to you about it."

The weather remained very dry, which was perfect for harvesting. All the wheat had now been cut and it was time for the threshing to begin. The three steam threshers that the farm owned were driven out to whichever field had been cut first and the operation began.

Carrie rode with Corky to bring dinner out the first day. He had to explain to her, again, what was going on.

"Those wagons there, they're called bundle wagons. It takes eight of them for each threshing machine." He pointed toward one of the wagons. "You see Swede over there? He's what we call a field pitcher. He loads the bundles of wheat into the wagon. The wagon takes the bundles to the thresher. Then the spike pitcher pitches them into the machine."

He pulled the wagon a little closer to the action while trying to stay out of the blowing chaff. "There's another wagon over there to catch the grain as it comes out of the machine," he continued. "That, of course, is hauled back to the yard and unloaded into the elevator. There's two wagons for each thresher."

Just then the big machine blew its whistle and it startled both Carrie and the horses. Corky had to hold the reins firmly until the animals settled down.

"That was a signal for more bundles," explained Corky. "One short whistle. When you hear one long one, that means more water. Two short whistles mean they want a grain wagon."

"Aren't they going to stop for dinner?"

"I'm sure they will in a few more minutes. Then we'll hear three short whistles. That means stop to eat. That's the one the men like to hear!"

Sure enough, about five minutes later, Carrie almost jumped again when the mighty machine blew out three shorts in quick succession. She and Corky scrambled down from the wagon and started to unload the noon meal.

Wagons brought the men from the other end of the field as well.

As hungry as the men were, they waited politely until Carrie and Corky could serve all of them and pour coffee for everyone. They came back for seconds, all the while eyeing the peach pie that Carrie had started to line up on the edge of the wagon.

There was a lot of joking and teasing among the men after they had filled their stomachs and were enjoying some more coffee. They all found some place to sit down in the shade of the wagons to have a little rest. Some were even able to catch a few winks of sleep. The horses needed feed and water and rest, too.

A whistle called them all back to work and Carrie and Corky turned the loaded wagon back toward the farm.

"Another hot day!" Corky wiped his brow with his sleeve. "Great for threshing, though. This sure has been a dry summer. Hope it holds for a spell."

When they returned to the yard, they met the meat wagon going out.

"Looks like the boys from Helendale have been here with some more meat," remarked Corky as he waved a greeting. "It sure takes a huge amount during the harvest time."

"It sure takes a huge amount of everything here!" exclaimed Carrie.

With some extra help, they unloaded the food containers and the dirty plates, cups and silverware in the kitchen. Mrs. Schmit, the laundry woman, was sharing a cup of coffee with Hilde and Cora. Pauline and Stella were already starting in on the ironing in the laundry room.

"I can't believe how fast the wash dried today!" exclaimed Berta Schmit.

"Yah, that hot, dry wind is good for something," remarked Hilde. Then she got up and began mixing up a large batch of cookie dough.

"What kind of cookies is it today?" questioned Corky as he was heading out the door.

"It's cracked sugar cookies today," Hilde called out after him. "You can stay and help roll them into balls for us."

"That's women's work!" he called back. "I'd just make a mess of things. I'll be back to test them for you, though. Good day, ladies. See you later."

It was so hot in the kitchen, Carrie didn't know if she could stand it any longer. And then they had to bake the cookies yet! She and Sally rolled the dough into balls and then dipped them in sugar and placed them on the oversized cookie pans.

While the cookies were baking, Carrie started slicing bread for the lunchtime sandwiches.

"What shall we put on them?" she inquired.

"Why don't you put summer sausage on some and cheese on the others," suggested Cora. "Betsy, you run out to the cooler and fetch the cheese."

"Get some more butter, too, while you're out there," Hilde called after the girl.

It was Pauline's turn to go out with the lunch wagon and Carrie took over the ironing for her. It was just as hot in the laundry room. The sweat just poured down Carrie's face and it ran into her eyes. She had to stop and wipe her face several times in the course of ironing one item. She finally finished the job and went back into the kitchen.

"Here, have yourself a little rest and a cold glass of lemonade," offered Hilde.

Carrie didn't know when anything had sounded so good! She held the cool glass up to her face before she took a big swallow of the tart liquid. She drank it down fast and poured herself some more to go with the fresh cookies.

"I sure hope it cools off better tonight," Cora remarked. "It was hard to sleep last night."

"Yah, you can say that again!" Hilde agreed.

Corky and Pauline returned from the field and soon it was time to start preparations for supper.

All we do is cook, eat, clean up, and cook, eat and clean up some more, mused Carrie, but she didn't voice her thoughts out loud. She didn't want to seem like a complainer. Everyone else was just as hot and tired as she was. Especially Hilde. The large woman was very red in the face and was moving extra slow. How can she put in such long, hot days and always be so cheerful, Carrie wondered.

That night a cool, refreshing breeze did indeed blow up, to everyone's relief. The next morning, even the men seemed to have benefited from the change in the weather. They ate a hearty breakfast and were anxious to get on with their work.

When Sunday came around, the men were grateful for a full day of rest. Many of the men slept in, but Amund and Peter came by in the buggy and picked up the girls for church.

"We couldn't shake Emory awake this morning," Peter teased Pauline.

Pauline found that she was disappointed that he would not be going along with them.

After services, the four young people decided to drive down to Kindred to the cafe there for dinner for a change. They saw several other men from the farm there, too.

"It must be a good place to eat," remarked Peter. "I see Big Joe over there. Eating is one of his favorite things so if he likes it here it must be good!"

"Or else they give large portions," laughed Amund.

It was a lovely, late summer afternoon, so after they ate, Peter took them for a drive east of town, down by the Sheyenne River. They went by a beautiful country church. The sign said Norman Lutheran Church on it.

"We should go here some Sunday," suggested Carrie.

"Well, it's quite a bit further to go so early in the morning," Peter answered.

"We would just have to get up earlier," Pauline said.

"Carrie, I think that this is the area where Engebret said his brother, Elling Ulness came and started a store in the early 1880's. Before the town of Kindred was established, even."

"That could be," remarked Carrie. "I remember him saying that the first settlers to this area built log cabins along the river here and they called the little settlement Norman."

"That's interesting," said Peter. "But there's only a church left here now."

"The mill was here for a time and then they moved it south of Kindred, by Ulness."

"That's progress, I guess." Peter turned the buggy around and they headed west again and then north back to the Daud farm.

"How much longer do you think the threshing will go on?" Carrie inquired.

"Well, Mr. Thompson told someone yesterday that we were over half done," said Peter. "I figure by the second week in September, we should finish. That is if it doesn't rain."

"I think it's forgotten how to rain," commented Pauline wryly.

"At least it cooled off some. Those were some really hot days for a week or so."

They turned into the farm. It looked very quiet, with not a soul around.

"Either everyone's napping or is gone someplace."

"This has been a lovely afternoon," Carrie told Peter and Amund as she was helped down from the buggy. Pauline agreed and the girls went into the house.

They found Hilde sleeping in a chair, a newspaper in her lap. They tiptoed toward the stairs and went up to change their clothes.

True to Peter's prediction, the threshing was winding up by the end of the first week in September. The field nearest the farm was saved till last. One of the threshing machines was set up in the yard, by the barns, so that there would be some big straw piles formed for the horses to feed from during the winter.

The Saturday after the end of harvest, there was a Harvest Ball held in Davenport. Most of the workers attended. They were ready to celebrate with some dancing and, for some, a few drinks. There was a keen shortage of girls to dance with, even with many of the young, local females attending.

Pauline danced most of the evening with Emory, but Carrie danced with someone different almost every set. One of her partners was a young fellow named Fred Shutz. He was from town there and worked for one of the local businesses.

"I noticed you were dancing with that Shutz fellow quite a bit, Carrie," teased Peter on their way home.

"Only one set, Peter," she laughed, "And how did you have time to be watching me when you were obviously quite busy with Miss Murphy?"

The teasing went back and forth all the way home. Pauline and Emory sat in the back of the buggy with only eyes for each other.

"It's pretty quiet back there!" Peter said loudly, as they were turning into the farm.

Emory laughed and hit him over the head with his hat.

Carrie hurried into the house, leaving Pauline and Emory lingering on the porch.

When Pauline came into the bedroom a short while later, Carrie was undressed and had her Bible open on her lap.

"I don't need to ask if you had a good time tonight, do I?" Carrie teased her friend.

"It was fun, wasn't it?" she answered dreamily.

"Just how fond of Emory are you becoming, Pauline?"

"Well, we seem to be getting very close to each other."

"Getting very close?" exclaimed Carrie. "Just what does that mean? That you're falling in love with each other?"

"Well, I don't know about that. I've never been in love so I don't know what it feels like."

"I guess I don't either," conceded Carrie, laughing. "Anyway, I'm no authority on the subject as you well know!"

The next several days the men spent cleaning and repairing the harvest machinery before putting it away. It rained finally, so one evening as Carrie and Pauline were getting ready for bed, Carrie turned out their light and opened their shade and, gasping, she said, "Oh my! What's that?"

Pauline hurried to join her at the window. They could see fires everywhere, in all directions.

"Oh, I think the men were burning the fields tonight," she explained. "To get rid of the straw. It was too dry to do it earlier."

"It looks like a big army campground!" laughed Carrie.

"Lucky that the wind is from the south. At least the smoke won't blow into our window."

One morning at breakfast, Carrie told Amund that she had received a postcard from Gilla Ulness, the oldest daughter of Engebret and Lena.

"She told me that her mother asked her to write us and tell us that the new baby had arrived. It was a girl. It would be fun if we could go and visit them sometime again soon, don't you think?"

That evening, Amund told Carrie as they were sitting on the porch, that the next day he was going to take one of the wagons full of wheat and bring it down to the mill and have it made into flour.

"I heard that Mr. Thompson was looking for some fellows to drive the wagons, so I volunteered. Maybe you could come along and we'll stop in and see the Ulness family for a short while."

"Oh, that would be fun!' Carrie exclaimed with delight. "I'll talk to Hilde or Mrs. Daud and see if I can be spared for part of the day. I'll let you know at breakfast time."

It was arranged that Carrie could go with Amund and she was excited as she sat on the wagon seat next to him. Three other wagons were ahead of them.

"How much flour will they be able to get out of these four wagons full?" Carrie inquired.

"Probably enough to last the whole year."

Amund let Carrie off by the store at Ulness and said he would find her as soon as he dumped his load. She went into the store to see who was in there. Randolph was behind the counter and greeted her with a smile and a look of surprise.

"Well, what brings you here, Miss Amundson?"

Carrie explained their errand and asked if it would be all right if she just walked over to the house to see his family.

"I'm sorry that we couldn't let you know that we were coming but this just came up and I wanted to come along."

"That's all right. You just go over there and Mama will be very pleased to see you. She just had the baby last week, did you know that?"

"Yes, your sister Gilla wrote us. That's why I wanted to come along so badly."

Carrie walked the short distance to the Ulness home and knocked on the front door. Hannah came and peeked through the screen door and made a sound of delight as she saw Carrie.

"Oh, Carrie! What a surprise! Come in, come in. Ma is up today for the first time and she is sitting in the parlor with the baby. Did Gilla write to you about the baby coming?"

"Yes she did. She said it was a girl. How nice."

Lena looked up with surprise at Carrie standing in the doorway of the parlor.

"Well, look who we have here! How in the world did you get here? Did you come alone?"

Carrie explained once more and sat down by the new mother and baby. "Oh, isn't she sweet and so tiny! What did you name her?"

"Alice," said Hannah. "Alice Tilda."

"Oh, that's a pretty name," said Carrie. "I wish we had a gift for her, but this visit came about in a hurry."

"Do you want to hold her?" asked Lena.

"Oh, do you think I should? She's so...so...new and...and... little."

Lena laughed her tinkling laugh and handed the tiny bundle to Carrie. "You need to get some practice."

Carrie looked at her questioningly.

"Well, you know, you'll be a mother someday yourself."

Carrie just laughed but said, "When we go back home to Spring Grove, I'll be able to hold my new little niece, Manda, who is just over two months now. I can't wait to see her. Ma writes about her all the time!"

"Go and put the coffee pot on, Gilla," said Lena. "I suppose Amund will be along soon."

The baby started crying so Carrie handed her back to her mother.

"I think she's hungry so I'll feed her before we have our coffee." Lena opened her dress front and began to breast feed little Alice. She began suckling noisily and Carrie laughed.

"I guess she really was hungry, wasn't she?"

After awhile they heard a wagon come in the yard and soon Amund presented himself at the front door. Hannah let him in and he joined the ladies in the parlor.

"So there's the new arrival!" he exclaimed, looking down at her in awe. "How little she is!"

When the baby had fallen asleep and Gilla announced that coffee was ready, they all went into the dining room and sat around the big table.

"Too bad Engebret isn't around today. He went down to Walcott to see how things were going on the farm there. He'll be sorry he missed you."

"Mama, shall I run over to the store and stay there so that Randolph can come home and visit with Amund?" asked Hannah.

"Yah, that would be a good idea," Lena said, and the young girl hurried out the door.

When Randolph joined them, the talk turned to farming. Randolph didn't enjoy that occupation, but he was interested in the big bonanza farming operation.

"So, you hauled in some of your wheat to the mill here?"

"Yah, that we did. Four wagons full. Our cook likes that Queen of the Valley flour and it takes a lot of it to keep us all fed!"

"Can you believe," said Carrie, "that during the harvest season we were baking about 40 loaves of bread a day!"

Lena just shook her head. "No, I can't even imagine that."

"And, of course, it also took many batches of cookies, cakes, pies and doughnuts, too."

"How many men were there to feed?" inquired Gilla.

"We were feeding about eighty just last week. Some of them have left now."

"After the fall plowing most of the men will leave," added Amund.

Just then 4-year-old Carl and little Gladys came down the stairs. They had been napping.

"Company, Mama?" asked Carl.

"Yah, you two can sit down here and have some cookies. Get them some milk, will you, Gilla?"

"Baby sleep?" asked Gladys as she gently patted the infant's head.

"They sure do love the new baby," Lena told them.

"How are you feeling, Lena?" asked Carrie.

"Oh, pretty good now. It took me a little longer to recover this time. I'm getting older, you know," she laughed.

"I hate to say this, Carrie, but we better be heading back to the farm. It's a long drive." Amund stood up and, picking up his cap, he thanked Lena and Gilla for the coffee and Carrie did the same.

"It was so much fun to see you again," said Lena, rising, too. "When will you be going back to Spring Grove?"

"I'm not sure," answered Carrie. "Probably in November sometime."

"Well, maybe you can come again before you go."

"We'll try," Carrie and Amund both answered together.

CHAPTER 15

October was another dry month, which was welcomed by Mr. Daud and his foreman, as rain would really mess up the fall plowing. Ten two-bottom gang plows, each pulled by six horses, were used to cover all the acres and turn over the stubble. About half of the crew had left right after the threshing was finished. The rest of the men would stay until after all the plowing was done.

Train cars arrived several days in a row to load up wheat from the Daud farm elevator and take it east to Minneapolis.

The women no longer had to feed the men out in the fields. This decreased their workload considerably.

"With only half as many men to cook for now, things sure go faster, don't they?" Carrie observed one day.

"Yah, we can even find a little time for ourselves now," agreed Hilde.

It was Carrie's turn to accompany Mrs. Daud on one of her shopping trips again. This time they went to Davenport to the Tuskind Store. Carrie ended up buying two baby dresses, one for the Ulness baby and one for her new little niece, Manda.

"I hope we can make a visit to Ulness again before we leave for home," she told Amund that evening.

"I've been meaning to talk to you about going home, Carrie. Mr. Thompson asked me if I would stay for the whole winter. I told him I'd like to go home for awhile anyway. When do you want to go home?"

"I was thinking the middle of November. Mrs. Daud talked to me about it and there won't be very many men left by then. She asked me if I would be interested in coming back next spring. I said I'd give it some thought when I'm home and let her know."

"Mr. Daud is going to rent out about 100 of his horses for the winter to one of the lumber companies in Minnesota. Peter asked me if I'd like to come with him and two other fellows to help bring the horses over to Bemidji and then I'd go home from there."

"You mean we wouldn't be going home together then?" asked Carrie.

"No, do you mind?"

"Well, no, I guess I can do that." Then she asked, "Why is he renting out his horses?"

"It costs plenty to feed so many horses all winter long, so a couple years ago he started doing this. We'll load up the horses in train cars that will come right to the siding here."

"How long does that trip take?"

"Oh, Peter said that we'll take three days going there and getting the horses settled in their new surroundings."

On the last Sunday of October, Carrie and Amund made a trip down to Ulness and on the first day of November, North Dakota had its first blizzard of the year. Roads and railroads were blocked for several days. By the next week, though, all the snow had melted and mild temperatures prevailed for a time. Peter, Amund and two other men loaded up the horses and made for Minnesota.

Carrie left the next day, after tearful goodbyes to all her new-found friends. Pauline had been asked to stay and work for the winter. Cora always left in November and came back in the spring, so Hilde needed at least one girl to help her. Pauline promised to write, as did Carrie.

Two days later, Carrie was sitting at the table with her family, telling them all about her experiences on the big bonanza farm in North Dakota. It was good to be home. Sylvia was excited to have her back to help with wedding plans. Olaf and Mattie were proud to show off their new baby.

Amund arrived home the next day. He helped his father and Olaf with work around the farm, repairing things and the like, but Carrie noticed that he seemed restless. She talked with him about it one evening when the rest of the family had gone to bed.

"I guess there just isn't enough to keep me busy around here, after having so much to do for so many months," he tried to explain to his sister. "My work never got done back there."

"When do you plan to go back?"

"I'll probably go the middle of January."

"Really?" Carrie was surprised. "That soon?"

"Yah, they need me to get machinery ready for spring planting. How about you, Carrie, are you going back there?"

"I haven't decided yet. Let's get the wedding and Christmas over with first. Then I'll see."

The wedding for Sylvia and Rudy took place on the second Saturday of December at the church in town. It was a cold, crisp day but the sun was shining and the little bit of snow that had fallen the month before had all but disappeared.

Sylvia, being the good seamstress that she was, made her dress herself. It was an ivory faille two-piece dress with long sleeves and a high neck. There were twenty-two tiny covered buttons up the front of the bodice. She wore a floor-length white veil which had a headdress of small satin roses on it.

Carrie was her sister's only attendant, wearing a dress that was quickly made upon her arrival back home. Hers was a deep burgundy and was similar in design to that of the bride's. Carrie sat up late many an evening covering the little buttons and finished just the night before the wedding.

After the ceremony, the small group of family and a few friends were invited back to the farmhouse for supper. Carrie, her mother, and sister Rosina had spent many days preparing food for the group. They served sliced ham and turkey, mashed potatoes, creamed corn, lefse and rolls. Mattie and her mother had volunteered to make the wedding cake, much to the relief of Mrs. Amundson.

The newly married couple went on a short wedding trip to St. Paul but were anxious to return and get settled in their little house in Spring Grove. Then there was Christmas to get ready for. An extensive housecleaning had already taken place in the Amundson home prior to the wedding so the time remaining was spent making last-minute gifts and baking some of the traditional holiday goodies, like rosettes, fattigmon, strull and julekakke.

Carrie spent an afternoon in Spring Grove shopping for her family. It was nice to have a little money of her own to spend, she mused. She bought string ties for the men in the family, which now included her new brother-in-law, and for her two sisters and Mattie, she picked out some nice-smelling dusting powder.

Carrie had purchased her mother's gift back in North Dakota on one of her shopping trips with Mrs. Daud. She bought a pair of kid gloves, much like the ones she herself had received as a gift from her employer. She hoped her mother would like them and not think them too extravagant.

Christmas was especially fun this year with five-month old baby Manda. She had just learned to sit by herself, with a little propping, and she liked playing with the paper, which had been strewn around after the opening of the gifts.

Sylvia and Rudy joined the family on Christmas Day after church services. Acting like typical newlyweds, they were excited about their new home and all the nice wedding gifts they had received. Sylvia was planning to continue with her seamstress job and Rudy was doing well at the hardware store.

A week after Christmas, Carrie received two letters the same day. One was postmarked Chicago and was from Mrs. Daud. The other was from Pauline. Carrie first opened the one from her former employer. Mrs. Daud was wondering if Carrie had made up her mind yet about returning to North Dakota for another season. Carrie laid that letter aside while she took Pauline's and went to sit in the big rocker.

Pauline started in right away with some startling news. Emory had proposed to her through the mail and she had accepted.

"Oh, my!" Carrie uttered aloud. "I thought she didn't want to marry a farmer."

"Who are you talking to, Carrie?" She and her mother were alone in the house.

"One of these letters is from someone I worked with at the Daud farm. A fellow who worked there was sweet on her but she said she wouldn't marry a farmer," explained Carrie, getting up and moving towards the kitchen. "Now, she says here that he proposed in a letter and she said 'yes'! I just can't believe it!"

"Well, love is funny, you know. It makes you do things you didn't think you would." Mrs. Amundson was giving the soup on the stove a gentle stirring.

Carrie continued reading in silence as she returned to the rocker. She picked up Mrs. Daud's letter again and reread it. She was leaning back in the rocker, deep in thought, when she heard the men coming in the back entrance. The table needed setting so she jumped up to help her mother.

"So Carrie, I hear you were pretty popular with the mailman this morning. Two letters in one day!" joked Papa.

"Yes, I heard from a girl I worked with in North Dakota and I also heard from Mrs. Daud. She's still in Chicago." She paused here before continuing. "She asked me if I had made up my mind yet about going back and working for them again in the spring." She looked straight at Amund but all eyes were on her.

After a long pause, Carrie's father finally said, "Well? What are you going to tell her then?"

"I...I...haven't decided yet."

"Do you want to go back?" asked Rosina.

"Sometimes I do and sometimes I don't."

"Well, I suppose she needs to know soon, doesn't she?" asked Papa.

"Yes, I need to answer her this week."

Exactly two months later, Carrie was bouncing along on the train, headed for North Dakota. Amund had left a month earlier. What finally helped make up her mind about returning was the restlessness that she, too, had felt ever since the hustle and bustle of the wedding and the holidays were over.

Upon making her decision, she got busy and made herself some clothes to bring along. She especially wanted to make a pretty dress, suitable for the dances she was anticipating. She had accompanied her father on a trip to Decorah one day and had picked out a beautiful piece of material for just such a dress. It was a pale-blue lawn fabric and she purchased a new, stylish pattern. Sylvia had helped her with the sewing.

When she had said her goodbyes to her parents on the platform in Spring Grove, Carrie had the feeling that things would never be the same again. She was turning a new chapter in her life. She was an adult now and had to have something meaningful to do, she reasoned to herself. If she had remained at home, just helping her mother, what would her future have held?

She was jolted out of her reverie when the train stopped and the conductor announced Breckenridge. Carrie rose and grabbed her overnight bag and hurried off the train. She stayed in the same hotel that she and Amund had stayed in a year earlier. The next day was a short traveling day and as they stopped at the water tower near Ulness, Carrie peered out the window, hoping to catch a glimpse of one of the Ulness family. She could see their house and the store.

When she arrived in Davenport, Amund was there to meet her. Again they went to the cafe for dinner. Carrie noticed a familiar face a couple tables away.

"Do you see that fellow sitting over there with that older man?" she nodded toward their table. "That's Fred Shutz. I met him at a dance here last fall."

Shortly after, Fred and the other gentleman got up and, on their way out of the cafe, walked by their table. Fred stopped short as he recognized Carrie.

"Why, Miss Amundson! I didn't know that you were back in this area."

"I just arrived a half hour ago!" she answered.

Fred introduced the older man as his father and Carrie in turn introduced them to her brother. Fred seemed like he wanted to say more, but instead he said they both better be getting back to work.

"Where does this Fred work?" inquired Amund.

"I think he said he worked at the newspaper office here in town and his father is the depot agent."

They finished their meal and declined offers of apple pie.

"I'm feeling too stuffed for dessert," remarked Carrie. "I had a large breakfast in Breckenridge this morning."

Before returning to the farm, Carrie told Amund she needed to stop in the Tuskind's store for a few minutes. He went to get the buggy and waited outside for her. She wanted to pick up a few little things for her friends at the farm. She bought embroidered handkerchiefs for Hilde and Cora and a hair comb for Pauline, which she thought would look nice in her thick, auburn hair. Mr. Tuskind welcomed Carrie back and he quickly wrapped the small gifts for her.

When she hopped up into the buggy, she had a satisfied smile on her face.

"What are you looking so smug about?" asked her brother.

"I just bought some little gifts for three dear friends and I can't wait until they open them!"

As they were driving out of town, Carrie said, "Mannie, I think I made the right decision to come back. It seems that this area and the people here have a strong pull on me. Do you feel that way, too?"

"Yah, I could hardly wait to get back here."

"Well, then, let's hope that this is a good year for both of us," Carrie said, still smiling with anticipation.

"Oh, I almost forgot to tell you something, Carrie!" exclaimed Amund on their ride out to the farm. "Guess what Mr. Daud brought back with him this year!"

"I don't know, another new buggy?"

"No, better than that. He had an auto car shipped by rail and it came about two weeks ago. You should just see it!" Amund's eyes shone with excitement. "It's a 1908 Cadillac. Last year's model. He bought it there in Chicago."

"Have you ridden in it yet?"

"Yah, sure, I've even driven it about some. We're waiting for the roads to dry up a little better before we take her very far."

When Carrie entered the house, by way of the back door, the welcome she received was overwhelming. Hilde held her in a long embrace and when she was released, Carrie saw tears in the older woman's eyes.

"You girls are like my children, you know," she said in explanation for the show of emotion.

Cora gave her a big hug, too, and when Pauline came downstairs she squealed in delight and the two young women hugged and laughed and hugged again.

"My, my, what's all the commotion down here anyhow?" said Mrs. Daud, laughing at the spectacle as she also entered the kitchen. She, too, gave Carrie an affectionate embrace.

"We're so happy that you decided to come back to us," she told Carrie. "Girls like you and Pauline here are hard to find."

A couple hours later, Carrie was right back in the routine of things as she helped prepare supper. Only about fifteen men had been hired on so far this spring, but, along with the ones who stayed the whole year, there were about twenty to cook for thus far.

Later that night, in their bedroom, Pauline and Carrie had so much to talk about. Especially the upcoming marriage.

"Pauline, what made you change your mind about Emory?" Carrie inquired. "I thought you said you wouldn't think of marrying him."

"Well, they say that absence makes the heart grow fonder," she laughed. "The longer we were apart the more I thought about him and missed him. I began to realize that I was in love with him."

"How did you know?" pressed Carrie. "I mean, how can you tell if you're in love with someone?"

Pauline sat down on the bed and began to unroll her hair from its thick coil and braided it loosely to one side for the night. "I guess it's hard to explain. You just want to be with that person and when you are, you're happy. I don't know how else to describe it. I want to make a life with him," she went on, "and grow old with him."

"Well, he's a fine man, that's for sure," commented Carrie.

"Yes, that he is. And he's very kind and considerate and he's a hard worker. He'll be a good provider. And you know what else?" Pauline said. "I just know that he will be a good father."

"I hope I meet a man like that someday. And I hope that I'm as sure about him as you seem to be about Emory."

"Oh, you will. Just be patient."

"I wonder what ever happened to Alphie," Carrie wondered aloud.

"I never heard, but he sure wasn't the type of man for you. He was a real cad, that one."

The girls settled down and it was quiet for awhile. "I'm half expecting to hear harmonica music," chuckled Carrie, nodding towards the slightly opened window. "I wonder if Karl will be coming back."

The next weeks passed quickly. The month of April started out cold and windy but finally the fields were proclaimed dry enough so that the men could start the harrowing. The harrows had been dragged from the machine shed and lined up in the yard, ready to go. Carrie had never seen such a sight. There were forty of these machines and they each, when spread out, reached 25 feet across.

The morning that they all left the yard, each machine was pulled by five horses. Behind each harrow there was a two-wheeled drag cart on which the driver sat, controlling the reins. Peter told Carrie that each machine could cover about 50 acres in a day. Each field would be harrowed two or three times before it was fit to seed.

One afternoon, after Carrie had picked up a letter at the store addressed to her and Amund, she went in search of her brother. She headed towards the machine shop where he usually could be found. He was just heading out the door.

"We have a letter from home, Mannie," she called to him.

"I have to hurry over to the elevator right now. They're having trouble with the wheat cleaner. Why don't you come along with me?"

Carrie had to practically run to keep up with her brother's long stride as they hurried along. She stood to one side as he examined the machine. He reached into his bag of tools and after a few minutes, had the mechanism working again.

"Here, Carrie, you may want to watch this for a few minutes. They're cleaning the wheat seed for planting. The wheat is shoveled into this cleaner. See that little gas engine? That runs the motor and keeps it going. The cleaned grain comes out this end and runs into those bags there."

The bags were 3-bushel cloth bags and it took two men to hold one upright until it was filled to three-fourths full. It was folded over and loaded onto a waiting wagon. Two men were ready with another bag to fill and so it went. Carrie watched with fascination at how fast things were done. She could see that several wagons were already filled with the bags.

Amund motioned for her to follow him back to his workshop. They sat outside on two stumps and Carrie opened the letter. She read it aloud while Amund leaned back against the wall to have a little rest.

Their mother had written that Pa and Olaf had just started planting their wheat. It had been cold and windy there, too. Marty wanted to quit school and just help on the farm so they were having quite a time convincing him that he had to finish, she wrote.

"Let's see now, has he got one more year left in the country school there?" inquired Amund.

"Yes, and I was hoping he would go on to high school, like Rosina is, but I bet Pa will never get him to do that!"

The sunshine, which had been noticeably absent for so many weeks, felt good on the sister and brother as they sat and thought of home.

"Well, I better get back to the house," Carrie said, folding the letter and putting it in her apron pocket. "I hear we had some more new men come today."

"Yah, it takes so many men to drive all those harrows and then with the wheat cleaning and all. It's going to be real busy around here for sometime now."

"See you at suppertime," called Carrie as she hurried off.

The fieldwork went full speed ahead for the next few days, but on Sunday, everything came to a standstill. That afternoon Mr. Daud got his new motor car out of the shed and Carrie saw it for the first time. He drove it up in front of the house and Mrs. Daud told all the women to come outside and see it. "Maybe even ride in it!" she told them.

It was a topless roadster in a black finish so glossy that one could see their image in it. The wheels were spoked and the front grill and headlamps were a shiny gold. The upholstered seat was of black leather and would accommodate only two people.

Mr. Daud sat proudly in the driver's seat and motioned for one of the women to hop up and have a little spin around the yard. Pauline went first and then Carrie.

"This is my first auto ride," she told her employer. He stepped on the gas pedal and they went zooming down the driveway, turned around and then came back. Carrie got down reluctantly and the women tried to talk Hilde into riding. At first she refused, but when Cora went and said it was great fun, she finally relented and they had to push her from behind as Mr. Daud pulled her arm and finally she was seated on the seat beside him.

The women laughed at the smug look she gave them when she went whizzing by them on her way down the driveway. She was waving and trying to hold onto her hat and laughing gleefully.

"Hilde needs to have some fun for a change!" exclaimed Pauline. They all agreed and laughed some more when she returned and didn't want to get down.

"Why, Mrs. Daud, you can drive this thing to town when you go on your little shopping trips!" she said when she had been handed safely on the ground beside the other women.

"Have you ever driven it?" Carrie asked Mrs. Daud.

"Yes, I drove it in Chicago a little, just around the block a few times. I guess I could drive it here, but it isn't so easy to crank it up. I may need a man along for that," she chuckled.

Some of the men sauntered over to the house and a few of them were given rides, too. Mr. Daud remained the only driver, though.

"I'd sure like to drive that thing again," Amund said to Carrie. He had come to watch the goings on. Mr. Daud had been blowing the horn each time he took someone new out.

"Maybe he'll let you, when there aren't so many others around."

"I'm going to have one of those myself someday," he said thoughtfully, as he watched Mr. Daud drive the vehicle back to the shed.

Something in his serious tone made Carrie look up at him. "I believe that you will, dear brother. You really will."

CHAPTER 16

After a week of bright, sunny days, Mrs. Daud declared it was time for the dreaded spring cleaning. All the women were put to work on the task and also some of the men who could be spared: Corky, the Thompson boys after school, and several other men.

Rugs were taken out and hung on the line to be whacked with the rug beaters, mattresses were turned, curtains taken down, washed, starched, and stretched, furniture was polished, floors waxed and windows cleaned. The window-cleaning job was a joint effort, with the men washing from the outside, some standing on ladders to reach the second story, and the women cleaning them from the inside. Then the storm windows had to be cleaned, polished, and put in place.

After three days the house was shiny and spotless and the women were worn out completely. But Mrs. Daud, who pitched right in there herself, was satisfied and happy and "if she's happy, then everyone's happy," remarked Hilde.

That happiness was short lived, though. The wind and dust started blowing again and with the newly harrowed fields, the topsoil was light and dry and blew around easily. On top of all that, rain added itself to the dirt in the air and it was almost like a mud storm before it was over. Mrs. Daud was beside herself when she saw what the windows looked like.

A few days later, she pulled herself together and commissioned the men to do the windows all over again. At least the insides didn't have to be gone over. Just a dusting of the windowsills was all that was required.

Mr. Daud told his wife that if she had waited until the crops were planted and had started to come up, then the topsoil wouldn't have blown around so much. Mrs. Daud was in a little bit of a huff for awhile after being told that. I guess she knew that he was probably right, thought Carrie.

Finally the ground was ready for the seeding so the drills were put into action. There were many of them, too, of course. They were 12 feet wide and it took four horses to pull them. The wagons filled with the cleaned seed were driven out to the field and the bags were emptied into the drill boxes. These boxes had to be filled at each end of the field. This planting process took about three weeks, so it was about the middle of May when it was completed.

Now it was time for some fun, Peter and Amund told the girls one evening. They heard of a big dance that was going to take place over in Horace on Saturday night.

"I think the five of us should go," said Peter. It would be he and Amund, Emory, Pauline and Carrie.

The girls thought this would be great fun, too, so they began to make plans. Carrie was hoping to wear her new lightweight dress that she had made back home but it was still too cool for it, she decided.

"I guess I'll just wear my new skirt and long sleeved white shirtwaist. How about you, Pauline?"

"Well, I did some sewing, too, this winter so I have a new dress that I think will be suitable."

The evening of the dance was fairly warm and balmy. "A beautiful, spring evening," Peter declared, as the five friends drove off in the biggest of the Daud buggies.

"Too bad we couldn't take the Cadillac!" exclaimed Amund. They all laughed at this.

"Only two of us could have gone then," Peter reminded him.

"Yah, Pauline and I!" stated Emory. This brought another big laugh from the group. The men spent the rest of the trip discussing automobiles and what was going to be the future for these vehicles.

"I don't think they'll ever replace the horse," stated Emory.

"Oh, don't be so sure of that," countered Peter.

"I've always said that they would be the thing of the future," said Amund with conviction.

About a half-hour later, they reached town and Peter let them off in front of the Thue store where the dance was being held on the second floor of the building. They waited for Peter to come back before they ascended the long stairway together.

"I wonder what group is playing tonight," remarked Peter. "They sound pretty good, don't they?"

The large room was crowded with people of all ages. The orchestra was playing a polka and many couples were giving it their best effort.

Emory whisked Pauline onto the floor when he saw an opening. The other three stood and watched for awhile and then went looking for a place to sit. They found only two vacant chairs so Carrie sat on one and they saved the other for Pauline.

"Oh, that was fun, but I'm out of practice!" exclaimed Pauline, breathing hard after the exertion of the lively dance.

They had been sitting there for only a little while before Carrie saw Fred Shutz coming toward her. Her heart lurched a bit and she felt color coming to her cheeks.

"Miss Amundson, I'm glad you're here tonight. I must have a dance with you!" he said enthusiastically.

She rose and said, "Why, I would like that very much!"

The orchestra was now playing a slow fox trot so the two were able to converse as they danced.

"Do you remember we danced together at Davenport last fall?" he asked Carrie.

"Oh, yes, I remember. I remember, too, that you were a good dancer."

"No better than yourself," he stated.

"Who are you here with?" he asked. He had recognized her brother but didn't know Peter or Emory.

"Oh, my brother and his friend Peter and my friend Pauline and her friend, or I should say fiancé, Emory. How about you?" she asked, almost shyly.

"Oh, just some young fellows from Davenport."

Awhile later, Carrie and Pauline were standing near the punch table talking to someone that Pauline knew. Carrie heard a familiar voice behind her and she whirled around to find Alphie Kastet standing there, sneering at her.

"Well, if it isn't my little Bonanza Belle!" he said, sarcastically.

Carrie's one hand flew to her mouth and the other clutched Pauline's arm. Carrie couldn't find her voice.

"So, Mrs. Daud let her little girls out for the evening, eh?"

Pauline grabbed Carrie and guided her away from the man. They couldn't see Amund or Emory so they went to the far end of the room and found two empty chairs.

"Oh, I can't believe he's around here again!" groaned Carrie.

"That cad!' Pauline said, vehemently. "I'd like to have slapped his face!"

"He better not come and ask me to dance! I wish the fellows would come back."

The music started up again and soon they spotted Amund and Emory walking toward them.

Amund took one look at his sister and asked, "What's wrong, Carrie? You look like you've seen a ghost."

"Well, in a way, I guess I have. Alphie is back!"

"He's here? At the dance?"

"Yes. He came up behind me over by the punch table and made some nasty remarks."

"Oh, I'd like to punch him in the nose!" said Amund hotly.

"Why don't you guys see to it that Carrie dances every dance," suggested Pauline.

"Good idea! Let's go waltz!" Amund led his sister out on the dance floor. Emory and Pauline followed.

"Where did you three go during intermission?" asked Carrie, when she had calmed down some.

"We went outside for awhile and then a fight got started behind the building so we were watching that for awhile."

"Who was fighting?"

"Oh, just some guys who had a little too much to drink. When you mix liquor and hot tempers together you get trouble."

"Didn't Peter come back in with you?" asked Carrie.

"Oh, he was talking to some fellows from Davenport. Your Mr. Shutz was one of them."

"He's not my Mr. Shutz," Carrie laughed.

The music stopped for a few minutes and Emory came up to Carrie and asked if he could have the next dance. When Peter came back in, Pauline told him what had happened and he, too, kept Carrie on the dance floor until the last song was played.

On the way home, they all discussed the happenings, including the surprise appearance of one Mr. Kastet.

"I thought I'd never see him again!" Carrie lamented.

"He must have gotten a job around here again for the summer," Peter proclaimed. "Let's hope he never has the nerve to come near Davenport."

The month of June brought more men to help on the farm and also the beginning of a long, hot spell. Carrie's birthday, June 3, fell on a Saturday so the young people decided to go into Davenport for an outdoor concert. Carrie was pleased that it was warm enough for her to wear her new summer dress.

Peter had suggested bringing a blanket to spread on the ground so they all five crowded together and settled down to listen to the fine music. It was the community band that was performing. The stores were open so people were walking in and out, shopping, listening to the music and in general, having a pleasant Saturday evening.

Carrie was hoping that she would see Fred Shutz and it wasn't long before her wish was realized. He had spotted her and was making his way toward the group on the blanket.

"Hello there, all of you!" he nodded to each of them. He came and plopped himself down on the grass by Carrie. "So you came to take in our first outdoor concert of the season, did you?"

"We had to think of something to do to celebrate Carrie's birthday," announced Peter.

"Oh, is it your birthday today?" he asked Carrie.

"Yes, and the fellows felt sorry for me. I had to work so hard all day that they thought I needed some entertainment tonight," she laughed.

"Well, after the concert, can I treat you to some ice cream over at Teigen's?" asked Fred.

"That sounds like a good idea for all of us," commented Amund.

Later that evening, the group crowded into a booth at the ice cream parlor. The guys got into a lively discussion about automobiles again. The girls just rolled their eyes.

"So when do you think Mr. Daud will drive his new rig to town then?" asked Fred.

"I'm surprised he hasn't already," remarked Emory.

"I wonder who will be the first one in Davenport to get one?" pondered Peter.

"Well, someone said that Mr. Broten--he's the hotel owner-- may be thinking about getting one," said Fred.

When they all finished their ice cream, they got up to make room for more customers coming in.

As they were walking towards their buggy, Fred asked Carrie if he could come calling on her out at the farm some Sunday afternoon.

She answered that that would be all right.

"How about tomorrow then?" he asked anxiously.

"Well, I guess you could do that."

"Good night then, everyone," Fred said. "I'm going to stop in the depot here. My father is working tonight. I hope you didn't mind sharing the evening with me."

"Anytime, old fellow," said Amund, giving him a friendly slap on the back.

When everyone was squeezed into the buggy, Peter made a remark about Carrie having a new beau now. She just laughed and told Peter that it was about time that he found himself a lady friend. She and Pauline spent some time naming different possibilities for him. He had an excuse for rejecting all of them.

"I think Peter's married to his work and his horses!" commented Emory.

"There's plenty of time! Plenty of time!" he told them. "Anyway, why aren't you picking on Amund here? He's such a handsome fellow, he wouldn't have any trouble finding a girl."

"I think the Monson girl had her eye on him at the dance at Horace, but Amund was too blind to see!" said Pauline.

The good-natured bantering continued the rest of the way home. Everyone was tired and very ready to turn in.

The next afternoon Carrie was in the parlor waiting for Fred to come. Pauline and Emory had gone off on a buggy ride and Amund and Peter were going to just rest, they said, and maybe get a baseball game going later on. There hadn't been much baseball played around there since the big fight the year before.

Carrie heard a buggy come into the yard but resisted the urge to look out the window. Hilde got up and looked and announced, "That must be your young man. He's stopping right out front."

He came up on the porch and knocked on the screen door. Hilde went to the door and invited him in. Carrie greeted him and introduced the two and then led him out onto the porch. They sat down on the settee.

"I'll bring you both some lemonade," Hilde called to them from the door. "Mr. Shutz must be hot and thirsty after his long ride on such a warm day."

"Oh, I should have thought of that," remarked Carrie. "I guess I just wasn't thinking."

"That's OK." He removed his hat and loosened his tie a bit. "Do you mind if I remove my coat?"

"Go right ahead. It's really too hot for a coat today, isn't it?"

"You're looking mighty... nice... this afternoon," Fred stammered.

"Why, thank you," she said, a little flustered.

"I wanted to tell you last night how pretty you looked in that dress but I didn't want to say it in front of everyone else."

Just then, Hilde came to the door with two glasses of lemonade.

"Here you go!" she announced.

Fred jumped up and opened the door and took the two glasses from her. "Oh, these feel nice and cold!" He handed one to Carrie.

When the two had finished their drinks, Fred asked Carrie if she would like to go out for a buggy ride.

"Well...I...don't... think so," she answered slowly. She was thinking about another buggy ride a year ago that ended badly. "Why don't I show you around the farm?" she suggested.

"Oh, I'd like that!" he said, jumping up. "I've driven by here several times, but never been on the place before."

An hour later, after they had explored almost every building on the farm, they could see that a baseball game had started so they sauntered over to watch for awhile.

"Do you like to play baseball?" asked Carrie.

"Oh, yes, I like it all right. I play on a Davenport team sometimes."

Later, Carrie invited Fred to stay for supper and the young people all ate out on the porch. Hilde had made potato salad and sandwiches. The group of friends had a jolly time. Peter and Amund were in high spirits because their team had won the game.

"I'm glad you didn't have any fights today, like last year," commented Pauline.

"It seems that the fellows all get along better this year. The main trouble makers didn't come back this season."

After Fred had left to go back to Davenport and the other fellows left for the bunkhouse, Pauline told Carrie some news.

"I could hardly wait for us to be alone. I wanted to tell you that Emory and I set our wedding date for the last part of October!"

"Oh, that's wonderful! Where are you going to be married?"

"We decided we'd get married here in Davenport before we go on over to Wisconsin where we'll be living. And Carrie," she went on excitedly, "I want you to be my maid of honor."

"Oh, I'd love to be!" said Carrie, just as excited.

The girls went to the kitchen in search of Hilde to share the news with her.

A couple mornings later, Mrs. Daud entered the kitchen and asked if her help was needed for anything. Then she said to Pauline, "I hear that you and Emory are getting married in October. We'd like to suggest that you get married here, in this house."

"Oh, well, I...we...will have to talk about that. Thank you very much for offering."

After Pauline and Emory had talked it over, they told Mrs. Daud that they would be very happy to have their wedding here at the house. The rest of the summer, the women could talk of little else and were busy making many plans for the event. Eunice Daud's wedding had taken place in this house so Mrs. Daud knew just what to do to make it a splendid affair.

"Is that all women can talk about is weddings?" joked Peter one evening as the group was sitting on the porch.

"Yah, how much planning can it take anyway?" Amund joined in.

"Have you bought your new suit yet, Emory?" Peter asked, mocking the girls.

"Oh, you guys, you just leave us alone, why don't you!" Carrie said sternly.

The weather was very favorable during August and September and the harvest went well. Some of the workers left then and some stayed to help with the fall plowing.

The last Saturday in October was the long-awaited day for Pauline and Emory. This, too, turned out to be a nice, fall day. The ceremony took place in the front parlor. Eunice and her family came from Casselton and she played the piano. The bride and her maid of honor came down the open stairway and Mr. Daud escorted Pauline down the "aisle". Reverend Lium had consented to come out and perform the ceremony.

The bride wore a white, cotton batiste ankle-length gown with a long veil and carried a bouquet of flowers from Mrs. Thompson's garden. The gown had been purchased in Casselton on one of the shopping trips with Mrs. Daud. In fact, Mrs. Daud insisted on paying for the gown, as she knew that Pauline could not afford anything very expensive. Pauline had protested at first but Mrs. Daud insisted on it. She suggested that Pauline just pay for the veil and white shoes.

"I only had one daughter to buy a wedding dress for so I want to buy yours," she had said to Pauline.

Carrie wore the dress that she had worn at her sister, Sylvia's wedding. She had written to her mother and asked her to mail it to her.

After the ceremony, Hilde and Cora, with the help of Stella, served a very fine supper. They ate in the Daud's private dining room. Seated around the table with the bride and groom were the Dauds, the minister, Amund, who was the best man, Eunice and her husband, and Fred. Carrie and Fred had been keeping company all summer long and he had become a good friend of Emory's, also.

After the supper, Carrie was upstairs helping Pauline change and get ready for the wedding trip.

"Do you feel really bad about your family not being here for your wedding?" asked Carrie.

"My family couldn't really afford to come. There are so many of them! We plan to go there for Christmas," replied Pauline, adjusting her traveling hat in the mirror. "I'm anxious for them to meet Emory."

Downstairs, the bride and groom were finally ready to leave. They would be driven to Davenport to catch the train to Fargo, where they would spend the night. There were many tears from the women as they said goodbye to the young couple. Mrs. Daud wrapped her motherly arms around the bride and told her that she would be greatly missed. Hilde could hardly talk; she was so choked up. Carrie followed Pauline to the door and the two embraced and promised to keep in touch.

Two days after the wedding, Carrie received a letter from Hannah Ulness. She had very sad news. Eight-year-old Louis had died on the 27th of October of rheumatic fever. Carrie couldn't believe it. She read and reread the short note several times.

"Oh, how terrible for the family," she shook her head back and forth. She hurried out to find Amund. He was in the blacksmith shop talking to Hogie.

"Mannie, come out here. I have something sad to tell you." She related the news to her brother.

"Just think," he said, "when we were there about a month ago, he was so healthy-looking, and remember how he and Carl were having so much fun playing on the bag swing."

"You just never know, do you?" Carrie said sorrowfully. "Hannah writes that he was taken to the hospital in Breckenridge and was there for a couple days but they couldn't do anything for him. Oh, how sad, how sad."

"On the bottom here she's added that the funeral will be Thursday at the Gol church. I think that we should try and go."

"Yah, I suppose we should," he agreed. "We really should."

CHAPTER 17

Carrie was asked to take Pauline's place and stay on through the winter. She decided she would try it, as Amund would be staying, too. It would be different not being at home during Christmas, she thought.

By December the population of the farm decreased dramatically. Cora had left in mid-November. She went to help out her two bachelor brothers and would not return until March. Stella left when the Dauds left for Chicago the first part of December. The only men left were Amund, Peter, Hogie, and three others, and of course, the Thompson family.

"Don't you ever go home, Hilde?" asked Carrie.

"I don't really have a home anymore. My brother who lived just west here now lives with my married sister in Minnesota. The rest are all gone. Out of eight children, there's only the three of us left. Only two ever married." She took a sip of her hot coffee. "Yah, this is my home now."

Carrie was elated to finally receive a letter from Pauline. She and Emory were busy getting settled in their little house on the family dairy farm. They lived near the small town of Hammond, Wisconsin.

"They took the train to St. Paul," Carrie told Amund later, "and then it wasn't too far east of there to their farm." She put the letter down and said, "I wonder if I'll ever see her again."

Carrie was beginning to think that maybe she had made a mistake, consenting to stay the winter to help Hilde. It was pretty quiet with so many people gone. Would she get awfully homesick, she wondered?

Amund drove Carrie and Hilde and Ida Thompson to Davenport one nice, sunny afternoon so the ladies could do their Christmas shopping. Carrie bought gifts for everyone back home and for Amund and Hilde and Ida. Carrie wrapped those for her family the next day and got them in the mail.

Hilde promised that they would have a nice Christmas, in spite of the distance from their families. She and Carrie baked cookies and Hilde taught her to make some German specialties. Peter and Amund went out and found a pine tree, down by the Maple River, and set it up in the front parlor. Hilde found the old, family decorations and so, on the Sunday before Christmas, they had a tree-trimming party.

Fred had come out that afternoon to see Carrie so he got in on the project. Hilde served coffee and hot chocolate and a big array of goodies. They sang some carols, without the aid of the piano, and then Fred said that he better be getting home. It was already dark and turning quite cold.

On Christmas Eve, Hilde and Carrie made a supper of spareribs and meatballs, with potatoes and mashed rutabagas and a rice pudding for dessert.

"They're probably having a similar meal back home tonight, don't you think, Mannie?" Carrie asked her brother when they were all seated around the kitchen table. The Thompson family was having their own Christmas Eve supper but Corky, Hogie and the three other men had joined them in the big house.

"I hope the weather will be nice tomorrow so that we can make it to church," Hilde commented.

"Oh, I think it will be nice, all right," Peter assured her. "We'll get you there!"

True to their word, Peter and Amund stopped in front of the house on Christmas morning and helped Hilde and Carrie into the buggy. The women had brought along hot bricks for their feet and Peter had two fur robes for them to cover their legs.

"Are you all nice and cozy back there then?" he asked, a few miles down the road.

"I'm glad it isn't much further," remarked Carrie, covering her nose with her mittened hand.

The church was packed and they had to split up in pairs to find a place to sit. The singing was uplifting and the service was very beautiful and meaningful for Carrie. She tried not to think of her family too much. This was her family for now. At least she had her brother here with her, and Peter was like family. And wasn't Hilde almost like family, too?

On the way home, Peter mentioned that he hadn't seen Fred at church.

"Oh, he and his father go to the German Lutheran Church in town," Carrie told him. "Immanuel Lutheran."

Ida had invited the whole bunch to come over to their house for Christmas dinner. This was a nice treat for Hilde, not to have to cook. Ida had prepared a big ham and had boiled potatoes and ham gravy, corn and apple pies for dessert. Everyone was in a festive mood and they had a jolly old time.

One of the three other workers to spend the winter there, named Ollie, kept them all laughing. He had many funny stories and jokes. The Thompson boys, Billy and Joey, were almost rolling on the floor, they were laughing so hard.

After dinner, all pitched in to help clear the table and do the dishes. Then the whole group moved over to the big house where the Christmas tree was and the two young boys passed out the gifts. Carrie had forgotten to buy gifts for them in town so she found two silver dollars and wrapped them up in a big package for each of them. They were immensely pleased when they finally got through all the paper and cord to find the precious coins.

Amund had bought a little something for Ollie and the other two men, Lars and Gunther, so they wouldn't feel left out. Everyone had several packages to open and they took their time, taking turns and exclaiming over each gift.

They sang some carols and sat around and talked, each telling of their childhood Christmases. Corky shed a few tears, telling of a Christmas when his wife and two little girls were still alive.

Hilde told of one year when her family was so poor that they were lucky to have heat in the house, much less something to eat. Then, she told them, a knock was heard at their door and her father opened it to find their neighbors all had gotten together and brought them a meal, all cooked, and a few little gifts for each of them.

Lars went back to the bunkhouse to stoke up the fire in the stove and he brought back his fiddle. He didn't know any carols but he could play several other songs so the group ended their Christmas Day celebration singing, "She'll be Comin' 'Round the Mountain" and "Polly Wolly Doodle!"

Later that night, Carrie wrote a letter to her family, thanking them for the gifts that had come for her and Amund. She assured them that she and her brother were doing just fine but that they missed them all. She fell asleep dreaming about Christmases past.

Carrie thought that January would really go by slowly, but she and Hilde kept busy. They both had purchased material before Christmas and each began cutting out dress patterns. In the evenings, after supper, some of the men would stick around and play cards. Carrie and Hilde played dominoes every night and they kept a running tally of how many games each had won.

Amund volunteered to stay nights in the big house so that he could keep the furnace going. Carrie felt better about having him there. The other men stayed in the bunkhouse but they had curtained off a small area so it wouldn't be so much to heat.

The weather in January and February was quite nice so it was possible to make it to church in Davenport almost every Sunday. Fred was able to come out to see Carrie at least once every week, usually on Sunday afternoons.

"I think this is getting serious," Peter would tease her.

Carrie would just glare at him and he'd laugh. Was she getting serious, she wondered? How did one know? She wished that Pauline were here to help her sort out her feelings. Thinking of her friend made her remember that it was her turn to write so she took out pencil and paper and she soon had three pages filled up.

One evening in February, Peter told the group around the supper table that he had heard from Mr. Daud that day.

"When are they coming back to the farm?" asked Corky.

"About the second week of March, he said," replied Peter.

"I wonder what new thing he'll bring back this time!" said Hogie. "Last year it was that Cadillac."

"Remember last fall," Amund began, "when Mr. Daud made that trip over to Dickey County? To that big, bonanza farm down there? I think it's by the town of Fullerton. Well, anyway, that farm has all steam-powered machinery now. Just think of that! They don't use horses to pull anything anymore!"

"Some of the big farms up north here are trying that out, too," Peter added.

"Do you think Mr. Daud will go that route?" asked Carrie. "He'd have to buy all new machinery, wouldn't he?"

"Well, I don't know what he decided. I suppose he's been looking into it in Chicago now," Amund declared.

"Maybe he'll be bringing home boxcars full of new stuff," remarked Hogie, shaking his head.

"What would you do with all the horses we have here?" asked Hilde, looking pointedly at Peter.

"I don't know," said Peter, a worried look on his face. "I wouldn't like to see it happen."

Amund, who had been silently thinking the last few minutes, chimed in. "Well, maybe that's progress. I think that someday we won't be using horses for anything anymore. Look at the automobile. Someday we'll all be driving them and the horse and buggy will be a thing of the past."

"Do you really think so, Mannie?" Carrie asked him.

"Oh, I don't agree with you there, Amund," said Corky. "You'll never replace the horse. Those automobiles are just a fad."

Amund said no more but Carrie could tell by the determined set of his jaw that he believed very firmly in what he had just said.

To change the subject, Carrie asked Hilde if she thought Mrs. Daud had hired someone to replace Pauline.

"Oh, I'm sure that she has been advertising for someone. We'll find out when she gets back."

The first week of March, Peter, Amund and Lars left for Bemidji to bring the horses back. The next week, the Dauds returned from Chicago. Mrs. Daud told Hilde that a new girl would be coming the first week in April. New men were arriving almost every day.

"With this warm, dry spring, we'll be in the fields real soon," commented Peter one day. He had just returned from Davenport where he had picked up three men and the new girl from the depot.

The girl's name was Emmy, short for Emmaline, and she was from west of Bismarck. Carrie offered to show her around after getting her settled in their room. It had been nice having the room all to herself during the winter. Cora and Stella were back so there were no extra rooms.

Mr. Daud had not brought any new vehicles or gadgets back with him this time. Peter asked him about the steam-powered machines but Mr. Daud said that he was biding his time about them. Peter was relieved, as he would hate to have to get rid of his horses.

The men had been seeding for nearly a week when it turned cold and began to rain. The next day, April 15, a terrible blizzard engulfed the southeast corner of the state. Ice and wind damaged many trees and the roads were impassable for many days. The leaves that had popped out extra early on the trees and shrubs were now frozen black.

"I've never seen anything like this before, in April!" exclaimed Carrie.

"Oh, I've seen it happen a couple of times," said Hilde.

Luckily the storm had not produced a huge amount of snow so about a week later, things were warming up and drying out again. Seeding was finished the first part of May.

One fine June Sunday afternoon Fred came out, as usual, and took Carrie for a ride. They drove over to the Sheyenne River and took out a blanket and spread it on the grassy banks. They were sitting there, throwing stones into the water when Fred cleared his throat and turned to Carrie. "I...ah...have something I...ah...want to ask you, Carrie," he faltered. "I was wondering if you would do me the ...ah...honor of becoming...my... wife?"

Carrie was thrown off guard completely as she had not suspected that this was coming. She didn't know what to say. She had to stall for time. "I...ah...don't know what to say, Fred. This is so sudden."

"Well, I guess it maybe is, but I know how I feel about you...I love you...and I hope that you feel the same about me."

"I'll have to think about this and give you an answer later."

"That's all right. I'm sorry if I sprang this on you."

When he had returned Carrie to the farm later and had supper with her, he said that he hoped that she would have an answer for him soon. "There's a concert in town on Saturday night. I'll look for you there. If you don't come, I'll drive out on Sunday afternoon."

Carrie tossed and turned in bed that night. What should she answer? If only Pauline were here to give her some advice. If I really loved him and wanted to marry him, wouldn't I know the answer right away? What had Pauline said about Emory--- "I miss him when he's not here and I want to spend the rest of my life with him."

She wanted to confide in Hilde but what advice could she give the young girl? Emmy would be no help, either. She was too young. Carrie fell asleep many nights with a prayer on her lips for help in deciding the matter.

Carrie asked Amund and Peter if they were planning to go to the concert Saturday night. They said they would see.

On Friday night, Amund came and visited with Carrie and told her that he and Peter would be going to Davenport the next night. She knew that she should have her answer ready. Or should she wait until Sunday? It's not fair to keep him waiting so long, she thought.

All Saturday she was extremely nervous. She still didn't have a clear answer ready so she decided that she would not go along with the fellows to town. She told Amund that she was too tired. She knew Fred would be very disappointed not to see her with her brother.

The next morning at breakfast, Amund told her that Fred looked stricken when he realized that Carrie wasn't with them. "He said that he'd be out this afternoon, as usual."

Carrie had reached her decision sometime during the night. When she heard Fred's buggy drive up and stop in front of the house, she went to the door and, when she saw him bound up the steps expectantly, she knew that she would tell him right away. No reason to let him wait and suffer anymore. She came out the door and the look on his face was of a small child, waiting to open a present that he'd been expecting.

"Fred, I'm going to tell you my answer right away!" she exclaimed. "It's yes!"

He was so relieved and happy that he picked her up and whirled her around the porch. He let out a "ya-hoo!" that could be heard around the whole yard. He didn't care if anyone was watching or not, he took her in his arms and they kissed their first long, lingering kiss. The few kisses heretofore had been quick pecks.

Hilde was sitting in the parlor and she came to the door to see what was the matter. Carrie spotted her and said, "Hilde, you're the first to hear the news. We're going to get married!"

"Glory be!" said the older woman. "I figured this would happen sooner or later."

The young couple went in search of Amund. He was found in his workshop. They related their news to him and he seemed happy about it.

"Put 'er there, old fellow," he said, shaking Fred's hand.

Next they stopped by the Thompson's and Ida was just coming out the back door. She was delighted for them, too. They went and sat down on the bench by the garden. Fred took her hand and asked, "When do you think we should get married?"

"Well, let's take one thing at a time," she laughed.

"Let's not wait too long," he implored.

Over the next few weeks they decided that they would have the wedding the end of October, like Pauline and Emory did. After some consideration, they decided that they, too, would have the ceremony on the farm in the Dauds' parlor.

Hilde and Cora were so excited and so was Mrs. Daud. The planning went on morning and night. They discussed the menu, the guest list and what everyone should wear.

"Carrie, I want to take you on a shopping trip to Casselton, just like I took Pauline, and you can find yourself a dress and everything," announced Mrs. Daud.

Carrie wrote to her family and asked if anyone would be able to come for the event. Her mother wrote back and said that she didn't think that they could make the trip but she was hoping that Carrie and her new husband would come there on their honeymoon.

Carrie tried to think whom to have for her maid of honor. If only Pauline was still here, she lamented. I wonder if Rosina could come, she wondered. She wrote to her but heard back that Rosina would be in school and couldn't get away. Sylvia wrote, congratulating Carrie and wishing her well. She announced that she was going to have a baby in November. She also said that Olaf and Mattie were expecting again, in December.

Carrie would have to have the wedding without any of her family, except Amund. Who would be her attendant? Who was she closest to here? One night, a thought struck her. She sat upright in bed. "Hilde!" she said aloud. She would ask Hilde. She could hardly get to sleep in her excitement.

"What?!" laughed Hilde, incredulous. "Me? A maid of honor?" She laughed until the tears began to roll.

"Are you done laughing now, Hilde?" said Carrie, seriously. "I wasn't joking."

Hilde wiped her eyes and looked at the girl who was sitting across the kitchen table from her. She sobered and said, "You aren't kidding, are you?" Now the tears began to roll again. "You mean you want me, Hilde Miller, an ugly old woman to be in your wedding?"

Carrie went to her and put her arms around her. "You aren't ugly and you aren't old and yes, I want you to be in my wedding. One's maid of honor is supposed to be someone very close to the bride. You have been so good and kind to me here. When I was homesick, you cheered me up. When that nasty business with Alphie happened, you were there for me to lean on. Please say yes, Hilde."

"Well, if you really want me to and you think that it would be proper, I guess I can't say no now, can I?"

"You mean you will do it then? Wonderful!"

"Oh, what would I wear?" Hilde looked horrified.

"We'll find something. Maybe Mrs. Daud will have some good ideas."

Carrie jumped up and went through the dining hall and toward the study to see if Mrs. Daud was around. She ran into Stella.

"Is Mrs. Daud around?"

"She's upstairs."

"When you see her next, tell her to come into the kitchen, please. Hilde and I want to talk with her."

Two weeks later, Carrie and Mrs. Daud were being driven to Davenport where they would catch the morning train to Casselton. This would be a two-day shopping trip. Carrie was so excited and Mrs. Daud seemed to be, also. They reached Casselton before noon and Eunice was there to meet them. They went right to her house where they freshened up and then they walked the two blocks up to the main street. Mrs. Daud treated them to lunch at the very elegant Occidental Hotel. Carrie had never been in a place so grand.

"Oh, this is so much fun!" she exclaimed over and over.

After lunch, they went to the department store and looked at wedding dresses. Carrie found one that she immediately fell in love with.

"Don't you want to look at some more?" asked Eunice.

"No, this is the one."

Mrs. Daud insisted on paying for her dress, as she had Pauline's and there was no talking her out of it. Carrie found a veil and a pair of soft, white leather shoes. By this time, it was late afternoon and they were all exhausted. They returned to Eunice's and rested before supper was served. Eunice had a maid who cooked and cleaned and helped with the children.

"Tomorrow we'll go shopping again to find some material for Hilde's dress," announced Mrs. Daud. "I wish we could have talked her into coming with us."

"She can be pretty stubborn, can't she?" laughed Eunice.

"She says that's the German in her!" remarked Carrie.

"She sure is honored and excited about being asked to be in your wedding, Carrie," said Mrs. Daud. "That was a very nice and thoughtful thing for you to do."

The two women returned home late the next evening, tired but happy because they had purchased everything they had set out to buy. Hilde was pleased with the material they found for her. It was a pretty, dark green fabric. Hilde had a pattern that would make up nicely out of the soft, supple material. They had even bought fancy gold buttons and a gold belt buckle for her. She cut out the pattern the next evening but than she said she would have to put it away until after harvest was over. Carrie would help her with it later.

The summer was warm and dry so harvesting started earlier than usual. Carrie had never worked so hard as she did that summer. Emmy could not quite hold up her end so Carrie had to do more that she should. If only Pauline were still here, Carrie thought for the hundredth time!

Emmy didn't like to go out to the field with meals for the workers. Especially after the men played a prank on the women. One day, after bringing the lunch wagon home and carrying the warming trunk into the house, Carrie lifted the lid and screamed. There was a dead rabbit inside! Cora said, "Oh, iiish!" Hilde said, "Uf da, nay da!" Emmy about fainted dead away! Mrs. Daud thought that a good retaliation for the men would be no lunch that afternoon. She was a tough cookie, thought Carrie.

Corky was enlisted to carry the carcass outside and he buried it in the garden someplace. Cora poured hot water from the teakettle into the trunk and added a little baking soda and let it sit awhile.

Hilde, having seen a trick of this sort a time or two, felt sorry for the men, thinking that they would be mighty hungry by mid-afternoon so she relented and made a lunch for them anyway. Carrie had to go out with Corky and the wagon. She told Corky that it would be fitting if they served the men rabbit stew that evening for supper! He got a good laugh out of that one.

In spite of some rain in September, the threshing was all finished by the third week. Some of the men started leaving so the workload for the women lightened somewhat. Plowing started and Emmy announced that she was leaving the end of October. Who would help Hilde when I leave, too? wondered Carrie.

In the evenings, Hilde and Carrie would try and sew a little on Hilde's dress. Carrie looked over her guest list and they also finalized the menu. She wrote to the Ulness family and asked if they could come for the ceremony. Lena wrote back and reminded Carrie that she was expecting another baby in October so they wouldn't be able to make it.

A week later, Carrie received a short note from Hannah Ulness telling her that her mother had just had her baby, another girl, born on the 14th. They all wished Carrie and Fred much happiness and hoped to see them soon.

The day of the wedding turned out to be bright and sunny. No rain in sight. A good sign, thought Carrie. The women hurried through breakfast and started getting the parlor set up for the ceremony. Eunice and her family would be coming about noon. Emmy, who had done some singing for church functions, would sing a couple of songs. She and Eunice could practice before any of the guests showed up.

Pastor Lium came from Davenport and Fred and his father rode out with him. Amund would be Fred's best man. The rest of the guests included Peter, Cora, Stella, the Thompson family, Lars, Ollie, Corky and Hogie.

Hilde was not allowed to fuss with the food once breakfast was over. She was to just relax and get herself ready. Her dress had turned out well and she looked very nice in it. She was nervous and kept looking in the mirror and fussing with her hair.

Fred was nervous, too, but tried not to show it. He looked nice in his new, navy blue suit, it was reported to Carrie, who was dressing upstairs. She wasn't nervous at all. She was actually enjoying all the fussing and stewing. At 2 o'clock she was ready to descend the stairway and meet Amund. He would walk her up the aisle and then take his place next to Fred.

After the short sermon by Rev. Lium and a song by Emmy, which really was quite good, the couple repeated their vows. Thus Miss Carrie Amundson and Mr. Fred Shutz were united in marriage on the 25th day of October,

1910.

After the wedding supper and the opening of some gifts, the couple prepared for their trip. Carrie changed into a traveling suit and they lingered over the goodbyes. This was going to be hard, Carrie knew. Hilde was weeping openly and Mrs. Daud even had trouble controlling herself.

"I'll come out and see you often," Carrie promised. "We'll be just a few miles away, you know."

Corky loaded their luggage and Mr. Shutz accompanied them out to the buggy. He grasped each of their hands tightly and, unable to say anything, he let go and waved them on.

"We'll see you in a few days, Pa," Fred told his father.

Corky drove them to Davenport to catch the train to Fargo. He, too, had trouble saying goodbye to the newlyweds. Carrie, noticing a few tears glistening in his eyes, stepped forward to give him a long embrace. He had become so dear to her.

With excitement very evident, the young couple boarded the train for Fargo and a whole future ahead of them.

CHAPTER 18

Carrie and Fred had decided to delay their honeymoon trip until Christmas at which time they would go out to see Carrie's family. So after a couple days in Fargo, they were glad to go back to Davenport and get settled into their little home. Fred's father had helped them buy a small house that had been recently vacated. It was their intention to have him move in with them but he said he wouldn't do that right away. He thought that the newlyweds should have some time alone. Anyway, he said, he didn't mind staying on in the living quarters above the barber shop where he and Fred had lived ever since they came to town five years earlier.

Whenever Carrie would ask Fred about his mother, all he would say is that she died when he was about 12 years old. Then he would always change the subject so she learned never to bring it up. They had moved to Davenport from a small town in South Dakota.

Fred and his father had done some painting in the house and had taken out the old kitchen flooring and replaced it with some nice, new floor covering.

"Oh, that looks so pretty!" Carrie exclaimed when she first saw it. The parlor needed something new on that floor, too, but that would have to wait. The house had only one story with a kitchen, parlor and two small bedrooms.

"This will do us just fine to start with," Carrie assured Fred. She was so excited to have a home of her own to fix up. They needed furniture but they would take their time. A new kitchen stove was an immediate necessity, however, so the first day that they were back, Fred went over to the hardware store and negotiated with Mr. Fredrikson and by late afternoon, a shiny black wood-burning stove was moved from the store to their home. Their house was only a block off Main Street so the stove was loaded up on a trolley cart and pulled over by a couple of men.

Fred and Carrie had done some furniture shopping in Fargo while they were there and had bought a bedroom set with money they had received from Carrie's parents. It would be delivered in a few days. Meanwhile, they were making do with the old fallen-down bed that had been left in the house.

Fred had to return to work the day after they came back. He worked two places. Part time at the newspaper office and then he would go and work at Myhra's implement store.

Amund came over on Sunday after church with the wedding gifts that Carrie and Fred had left at the farm.

"It's fun seeing them again!" exclaimed Carrie. They had opened them in such haste the day of the wedding. Amund had given them a beautiful mirror, and they had received a pretty bowl and a vase and some bed linens. They had also received some money so they had bought a set of dishes at the store in town. Carrie made dinner for Amund, and Fred's father also came over.

"We'll have to decide which church we should go to," Fred mentioned after the meal. "If Carrie goes with me to my church, she won't understand a word of the German, and if I go with her, I don't understand Norwegian," he laughed. He shrugged his shoulders. That day, they had each gone their separate ways but Carrie didn't like doing that either.

The next afternoon, a delivery wagon stopped out front of their house. When Carrie looked out, she could see that it was from the furniture store in Casselton. "What in the world are they stopping here for?" she said aloud.

They came to the door and said they had a delivery for Mr. and Mrs. Fred Shutz.

"Well, what is it and who is it from?" she inquired, puzzled.

He looked at his invoice slip. "It says here it was purchased by a Mrs. Daud. We'll bring it in and set it up for you, ma'am."

Carrie couldn't believe her eyes when they brought in a beautiful china cupboard with curved glass doors! She wept with delight. The men didn't know quite how to deal with her reaction.

"Oh, it's just so beautiful!" she exclaimed over and over.

She had to sign for it and then they left her to admire the new piece of furniture. She could hardly wait until Fred came home for supper.

He was surprised and delighted, too. "I can't believe they gave us such a wonderful, generous gift."

"I thought the wedding dress was enough, but you know Mrs. Daud! She loves to buy things for people. I must send her a note right away and thank them and tell her how much we appreciate it."

That evening, Carrie placed their new bowl and vase into the cupboard and admired it. "My, don't they look nice in there! It may take awhile to get it filled up with pretty things. Oh, won't this be fun!" She clapped her hands for joy.

Fred pulled his wife to him. "It's good to see you so happy." He gave her a quick kiss and said, "I have to get back to the newspaper office. Deadline tomorrow, you know."

They left on the 22nd of December by train for Spring Grove. Carrie was so anxious to see her family again after almost a year and also, to show off her new husband. They arrived late the next day and Mr. Amundson was there to meet them. Marty came along, too. Sylvia and Rudy came up to the station just as they were about to leave.

"Oh, I'm so glad we didn't miss you," said Sylvia, out of breath. "Your train must have come in early."

Carrie hugged her older sister and stood back to have a look at her. "Motherhood becomes you, Sylvia!"

She had had her baby exactly one month ago. It was a boy and they named him Johan. "But we call him Johnny," Rudy piped in proudly.

They had left the baby with a neighbor because they thought it was too cold to bring him to the station. They only stayed long enough to say hello and meet Fred and then they were off again. "We'll see you again soon," Sylvia called back to them. They would be coming out to the farm for Christmas.

When they reached the Amundson farm, every light in the house was on. Carrie's mother shed tears of happiness when she saw her daughter. "Oh, Carrie, it's so good to have you home again," she said, wiping at her eyes. "And this must be Fred." She gave him a hug, too, and told them both to take their wraps off and warm up by the stove. She had coffee ready so they all sat around the kitchen table and talked until almost midnight.

The next day, Carrie wanted to make a quick trip over to Olaf and Mattie's. They had had their new baby just about two weeks ago. It also was a boy and they named him Burton. They were thrilled to see Carrie and Fred and happy to show off their new baby. Two-year-old Manda was trying hard to keep the attention on herself and away from the baby.

"I think we're going to have a little trouble with her!" exclaimed Mattie.

Next, Carrie wanted to make a trip into town and finish her Christmas shopping. They stopped back at the farm and picked up Rosina, who wanted to go along as well. Carrie enjoyed seeing so many people she knew and introduced her husband to all of them. She bought some items for the two new babies and then some grocery items that her mother needed.

They stopped in to see Sylvia for a short while, too. Carrie got to hold little Johnny and it was fun to see Sylvia and Rudy's home. It was small, like Fred and Carrie's, but it looked very cozy and comfortable. They had a decorated tree in the parlor with several gifts under it.

"We'll see you this evening then," Carrie called, as they left the house.

They made it home just in time for dinner. It would be a simple meal as Carrie's mother was busy getting a meal ready for the evening. The whole family would be coming for Christmas Eve.

"I told everyone to come about 6 o'clock. The men will start the milking a little earlier than usual."

"It will be so much fun having everyone together tonight," remarked Carrie. "I just wish Amund could be here, too."

"Yah, we sure missed both of you last Christmas," said Carrie's mother.

That night, with the whole family gathered around the big table, Mr. Amundson prayed at length and thanked God for these loved ones, for the new babies, the newlyweds, and for good health. The food and fellowship were savored slowly, with no one being in a hurry for it to end. Carrie had so much to tell everyone and so much to get caught up with.

"Well, I think Santa Claus may be on his way," Mr. Amundson said, looking at Manda who was starting to look a little droopy. She started banging her spoon on the highchair tray and wanted to get down and see "Sanda Cause" as she called him.

The gifts were piled up high around the tree and Mrs. Amundson just shook her head. "So many presents! Why, when I was a girl, we were lucky to get one thing and maybe it was just a piece of fruit."

"Things have changed now, mother," Sylvia reminded her.

"Yah, they sure have, haven't they, Knute?" she said, looking at her husband. The two looked at each other in understanding.

"It's changed for the better, I'll have to say that!" Mr. Amundson said.

After the gift opening and then some coffee and cookies, the guests decided it was time to head for home. They bundled up the babies and braced themselves for the cold ride home. Luckily, neither family had very far to go.

The next morning, the families met again at church for Christmas Day worship services. As soon as Carrie sat down, she noticed Ted Gunderson sitting with his mother. Sylvia had told her the day before that Ted never did get married to the woman named Birdie. She had broken off the engagement. He was now working at the bank in town. Carrie wondered secretly if he ever thought about her and what might have been.

After the service was over, Carrie clutched Fred's arm tightly as they were ushered down the aisle. Let him see how happy I am, she thought to herself.

On the train ride back home, Carrie leaned back and closed her eyes.

"What's my wife smiling about?" asked Fred, gently.

"Oh, just how much fun it was to be able to go home for the holidays. I hope that we can do this again some other year."

"I hope so, too. I enjoyed meeting your family. They really are all wonderful. Just like you and Amund. You come from a good family."

He turned silent after this. Carrie wondered if he was thinking about his family, when he was younger. It would do no good for her to ask him about it. He had an older sister, married and living in South Dakota. He rarely talked about her, either.

After they had been home a couple months, Carrie started to become restless. She didn't have enough to do to keep herself occupied. She was used to being so busy, working on the big farm. She found out that Mrs. Carr at the cafe was looking for some help during the noon hour. She mentioned this to Fred and it was decided that she would go and inquire about the job.

She did this the very next morning and found herself employed immediately! She would work for two hours, from 11 o'clock to 1 o'clock, waiting tables and helping with the dishes. She found that she liked doing this. It gave her a chance to get out every day and talk to people.

Carrie was asked to join the Ladies Aid of the Norwegian church and, also, a sewing club in town. This kept her busy and she made many new friends. She would be expected to take her turn in hosting a meeting once in awhile. She hoped that they would be able to get some more furniture before then. They needed a sofa and some chairs and also a new kitchen table. For a table, they were presently using a broken down one that had been found in the shed in the back yard. Covered with a cloth it didn't look so bad, but it was quite wobbly.

Carrie would stop in at Fredrikson's store once or twice a week and look around. She looked longingly through the large glass showcase containing a wonderful display of cut glass and silverware. Someday, she thought, I'll have some of those pretty things.

She also looked at the furniture there. Mr. Fredrikson kindly let her look in the store's catalog and there she found a sofa that she would really like to have. She had Fred come in and look at the picture, too. He liked it but didn't know if they could afford it.

Carrie still had some money in savings from when she worked at the farm. If she drew it all out, they would have enough to pay for the sofa and maybe a chair to match. Should she take all her money out, though, she wondered? Finally, they worked out a deal with Mr. Fredrikson where they would pay for half, with her taking some of her savings, and then they could pay the rest a little bit monthly.

Fred was reluctant to do this, but he realized that they really did need to have something for people to sit on in their home.

"We'll just get along with our rickety old table for a while longer," Carrie told him.

After working at the cafe only about a month, Carrie realized that she was going to have a baby! She felt a little sick right away in the mornings for a week or two, but then was all right after that so she kept working at the cafe.

Mrs. Carr let Fred eat his noon meal there for free so he'd be in every day, checking on Carrie to see if she was feeling all right and not working too hard. He was very excited about the baby and so was his father.

All spring the town of Davenport was busy planning for a big celebration which would be held the last of May. They were going to call it Farmer's

Day, honoring the farmers of the community and surrounding areas. Many committees were formed and almost everyone in town was on one of them. Fred was to help with organizing the auto race and Carrie would be helping with food.

The day of the celebration began with fair skies. The morning was devoted to a band concert and several speeches by members of the faculty of the North Dakota State Agricultural College. There were speeches on farming, education and domestic economy.

At noon a free lunch was served to the huge crowd. Some of the people chose to eat in the two cafes in town, so Carrie was very busy helping Mrs. Carr.

The afternoon activities consisted of races, contests, a tug-of-war and a baseball game. People were encouraged to bring in everything from homemade jam to horses to be judged and awarded prizes.

Carrie noticed that Mr. Daud had won a prize, a very nice bridle, for the best appearing stallion. She talked with both he and Mrs. Daud afterwards. Hilde and Cora were along, too, and she got to visit with them some.

There was an auto race, which Fred had helped plan, but there were only two entrants! Mr. Plath won with his auto and Miss Cullen, the other driver, drove an Overland. The course was four miles and Mr. Plath took it in 7 minutes 30 seconds. He won a nice auto robe for his effort.

Carrie didn't stay for the baseball game. Fred wasn't playing in it but he wanted to watch it. She went home to rest. She found out later that Davenport was victorious over the Dakota Business College team from Fargo, 6 to 3.

"It was a very successful day today, don't you think?" she said to Fred as they were relaxing in the parlor on their new sofa that evening.

"I'll say! It's estimated that we had about 1500 people in town for it! Imagine that!"

"I thought that the best part of the whole day was when the Norwegians won the tug-of-war!" teased Carrie.

"Oh, we'll get back at them next time," countered Fred. "You know" he went on, "they're thinking of doing this again next year. Making it an annual event."

"I talked with the Dauds for a few minutes. Did you see that nice bridle that he won for entering his horse?"

"Yah, he sure needed to win that, didn't he?" laughed Fred.

"I had a nice visit with Hilde and Cora, too. I wish we could see them more often. I told them our exciting news!" Carrie said. "They were very thrilled."

"Now that the weather is nice, we can take a drive out there some Sunday."

"I'd like to go and see the Ulness family sometime soon, too. Maybe Amund can come along with us."

"Carrie," Fred called as he came in the door one evening. "Shall we go out to the barn dance at the Plath farm tonight, then?"

"Oh, I forgot about that," answered Carrie, hurrying to set the table for supper.

"Yah, they're going to get that new barn off to a good start!"

"I don't know what I'd wear," Carrie lamented. "My clothes aren't fitting too good anymore."

"Well, that's all right," Fred stated. "I'm almost too tired to go anyway."

As they were eating, Fred said conversationally, "Speaking of barns, I heard today that the Jensven barn was struck by lightening on Saturday. I guess it only took just a few pails of water to put out the fire, though."

Fred helped himself to a big helping of potatoes. "I heard a good one about Dr. Haugen today. He was driving his new auto and was trying to pass a team of horses with only one hand on the wheel and he had an accident! They were teasing him that he was busy looking at the pretty girls in the buggy!"

"You always have so many interesting things to tell me every night. I don't hear near as much at the cafe," complained Carrie.

"Well, it pays to work at the newspaper office. 'We get the news first,' is our motto," he laughed.

"Another auto agent came to town today," Fred went on. "He's with the Ford Company. He'll be offering free rides for several days."

"I'll bet that was the man who came into the cafe at noon today," Carrie remarked. "He mentioned he was staying at the Hotel. Very nicely dressed."

"Last week when the Olds auto agent was in town, he sold a couple of his

Oldsmobiles, I heard."

"Really?" inquired Carrie. "I wonder who bought them."

That summer passed quickly. Fred and Carrie made a couple trips out to the Daud farm and they went down to Ulness once, in July. They had to rent a horse and buggy from the livery every time they wanted to go out of town. It would be nice to have our own vehicle, maybe even an automobile, thought Carrie, but she didn't express this out loud. They couldn't afford it. There were too many things they needed.

Sometimes, on Sunday's, Amund would come and drive them in one of the Daud buggies. One fine Sunday, he actually came in the Cadillac and drove them about town.

How's the implement business now, Fred?" asked Amund, as they were cruising down Main Street. "Is Mr. Myhra selling anything these days?"

"Well, it's not going too bad," answered Fred, who worked part time for the machinery dealer. "The crops are looking good so many farmers have been in. Sold a couple Deere & Weber plows the other day."

"Yah, the crops are looking good. The grasshoppers were pretty hard on some fields, though."

As Amund dropped his sister and her husband off at their home, he asked, "Are you folks going to the outdoor concert and dance on Saturday night?"

"We might," answered Carrie. "We'll see when the time comes."

The concert, put on by the 1st Regiment State Band of Lisbon, was well attended. Fred and Carrie walked uptown and found a place to sit on some benches that had been set up. Amund and Peter came and sat by them.

"Those boys can really play, can't they?" exclaimed Amund.

"Yah, I've heard them once before and they are really good," remarked Peter. "They will be playing for the dance, too, up in the hall. Are you staying?" he inquired of Fred and Carrie.

"We'll probably go up there for awhile. Maybe dance a few slow ones," said Fred, taking Carrie's hand. "My wife tires pretty easily these days," he teased.

Carrie quit at the cafe in August as she was getting too big and uncomfortable. When she thought about threshing time at the farm, she sure didn't miss that one bit! She spent her time sewing and knitting for the baby.

One day in early September, Fred came home with an amusing story. "I heard that the new school teacher, who just came, stayed only one day and then got so homesick that she quit! Before school even started! The board had to hustle and find a replacement in a hurry!"

"Oh, my! I hope they didn't hire just any old teacher.

"I guess it can be a real headache, being on some of these boards."

In early November, the next-door neighbor lady came over with a cradle and a baby scale that they could use. Carrie invited her to stay for a cup of coffee.

"My, you certainly are big!" exclaimed Mrs. Gust. "It shouldn't be too long now."

Dr. Bernard, the new doctor in town, was called to the Shutz home on the night of November 9. He assisted in the delivery of their fine, baby boy, and he remarked that it was one of the easiest deliveries he had seen in awhile.

"Your wife and baby are doing just fine," he told Fred as he went out the door. "Oh, I see it has started to snow. I hate to see snow so early. It makes for a long winter."

It was a long winter and a very cold one at that but Fred and Carrie were content to stay in their cozy home and admire their new little son. They named him Frederick, after his father, but called him Freddie. Mr. Shutz came over often to see his grandson and he often stayed for supper. He was always good to bring over some meat and other groceries.

A few days before Christmas, Fred came in the back door, stomping snow off his boots. "Boy, is it cold out! The thermometer over at the implement store said 40 degrees below zero this morning when I went to work!" He stood by the stove to warm up.

"It may be too cold to take little Freddie out to church on Christmas Day," remarked Carrie. "I sure would hate to miss church that day. It wouldn't seem like Christmas."

On Christmas Eve, Mr. Shutz came over for supper. Amund and Peter had to decline the invitation because it was still too dangerously cold to be out. After the meal, which consisted of both German and Norwegian dishes, the three adults opened their gifts to each other and admired their little tree which Mr. Shutz insisted on getting for them. Carrie had made some decorations, calling on her memory of her school days to come up with ideas. Mr. Shutz had stopped by Fredrikson's and bought a box of glass tree ornaments, also. They were beautiful, Carrie had told him, and she would treasure them forever.

From mid-December to mid-January the temperature hovered around 30 below the whole time. Neither Fred nor Carrie had ever experienced such a cold spell but some of the old-timers recalled other similar years way back when.

In March, the community felt the need for a social doings after such a beastly winter, so a masquerade ball was planned. Mr. Shutz offered to stay with little Freddie so that Fred and Carrie could "go out and have some fun" he told them.

For those people not having their own masks, some could be rented at the Fredrikson's store prior to the affair. The day before the ball, Fred had brought home masks for them to wear. Carrie found some old clothes of theirs to add to the costumes. The ball was held up in the community hall. Malchow's orchestra provided music and there was a large crowd of both dancers and spectators. Prizes were awarded in different categories, including one for the most comical costumes for both men and women. A late supper was served at the hotel after the dance.

It was very late when Fred and Carrie slipped quietly in the back door of their home. Mr. Shutz was asleep on the sofa but, when awakened, he reported that little Freddie had been very good for his grandpa.

One Sunday afternoon when Amund was visiting, he and Fred were talking about the recent sinking of the big ship, the Titanic.

"I thought that it was supposed to be unsinkable," remarked Fred.

"Yah, I thought so, too. Did you hear that Mr. Chaffee was on board and went down with the ship?"

"We were reading about that just this past week. That sure was too bad. It said he was only 46 years old."

"The Dauds knew him and his wife. They had been out to the farm a time or two," Amund informed them.

"I guess they were returning from a trip to Europe. Mrs. Chaffee was saved, though."

"He's going to be greatly missed," Amund went on. "The Dauds are feeling pretty bad about it."

In June, there were two big events scheduled. One was the now annual Farmer's Day on the 12th, which, it was reported, drew a crowd of about 3000 people!

"That's almost twice as many as last year!" exclaimed Carrie.

"Well, they might have stretched the truth a little bit," laughed Fred, "but I know there were more people this year. The ladies prepared 2000 free lunches ahead of time but had to hustle up about 1000 more," he added, "so, you can see right there how many more there were."

Carrie had not been able to take in everything but enjoyed a visit from Hilde and Cora, who stopped by the house for a short time.

"Who won some of the biggest prizes this year?" Carrie asked Fred that evening.

"Well, Oscar Liudahl won the walking plow."

"Oh, my, that's a nice prize, isn't it?"

"And Mabel Evingson from Kindred won the pair of ladies shoes. Her family owns a department store down there so she really didn't need to win those!" Fred joked.

Fred and Carrie went up to the dance in the evening but it was not very well attended.

"I guess everyone was too tired to stay after all the activities during the day," remarked Carrie.

The next big event in Davenport, just five days after Farmer's Day, was a big tent show. It was a play, "The Girl From Over There," and it was billed as a 'big western comedy drama'. It included a cast of 30 and they traveled in their own Pullman train cars, which stopped in town for a couple days. The big tent had to be set up and it boasted 1800 seats!

Fred and Carrie attended this event, as did most of the town, but the tent was not entirely filled.

"I think it was too close to the big Farmers' Day celebration," suggested Carrie.

The evening was very enjoyable, however, and Carrie was glad they had gone.

"This town is sure full of events and things to do, isn't it?" remarked Amund after the show.

And so it was, that Fred and Carrie lived their life happily in this small mid-western town in the early 1900's. Could life get any better than this? Carrie wondered many times.

CHAPTER 19

When little Freddie was two years old, Carrie started thinking that it was time to have another baby. Just before Christmas, she realized that she was, indeed, in the family way again and she and Fred were so thrilled. This exciting news helped make Christmas that year a little merrier. She was so hoping that they could have gone back to visit her parents and spend the holidays with them. They really couldn't afford to make the trip and Fred didn't feel that he could be off work that long.

I am missing so much back home, Carrie thought. Sylvia and Olaf's new babies were growing up and she hadn't seen them since they were born. And her parents had never even seen Freddie! "Oh, families shouldn't live so far apart," she often lamented. Amund reminded her that if she hadn't come out here, she would never have met Fred and wouldn't have little Freddie. I'll just have to be content here with my new little family, she told herself.

Amund was going home for Christmas this year, he had told them one Sunday. Mr. Daud was sending Amund to Chicago to an auto mechanics school which would last for two weeks in January so he would stop by Spring Grove for about a week and then go on to the big city.

How exciting! thought Carrie. Amund hadn't seen his family for several years. His fascination with the automobile was not lost on Mr. Daud. He could see the potential in the young man and he also realized, like Amund did, that the automobile was something that was not going to go away. Mr. Daud had brought back another new car this past spring. It was a 1913 Chevrolet, a four-passenger with a top. He let Amund take it into town some Sunday afternoons.

The general interest in the auto cars was growing so great locally that an automobile club was organized in Davenport. Sunday afternoons one could see quite a number of them in town, "showing off," as Fred would say.

"If you had one, you'd be showing it off, too," laughed Amund.

Farmer's Day was again a huge success in Davenport and baseball was truly becoming the all-American pastime. Fred played regularly on the Davenport team now so this occupied many of their Sunday afternoons. Even the Daud farm had their own team, now. They called themselves Daud's Dodgers.

The town of Davenport was still progressing and growing. A new, second bank was just organized, called the Farmer's & Merchants Bank. Due to several good crop years, the farmers were doing fairly well which contributed to the overall economy of the area. Fred was doing well at the implement dealership. He was a good salesman, "good with people," his boss, Mr. Myhra said.

In fact, on the last day of August, Fred hurried home at noon and was going to tell Carrie that he had just sold another plow, when she met him at the door with news of her own.

"It's time, Fred. Can you go and fetch the doctor?" She laid herself down carefully on the sofa and made it through another sharp labor pain.

"Remember how fast the last one came!" she reminded him. This put fear into him and he didn't even stop to have his dinner. He hurried out the back door and ran the block to Main Street. The doctor's wife said that her husband was on a call but should be home soon. She'd send him over. Amund looked so terrified that she offered to come over herself after she'd left a note for her husband.

After the doctor's wife came, Fred hustled little Freddie over to the neighbor's house and returned to find that the doctor had just stopped by. Carrie was now in the bedroom and after the doctor had examined her, he said that it wouldn't be long now. He rolled up his sleeves and prepared to bring another baby into the world.

Little Joseph Helmut was born by mid-afternoon and he was healthy and good-sized, the doctor told the nervous father, who had been pacing outside the bedroom door. Carrie felt good after such a short labor again and the new parents beamed down at their new son.

"We'll call him Joey, for short," Carrie said. "Now we have two fine sons."

Carrie received a letter from Lena Ulness shortly after Joey was born. The Ulness family wanted to congratulate the Shutzes on their new little boy.

Lena said that their daughter, Gilla, had just wed, a few weeks earlier, a young man of the community named Hank Hertsgaard. They were living on a farm not too far away. Their other older daughter, Hannah, had been married in January to a neighboring farmer, Louis Perhus.

"Their family is certainly growing up, isn't it?" Carrie remarked to Fred that evening. "Imagine, having your children getting married already!"

The following summer, in June, Carrie decided it was time for her to take the boys over to Spring Grove to meet their grandparents. Fred couldn't get away but she felt that she could make the trip by herself. Freddie was almost four now and a big help to his mother and the baby, she felt, would be a good traveler.

Her family was overjoyed to have her come and bring the little boys. With Sylvia's little boy and Olaf's two children, the Amundson household was brimming with the sounds and laughter of little ones. Carrie stayed for two weeks. Sylvia reported that she was expecting again in a few months and Mattie confessed that she thought that she might be in the family way again, too.

Rosina had finished high school and was planning to go to a teacher's college in the fall. Marty had shot up to be almost six feet tall and was loving every minute of farming.

As much as Carrie hated to leave everyone, she was anxious to get back to her own home and her husband. Joey was a little fretful on the trip home but perhaps he was teething, she thought. When they reached Davenport, Mr. Shutz gave Carrie and the children a ride home in a buggy and Fred came home soon after. The little family was reunited and very happy to be together again. Mr. Shutz came over for supper that evening and Amund dropped by later.

"I think Amund will be coming to Davenport more often than usual, now," Mr. Shutz told Fred and Carrie. "He's found some feminine attraction here, haven't you, my boy?" he joked.

"That's what I've been hearing, too," added Fred.

"Oh, really," Carrie spoke up. "Tell us about it."

"Yah, well, I've been seeing a bit of Edith Moehler. She lives on the east edge of town. I think you all know her."

"Oh, course we know her!" exclaimed Carrie "We know everybody in town. And she is a very nice young lady, Mannie. You couldn't do better."

"I'm actually on my way to see her right now, so I better be going."

"So, you didn't come to town just to see us, then, did you?" teased Carrie.

"Well, it was a two-fold mission," he confessed.

About a month later, Joey's fussiness returned and Carrie could no longer blame it on teething. She called for the doctor, finally, and he was grim after examining the small child.

He didn't reveal what was in the back of his mind, but he just told them that he would send around some medicine from the drug store. "If his breathing becomes labored, call me at once."

The medicine arrived and Carrie gave Joey some of the foul smelling stuff and laid him down for a nap. Two hours later, when he hadn't awakened yet, she became alarmed when she stood over his crib, watching him. She sent Freddie to fetch his father.

"Tell him to come home right away. Tell him to stop by and get the doctor, too," she added.

Joey's forehead was burning hot and he looked a little blue around the mouth. She picked him up and gently shook him to wake him up. His little eyes opened slightly and then they rolled back. This terrified Carrie.

"Joey, Joey! Wake up! Wake up!" She continued to shake him, not quite so gently this time.

He awoke fully and began crying but gasped, seeming unable to get his breath. Just then Fred came running in, Freddie close at his heels.

"The doctor's coming! How is he? Is he worse?" Fred took one look at Joey and he felt fear as he'd never felt it before. "Here, let me take him," he said.

Carrie ran to the kitchen to get a cool, wet rag and she brought it and applied it to his forehead. He was so listless that he just lay in his father's arms. As Carrie looked down at him, she, too, felt that this was very serious and her stomach lurched with an unnamed fear.

The doctor came in the door without knocking and hurried to the child. He checked him over briefly. "It's as I feared. I think he has diphtheria."

"Diphtheria!" the parents chorused together. They each had a question that they dared not ask. Would their child live?

"How... bad.. is it?" Fred finally stammered.

"I'm afraid it's not good," Dr. Bernard told them. "We'll do what we can and the rest is in God's hands." He turned to Carrie and said, "You maybe should send Freddie over to a neighbor's for a few days. We don't want him getting it, too. It's highly contagious."

What he didn't tell them is that a little girl had just died the night before. A girl from over by Litchville that he had attended. He ran his hand through his hair in a helpless gesture and sighed.

"Here, Doctor, have a chair," said Fred. "You look so tired."

Carrie hurried up and gathered a few of Freddie's things together and ran with him next door to Mrs. Gust. When she returned, Joey was asleep again, but fitfully. He whimpered and gasped repeatedly and then he would awaken. The three adults sat around his crib, feeling very helpless.

The doctor stood and said he should go home for awhile and he would check back in about an hour. Mr. Shutz came over after his shift was done. Word had spread around town by now. A couple neighbors came to the door, but, not wanting to come in, expressed their concern and said that they would be praying for the little boy.

The next day, his condition had worsened and the doctor stayed there and helped keep vigil. Fred and Carrie took turns snatching a little sleep now and then. The doctor could be seen shaking his head in despair when he thought the distraught parents weren't looking. How helpless he felt. This was an insidious disease that shouldn't happen to little children, he thought to himself.

The baby awakened and attempted a weak little gasp, and then another and then there was silence. A deafening silence. Carrie and Fred stood there, willing their child to breathe another breath. The minutes dragged on; Joey's little face was turning blue. He gasped again and then there was silence again. This time, as they watched, his face turned from blue to a deathly white. They waited. The doctor rose and felt for a pulse. He couldn't feel any. Carrie stood there in shock. Could this be happening to them? Won't he start crying and be his old self again soon? Fred started weeping and Carrie looked at him sharply.

"He's only sleeping," she told him. "He'll be better soon." She was in total denial.

The doctor put his arms around both of the parents and wept himself. "I'm sorry. I couldn't save him. He's gone."

And so, the obituary in the next week's *Davenport News,* which Fred had to help typeset, read as follows: 'We were all saddened to hear that Joey Shutz, 10-month-old son of Mr. and Mrs. Fred Shutz, passed away last Wednesday. Dr. Bernard said that it was diphtheria that took the life of the cherished little one. The Shutz family has the sympathy of the entire community.'

That same issue of the paper stated that there were three other cases of the dreaded disease which also ended in the deaths of young people from the area.

Fred and Carrie were devastated. Amund had to come and take care of certain things, like making the funeral arrangements and letting his parents know the sad news. The funeral was held in the German Lutheran Church with burial in the cemetery east of town. Carrie couldn't understand anything the minister said, as it was in German, but it didn't matter to her. No words could console her, anyway.

Fred and Carrie moved around as if in a fog for the next several days. Freddie would ask where the baby was. This would set Carrie to crying again. Amund came in as often as he could but was unable to get through to his sister. He was worried about her. He stopped and asked their pastor, Rev. Johnson now, to go and talk with her.

The Sunday after the funeral, a buggy pulled up in front of the Shutz house. It was Lena and Engebret Ulness. Amund had contacted them a few days earlier. Carrie was glad to see them and she and Lena embraced and went into the bedroom to talk together.

"I can honestly say that I know what you are going through, Carrie," Lena began, "and I can also tell you that only God can get you through this. If you will but ask, He will send his Holy Spirit to comfort you and guide you through these next dark weeks and months."

"Fred and I," Carrie sobbed, "we don't know how to comfort each other. He is blaming God for taking our little boy, and I say that it's not God's doing. I can't help him and he can't help me."

Lena pulled out a worn Bible from her handbag. She paged through it until she came to the Psalms.

"Carrie, here in Psalms 40, let me read to you: 'I waited patiently for the Lord; he inclined to me and heard my cry, He drew me up from the desolate pit, out of the miry bog and set my feet upon a rock making my steps secure. He put a new song in my mouth, a song of praise to our God.'"

Lena went on, "This pit it talks about, is where you are right now, Carrie, just like it says in Psalms 23, 'Yea, though I walk through the valley of the shadow of death.' God will come and comfort you."

Lena talked with Carrie for sometime. She told her of her recent loss when Louis died and she also told her of past sorrows. She had lost another son, Adolph, as a small baby and then she lost a baby girl about two years after that.

"How did you get over all that?" Carrie wanted to know.

"Well, you don't ever get over it, but God helps you get through it."

"What can I say to Fred, when he thinks that God has taken our baby because of some sin we've committed? He's inconsolable and I can't talk to him," Carrie wept again. "I don't know what to do."

"You must pray every waking moment for God's help and pray also for your husband, that God will open up his eyes."

After about an hour, the women emerged from the bedroom. Fred was sitting, with his head in his hands, and Engebret was pacing the floor.

Engebret expressed his deepest sympathy once more to Carrie and grasped her hand before heading out the door.

"I'll be praying for you," Lena told Carrie.

The house was silent. Freddie was over at a little friend's house. The only sound was the ticking of the clock. Carrie sat down and opened her Bible and found the passage that Lena had read to her. She read it over and over and then turned to Psalm 23.

Fred looked up and asked her what she was doing.

"I'm trying to find comfort in God's Word. Lena helped me so much. It was so good to talk to someone who understands. Here, let me read from Psalms 40."

"No!" Fred fairly shouted. He stood up and started pacing. "I don't want to hear what your God has to say. He took my son. He can't be a God of love."

Carrie stood up now, too. "God didn't 'take' our son, Fred. It just happened. He got sick and he couldn't be cured and so he died. We have to accept that. People get sick, people have accidents, things go wrong, but it isn't God's fault." She was fairly shouting, too, now.

Fred stomped out of the house and Carrie watched him go out to the little shed in the back yard. "I must pull myself together, even if he can't," Carrie declared out loud. "God, please help me to do that."

She left the house, too, and walked over to find Freddie. It was time for him to come home. "Help me get out of this pit, Lord, so I can be a mother to my dear little son who is left."

Carrie was able, with God's help, to overcome her grief somewhat and, an attempt at some kind of normalcy and routine was established in the household.

Fred, however, would not allow anyone to speak Joey's name but sometimes Freddie would ask about him and his father would go into a rage. The little boy became afraid of his father.

Mr. Shutz came over less frequently because he couldn't deal with his son's behavior. Carrie finally went and had a talk with him one day when Freddie was again playing with a friend.

She walked into the depot and found her father-in-law alone behind the counter.

"Mr. Shutz, I need to talk to you, please," Carrie said quietly.

He rose and came around into the waiting room and they both sat down on the bench.

"I don't understand Fred's behavior; he's so angry. It seems like it's more anger than grief. That doesn't seem....normal. I don't know what to do." She tried to stifle the sob in her throat but was unsuccessful. Mr. Shutz could see that she was very distraught.

He sighed and said, "I've noticed that his grief didn't seem...quite...right. I'm wondering if it has anything to do with his grief over his mother's death. Perhaps he's never told you about it."

"No, whenever I've ever brought up his mother, he changes the subject. He won't talk about her."

Well, his mother was ill and I had to go to work everyday at the depot so that summer, Fred was supposed to stick around the house while I was gone. One day, the day that she died, he left the house for awhile because she was sleeping, and he was gone, oh, I suppose about an hour, he said. When he came back in the house, he looked in on her and she....she was gone." Mr. Shutz paused for awhile and collected himself.

"She had evidently tried to get up or call out for someone because she was...she was half out of the bed. Fred never got over the guilt of not being there. So, in addition to blaming himself, he has also blamed God ever since. And now, with Joey's death...well, maybe he feels some sort of guilt there, too, but he's blaming God again."

Carrie looked hard at Fred's father and saw a tired, old man. "What can we do to help him?" Carrie asked.

"I don't know. I quit trying to talk to him about it years ago."

Someone came in the door, so Carrie stood and said, "I better go now. Thank you for telling me all this. It will help me to understand the situation better."

That evening, she decided that she would confront Fred. After Freddie was asleep, she came into the parlor where her husband was sitting, reading.

"I had a talk with your father today, and he told me about your mother's death," she came right to the point, "and how you blamed yourself for it."

Fred stared at his wife in disbelief that she would say this to him.

"And now you're blaming God for what happened and also for Joey's death."

He put his hands over his ears. He didn't want to hear this.

Carrie stopped and waited for him to say something. Anything. Finally he turned on her and there was something in his look that turned Carrie cold inside.

"I think God was punishing us for something that you did! Some past sin of yours!" He hissed and then just glared at her.

Carrie was struck dumb. She couldn't believe what he was saying. She felt a numbness start in her belly and move up to her chest. It was like something died inside of her at that moment. She sat down on a chair opposite her raving husband.

"You don't know what you're saying!" she finally got out. "You're talking like a crazy man! God isn't punishing us...me...for anything. That isn't His way." Carrie could take it no longer. She got up and fled to the privacy of their bedroom. Little Freddie came out his door and asked what was the matter.

"Why are you crying, Mommy?" He looked scared.

"I'm sorry if we woke you, Freddie. Here, let's go back to your bed now." She got him settled again and he soon fell asleep. She sat on the edge of the bed, looking down at him. "Oh, God, I thank you for this precious little boy. Please don't let anything ever happen to him."

For the next few weeks, the relationship between husband and wife was very strained. They wasted very few words on each other. Only when Freddie was present did they speak at all and then it was short and clipped. Freddie, who had always been a very good boy, was now acting up and he seemed nervous and melancholy at times. Carrie was very worried about him.

One afternoon, when he was napping and Fred was home for dinner, Carrie decided that this could go on no longer.

"We can't go on like we've been doing, Fred. We must talk and settle some things. Can't you see how this is affecting Freddie? It's bad enough that he lost his little brother but now I'm sure he feels like he's losing his mother and father, too. Your father is the only one who brings a smile to his face nowadays."

She waited for him to say something. He continued eating in silence for awhile. He got up and was heading for the door and Carrie hurried to block his way.

"Oh, no, you're not going until we settle this!"

He could tell that she was very angry indeed. He turned and sunk down on a chair and bowed his head and wept silently. She waited.

"I'm sorry," he finally said. "I shouldn't have said those things to you."

"And do you really still believe that it was something I'd done that caused Joey's death?" When he didn't answer, something snapped inside her. "Well, do you?" she screamed at him. "I have to know."

He looked up at her and answered in a low voice, "No, I guess it wasn't your fault."

"And do you still blame God for what happened to Joey, and to your mother?"

"Well, I don't know about that yet." He stood up then and said, "I have to get back to work now." With that he left the house and Carrie was drained. She left the dinner on the table and went and lay down on the sofa. She wept and prayed and slept a little.

When Fred came home that evening, she could tell that he was trying to make some kind of effort to be more civil. Freddie noticed it, too, and asked his daddy to play with him on the floor while Carrie cleaned up after their supper. Carrie heard laughter come from the parlor and it sounded good. No one had laughed in this house for, oh, so long.

Maybe things will work out now, she told herself as she prepared for bed later that evening.

CHAPTER 20

Things did not improve much in the Shutz household. Fred immersed himself in his work and everything else except in being a good father and husband.

"He's joined every organization in town and is never home in the evenings," she told Fred's father one night when he had come over for supper. Fred had hurried through his meal and run off. "It's as if he can't be idle even one minute, he has to be in constant activity so that he won't have time to sit and think."

Mr. Shutz just shook his head and looked very sad and disappointed in his grown son. "I don't know what to tell you."

"He doesn't want to think about Joey's death, or talk about why he's blaming God and me for everything that went wrong. I want him to speak with your pastor but he won't. He doesn't go to church anymore, as you know."

Carrie stood and started to get the dishes gathered up for washing. She poured hot water into two dishpans, which she set on the table. As she began to wash, Mr. Shutz grabbed the towel and prepared to wipe.

"He's just joined the fire department in town here now. That's where he went off to tonight. They have meetings once a month, I guess."

Carrie was silent for awhile and then went on. "When he doesn't have any meetings or baseball practice or something at work, then he goes up to the pool hall and plays cards with the other fellows. At least he doesn't gamble, but he could be home those nights with us."

Carrie started to cry, and she quickly wiped her hands on her apron and went and sat down at the table. She put her face in her hands and let the sobs come freely.

Mr. Shutz didn't know what to do so he just continued wiping and then took over the washing. Then he, too, sat down across from his daughter-in-law, whom he had to come to love dearly.

"I know anything I say to him won't do any good," he said. "I haven't been able to reach him since his mother died."

Amund stopped by later that evening and Carrie told him that she wanted to go down to see Engebret and Lena sometime soon. "I feel like I need to have a good talk with Lena again. She helps me so much."

"Well, the weather has warmed up nicely now; maybe we can go next Sunday afternoon," he volunteered.

Amund stopped by, as promised, the next Sunday afternoon for Carrie and Freddie. Fred declined the invitation to go with them. Next they stopped by the home of Edith Moehler, as Amund wanted her to go along, too.

It was a lovely May afternoon and Carrie's spirits lifted. Edith was a very agreeable companion and had a sharp wit. They talked and laughed on the way down to Ulness.

Engebret was in the yard, trimming some bushes when they arrived and he was very pleased to see them. He ushered them up unto the porch and told them to go right on in.

Lena gave Carrie a warm hug and Amund introduced his lady friend, Edith. A little boy toddled up to Lena and grabbed at her legs.

"Oh, my! Who is this?" asked Carrie.

"This is little Orville" Lena announced, stopping down to pick him up. "Didn't I write and tell you that Hannah and Louis had a baby last January?"

"So you are a grandma now then!" exclaimed Amund.

"Yah, and my own baby, Luella, is only six years old!" She laughed her tinkling laugh.

They sat down in the parlor and Hannah came in from the kitchen. She and the baby were visiting for the afternoon, she said. Gilla and Hank would be coming over later, too.

"This house gets pretty full of family sometimes!" Lena said, chuckling. "I probably didn't tell you, either, that Alfred got married last summer, too."

"I read that in the paper," said Carrie. "You are sure getting them married off, aren't you?"

"He married a very pretty girl named Alma Anderson, from town. They're going to have a baby later this summer."

"Oh, my, things have really changed since we came here the first time, haven't they?" Carrie remarked.

Later that afternoon, Carrie mentioned to Lena that she would like to have a talk with her alone sometime.

"Well, let's you and I take a little walk down by the river and we can talk alone then."

When they started out, Luella wanted to follow the two women, but Lena scolded her and sent her back to the house.

They walked along until they came to a log, which had fallen, forming a perfect bench for them to sit down on. "Now then, Carrie, what's on your mind?"

"I don't know what to do with Fred. He's so changed these days. Ever since....Joey's death." Tears welled in Carrie's eyes. "He's so distant to Freddie and me. He's still blaming God for what happened but I think it goes beyond that. He blames himself for his mother's death many years ago and I don't think he has ever forgiven himself. He involves himself in a frenzy of activity so he doesn't have to think about what's troubling him."

"I'm having similar trouble with Engebret right now, too. A few years back, he was diagnosed with epilepsy. He has fits now and then. He blames God for that and for the death of Louis, too." Here she had to wipe the tears that were forming in her eyes, too.

"Why do these men have to blame God for everything that goes wrong, anyway?" Carrie asked.

"I think they like to be in control of everything that happens to their family and when something like this comes along, they can't just accept it and go on. That's what I think, anyway," Lena stated.

"You may be right. I never thought of it that way. But how do we get them to see that what they're doing to their family is wrong?"

Lena shook her head. "I don't know. I pray for Engebret daily. He doesn't go to church very often anymore. We argue about this almost every Sunday morning." Here she sighed.

Carrie looked at her cousin's wife and saw a woman who had borne many sorrows and disappointments in her life.

"We'll continue to pray, that's all we can do, and keep on doing our best to cope," Lena went on. "We must pray for each other, too."

The two women talked for awhile longer and then they heard a buggy come in the yard.

"Oh, I bet that's Gilla and Hank. Now you can meet Gilla's husband."

They hurried off in the direction of the house.

On the way home, Carrie felt somewhat better. She would just make the best of everything. Little Freddie was still her greatest joy. She hugged the child to her and he was getting very sleepy, almost nodding off. She laid his head in her lap and rubbed his back gently.

The town of Davenport was getting ready for another Farmer's Day celebration but Carrie couldn't get her heart into it. Almost a year had gone by since Joey's passing. Fred was more distant than ever. Maybe as more time goes by, thought Carrie, he will come around. Mrs. Carr asked Carrie if she would help out in the cafe that day so she was there for several hours. Freddie had to go with his daddy.

On the Fourth of July, the three of them went with Amund and Edith down to Kindred for the parade and speeches. Amund had bought himself a Model T car a few weeks earlier.

"I knew it wouldn't be long before you had one yourself one of these days," Fred teased Amund. Fred was always in a jollier mood when Amund was around.

"Yah, well, they finally became affordable to someone like me," commented Amund. "After Mr. Ford figured out how to make these cars assembly-line fashion, he can sell them so much cheaper." Warming up to his subject, he continued. "Did you know that it used to take the workmen over 12 hours to assemble one car but now it takes only a little over an hour? Imagine that!"

"I think you've been reading too much again, Amund," joked Fred. They all laughed at this. They knew that Amund would rather talk about cars than most anything else.

The group had a fun time that day, almost like it used to be, thought Carrie. That evening they hadn't been home very long before they heard the fire bell ringing. Fred grabbed his hat and ran out the door.

"Daddy, don't go!" Freddie shouted after him. "I want Daddy to play with me."

Carrie soothed him and soon got him ready for bed. Then she went outside and stood on the sidewalk, trying to see where the fire might be. There were others looking, too, so she crossed to the other side of the street to see what they knew.

"They say it's someone's barn out west there," Mrs. Fredrikson said, pointing. They craned their necks to see if they could see smoke.

Later Carrie went in to check on her sleeping son. She tidied up the house and waited. She sat down to read a little and waited some more. It was now past midnight. What could be taking the men so long?

She stepped outside as a buggy was driving by. "Maybe they're coming home now," she said aloud. She sat on the front stoop and waited some more. She felt an eerie feeling, like something was wrong. She shrugged it off. Maybe she should just go in and go to bed, she told herself as she yawned again.

Just then she heard another buggy and it turned down her street and came and stopped in front of the house. They're dropping Fred off, she told herself. Two men got out slowly and deliberately but Fred was not one of them. Her heart started thudding in her chest.

They were surprised to see her outside. They stopped and removed their hats.

"I'm afraid we have some bad news, Mrs. Shutz," one of the men said. It was Mr. Myhra, Fred's employer. Carrie didn't know the other man.

Carrie swallowed hard and felt weak in the knees. "What is it? Do you want to come in?"

"Perhaps we better," Mr. Myhra replied. They followed her in and shut the door.

"Have a seat," she offered the two men.

They remained standing and so did she. "Ah, Fred had an accident trying to put out the fire out at the Muir farm." It was hard for him to go on. "He...ah...was struck in the head by a burning beam and he...ah...was ...killed." Here his voice cracked and he began sobbing.

Carrie couldn't believe what she was hearing. Had she gone to bed and this was all a bad dream? She couldn't seem to find her voice. And something heavy was pressing on her chest. She stumbled and the other man helped her to the sofa. Mr. Myhra sat down beside her and took her hand.

He was very distraught, too.

"I'll stay with her," Mr. Myhra said. "Why don't you go and fetch my wife to come over."

Just then, Fred's father burst in the back door. He had just heard the awful news, too. He came to Carrie and sat down on the other side of her. What am I going to say to comfort this young woman who has already had her heart broken, he thought to himself. He broke down and sobbed.

"We'll have to call her brother at the Daud farm," remarked Mr. Myhra.

Carrie was aware of very little of the next twenty-four hours. She vaguely remembered Amund being there and then Mrs. Daud and Hilde. Hilde sat and held her for long periods of time. Freddie was curled up on her lap for much of the next day. He looked bewildered by all the comings and goings.

When's my Daddy coming back?" he asked repeatedly. "Is he still at the fire?"

The funeral was held at the German church, but again, it didn't matter to Carrie. She heard none of it anyway. Fred's body was put into the black, horse-drawn hearse and brought out to the cemetery east of town. The family and mourners followed in buggies. His coffin was put down next to little Joey's.

Lena and Engebret Ulness were there and they stayed at the cemetery with Carrie and Amund for quite a length of time. Lena and Carrie walked a short distance from the rest of the group. They wept together and Lena tried to leave Carrie with some words of comfort.

"God will never leave you, Carrie, just remember that. Count on him for everything, each day. He will see you through this, too."

Two days after the funeral, Carrie's mother arrived by train from Spring Grove. She planned to stay about a week.

Amund came in every evening and he and his mother tried their best to console the grieving young woman. She told Carrie about the grandchildren back home but Carrie was only half listening.

Mrs. Amundson didn't know just how it was going to go with Carrie when she left.

"I'll be all right, Ma," Carrie assured her. "I still have my faith in our loving Father, even if I don't understand why this had to happen, too, but I know he loves me and will help me."

"Thank God for that!" Mrs. Amundson said.

When she left, it was indeed very quiet in the house. Mr. Shutz came over every evening for supper. Carrie insisted on this. It gave her something to do with her time.

One day, the pastor of the Norwegian church came over.

"I'm glad to see you, Rev. Johnson," she said as she invited him in and offered him a cup of coffee. He sat down at the kitchen table and Carrie sat across from him.

"I have something to ask you," she said. "Remember when I told you that after Joey died, Fred blamed God and he was still blaming God up to his last day. Do you think that perhaps, in his last moments, he asked God for forgiveness? The other fireman said that he was conscious for a short while after he was struck."

"That could very well be possible, my child" the pastor said gently. "We'll have to hope that he did that in his last minutes."

"It's very important to me that he did ask for forgiveness," Carrie said, starting to weep. "Oh, I'm surprised that I have any tears left," she apologized as she tried to wipe her eyes with her apron.

"That's all right," the pastor assured her. "It's the people who can't cry that I worry about."

Pastor Johnson read some scripture to Carrie and they prayed together and then he left. She felt better than she had in a long time. When Freddie came in from outside she suggested that they take a walk. She would pull him in his little wooden wagon.

"Oh, boy!" he cried. He smiled the first smile she had seen in many days.

The days dragged and were very lonely for Carrie and the child but she managed to get through them, taking each one at a time. One afternoon an automobile stopped in front of the little house. Carrie looked out the window to see Mrs. Daud and Hilde coming up the sidewalk. She hurried to the door to welcome her dear friends.

"Oh, it's so good to see you two!" she exclaimed, holding the screen door open. "Come in, come in."

After coffee was served and much small talk was exchanged, Mrs. Daud came to the point of their surprise visit. "Carrie, we want you and Freddie to come out to the farm and stay for awhile." Before Carrie could open her mouth in protest, Mrs. Daud continued. "You could help us in the kitchen again. We need you during the upcoming harvest."

"Oh, I don't think I should do that," she answered slowly.

"Just think about it," Hilde interjected. "Work is a good healer and it would be good for Freddie. He would have so much to do on the farm. Please say you'll come."

After about a week of thinking about it and talking it over with her brother and Mr. Shutz, it was decided that she and Freddie would go out to the farm for awhile. Amund moved her and a few of their things the very next Sunday.

"Just in time for the harvest!" he exclaimed. "The women could really use your help, too, I understand. The two girls they have now, that replaced you and Pauline, aren't exactly balls of fire!"

Carrie and Freddie were put in the guest bedroom in the Daud's private quarters. "Oh, I didn't expect anything this grand!" she exclaimed. "Are you sure this is all right that we stay in here?" she asked Stella over and over again.

Stella just laughed and told her to enjoy it as Mrs. Daud was enjoying playing the role of mother hen, as usual.

The very next day, Carrie got back in the swing of things. It was good to be real busy and it was nice to be around Hilde and Cora again. Amund was right about the two new girls. They didn't like to work very hard. They won't last here very long, she thought.

Freddie became Corky's little shadow, each adoring the other. He also liked riding along with Joey Thompson wherever he went. And, of course, he liked running over to his Uncle Amund's workshop. He never lacked for things to do.

"I think this farm life is very good for Freddie," Carrie remarked to Hilde one day.

"I think it's very good for you, too," the older woman answered.

Carrie went to bed each night totally exhausted, but that was good, she thought, because then I sleep so good all night and feel really rested the next morning.

Mrs. Daud asked Carrie if she would stay the winter with Hilde again. After much deliberation, she decided that she would like to. It would be too lonely back at the house in town with just the two of them, and so many memories that she wasn't ready to face yet.

Mr. Shutz told her one Sunday, when she and Freddie came to town with Amund, that he should probably move into the house for the winter to keep heat in it. Carrie agreed that this would be a good idea. Mr. Shutz would give up his tiny living quarters uptown.

Just before Christmas, Amund told Carrie of his plans to quit his job at the farm and move to Davenport and open up a garage. "I can fix people's automobiles and sell gas, oil and tires."

He seemed so excited about the idea that Carrie had to be happy for him. He would stay on the farm until March sometime. "I'll get the machinery all fixed up before I go," he told her.

"I bet Mr. Daud wasn't too happy to hear that you're leaving, Mannie," Carrie remarked.

"No, he wasn't at all, but he understands my ambition had to extend beyond this farm one day."

"So, where are you going to have your garage?"

"I'm going to put up a new building on Main Street. I've already talked with Mr. Nokleberg and he will have time to build it first thing in the spring."

"Where are you going to live then?" Carrie asked.

"I don't know yet. I'll start looking after Christmas, I thought."

Carrie was silent for awhile and then she said, "Why don't you move into my little house with Mr. Shutz for awhile, until you can get something else?"

Amund mulled this over for a time. "When are you planning to go back there?"

"Well, I thought I'd stay here until next fall. Then Freddie will be starting school so I'll move back into town again."

"Well, you may have a good idea there," he told her. "I'll give it some thought."

Christmas was very lonely again for Carrie but Hilde did her best to make it a happy time for all. The winter was cold and stormy, with lots of snow. There was a bad blizzard on February 4. It was good sleighing weather, though, and Freddie lived for each day that he could go out with Joey and Corky.

Corky and Hilde taught Freddie every card and board game that they knew. "That kid is sharp as a tack!" Corky would remark with pride. He spent many an evening in the big house, entertaining Freddie and teaching him all kinds of things. "You'll be too smart for first grade!" he teased the boy.

Amund moved to town the middle of March and work started on his new garage the end of the month. "It should be up and running in about a month or so, he announced.

"I suppose you could have made some living quarters above and moved in there," Carrie suggested to her brother.

"Well, you see...I....ah...don't think that would be a good place to bring a new wife."

"Mannie!" Carrie shouted. "Are you trying to tell me something?"

"Yah, I guess so, but I haven't actually asked her yet, so that's why I haven't said anything to you. I'm going to do it soon, when I get up the nerve!" he laughed. "Actually, I think she'll say yes so I don't know what I'm so nervous about."

"Well, you hurry and ask her and get a wedding planned, you hear?" Carrie scolded her brother.

CHAPTER 21

The war in Europe was heating up and it looked like the United States might get involved. Mr. Shutz and Amund talked about the situation overseas often. Mr. Shutz was very concerned about the role that his homeland, Germany, was taking. He did not agree with its politics and was very worried for both his old country and his new country.

On April 6, 1917, after listening to President Wilson exclaim, "The world must be made safe for democracy," Congress declared war on Germany. The US, aligning itself with the Allies, stepped up its defense program and Congress also adopted a selective-service act that required all men between 21 and 30 to register for the draft.

Carrie feared for Amund who had just turned 29. Hopefully he would not be called. Peter was a year older so his chances were even less likely.

Amund's marriage proposal to Edith was accepted but the wedding date had not yet been set. Things were up in the air with the war just starting and Amund opening his new business.

Several times that spring, Amund and Edith would pick up Carrie and Freddie out at the farm and they'd go visit the Ulness family. One time when they came in the yard, Amund spotted a shiny new automobile.

"I wonder if Engebret has finally bought himself a car!" he wondered aloud.

"Oh, I doubt that," remarked Carrie. "He was always so against them."

Lena welcomed them and told Amund that Engebret was over looking at the ruins of the mill which had burned a short time earlier. Amund said that he would take a walk over there and have a look himself. The women were ushered into the parlor.

"We read about the fire," remarked Carrie. "That was too bad.".

"Well, as you know, it had gone out of business about 7 years ago," Lena commented.

"What caused the fire?" asked Carrie. Thoughts of another fire a year ago still haunted her.

"We don't know but there seems to be something suspicious about the whole thing." said Lena. She didn't elaborate so Carrie didn't pry.

Nine-year-old Alice came up to Carrie and shyly asked her if she would like to come upstairs and see the "schoolroom." Carrie raised her eyebrows in question and looked at Lena.

Lena laughed and said, "Yah, Alice, take her upstairs." Then by way of explaining, she told Carrie that Engebret wanted the children to have a place to learn and play so they took one of the bedrooms and turned it into a combination playroom-schoolroom.

Carrie followed the young girl upstairs and was surprised when she went into the room. It was painted a bright blue and had a blackboard on one wall and there was a table with some pockets on the sides, evidently a game of some kind. There were bookshelves and books and two homemade school desks. There were other toys and games sitting around. Two big windows provided the room with plenty of natural light.

"This is very nice, Alice," Carrie told the girl. "Do you children spend lots of time up here?"

"Oh, yes, sometimes." Alice answered. "Papa thinks it's very important that we be learning all the time." She sighed here. "Sometimes I just like to play, though."

When Carrie was back downstairs again, she heard the men come up and sit on the porch. She repeatedly heard the voice and laughter of a man she didn't know.

"Who's out there with Amund and Engebret?" she was curious to know.

"Oh, that's a neighbor, George Johnson. That's his car out there."

"We were wondering if it was yours," remarked Carrie.

"Oh, goodness, no!" Lena laughed. "Engebret says he won't have one of those new-fangled things!"

They heard the hearty laughter again of the neighbor. Carrie thought it was so good to hear a good belly laugh again. It reminded her of her father and of happier times.

At coffee time, the men joined the women folk in the dining room and George Johnson was introduced to Carrie and Edith. He was a young man, about Amund's age, Carrie guessed, with a head of thick, wavy blond hair and a pleasant smile. He sat across the table from Carrie and seemed to pay her quite a bit of attention, Lena noticed.

Aha! Lena thought to herself. Those two would make a good pair. And so it happened that Lena Ulness, wife, mother, grandmother and midwife, now became matchmaker, also.

At every opportunity she contrived to get the two together. About a month after their initial meeting, she invited Carrie and Amund to come for Sunday dinner. She had also invited George and his widowed mother.

In the afternoon, the young men and boys got a baseball game going with some of the other neighbors. Lena encouraged Carrie to go and watch.

Later, after the game, as Lena was serving a cold drink and cookies to her guests, George asked Carrie if she would like to go out on the porch and eat.

"It's cooler out there," he said. Lena and George's mother exchanged sly smiles.

Later, as Carrie and Amund were leaving, George mentioned that he was going to come to Davenport for Farmer's Day. "Maybe I'll see you there," he said.

On the way home, Carrie was wondering how Freddie was getting along. He had stayed back on the farm as he and Corky had something planned.

"Oh, I'm sure they're doing just fine," Amund assured her. Amund felt that perhaps his sister was too over protective of her remaining child.

The war in Europe raged on and they heard of several young men who had been drafted. Amund's business was struggling some because of the war, but he and Edith had set a wedding date anyway, for late November.

Carrie saw George Johnson several times over the summer, sometimes at the Ulness home and twice in Davenport at various doings. One Sunday when George was visiting, the talk was all about the attempted theft of the bell from the Christiania Church, which was located several miles south and west of Davenport.

"I don't see how the thieves got the thing down. I understand that it weighed over 1300 pounds!" exclaimed Amund.

"Yah, and then I read where their trailer, which they were transporting it on, broke down south of Davenport!" added George. "Can you imagine their dismay?" he laughed.

"They just left it there, then, didn't they?" asked Carrie.

"Yah, it was found the next day. It was quite a job to get it back up in the belfry!"

"Why do you suppose anyone would want to take the bell?" asked Carrie.

"Well, with this war going on, metal is very expensive and maybe they thought they could get a handsome sum of money for it," reasoned Amund.

"Do you think they will ever catch the ones who did it?" asked George.

Carrie was planning to move back to town in early September in time for Freddie to start school. She wondered who would help at the farm during harvest and she also wondered where Amund would move, as he and Mr. Shutz were living in her little house. She would leave all this in God's hands, she thought. Something will work out.

As it happened, Mr. Shutz announced one Sunday afternoon that he was being transferred back to South Dakota to a depot there and that he would have to leave the end of July. This was rather a jolt to Carrie. She realized then just how much she had come to depend on the kindly, older man.

"Then Amund can stay here with you until he gets married," Mr. Shutz told her. God was already working things out, she thought.

Mrs. Daud told Carrie not to worry about staying and helping. They were just happy that she had stayed as long as she had. Stella and Mrs. Thompson would fill in for her. She and Freddie moved the last Sunday in August. They both felt a little lost for awhile as there just wasn't as much to do in town. But soon Freddie started school and was very excited about that. Corky's prediction about him being too smart for first grade came true so he had an easy time of it.

George sent Carrie a postcard in early October and asked her if she would accompany him to the dance that was to be held in Davenport the following week. She answered that she didn't think that would be proper yet, as she was still so recent a widow. He then wrote again and asked if he could come calling on Sunday. She answered that he would be welcome to do that.

Young Freddie seemed to like George very much and the feeling was mutual. George knew just what to do to entertain small boys.

"I sure like that George," Freddie told his mother after one of the Sunday afternoon visits. "He's so much fun."

Carrie, too, felt that she was thinking along the same lines. He was a nice man. So kind and very much fun indeed. He laughed easily and often and made others around him do the same. But he had a deeper side to him, too, Carrie noticed. He was very compassionate and he asked Carrie to tell him about her husband and little boy, Joey. One Sunday he even drove her out to the cemetery and she showed him their graves. He stood beside her with tears in his eyes. She was so moved by this that she touched his hand in gratitude and they walked silently back to the car.

"I can't imagine what it must have been like for you, to lose both a child and then your husband," he said kindly on their way back to town.

"It was the hardest thing in the world," she answered. "I had to rely on God every single day or I don't know how I would have gotten through it. Lena helped me so much, too."

"Yah, she surely has gone through some trying times, too, I understand."

When they returned to Carrie's house, Freddie was just coming up the walk with Amund. They had walked over to Edith's. The four of them had an early supper together and then George had to hurry back to his farm to do the evening milking.

"Those cows don't milk themselves, you know," he laughed.

Amund told Carrie that he thought he and Edith had found a house to live in after the wedding.

"You know that house on the north side just past the school? The one with the lilac bush you always admire so much? Well, the man who lives there wants to sell it and move in with his daughter west of town as he's getting up in years and can't care for it anymore."

"Well, that sounds wonderful, Mannie!" exclaimed Carrie. "Edith won't be far from her parents then, either."

"We were over looking at it this afternoon," he added. "We just have to negotiate a price agreeable to both parties."

"I suppose you are a little strapped for money, what with the new garage and all," remarked Carrie.

"Well, I thought I'd try and get a second job for the winter. The garage business will slack off then. Edith will continue to take in sewing. She thought she might also help out in her uncle's store some."

Amund and Edith's wedding took place in November in the Norwegian

Lutheran Church and a small reception was held at the Moehler home. The couple moved into their new home that very night. They took no honeymoon, rather spending that money on their house.

George had been invited to the wedding and afterwards he stopped in at Carrie's for awhile. As usual, he had to hurry home to do the milking.

"I hate this having to hurry home every time I come here," he said as he left.

I do, too, Carrie found herself thinking.

The area had received very little snow up until Christmas, so George was able to make several auto trips to Davenport to see Carrie.

"The roads are frozen hard now so it's good driving," he remarked as he arrived one Sunday afternoon.

As she took his coat and hat, she noticed that he was shivering. "Oh, my, I bet it's really a cold drive for you! Here, I have the coffee ready. Let's get you warmed up." She led him into the kitchen and poured him a large cup of the hot liquid.

"You shouldn't be driving such a distance when it's so cold," she admonished him. "Maybe you better wait until spring before you come again."

"Well, I suppose it will soon come to that, especially if we start getting a lot of snow," he answered slowly. "I like coming here to see you though, Carrie," he went on shyly.

"Well, we can't have you freezing to death or catching pneumonia!"

He wanted to say more, but Freddie came into the kitchen and sat down by him and wanted some coffee, too.

"Well, just a little bit then," said Carrie, pouring a small amount into a cup and setting it down in front of her son.

"Can I have a sugar lump, too, Mama, please?"

She laughed and said, "Well, just one and that's all."

The boy dunked it into his coffee and sucked it slowly, savoring its sweetness.

"How's school going for you, Freddie?" asked George, tousling the boy's hair.

"Oh, I like it very much! My teacher is very nice, too. She says that I'm the smartest kid in the class!"

"Oh, really?" he and Carrie exchanged amused glances. "Does she tell you this in front of everyone else?"

"No, just to me. The other kids might not like me if they heard what she said."

"That's right, Freddie. No one seems to like the smartest kid in the class."

There was a knock on the door and Freddie's playmate from across the street came in and Freddie got dressed to go outside and play.

"Don't stay out so long now this time, Freddie," his mother told him. "I don't want you getting sick."

Carrie and George settled themselves in the parlor for a visit.

"How are the newlyweds getting along?" George asked.

"Oh, just fine. Maybe we could go over and see them for a little while. They'd like that."

"That would be fun, but, Carrie, I...ah...have something I want to talk to you about first."

Carrie looked at him with interest and saw that he looked nervous, which wasn't like him, she thought.

"What is it, George? Is something the matter?"

"Well, you might say that," he laughed. "Ah...I don't know just how to say everything that's on my mind." With that he jumped up and said, "Darn, I knew I would flub this up. I practiced all the way over here and now I can't think how to start." He ran his hand through his hair and then sat down again.

He took a deep breath and proceeded. "The reason I'm so nervous is that I don't quite know how you're going to take this."

"Well, George, we're close friends," she said gently. "Just spit it out. I don't bite!"

He laughed and stalled a bit more. "All right, I'll just come out and say it. I'm in love with you!" He quickly glanced at her to see if her reaction was favorable before he continued. He couldn't read her face, which had gone blank.

"I'm...ah...hoping that you feel the same way. I'd like you to become my wife. There! I've said it." He slumped in his seat, like a great weight had been lifted from him.

"I...ah...don't know what to say, George!" She was remembering another proposal a few years back when she wasn't able to give Fred an answer for a whole week. She played with her wedding ring, which, she noticed, was fitting quite loosely.

Neither one was prepared for what she did next. She put her hands to her face and burst out crying. George sprang from his seat and joined her on the sofa. He didn't know exactly what to do with the crying young woman but he knew what he wanted to do and that was to take her in his arms. So that's exactly what he did.

Carrie cried on his shoulder for some time. Then she pulled away and tried to wipe her tears. He gave her his handkerchief. After she had composed herself, she looked at him and then they both burst out laughing.

"What a picture we make!" Carrie said. "Here, you're asking me a most important question, one that it took a lot of courage on your part to ask, and what do I do? I start crying like a baby!" They laughed all over again. The tension was now relieved for both of them.

"I don't know why I started crying, George. That's not like me at all. I can't even explain it."

"Well, I don't know what I was expecting, but it wasn't that!" he joked.

They both paused, and he, turning serious once again, asked, "Shall I start all over again or do you want me to leave?"

She looked at him for quite some time, not knowing what her answer would, or should be. "Maybe you should wait and ask me some other time, George. I....don't know what my answer would be yet." She could see the disappointment in his face and that saddened her deeply. She didn't want to hurt him, ever. She took his hand and held it gently in both of hers.

"You've become very dear to me, George. But I can't give you an answer yet. Please understand."

"I do understand, Carrie. I know I may have rushed you but I couldn't hold back my feelings any longer. I know we only met a few months ago." He brushed her hair back from her face with his big, but gentle hand. "I just know," he went on, "that I want to spend the rest of my life with you....and little Freddie, too, of course. I want to love and take care of you both. There! Now I've said all that's in my heart."

He rose and walked to the window. "Now then," he said, "let's go over and see Amund and Edith. We'll wait awhile before we talk more about this."

As it turned out, they had to wait quite awhile before they saw one another again. The weather turned bitterly cold and the snow came heavily. Carrie wished that she could have gone back to Spring Grove for Christmas but she hated to travel in the wintertime. She had heard of some trains that had gotten stuck in snowbanks for days!

She and Freddie joined Amund and Edith and Edith's family for the holidays and before she knew it, it was January and Freddie was back in school. The days got long for Carrie. She inquired of the new cafe owners if they needed any help and they said they could use her for as many hours as she could put in. She decided that she needed the money and something to occupy her so she worked from late morning till just before Freddie came home from school. She did her housework before and after and this arrangement seemed to work out fine.

She didn't know what to do about the question that George had asked her early in December. Why is it, she asked herself, when a man proposes to me, I can't already know how I feel about him and answer him on the spot. That's how it is in the few love stories I've read!

She wished she could talk to Lena about it but that looked impossible for some time to come. So she decided to write her and tell her about it and ask her advice. Lena wrote back immediately and she was all excited that George had proposed to her.

"Carrie," she had written, "I think that God has sent this fine, young man to you to love and care for you and I think that you should accept." Carrie prayed about it every night asking God to show her what she should do.

One night, as she was hearing Freddie's prayers, her son surprised her when he asked God to watch over George Johnson.

"Mama, why doesn't George come here anymore?" he asked as he was snuggling under the quilts. "I sure did like him. I wish he was my daddy."

Carrie hardly knew what to say. "You mean, you would like George to be your father? Why do you say that?"

"Because I want a father and I like George. He's fun and he makes me feel.... happy. Don't you like him, Mama?"

Carrie hesitated a little before saying, "Yes, I like him very much, too." Then she said, "What would you really think if I. ...ah....married him one day?"

Freddie sat up in bed and threw his little arms around his mother. "Oh I'd like that very much, Mama. When can you do it?"

She laughed and untangled his arms and pushed him gently back down and covered him up again. "Well, we'll have to see about that. I'll have to speak with George now, won't I?"

"Oh, I'm sure he'll like the idea all right. I think he likes you a lot!"

"Why do you say that, Freddie?" asked Carrie.

"Well, I heard Uncle Amund and Auntie Edith talking one day and I was hoping that it was true."

"Well, you go to sleep now. We'll talk about this some other time," Carrie said as she kissed him gently on the forehead. What a child, she chuckled to herself on her way out of his room.

That night, when she herself was snuggled under her quilts, she lay there thinking. Is this my answer, God? I guess it couldn't get any plainer than that. Out of the mouths of babes, she thought. She lay awake long into the night, thinking and praying.

On the first of February, Carrie and Freddie were over to Amund and Edith's for Amund's 30th birthday. "It doesn't look like you'll have to worry about the draft now, will you, Mannie? she asked him.

"No, I don't think so, he answered. "I just heard yesterday of a young man from the Kindred area who was reported killed in action in France. I wonder when this war will end, anyway."

Amund had been working all winter at Mr. Berg's blacksmith and engine repair shop besides running his own business. Work at both places was slow this time of the year.

"The garage business won't be too good as long as this war continues," he remarked. "The government's been restricting the use of gasoline and rubber." He shook his head.

"It's a good thing that I have a job, too," Edith said. "We're able to make the payment on the house and keep food on the table." She cut the birthday cake and passed it around.

"At least the garage is almost paid for," Amund said. "I had saved enough from when I worked at the farm to just about pay for that."

"We haven't seen George around lately," Amund said, changing the subject. "Is it the weather or is there some other reason?"

"It's the snow and the cold, I think," Carrie laughed. "I get a postcard about once a week, though," she divulged.

"Well, I hope we see a lot more of him after the weather warms up and the roads get passable again."

"I told Mama that I want George to be my new daddy!" Freddie blurted out.

"Freddie!" Carrie said, shocked at her son's precocious statement.

Amund and Edith laughed. "I was thinking along those same lines, Carrie," her brother said.

Carrie felt her cheeks burning but she had to laugh with them. All she would say is, "Time will tell. Time will tell."

CHAPTER 22

On Valentine's Day, George sent a pretty card to Carrie. He said if the roads didn't clear off in the next few days, he would take the train from Kindred to Davenport to see her. It had been too long, he wrote.

Thus, early the following Saturday, Carrie heard a knock on her back door and she opened it up and it was George standing there with a big grin on his face!

"Why, George! Is it really you?" she cried.

"Yah, it really is me! I thought if I didn't come soon you would forget what I looked like!" he laughed as he came in, stomping the snow off his boots. "I caught the early train."

When she helped him off with his heavy overcoat, the very nearness of him overwhelmed her. She realized then just how much she had missed him. She stood back and took a long look. He was of average height, but stoutly built. His face, while not strikingly handsome, was a very dear face to her. He had light blue eyes that always held a sparkle and a ready smile.

"Have you got any coffee ready?"

"No, but I soon will. I was just stirring up a batch of doughnuts to fry. Freddie just loves them."

"Well, you go on with those and I'll start the coffee," he told her.

It seemed the most natural thing in the world to work side by side in the kitchen with this man, thought Carrie. She finished rolling out and cutting the doughnuts and he helped her fry them.

Freddie woke up and walked into the kitchen. "I smell doughnuts!" he exclaimed and then he stopped short when he saw George there. "George!" he said and ran into his arms. "What are you doing here?" He looked at his mother for an explanation.

"Well," George began, "I was so lonesome for my two favorite people that I couldn't wait any longer for the roads to clear off so I just hopped on the train and here I am!"

"Oh, boy! This will be a great day!" cried Freddie as he jumped up on the chair and grabbed a hot doughnut.

"Here, I'll give you some milk to go with that, Freddie. And then I think you should have some oatmeal for your breakfast." Turning to George, she asked, "How about you, George, do you want some oatmeal, too?"

"Well, sure, if Freddie's going to have some, I will, too."

Freddie beamed up at the man as he slowly ate his doughnut.

After the two had eaten their oatmeal and still another doughnut each, Freddie went to get dressed. Carrie decided that she was going to tell George her answer to his proposal before he had to ask her again. She would spare him that.

"George," she turned to face him and said, "I have something to tell you. My answer to your question is 'yes'! I will marry you!"

George looked so surprised and startled that Carrie had to laugh. "Well, you haven't changed your mind now, have you?" she teased.

"Of course not! It's just that I was fussing and stewing all the way here how I was going to go about asking you again and here you made it so easy for me!"

"Well, I thought I would save you the agony of doing it all over again. I'm sorry that it took me so long but I hated to tell you in a letter."

He stepped closer to her and took her in his arms and held her close. "Ah, Carrie, you have made me the happiest man alive, that's for sure!"

Freddie came running into the kitchen again and stopped and looked at the grownups. "Are you kissing or what?" he asked them.

"I guess we are, young man. Your mother has something to tell you."

"Freddie, George and I are going to get married and the three of us will be a family."

"Whoopee!" Freddie cried. Now I'll have a daddy again!"

George went to him and picked him up and hugged him hard. "I'm going to love being your daddy, son," he said, with tears forming in his eyes. He reached out his arm for Carrie to join the embrace.

Before George went home on the evening train, the two of them had set June 5, two days after Carrie's 27th birthday, as their wedding date. George wouldn't hear of waiting any longer. The weeks and months ahead went fast with wedding plans for Carrie and spring fieldwork for George. Everyone was excited about their news.

Lena sent a letter, offering the couple their home for the wedding. However, Carrie wanted to get married in the church this time so they had the ceremony at the Norwegian Lutheran Church. Also, this time, Carrie's parents and Rosina came for the wedding. Several folks from the Daud farm came, including Hilde, Cora, Mr. and Mrs. Daud and Corky. Lena and Engebret were there with their three youngest daughters.

It was a simple but lovely affair. The lilacs were still in bloom so Edith brought many bouquets from the bush in front of their home to decorate the church. Many of the townspeople were invited so the church was well filled.

As Carrie and George were kneeling before the altar of the Lord, Carrie stole a glance at her new husband. Thank you, Lord, Carrie thought to herself, for this wonderful man and this second chance at happiness. Thank you for answering prayers. George gave her hand a squeeze and she responded with a smile.

Amund and Edith hosted a small reception afterwards in their home. "Keep it simple!" Carrie had admonished them, so it was just cake, sandwiches and coffee. It was so wonderful, Carrie thought, to have her parents there and her father to walk her down the aisle this time. Rosina was excited to be called upon to be her sister's maid of honor. She had grown up so, into a very lovely young woman. She was going to be teaching come fall.

The newlyweds decided against a honeymoon. Carrie wanted to spend some time with her parents who were only staying a couple days after the wedding.

"Marty is taking care of things back home," her father had told her, "with Olaf there to help if needed."

After the reception, George and Carrie were given a noisy goodbye with rice being thrown and wishes of happiness called after them.

"You don't have to milk the cows tonight, do you, George?" teased Amund.

"No, I have a neighbor doing them for me today," laughed George.

The young men had been busy hanging old shoes and things to the back of George's car so about a mile out of Davenport, George stopped and removed the noisy things and threw them in the ditch.

They went straight to the Johnson farm. George's mother had moved out the week before and Carrie's furniture and things were moved over just that morning. She didn't have much. Just the bedroom set that she and Fred had bought. George said that they could put that in the spare bedroom. She had her fairly new sofa and, of course, the beautiful china cabinet from the Daud's. George was very understanding about moving in things that had belonged to her and Fred.

The house, which Carrie had only seen a couple times, was about fifteen years old. It was a big, square two-story, painted white. It had a large, sunny kitchen, a dining room, parlor and a downstairs bedroom. There were four bedrooms upstairs. George's father, who had built it for his family when they had moved to the area from Iowa, must have anticipated a large family. Mr. Johnson had died of a heart condition five years earlier.

Carrie thought it would take her several days to get used to calling this her home now. She and George unloaded their newly opened wedding presents and found a place for everything. Her china cabinet was getting filled up by and by.

Carrie's parents and Rosina, Amund and Edith stopped over two days later, before the Amundsons had to leave for Spring Grove.

"It's so wonderful having you here," Carrie told her parents and sister. Freddie was becoming quite attached to his grandfather whom he hardly remembered.

"I took Pa out to the Daud farm this morning," related Amund. "I could hardly get him away from there!"

"Yah, that's quite a place, that's for sure," Mr. Amundson commented. "I can't believe all that machinery and horses for one farm." He was shaking his head in wonder.

"I think you have a very nice farm here, George," said Mrs. Amundson. "Now when I think of Carrie I can imagine her in these rooms."

There were many hugs and tears when the family had to say goodbye. Freddie was almost crying and Carrie was, too.

"Well, now that you know the way here, we'll expect you to come often!" George joked with his new in-laws.

"Well, we'll have to see about that. It wasn't as bad a trip as I thought it was going to be," admitted Mr. Amundson.

Young Freddie absolutely loved farm life. He shadowed George all day and learned many new things. He enjoyed being in the barn with the animals. They had a few milk cows, several sheep and some hogs. Their four horses had names like Lady, Barney, Fannie and Colonel. The chicken coup had enough hens to keep the family in eggs and it was Freddie's job to look for eggs daily.

Mrs. Johnson had started a garden for Carrie so there were vegetables already growing. She had a fair amount of flowers, too, which Carrie looked forward to enjoying. "I'll put fresh flowers on the table every day," she told George.

Carrie, who never thought she would want to marry a farmer because it seemed like such a hard life, just loved their farm. It was about a mile from the Sheyenne River and the soil was the "best in the country," bragged George. He farmed a quarter of land, which he owned, and he rented another eighty from some retired neighbors.

The farm buildings were in good repair, just recently painted a year ago. All in all, it was an attractive place, with some stately, old trees for shade and beauty. The Ulness home was just across the river but to get from one place to the other, one had to drive about 5 or 6 miles around to cross the bridge.

Lena and Carrie visited as often as they had time for and saw each other many a Sunday. George and Carrie went to the same country church as the Ulness family, the Gol Lutheran Church, just two miles away from the Johnson farm.

After a couple of Sundays attending this church, Carrie commented on the way home that there sure were a lot of Ericksons there! "They should have named it the Erickson Church!" laughed Carrie.

"Yah, we've teased them about that before. There are plenty of Erickson families, that's for sure."

Carrie, like Lena, became active in the Gol Ladies Aid. That summer the group was trying to raise money to help pay for a basement which was being put under the church.

One Saturday evening in July, the ladies put on a supper and then held an auction for their many handmade items and homemade jellies and such. Engebret always donated his services as auctioneer and Carrie thought that he did quite well at that job. Carrie donated some dishtowels that she had embroidered on the winter before and she also made some pies and doughnuts.

"The best doughnuts in these here parts!" Engebret announced, as they came up to be sold. "I've tasted them several times and I'll stand behind them. Who'll give me a dollar to start?"

By the time the church basement was finished, the Ladies Aid had $500 to donate towards the project. "What would we do without the ladies?" Engebret said one Sunday afternoon as they were visiting.

"Well, you can take a lot of credit, too, Engebret," Carrie told him. "You manage to get money out of people before they know what's happening!"

When Lena and Carrie were alone, Carrie mentioned that she thought that Engebret didn't look well.

"It's his kidney condition acting up," Lena explained. "The doctor told him several years back that he had something wrong with both of his kidneys. He won't slow down and take care of himself, either," she complained.

The threshing crew came to the Johnson farm the end of August and spent about a week there. Carrie didn't mind cooking for all of them as she was used to feeding a large crew. George's mother, Olivia, came and spent a few days to help her and then she had to get back to her daughter's farm where she was now living.

One Sunday as George was driving his family around the area, they passed the school that Freddie would be going to. It was the Barrie Township School #2 but everyone in the neighborhood called it the Overboe School.

"I thought that he would be going to the same school as the Ulness children, the Riverside School," commented Carrie.

"Well, we live in Barrie township and they live in another township so we have to go here," George explained.

The school was about a mile or so west of the Johnson farm. They passed a house that was right next to the school and George said, "The Nelius Iverson family lives there. You remember meeting them in church, don't you?"

"Oh, yes, I know who you're talking about."

"Well, his brother, Iver, started building that house a couple years ago but he fell into the basement one evening and he was killed. He was found the next morning." George shook his head slowly. "I'll never forget that. I had to help get him out. The house was finished later and his brother and family moved in. They say that Iver was sweet on the Overboe girl, who lives there across the road. Perhaps he had hopes of marrying her."

"Oh, how tragic," said Carrie. "Whatever happened to her?"

"As far as I know, she's still living at home there."

In September, Freddie started school and, being in the second grade now, he declared that he could walk to school by himself. That first day, Carrie watched him walk down the road. He turned several times to wave to her. She wiped a tear that had been threatening to run down her cheek.

"He's come a long way, that little boy has," she told George later that morning. He's so happy now." She came and put her arm on her husband's shoulder as he sat by the kitchen table having a cup of coffee. "He's not the only one who's happy," she added.

"That makes three of us then!" George exclaimed, as he rose and picked Carrie up and twirled her around the kitchen.

Later that day, her happiness was increased when the mailman brought the mail and there was a letter from Pauline. The two kept in touch by mail several times a year.

"Pauline just had her baby!" Carrie told George that evening when he came in for supper. They had two children already, a boy and a girl. "Oh, how I wish I could see them. Too bad they live so far away."

Carrie and Hilde exchanged post cards frequently, too, so she kept up with things on the Daud farm. Peter was still working there but Hilde thought that he might quit after this year.

Amund and Edith were occasional visitors at the Johnson farm but Edith announced that she was going to have a baby and was not feeling too well so their trips would have to end for awhile.

On November 12, the newspaper brought the good news that the war was over! Germany had signed an armistice the day before. "There was dancing in the streets of many American cities," the paper said. Carrie was relieved.

Now she didn't have to worry about any of the young men she knew going off to war.

One day, George took a wagonload of wheat to town to sell. When he came back Carrie asked him how much he got for it.

"Today it was $2.07. That's not too bad but I'm going to wait and see if the price goes even higher before I sell any more."

Their first Christmas together was a very happy one. On Christmas Eve, they drove down by Walcott to visit George's sister, Caroline and her family, and George's mother. They got home late that night and after church services the next day, they were invited over to the Ulness home. The house was full to overflowing with family and they all had such a good time.

The rest of the winter was what one would call an "open winter" as there was very little snow to block the roads. Therefore, George and Carrie were able to get around to visit neighbors frequently to socialize. They played cards, visited and sometimes there would even be a little house party where the rug was rolled up and someone with a fiddle would furnish music for dancing.

On confirmation Sunday in June, Carl Ulness was one of the confirmands. Carrie remarked afterwards to George that she thought the young lad looked very handsome in his new suit but also a bit uncomfortable.

George laughed. "I remember my first suit all too well!"

That afternoon the Johnson family drove to Davenport to visit Amund and Edith and to see their new baby. On their way, they stopped by the cemetery. Carrie and Freddie got out and walked over to the graves of Fred and little Joey. Freddie took his mother's hand and she blinked back the tears that were forming. Freddie was quiet and thoughtful on the way into town.

He cheered up when he got to hold the new baby, a girl, named Irene Arlys. She was only two weeks old and "so tiny and precious," Carrie commented.

When Edith and Carrie were alone in the kitchen, Edith said, "Well, you've been married exactly a year now. I suppose you'll be having a baby next!"

"Well, I hope it won't be too long. I'd really like to have some more children," Carrie answered.

Amund said that business at the garage was picking up considerably. "Now that the war is over, gas and rubber can be used domestically again," he told them. "I think we'll see a big increase in the number of people who will want to own an automobile. And that will be good for me!" he joked.

"They're going to have to do something about the condition of the roads, though," said George. "It's one thing to have a car, but it isn't every place that you can drive one. The road from Kindred to Davenport isn't anything to brag about, I tell you!"

"Well, that will come in time, too," said Amund.

After they left Amund's they took a drive out to the Daud farm. It was so good to see Hilde and Corky and everyone again.

Peter told George that he would be leaving after this season was over. Mr. Daud was going to be switching over to all gas-engine tractors before the next spring so many of the horses would be sold.

"I guess I'll go back to Minnesota and see what there is there for me."

Before they left for home, Carrie invited all of them to come down and visit their farm.

"That would be nice," Hilde commented, wiping a tear from her eye as she hugged Carrie and then Freddie.

The next two years went by quickly. They were happy years, the crops were good and the price of wheat was still up.

"Let's go out on the town tonight!" George suggested to Carrie and Freddie one Saturday noon. "They're showing a movie at the Anderson Hall."

"Oh, goodie!" exclaimed Freddie. "What's the movie?"

"The Great White Trail," answered George. "It think it's supposed to be real good."

"That sounds like fun," said Carrie.

"We'll have to go to town early and get our grocery shopping done first, I suppose," said George.

"Well, I better get busy with my housecleaning then, and I need to wash my hair, too." Carrie hurriedly washed up the dinner dishes and Freddie dried them.

On the way into town that evening, Carrie said, "Lena was talking about the eating place that Gilla and Hank just opened up in town. I guess farming didn't go too well for them."

"Well," George said quietly so that Freddie couldn't hear, "I heard in town that maybe he lost some of his land."

"Oh, no, that's too bad. Lena never told me that."

"Maybe she doesn't know."

"They're calling it the Ideal Restaurant," Carrie told him, getting back to the subject of the cafe. "Maybe we can go there after the movie."

"We'll see how late it gets," answered George.

The next weekend, George and Carrie asked a neighbor girl to come over and stay with Freddie and they went back to the same hall in Kindred, this time for a dance. There was a 6-piece orchestra from Casselton playing. The proceeds were to go for the baseball program.

Carrie saw that some of the fellows from the Daud farm were there. As Carrie was dancing with George, the thought struck her that what would she do if she saw Alfie there. She hadn't thought of him in several years. I wonder where he ended up.

"What are you thinking about?" asked her husband. "You're frowning."

"Oh, nothing important," she laughed.

One of the fellows from the Daud farm came up to them and asked them about Peter. "We haven't heard much from him since he left."

"Well, he's back in Spring Grove," George told him. "He got a job there with the lumber yard and we even hear from Carrie's mother that he has a girlfriend."

"No kidding! We thought he was a confirmed bachelor, for sure."

George surprised Carrie one day after he'd been in town by announcing that they would be getting a telephone. "We're going to get hooked up to the Kindred line."

"Oh, that will be so exciting!" Carrie exclaimed. "When will it be put in?"

"Sometime in the next month, they're saying."

Sure enough, by the end of May, they had a telephone and so did the Ulness home so Lena and Carrie spent many an hour talking every day. It was soon evident that some people liked to listen in on other people's conversations. Lena and Carrie devised a plan to outwit these "rubber neckers" by each of them picking up the telephone at exactly 2 o'clock every afternoon without anyone having to hear any ringing. Some days they would vary the time.

One day when George came in just after Carrie and Lena had finished their conversation, Carrie related something that Lena had told her.

"Did you ever hear Lena tell about how, many years ago her family had to run away from the Indians?"

"No, I don't believe I ever heard about that."

"Well, it was back in 1882 when Lena's sister, Rosina, was born. She was only a few days old and a rumor was spread that the Indians were coming to attack the white people around here! The men hurriedly made a bed for the mother and new baby in the wagon and the family drove to Fort Abercrombie. They stayed there until it was safe to return home. Lena was about 13 years old so she says she remembers it well."

"They must have been very frightened," George remarked.

"I guess they were. Lena said she had nightmares about Indians for many years after."

"So, what else did you learn on the telephone today?" he asked. He liked to tease her about her spending so much time on the new "contraption," as some people called it.

"Well, Gladys will be getting confirmed next Sunday."

"Little Gladys is being confirmed already?" he asked.

"Yes, they certainly are all growing up fast, aren't they?"

"Lena also said that Engebret has been feeling poorly again now," Carrie told him as she started to prepare supper.

"I ran into him the other day and he didn't look very good then."

Carrie's life was very good and she was happy, all except for the fact that she wanted a baby very much and that didn't seem to be happening. She longed so to hold an infant of her own in her arms again. George wanted a baby, too. They waited each month, only to be disappointed every time.

The middle of August, Lena called and told Carrie that Engebret was so ill that morning that he couldn't get out of bed. The doctor was called and medicine was prescribed. As the days passed, it seemed that his condition only grew worse.

Carrie and George drove over there one afternoon. Lena looked exhausted and worried.

"I don't think that Engebret is going to make it this time." She broke down and cried. "The doctor told us to expect the worst. His kidneys are failing rapidly."

A few days later, the doctor arranged for a nurse from Fargo to come out and stay with the family. This relieved Lena somewhat but she still couldn't sleep. She stayed by Engebret's bedside almost constantly. The girls did the cooking and household chores. The married daughters, Gilla and Hannah, came and helped when they could.

When the phone rang in the Johnson home at six o'clock in the morning, Carrie was almost afraid to answer it. She almost knew what the news would be. George had just come in for breakfast so he picked up the receiver. It was Randolph. He said that his father had passed away about an hour earlier.

Carrie and George both broke down and cried for the cousin and friend whom they had come to love so much. When they got Freddie off to school, they drove over to the Ulness home. There were several people there already. Mrs. Erickson, their closest neighbor, was in the bedroom with Lena. They were preparing the body.

Oh, my, Carrie thought to herself. I don't think that I could ever do that. But Lena had done it many times for others in the neighborhood. She had helped bring many babies into the world and she had prepared several others to leave this world. She is a remarkable woman, Carrie thought.

After finishing their task, the women came out and joined the others in the parlor. Carrie put her arms around her beloved friend and they both sobbed. The younger Ulness children were all sitting around in the room, not quite knowing what to do or how to act. Carl looked devastated and Gladys, Alice and Luella were all crying softly.

They're all too young to lose their father, Carrie thought. Just like Freddie was. What will Lena do now, with four younger children left to raise, she wondered?

Two days later, there was a small service in the home for the family and close friends and then they all drove to the church for another, bigger service.

The church was well filled. There were many of Lena's family there, the Bakkos from down by Walcott, and many others from the community.

"And so, on September 7, 1921," Pastor Ballestad intoned, "at the age of 57 years, Engebret O. Ulness, beloved husband and father left this world for another."

Carrie's mind wandered abit. Will Lena have to wonder, like I did, if her husband reconciled himself with God before he died? Where will he spend eternity? She wiped at her eyes with her hankie and tried to focus on the rest of the service.

The mourners all walked the short distance to the cemetery behind the horse-drawn hearse, where they lay to rest their husband, father, friend and neighbor. George put his arm around his wife, sensing that this funeral was perhaps bringing back painful memories for her. She leaned into him and was grateful for his love and concern.

CHAPTER 23

The day after the funeral, the threshing crew came to the Johnson farm so Carrie was very busy and totally exhausted every evening. This is good, though, she told herself. I'm too busy to dwell on the sadness of the past week. The day after the crew left, it rained heavily all forenoon.

"Well, we got done just in time, didn't we?" George remarked. "I think I'm going to sell all the wheat right away. From what I've been reading, I think the price will be going down."

He helped himself to a couple of doughnuts and as he was leaving the house, he asked Carrie, "Do you want to go to that Harvest Moon barn dance near Leonard tomorrow night? To celebrate the end of a good harvest?"

"Well, I don't really feel like celebrating so soon after Engebret's funeral. My heart just wouldn't be in it. Do you really want to go?"

"I don't really care, I guess. Pete asked if we were going. He and his wife are planning on it."

As it turned out, the Johnsons didn't go to the dance but the following week the circus came to Kindred so they took Freddie to that. There was a full day of events. There were auto races at the ballpark in the afternoon between drivers of "international reputation such as is seen at large fairs," the paper had read. After the races, the world's greatest aviacrobat, Al Blackstone, did some daredevil stunts from an airplane.

Freddie was mesmerized as he watched. The stuntman stood atop the plane during the loop-the-loop, and then he hung by his toes and teeth from a rope ladder beneath the plane. Next he walked to the edge, using no stirrups or handholds and then he made a parachute leap to the ground.

Everyone was awed and struck dumb for awhile. Never had they seen such a feat! It was talked about for weeks to come.

"I'm glad we took the time to go and take Freddie," remarked Carrie later that night. "This was something he'll never forget."

"I don't think I will either," laughed George, still shaking his head over what they had seen.

The end of September brought the potato harvest. George didn't grow potatoes but he usually helped his neighbors who did raise them. "It's a good potato crop this year," he told Carrie one day when he had come home from town. Albert Nipstad says he's getting 200 bushels to the acre."

Some of the schools in the area closed so that students could help pick potatoes. Freddie wanted to help this year. Carrie didn't think that he was old enough.

"He's almost ten and he's big for his age," George told her. "I think that he could try it. He can go with me over to Overboe's when I help them."

"Oh, goodie!" exclaimed Freddie when told that he could try it this year. "Now I can earn some money. They're paying 5 cents a bushel."

The next day, George and Freddie went over to the neighbors and Freddie got his first taste of potato digging. George helped drive the digger. It was a Hoover machine using two horses. Freddie and the other kids, most of them older and bigger, came behind with gunny sacks and filled each sack with potatoes. Then the sacks were loaded unto waiting wagons.

That evening when Freddie and George came home, Freddie was excited about his first day of work but the next morning he could hardly move, he was so stiff.

"Yah, I thought that would happen," said George. I remember my first day of potato picking a few years back."

Freddie wasn't quite so excited about going out to the potato fields the second day. He finished out the week and then school opened again and he had to go back there.

"I'm proud of you, son," George told him. "You stuck it out even when it stopped being fun."

The boy was mighty proud, also, of his first paycheck.

When George came home from town one day, he said, "I talked to Ole Braaten at the barber shop today. He said that we should come to Norman Church on Sunday night for their chicken supper. It costs 50 cents for adults and it's sponsored by the Mission Society."

"Oh, that sounds like fun," remarked Carrie. "We could take Freddie along, too. Maybe we could ask Lena to go with us."

"Yah, that sounds like a good idea. You call her and ask her."

Carrie called her right away and at supper that evening, she told George about their conversation.

"Lena told me today that Hank and Gilla's car was stolen in Fargo last week while they were there for the day."

"Really?" remarked George. "I hadn't heard that."

"His new fifty-dollar overcoat was in the back seat and he had no insurance."

"Oh, no! Well, they'll probably never see that vehicle again. Or the coat!"

When they picked up Lena on their way to the church supper, she told them that there was going to be an auction sale at the Ulness farm near Walcott on October 22.

"Oh, I'll have to plan on going there," George told her.

As it turned out, Carrie and George both went to the sale. It was a beautiful fall day so Carrie decided she would like to go along. She had never been out to the Ulness farm. It was located a couple miles east of the town of Walcott.

There was some farm machinery for sale and some workhorses. George was interested in them. There were also chickens-- about 70 Plymouth Rocks--and George bid on them, too, but didn't get them. He did go home with one of the horses, however.

When they got back to the farm, George said he had to make a quick trip into town. "Do you need anything?" he asked Carrie.

"Remember to stop by the Evingson's Store and get that flour that's on sale for $4.45," she reminded him. They had advertised in the Kindred Tribune that a railroad car would be sitting on the tracks for the next two days with 100# sacks of Pillsbury flour, and would be sold at "rock bottom prices."

About a month after the theft of the Hertsgaard car, Lena called Carrie one day to tell her that Hank's car was found way up by Sherwood, a town near the Canadian border. Carrie related the news to George at supper that evening.

"A farmer had come across it in his field. It was damaged and the battery was gone and all identifying numbers had been erased," she told him. "However, they found a gas-measuring stick with the name 'M.J. Elefson, Kindred, ND' printed on it so the farmer wrote to Elefson. That's where Hank had bought the car. When Hank heard the news," she went on, "he wired the farmer and told him to hang on to the car, and that he'd be up to get it as soon as he could."

"Boy, I sure didn't think they'd ever see that car again! I wonder how badly it's damaged."

George read in the newspaper one day that the price of wheat had gone down to under a dollar. "The lowest since the war," he quoted. "I sure am glad that I sold all my wheat before this happened."

"How did you get so smart?" Carrie teased him.

"I don't know, I just had a hunch."

He read on for awhile and then spoke up again. "It says here that they've decided where the new Kindred School will be built. They're going to buy some of the Ottis land east of town, at the end of Main Street." He glanced down at the article again. "They'll be paying $225 an acre for 3 3/8 acres."

"Well, Freddie, when you're ready for high school, you'll get to go to a brand new school."

"It won't be brand new then. I'm only in the 2nd grade!" the boy reported. George just laughed.

A few minutes later, George looked up again. "I'm learning all sorts of interesting things in this issue! Next week there's going to be a "cap" social."

"What in the world is a cap social?" asked Carrie.

"Here it says, 'each girl is to bring two identical caps. One will be sold and she keeps the other. After all caps are sold, partners are found by all putting on their caps." George looked up again and he and Carrie started laughing.

"Well, that sounds like it might be kind of fun at that," said Carrie. "What will they think of next to pair people up."

"If we were still young and single, maybe we'd go to something like that." George told her.

Reading on, he announced that "a Sons of Norway Lodge would be organized here in Kindred. We'll have to find out more about that later," he said, laying the paper aside. "I think that's all the news I can hold for one night," he chuckled, and then announced that it was time for bed.

During that winter, Carrie found herself suffering from the "blues," as she called it. She and Lena talked often, on the telephone and in person, and they reminded each other to read Psalm 9: 'The Lord is a stronghold....in times of trouble. And those who know thy name put their trust in thee, for thou, O Lord, hast not forsaken those who seek thee.'

Carrie worried about Lena sometimes. Carl had been sick after the new year and the doctor thought for awhile that he had tuberculosis but it turned out not to be. Thank you, Lord, for that! thought Carrie. How much more could the woman take?

George had been hearing rumors in town that Alfred, Lena's son, had left town unexpectedly and no one knew where he went. Lena never would talk about it, even though Carrie gave her the opportunity to do so. Alfred and his wife, Alma, had two daughters now, Lorraine and Margaret.

"How terrible for Alma," Carrie said to George. "And for those little girls. I wonder where he went and why?"

"That's what everyone's wondering," George said. "You know, Alma's father, Pete Anderson, never liked Alfred and did everything to discredit him. I understand that Alfred stopped in at Pete' house in town, where Alma and the girls were staying, to say goodbye."

Carrie shook her head in wonder. I sure hope nothing bad has happened to him and that he comes home soon. What do you suppose could have driven him away?"

"Well, I don't know," George replied slowly, "but I hope it didn't have anything to do with gambling."

"That gambling sure can get people into trouble, cant' it? I'm so glad that you don't indulge in that," Carrie told her husband.

In March, Hannah and Louis had a baby, another boy, and they named him Leon. This helped cheer Lena up some. She went over to the Perhus home to help out for a week or so. She didn't have to deliver this one. The doctor had made it out there in time.

While Carrie was concerned for Lena and family, she was also troubled by the fact that she was apparently not going to have another baby. "Forgive me, Lord, for self pity. Help me to accept my circumstances and be happy and thankful for what I do have." She prayed this often and it made her feel better to mentally list all her blessings.

The increased physical activity that spring brought with it made her feel better, too. There was housecleaning to do and gardening and yard work, cooking and baking. George often had a neighbor, Ole Olson, come and help him put in his crop and then Carrie would have an extra mouth to feed.

One day, the first part of April, and very early in the morning, Carrie saw a big, black automobile drive into their yard. "Now who in the world could that be?" she said aloud. Freddie was still asleep and George was out in the barn.

She watched as a woman came walking up the sidewalk to the back door. A man remained in the vehicle. "I sure don't know this woman," Carrie said, still talking to herself. She stepped up to the screen door before the woman could knock and looked inquiringly at the stranger.

"May I help you?" she asked, thinking now that perhaps the couple was lost and needed directions.

"Yes, I hope you can," answered the woman slowly, looking at Carrie very deliberately. "Are you Mrs. Johnson?"

"Yes I am. Please come in, why don't you?" Carrie held the door open for her.

The stranger looked around the room, as if checking to see if they were alone. "Is your husband at home?"

"He's out in the barn." Carrie glanced out the window and she saw George coming toward the house.

"I want to speak with both of you....about....something important," the woman stated.

"Here he comes now," Carrie said as George entered the kitchen. He looked from one woman to the next.

"George, this woman wants to talk with both of us. Here, I'll get us all some coffee."

"No, no," protested the stranger. "Don't bother with that. I think we all need to sit down, though."

They all took places at the table. "I'm sorry if I haven't introduced myself but I'm afraid that I can't tell you my name...ah...because of the...ah... nature of this visit. So," she took a deep breath, "I'll get right to the point. I understand that you both would like very much to have a baby and perhaps I can help you."

Carrie gasped and said, "Who are you and where did you hear that?"

"Well, I'd rather not tell you who I am except to say that I'm from the next county west of here and I can't tell you, either, who told me of your plight. But, please, let me go on. I know of a...ah...young girl... who is going to have a baby that she...ah...can't ...ah...keep. She isn't married, you see, and the child must be put up for adoption.

"The family is trying to keep this all very secret," she went on, "and when I heard of you, I thought that this was an answer to our problem and also to yours. Would you be willing to take the baby and adopt it?"

Carrie and George looked at each other and then at the woman. "This is all so startling!" George exclaimed. "We don't know who you are or anything about you or this...young girl."

"Well, all I can tell you about this girl is that she comes from a good family and she got herself into a bit of trouble and it would be a real embarrassment to have this get out. That's why all the secrecy and I'm sorry about that."

The woman rose and said," I know that you'll want to think about this for awhile. I'll call you in a few weeks and you can tell me your decision. The baby is due in less than two months."

Carrie looked at George and he nodded. They watched the woman leave and return to the car, which had sat there all the while with its motor running. Carrie could see that there was a man behind the wheel. It drove slowly out of the yard and headed west.

George and Carrie were too stunned to say anything for awhile. "Here, I'll dish up your oatmeal," Carrie said, and she also poured two cups of coffee. She noticed that her hands were shaking.

"Was this a dream and we're just waking up or did this really happen?" Carrie asked her husband. "Who is this mystery woman and where did she come from?"

"The biggest mystery is where did she find out about us, and that we wanted to have a baby?" George asked.

"I don't know. I can't even imagine who it was."

They didn't discuss it again the rest of the day until that night in bed. Carrie turned to George and asked, "Have you been thinking about this morning and that woman who came out of the blue?"

"Indeed I have! And you?"

"I've thought of nothing else!" she answered. "What do you make of it anyway?"

"Well, I guess it's just like she said. There's a young girl who has to give up her baby when it comes and this woman, perhaps she's related in some way, is trying to help find a home for it."

"Why wouldn't they just go through an adoption agency?"

"I don't know. I really don't know."

They both fell into a fitful sleep after that but in the morning, Carrie was up early. When George came down, she was sitting at the table, having her first cup of coffee. As he joined her, she looked into the face of her dear husband and seemed to be searching for something.

"What are you thinking about?" he asked her.

"About this baby. I can think of nothing else." She rose and busied herself frying up some eggs and bacon for their breakfast. She went to the hallway and called, "Freddie! Time to get up for school."

"George, I think that later this morning I'm going to drive over and see Lena. It always helps to talk things over with her."

"You mean you're going to tell her about this woman and the baby?"

"Well, yes, It won't hurt to tell her. She won't say anything to anyone else. Can you hitch up the small buggy for me?"

"You could take the car," George suggested.

"Yes, I suppose I could, but I have trouble cranking it up sometimes. If none of the boys are around over there, I may not get it started myself."

And so, when Freddie was off to school and Carrie had her kitchen straightened up, she hopped in the buggy. She lightly flicked the reins on the back of Lady and drove over to the Ulness place. Lena was glad to see her, as always. Her youngest girls were at school and Lena was home alone.

The two women settled down at the kitchen table with a cup of coffee. Carrie looked around her. How she loved this cozy room. The walls were painted a gray-blue and there was wainscoting on the bottom half. A large wood box stood by the range and the smell of burning wood was always in the air. A spacious pantry was off to the left.

Carrie finally plunged right in with the purpose of her visit.

"Lena, you won't believe what happened yesterday!" She told her about the stranger who appeared at their door in the early morning hours.

"Lena shook her head back and forth. "I wonder who she was and who could have told her about your wanting to have a baby?"

"That's what we've been wondering about ever since she came!" exclaimed Carrie.

"Lena, you know how badly I want a baby. Do you think it would be foolish to even think about doing this?"

Lena was silent for some moments. "You know Carrie," she said slowly, "maybe this is an answer to your prayers. God works in mysterious ways sometimes."

"I know, I've thought of that, too. But how will we know if this is from God or not? I don't want to be so desperate that I'd do just anything to get a baby."

"I know you wouldn't, dear," said Lena, patting the younger woman's hand. "When do you have to decide?"

"She said she would give us a call in a couple of weeks or so."

"Well, let's just keep praying about it and hope that God sends a sign for you to guide you in this important decision."

Later, as Carrie was driving home, she prayed fervently that God's will would be done in this matter. "I really want this baby, God," she said, aloud, " but 'not my will, but thine, O Lord.'"

"So, how did it go today at Lena's?" asked George, after supper that evening. Freddie had gone outside.

"Well, Lena says that maybe this is an answer to our prayers and that we should keep praying for direction."

They discussed the situation a while longer until Freddie came in the house.

"Lena told me that she had recently been down to the Walcott area to visit her sister, Rosina," Carrie said. "I think I told you sometime ago that she and Knute had twins back in January. A boy and a girl."

"I remember you saying something about that," said George, half-listening and half reading the newspaper.

"That was such a blessing to them. After all the tragedy in their family shortly before."

Here George put down the paper and gave her his full attention.

"About four years ago, their young son, Herman, was killed when his horse was startled by an automobile coming out of their yard. He was only 8 years old."

"That must have been very hard for the family," said George.

"Yes, but then, a year later, their 6-year-old son, Gilman, died of the flu!"

"Oh, I don't remember hearing that. Was that during the awful flu epidemic?"

"It probably was," Carrie said. "Just think, to lose two of your children, a year apart. Their daughter, Goody, was born a few months after the little boy died of the flu."

Carrie was deep in thought for awhile. Then she sighed and said, "Just think of the terrible things some families have to go through. Like Lena, for instance."

George rose and came and put his arm around his wife. "Well, you had to go through some pretty terrible things, too, didn't you? Losing your baby and then your husband." Carrie started to weep not only for herself but also for all the hurting people who'd suffered losses.

"There's so much sickness, and terrible accidents and so many people die. It's especially hard when it's the little ones." She tried to compose herself and reached for her hankie.

"I think I told you about what happened to the Arne Perhus family," George said. "Six of their children died in the diphtheria epidemic of 1890. They said that the neighbors couldn't make the little coffins fast enough!"

"Oh, how awful!" Carrie was remembering her little Joey, and standing above his crib, watching him die of that same disease.

"They're all buried out in the Perhus cemetery. We drive by there on the way over to the Ulnesses. They were the older brothers and sisters of Louis, who's married to Hannah."

"Oh, yes, I remember now hearing about that," Carrie said.

Freddie was watching his parents, taking it all in. "Why do people have to die?" he asked.

"That's a hard question to answer, son," George said.

"People are born, they live on this earth for awhile and then they die," Carrie said. "The short time that we're on this earth, we're supposed to live our lives as God would want us to. He's our creator and we're to love Him and obey his commandments and love others. Then when we die, as we all must, we'll go to Heaven to live with Him."

Freddie was thoughtful for some time, digesting this. "And that's where Joey and Daddy are, isn't it, Mama?"

"Yes, Freddie." Carrie hoped with all her heart that that's where Fred was.

About two weeks later, Carrie mentioned to George that the mystery lady, as they called her, would probably soon be calling them for their answer. They still didn't know what to do.

"I'm waiting for some sign from God, telling us what to do," Carrie told George. "This is too important a decision for us to decide alone."

That next Sunday in church, Pastor Ballestad mentioned the phrase, "and a little child shall lead them." Carrie's head jerked up and she could see that the pastor was looking straight at her and he held her gaze for sometime. She felt prickly up and down her spine. Is this your sign, Lord? she wondered.

After they had returned home, Carrie and George were both in their bedroom, changing out of their Sunday clothes. She told George about what had happened during the church service.

"Well, maybe that's our sign," he said.

"Oh, do you think so?" Carrie's heart started beating in her excitement. "Does that mean that we should take the baby, do you think?"

"Yah, I think so. I think that we should say that we'll take it."

They didn't have long to wait to act upon their decision. The mystery woman called them late that night. They had already gone to bed but George hurried to the telephone before it could stop ringing.

I hope no one picks up their phone to hear who is calling this late, Carrie thought to herself as she followed her husband to the kitchen. By the time she got there, the conversation was already over and he had hung up.

"Who was it?" she asked.

"It was her."

"What did she say?"

"She just asked if we had decided to accept the parcel."

"The parcel?" cried Carrie.

"Well, she's probably familiar with party lines and people listening in so she was being very discreet, perhaps."

"Oh, yes, of course. That was smart of her."

"Then what did you say?" Carrie urged him on.

"I said that, yes, we would accept it, and then she said that she would call when it's ready!"

"That's all she said?" Carrie was getting agitated. "I'd like to talk with her about it some more. When can we expect it, I wonder." She was wringing her hands.

"I don't know. Maybe she'll contact us again."

The end of the week, a letter came with no return address but it had been mailed from Kindred. It was from the mystery lady. It said that she was happy that they would take the baby and she was sorry she had to be so brief on the telephone. She was mailing this from Kindred as they passed through there so that her real hometown would remain unknown.

"Boy, she thinks of everything, doesn't she?" remarked George, as he read the note over his wife's shoulder.

She ended by saying that they should prepare for receiving a baby, buying all the things that they will need. She would call them upon the birth and deliver the child immediately, day or night.

Carrie grew weak in the knees. She had to sit down. "George, we're going to become parents soon!" He gave her an excited hug and said, "What do we need to get for it? I think my old crib is in the attic. I'll go up and have a look later."

"We'll need bottles and I'll buy some material and make some diapers and little blankets. Oh, George, I'm so excited."

"We'll have to tell Freddie!"

"Let's wait till it happens, just in case something unexpected... comes up," cautioned Carrie. "You never know."

"You're probably right," said George. "Let's see, we maybe have about six weeks left."

"I think I'll go to town with you this afternoon and buy the material I'll be needing. We'll buy the bottles later. We don't want people speculating."

"Maybe we could buy them in a different town," George suggested. "I could drive down to Walcott one of these days."

"Yes, maybe you should do that."

The next few weeks were full of excitement and preparation and secrecy. Carrie told no one except Lena. George got the bottles and Carrie made some baby things. George's little crib was found in the attic and they cleaned it up. When Freddie asked about it, Carrie said that someone who was having a baby would be needing it soon. He seemed to accept that evasive explanation.

Six weeks passed and still no word. "Do you think someone was just playing a prank on us?" asked Carrie one day.

"Oh, no, nobody would be that cruel!" exclaimed George. "We'll just have to have patience. Babies sometimes come late, you know."

In the wee hours of the morning of the 5th of June, the phone rang. Both Carrie and George jumped up and raced to the kitchen. George picked it up on the third ring.

The woman's voice on the other end said simply, "It's come. We'll deliver immediately." Then she hung up.

Husband and wife stood looking at each other and then the tears began to fall. They fell into each other's arms and cried and laughed at the same time.

"I'm so excited I don't know what to do with myself!" Carrie said later as they were getting dressed.

"Well, this is pretty new to me, being a father, you know," George admitted. "I won't know what to do with a little baby."

Carrie hadn't thought of that before, that this would be so new to George. "It will be all right, dear. I'll teach you." After a pause, she added, "It's been awhile for me, too. Hope I can remember what to do."

"I just thought of something," announced George. "Today is our wedding anniversary!"

"That it is! Isn't this a nice way to celebrate."

"We better wake up Freddie and prepare him for the surprise."

"We don't even know if it's a boy or a girl!" exclaimed Carrie later.

George looked at her, startled. "No, I guess we don't, do we?" They both laughed in their excitement. "This will be a surprise to us, too!"

CHAPTER 24

Little Olivia Oline Johnson was baptized on the last day of June in the Gol Church. Everyone said what a beautiful baby she was and how surprised they all were to hear that there was a new baby at the Johnson home!

Carrie and George stood by proudly showing her off to everyone. She was wearing a baptismal gown that Caroline, George's sister, had just used for her last baby. George's mother and Caroline were in attendance at the service. Mrs. Johnson was proud of her namesake. Her name was Olivia and the baby's middle name came from Carrie's mother. George and Carrie had already started calling their baby "Livvie" for short.

Mrs. Johnson had come several days after the baby arrived, to help Carrie. She was so surprised, as was everyone except Lena. Now she would be returning to Caroline's. She gave the baby one last hug and tearfully said goodbye to the family.

Livvie had been a good baby from the very start. She took to the bottle right away and was now sleeping through the night. George had proved to be a quick learner and he couldn't seem to get enough of looking at his new daughter. Freddie rather liked her, too, but was sometimes perturbed that his father paid her so much attention.

About two months after they had received Livvie, there came a letter with the legal adoption papers, just like the mystery lady had said. It was postmarked Lisbon this time.

"Isn't that the county seat of Ransom County?" asked George.

"I wouldn't know," answered Carrie.

They were instructed to fill out and sign both copies and send one back to the courthouse.

"I see that the mother and father's names are omitted. Is that legal?" George wondered.

"Under 'mother's name' it just says, 'underage girl' and for father's name it says 'unknown.' That doesn't tell us much, does it?"

"Well, we'll have to trust the woman that everything is on the up and up." They took their copy of the document and hid it well away.

George realized that he needed to spend more time and attention on Freddie now so he and the boy went to several baseball games together in the area that summer. They followed the New York Yankees team in the paper. They were especially intrigued by a player named Babe Ruth.

"He'll be a great one some day, just you watch, Freddie," George told him.

A real highlight for Freddie was when he and George went into Kindred to Joe Owen's Electric Shop to hear the World Series over radio. Mr. Owen received the signal through Fargo Plumbing and Heating Company, who received it direct from New York. The Yankees were playing the New York Mets. Several other fathers and sons were crowded into the shop. The Mets ended up taking the series, much to the dismay of the Yankee fans present.

Carrie was very happy and contented now with her little family. Livvie was growing and the next June, mother and daughter celebrated their birthdays together, being only two days apart. Carrie invited Lena and her girls over, and George's mother and sister came from Walcott. They had supper and a birthday cake with one candle on it and then they opened some small presents.

Later that summer, Lena called Carrie one evening to tell her that she had just gotten word that Alfred and Alma's little girl, Margaret, had taken ill and was very poorly. Lena's son, Alfred, had still not returned and no one had ever heard from him since he left. Carl was going to take his mother into town, where Alma was living with the two girls.

"Call me tomorrow," Carrie told Lena, " and tell me how things are going there."

The next afternoon, Lena phoned Carrie again, this time in tears. "Pete Anderson just called me to say that little Margaret died this morning." Here her voice broke and she could not go on. Carrie had to sit down. She was feeling weak in the knees. Little Margaret was only four years old. What if something like this happened to Livvie? And she thought of Joey and how she had felt then.

"The funeral will be on Thursday. That will be a very hard day," Lena sighed. "She was such a sweet child. I didn't get to see her very much, but Alma would bring her over sometimes." Here Lena cried afresh.

"What did she die of?" George asked Carrie that evening at supper.

"Lena said the doctor called it tuburcular meningitis."

"My, I've never heard of that before!" he said.

A couple weeks before Christmas that year, Lena called to tell Carrie that she had just been over to Chris Erickson's and delivered a baby girl. She had also been the one to deliver their three older boys.

"They were very excited to have a girl!" exclaimed Lena. "Alice will go over there and stay with them."

Alice, now fifteen years old, had quit school after one year of high school and had just been staying at home. Gladys was still in high school and would graduate come spring. She wanted to go on and become a teacher.

That spring, a travelling photographer came to Kindred by way of rail and his specially-equipped boxcar sat on the sidetracks for several days and people could come and have their photographs taken. Carrie decided to take Livvie there for her two-year-old picture. Freddie considered himself too old to have his picture taken but Carrie did get him to come along and pose once, holding Livvie.

She was excited when the finished pictures finally came in the mail about one month later. The photographs turned out very nice. She drove over to Lena's one afternoon and brought them along and gave one to the Ulness family. Lena had one to give Carrie, too. It was of Lena and her five daughters.

Carrie showed it to George that night. "Isn't that picture nice of all of them?" she exclaimed. Looking more closely at it, she realized how tired and worn out Lena looked.

"Look at Lena's eyes. She looks so tired," she told George.

"Well, she's gone through some tough times the last few years. Engebret dying, Alfred disappearing, little Margaret dying. It's been just too much for her."

"Yah, that it has," Carrie agreed.

"I wonder whatever happened to Alfred," mused George. "Nobody's heard a word from him. Do you suppose he met with some bad end?"

"And just think," added Carrie. "He doesn't even know about his little girl dying and that his father died!"

George just shook his head. "I can't imagine what happened to him."

Carrie sent a picture to Pauline and one out to the Daud farm for all to see. And, of course, a couple to George's mother and sister. She was planning to take Livvie and go down to Spring Grove in July, so she would bring pictures for her family then.

Freddie, who was almost twelve now, was torn between staying home and helping George or going along to see his grandparents.

"You better go, Freddie," George told him. "Pretty soon you'll be too old to have time for vacations and I'm sure your grandparents would very much like to see you."

So it was, the middle of July, Carrie and her two children boarded the train and headed for Minnesota. It was great to see her whole family again. It had been too long, she said. They were equally excited to see baby Livvie and they all marveled at how Freddie had grown into such a tall, young man now.

Olaf and Mattie's children, Manda, Burt and Agnes, were 16, 14 and 8. Sylvia and Rudy had just two, Johnny and Esther, 14 and 9. All the children had such a good time together and, of course, they all doted on the youngest, little Livvie.

Sylvia mentioned that she had talked to Ted Gunderson in the bank a few days earlier and he had inquired about Carrie. Sylvia told him that her sister and children were coming to visit in a few days.

Carrie's mother had been sending back issues of the Spring Grove Herald to Carrie so she was pretty well caught up with all the latest news. She had read that Ted had married and had three children. Why did she still even have any interest in the man after all these years? she asked herself. She couldn't answer that question.

One day, however, she met him outside of the grocery store and he stopped to talk with her. He inquired after her and her family. She had

Livvie with her and he admired the child. He had an unhappy look about him and he almost seemed to want to say more to Carrie but then he said he better be getting back to the bank.

That evening, Carrie mentioned the conversation to Sylvia. "I've heard rumors that he isn't very happily married," said Sylvia. "His wife, Vera, is a real shrew, I understand."

"Oh, that's too bad," replied Carrie.

"Why should you care?" asked her sister.

"Well, I hate to see anyone unhappy in their marriage. Even if that person dumped me!" she laughed then.

Rosina was home for the summer. She was getting married in the fall to a fellow teacher in a neighboring town. They would both be teaching at the same school, he in the high school and she in the grades.

All too soon, the visit was over and Carrie and the children had to board the train for the ride home. "I hope Livvie travels better going home than she did coming out here!" she told her parents, as they were saying their goodbyes.

As it turned out, Livvie slept most of the time. She was worn out from all the attention from her older cousins, it seemed.

The following summer was a good one. The crops looked promising and the price of wheat had gone up to $1.50. "That's not a terrific price but at least it's going up," George commented.

"I'd like to buy a new car, but I guess I'll try and get along another year," he told Carrie one day. "In fact, I was thinking that tomorrow I'd take a drive over to Amund's garage and have it tuned up. Do you want to ride along?"

"Oh, sure!" Carrie answered. "I could visit with Edith for awhile. That would be fun."

The next day, on their way to Davenport, Freddie asked if they could stop at the cemetery. It had been a couple years now since they had done this. The whole family got out and walked toward the two graves. Livvie ran around the tombstones but Freddie stood still and read the inscriptions. Carrie put her arm on her son's shoulder.

I'm sure he's wondering what it would have been like for him now if his father had not been killed and if little Joey had lived.

They all walked wordlessly back to the car. When they reached Amund's house, Carrie and Livvie got out and Freddie went with George down to Amund's garage. Edith and Carrie had a nice visit. Irene, who was now six, played nicely with Livvie. Kenny, who was only two, was taking a nap.

After a couple of hours, Amund picked up his wife and daughter. Carrie said she wanted to stop at the Tuskind's store for a few grocery items and then the family headed for home.

"Amund says he's as busy as he can be. He may have to hire some help, even," George told Carrie on the way home.

"Well, I'm really glad to hear that. His first few years at the garage were kind of slow, weren't they?"

One evening, a few weeks later, a car which Carrie didn't recognize came into the yard. She wiped her hands on the dishtowel and walked out onto the porch. She saw Lena getting out of the passenger's side and then her son, Carl, stepped out and proudly stood by the car. George came out of the barn then and both he and Carrie walked over to see what was going on.

Lena spoke first. "Carl got himself a car yesterday!"

"Well," George said, slapping the young man on the back. "Your first car! It's very nice." It was a new 1925 Model T Ford; black, of course.

"Just look at those glass windows!" exclaimed Freddie, now joining them, too.

"Did you get it at Westby's in town here?" asked George.

"Yah, I did. The great thing about it, it has electric start," said Carl.

"Oh, that would be nice," commented Carrie.

"Why don't you take George and Freddie for a little spin?" Lena suggested to her son.

"Sure! Hop in!" Carl said, grinning broadly.

The women walked up unto the porch and sat down. "Yah, Carl is sure excited about his first car. He has worked and saved for quite sometime for this."

"Well, that's nice that he could get one. I hear that he has a girlfriend, now, too."

"He's been courting the Heglie girl from over by Walcott," Lena volunteered. "Her family lives a couple of miles from our farm over there."

"What does she do?" asked Carrie.

"Carl says that she's going to attend the teacher's college in Moorhead in the fall."

"How about Gladys now. Did she find a teaching position?" She had just finished one year at Valley City Normal School.

"She just heard from a school over at Turtle Lake," Lena said. "She thinks she'll take that if she doesn't hear from anyone else pretty soon."

"Where is Turtle Lake?" asked Carrie.

"Well, Gladys said that it's north of Bismarck about 75 miles or so."

When the men returned, Carrie invited all of them in for a cold drink. She made up some orange nectar and added crushed ice from the icebox and filled some tall glasses.

"Oh, this tastes so good!" exclaimed Carl.

"Yah, it sure has been a hot one today, hasn't it?" George offered.

"Pa, do you think we could get a new car like that one?" asked fourteen-year-old Freddie, who was already very interested in cars.

"Maybe in another year or two," answered George.

The next day, George announced that he was going to take a couple hogs in and sell them. "Hogs are going for $10.80 now, so I thought this would be a good time to sell."

When he returned, he told Carrie, " I think we can't put off digging a new well any longer. I talked to a man from the North Dakota Well Company. He was in town, at the lumberyard. They can come here and dig ours next Friday."

"How much will that cost?" Carrie asked.

"Between $300 to $400."

"Oh, that much?" commented Carrie.

"Yah, nothing is cheap anymore," George said, shaking his head.

"Well, I guess if we need one, we need one."

The next couple years passed quickly. It was now 1927 and Freddie was almost sixteen. He didn't want to continue on in high school but his parents were urging him to go back in the fall and finish. They didn't know if he would be interested in farming or if he would like to do something else.

"If you get your high school diploma, Freddie," his father said, "you'll be prepared for whatever you decide to do."

"Lena's granddaughter, Lorraine, will be coming to live with her grandma for awhile, it seems," Carrie told George one evening, many months later.

"Why is that?"

"Her mother, Alma, has been diagnosed with TB and she has to go up to the San Haven sanitarium."

"Oh, that's too bad. I wonder how long she'll have to stay there?"

"I don't have any idea. Lorraine will have to go to school at Riverside and Lena says that the girl is not very happy about that."

"What else did you learn today from talking to Lena?" teased George.

"Well, you remember that Gladys had gone out to Turtle Lake to teach a year ago, or so?"

"Yah, I remember."

"I guess she didn't like it too well. Too many Russians there, she told her mother. Well, now she's accepted a job in Montana someplace."

"I don't suppose Lena is too keen on her going so far away," commented George.

"Well, no. She doesn't know why she can't get something around here."

"Maybe she's the adventurous type."

"That may be."

"I ran into Ole Braaten in town today and I told him that he and his family should come out sometime and visit, maybe on Sunday, I said," George told Carrie. "He said that he would ask Mathilde, but they'll call first, before they come."

"Oh, that would be fun. We haven't really seen them for a long time."

On Saturday, Mathilde called and said that the family would drive over the next day. "I'll have to fix plenty food," joked Carrie. "They have a pretty big family!"

On Sunday after dinner, Carrie finished doing the dishes. She wiped out the two dishpans and hung them on the nail behind the pantry door. Then she put on her "Sunday tablecloth" over the everyday oilcloth one. Then she went outside and picked some fresh daisies and snapdragons and put them in a tall vase and placed it in the center of the table.

She was standing back to admire her efforts when George came into the room. "How nice it looks," he commented, putting his arm around her waist.

"All except the floor," she said ruefully, and they both looked down.

"Yes, that floor is getting pretty bad, isn't it. It's almost worn through in some places, I see. You know what?" he said. "Tomorrow I'll go into the hardware store and get a piece of some of that new floor covering."

He reached into a drawer and pulled out a measuring tape. "Here, Freddie, hold this tape and we'll measure this room."

He jotted down the measurements on a piece of paper. To Carrie he said, "maybe you want to come along and help pick out something pretty."

"Well, tomorrow's wash day, you know," replied Carrie.

"I could wait until you're done. I'd like to have you along."

About mid-afternoon Sunday, they heard a vehicle come into the yard. "The Braatens are here!" announced George.

The family piled out of the car. When they were all welcomed into the house, Carrie told Mathilde that she would have to refresh their memory on the names and ages of all the children again. "It's been awhile!" Carrie said.

"Well, Glenda is the oldest at 13; then there's Mildred, Ingval, Florence, Helen and Delores, here, she's four."

"She's a year younger than Livvie," said Carrie. "They should have fun playing together.

At coffee time, Carrie put all the children at the kitchen table and the adults at the dining-room table. She had made a large cake, white with lemon filling and white icing, and a big bowl of red Jello. She had put two bananas in it to make it more special. She also made summer sausage sandwiches.

Soon it was time for the Braaten family to leave. The children didn't want to go so it was a struggle to round them all up. Some were in the barn playing with the kittens.

After a lot of laughing and goodbyes, the family drove off in their big Veeley.

"They certainly are a big, happy family," commented Carrie, wistfully. I wish we could have had more children, she thought to herself.

As if reading her thoughts, George said, "We are a happy family, too, don't you think?"

"Yes, and I thank God daily for our children."

Later that night in bed, she turned to George and said, "What if we had said no to taking Livvie. I can't imagine life without her. She's been such a blessing to us."

"She surely has been that," George agreed.

CHAPTER 25

After the 1929 crop was planted, George sat at the kitchen table working on his account books. He looked up at Freddie and said, "Son, I think that we can buy ourselves a new car this year."

"Whoopee!" hollered Freddie. "When can we get it?"

"We'll wait until maybe June or so. Then we'll see how the crops look," reasoned George.

"Oh, do you think we can really afford one?" asked Carrie, always the cautious one.

"Well, the one we have is getting old and needs repairs so often now that I think we'd be better ahead by investing in a new one. I was going to buy one last year, remember, but I bought the Moline combine instead."

"Can we just go and look at some cars, Pa?" asked Freddie. "Do you want to get a Ford again or what?"

"Well, we'll look around and see."

Livvie, who was now seven, came skipping into the kitchen. She liked to twirl around on the shiny, kitchen floor. Carrie loved it, too. It was so easy to keep clean and she liked the way it shone when just washed. She had helped pick it out and that was almost two years ago now, but she never tired of looking at it. It had a lot of red in it, which really brightened up the room. Shortly after it was laid, Carrie went to Larson's Store and picked out some red and white dotted-Swiss material and made curtains for the windows.

Carrie was busy making a chocolate cake, which was a Saturday ritual, it seemed. "I have a feeling that maybe the Nelsons will come over tomorrow. Then we can see their new, adopted baby."

"What does adopted mean?" asked Livvie.

Carrie looked over at George uneasily. Freddie looked at his parents. There had been some disagreement for some time about when to tell Livvie that she was adopted.

"Well, Livvie, that is when...ah...the baby's real mother can't keep her baby...so...ah...she thinks it best to give it to a family who will love it and care for it as if it was their own."

"Oh! I'm sure glad that I'm not adopted," said the child as she twirled some more around the room. She hugged her mother around the waist and then skipped outside.

Carrie was feeling weak in the knees and had to sit down. She looked at her husband in silent appeal. George ran his hand through his hair.

"When are you going to tell her?" Freddie asked his parents. He had always thought that she should have been told by now. "What if she finds out from someone else? Like from some of the kids at school?"

"I don't know," said Carrie, shaking her head. "When is a good time? It will be very hard on her when we tell her. We had thought we'd wait until she finishes high school and then tell her, but I don't know."

The next day, when the Nelsons did indeed come visiting, Livvie took one look at the baby and declared, "That baby doesn't look adopted!"

All the adults gasped and Carrie tried to shoo the girl away and changed the subject.

Later that night, when Livvie had gone to bed, Carrie and George discussed the matter again. They still decided that it would be best to wait until she was older.

Freddie graduated from Kindred High School in May. His parents were proud and relieved that he had stuck it out. He seemed to like school more this last year and even talked about going on to a business school in the fall. George had mixed feelings about this. He could really use him on the farm but he didn't want to stand in his way of doing something else.

Carrie received a call one afternoon telling her that Ole and Mathilde Braaten had just had another baby. This one, a boy, made a total of seven children now. Carrie couldn't wait to tell George about their friends.

"What did they name this one?" he asked, after she related the news to him.

"They named him Donald, but will be calling him Donnie. Boy, she sure has her hands full. She'll need two hired girls this summer!"

One morning in late June, George announced that they had waited long enough for a new car so he and Freddie took off for town to see what they could find. About noon they came home driving a new Ford and Carrie and Livvie had to hop in and they went for a ride.

George drove and he took them over by the Riverside school and then around to the Ulness place. Lena was home and Gilla was visiting with her little boy. After thirteen years of marriage, Gilla and Hank had finally had a baby. It had been quite an exciting event, Carrie recalled.

"I suppose he's about two years old now."

"Yes, in February," Gilla said proudly.

After showing off their new car there, they left, with Freddie at the wheel this time, and headed for home. "The dinner is probably burning in the oven," Carrie remarked.

That evening, Freddie was given permission to take the new vehicle. He wanted to drive over to see his friend, Oswald Swenson, who lived over by Barrie Church. They had graduated together.

"Freddie's a good driver and very responsible," George assured his wife.

"Yes, he surely has never given us any trouble, has he? And, George," she went on, "you have certainly been a good father to him."

"I've always felt like he was my very own."

That fall, after harvest was completed, Freddie and his friend, Oswald, both went to Fargo to attend a session at the Dakota Business College there. They stayed at a boarding house.

Livvie started back to school and was now in the second grade. A new teacher was hired and it turned out to be Beatrice Heglie, Carl Ulness' girlfriend. She was very good with all the children and Livvie just loved her.

"She's so nice to us, and so pretty, too," Livvie reported after only a few days.

Miss Heglie helped the children put on an elaborate Christmas program in the school. The parents all crowded in for it. The school board members had hauled planks to make a small stage and chairs were rounded up from various neighbors. Mrs. Iverson cooked coffee at her house and the men carried it over to the school for a delicious lunch afterwards.

"I think this was the best program ever!" declared Mr. Iverson. Carl was there, too, to see the program and he received a lot of teasing, being the teacher's boyfriend. He just smiled and didn't seem to mind.

Christmas was as merry as it could be in spite of the fact that the stock market had crashed in late October and the country's economy was in a panic. The people didn't really know just what to expect.

"We'll just have to wait and see what happens," George told Carrie.

Right after the first of the year, the members of the Gol congregation had a meeting to decide what to do about their church. It had been damaged in a bad windstorm a few years earlier in which it had been lifted off its foundation. It had been moved back in place but now it was deemed unsafe and it was voted on to build a new building on the same site.

George had stayed for that meeting and when he came home, he told Carrie all about it. "They're going to start tearing it down in the spring and they're getting the Brateng Brothers of Kindred to rebuild."

"How much will that cost, do you suppose?" asked Carrie.

"Well, they figure about $9,000, or so."

Carrie just shook her head. "Where will we have our church services then?"

"I guess Kindred Lutheran has said that we can use their church as long as it takes."

"That's certainly nice of them."

That spring was a wet one but George finally got his crop all planted. Freddie was home to help him.

In June, George and Carrie and Livvie went up to Davenport for Farmer's Day. They had missed the last couple years so it was fun to go again. They ran into Hilde and Mrs. Daud. Hilde had aged some, Carrie thought, but Mrs. Daud looked the same. She mentioned that Mr. Daud hadn't been feeling too well the past few months.

One day, shortly after the Fourth, George came into the house and slumped down in a chair.

"George! What is it?" Carrie cried. "Don't you feel good?"

"I heard some awful news from Ed today. He'd been to town early this morning."

"And what did you hear?"

"It's Mathilde. Mathilde Braaten," he said, and couldn't go on for awhile.

"What happened?" Carrie pressed. "She was pregnant again, I heard. Did something happen to the baby?"

"Mathilde died last night!" was all he could get out.

"What!" Carrie sank down into a chair, too. "Tell me what happened."

"Well, she and the family had spent the Fourth at the Ted Dawson Rodeo and shortly after returning home, she got violently ill. She was taken to the hospital in Fargo. They couldn't do anything for her. The baby, a girl, was born and died immediately and Mathilde died, too. They say it was possibly eclampsia, whatever that is," George said.

"That sometimes happens during a pregnancy," Carrie explained. She got up and started pacing and wringing her hands. "Oh, dear me, dear me, whatever are they going to do without her." She sat down again and put her head in her hands and wept for her dear friend.

That evening she and George drove over to the Braaten home. It would not be easy to walk into that home, Carrie knew, so she said a little prayer and braced herself.

There were many friends and relatives already there. The children were out of sight, perhaps upstairs. Ole was bereft and seemed in shock. After paying their condolences and staying awhile, the Johnsons left. They rode home in silence. Neither one could trust their voice to speak of what they felt. That night, in their bed, they clung to each other. Words were not needed. They knew what each other was feeling.

The funeral was held a few days later in Norman Lutheran Church. The sanctuary was filled with friends and family. Carrie wept frequently during the service, but especially when the family, all those young children, walked down the aisle behind the casket of their beloved mother.

"Another dear friend has left this world," Carrie commented on the way home. "Is there any end to the sorrows of this life?"

That evening, when she was talking to Lena on the telephone, Lena asked what would become of those dear children.

"I heard today that Ole's sister, Bella Braaten, has moved over there to help care for them. Also, Glenda, the oldest, has decided to quit school and stay home, too, and help."

"How old is she now then?" asked Lena.

"She's going to be sixteen. She would have been a junior in high school, come fall."

"Oh, that's too bad that she feels she has to quit school."

"Well, it's quite an undertaking to care for all those children."

In February of '31, Alice Ulness married Tollof Grant, a local farmer, and the Johnson family attended the wedding. This would be the first wedding in the new church. The congregation was very happy to be back in its own building again.

Up until this time, the services at the Gol Lutheran Church were all in Norwegian, but now they changed to mostly English. George, who was still on the church council, had pushed for this progressive change. A Sunday School was formed and Carrie was one of its first teachers.

Later that spring, Livvie reported that her teacher, Miss Heglie, would not be returning as she was getting married. Livvie felt very bad over this but was comforted by the fact that the Johnson family was invited to the wedding.

Carl Ulness and Beatrice Heglie were united in marriage at the Heglie farm home near Walcott on June 14, 1931. The ceremony was simple but lovely. The bride wore a yellow flowered chiffon dress and carried a bouquet of yellow tea roses and lavender sweet peas. Her attendants were her sister, Edna, and Carl's sister, Luella.

Little Bergliot Iverson, the youngest of the Iverson children, was the flower girl. Beatrice had boarded with the Iversons for the past two years, as they lived right next to the school, and had grown very close to the family. Buddy Hertsgaard, Hank and Gilla's son, was the ring bearer.

Before the service, Nelius Iverson sang "O Promise Me," and following the ceremony, Lorraine Ulness sang "I Love You Truly." A buffet supper was served to the bridal party and about forty guests. The couple left that same evening for Fargo where they would spend the first night. Lena mentioned that they were also going out to western North Dakota for a honeymoon trip.

On the way home, 9-year-old Livvie could talk of nothing except the wedding. She was so impressed with it. "When I get married, I want a wedding just like that," she told her parents.

"Don't you want it in the church?" asked her mother.

"Well, maybe. I'll think about it."

"You have lots of time to think about it, young lady," laughed her father.

"Well, Lena only has two children left now that aren't married yet-- Gladys and Luella," Carrie commented. Randolph had gotten married, too, the year before.

The day after the wedding, the community of Kindred was rocked with an unexpected and tragic incident. The banker at the Farmers and Merchants Bank was found early that morning, where he had hung himself behind the bank building. He had taken some rope and tied it to the fire escape ladder. His home was just kitty-corner across the street so his wife could see him when she looked out the window. She was heard to say, "Cut him down! Cut him down!" by some early-rising neighbors.

Everyone was shocked and the bank closed immediately and the books would certainly be examined in due course. Every time Carrie picked up the phone that day to make a call, she would hear her neighbors talking about it.

"People are certainly taking drastic measures nowadays, in these desperate economic times," said George that evening. "What will happen next, I wonder."

While the honeymooners were on their trip, Lena and her youngest daughter, Luella, were busy getting ready to move to Walcott and live in the apartment above Randolph's store. Carl and Beatrice were planning to live in Lena's house, the house that Carl grew up in.

"Oh, Lena, what will I ever do without you?" cried Carrie into the telephone the night before the move was to be made. "I'll hardly ever get to see you!"

"Yah, I'll surely miss you, too, Carrie," lamented Lena. "You've been a dear friend to me. You'll just have to come to Walcott often and see me."

When Carrie hung up the phone sometime later, she couldn't help the tears that began to fall. George noticed this and came and put his arm around her.

"I'm going to miss her so much," said Carrie into his shoulder. "She and I have been through a lot together."

"Well, she was a dear, older friend to you. Now maybe you can be a dear, older friend to Carl's wife."

"Yes, I guess I could, couldn't I?"

Later that month, George and Carrie attended the reunion of folks who had come to the area from Spring Grove. It was held at the Sons of Norway Park, which was near the Norman Church. There were several families from Kindred there, the Mullers, Anna Rustad, the Gubruds, to name a few and the Fredriksons from Davenport and some families from Hickson. It was fun for Carrie to get together with all these people from her home area. Some of them remembered her parents.

"When I see these people, it makes me rather lonesome for back home," said Carrie wistfully. "Maybe we can make a trip back there again sometime."

When Carl and Beatrice returned from their wedding trip, they got settled in their big house. Carrie and George drove over there one evening to welcome them back. Lena had left some of her furniture for the young couple. Beatrice had been saving her hard-earned teacher's salary, thinking she would buy furniture after they got married. As luck would have it, she had put all of it in the Christine Bank and when that town's only bank collapsed, as was happening to many banks, she lost all of her savings.

"I had about $300 in there," she lamented.

"Oh, that's too bad," Carrie told her. "It's a terrible thing that is happening to many people."

"I'm just glad I have a job," remarked Carl. He drove the Kindred Transfer Truck for Hans Herstad. He made many trips to Fargo and thereabouts.

Over cups of coffee and some cookies that Carrie had brought over, Carl told them of his surprise upon hearing about the banker in town.

"We spent the first night of our honeymoon in Fargo, as you probably knew, and the next morning when I went down into the hotel lobby, I glanced at the newspapers and the headline of the Fargo Forum was 'Kindred Banker Hangs Himself!' I bought the issue and brought it back up to the room to show Beatrice. We just couldn't get over it," he said, shaking his head, still in disbelief.

Late that fall, Carrie received a postcard from Lena. She said she was lonesome for her home but was getting along all right. Luella was working in Randolph's store. Randolph and Nora had just had a baby girl. They named her Louise. Lena said that she and Luella were planning to come and see Carl and Beatrice soon, before winter set in, so she would call Carrie from there.

In the spring, as soon as the roads dried up, the Watkins man could be expected. Carrie had her list ready for him. So, she wasn't surprised when Freddie came in one afternoon and said that he'd seen the peddler on the road in the neighborhood.

Along about lunchtime, she heard his vehicle come into the yard. She greeted him at the door and invited him in.

"How about a cup of coffee?" she asked him. It was a new man this year.

"No, no, thank you," he answered. "I just had a cup over at the Graff's."

"I'll find my list here, then," said Carrie. "There are several things I need."

While she was looking for it, Livvie came into the room and sat down and watched the old man take out some of his new wares. Carrie noticed that he kept staring at her. He asked her age and even when her birthday was.

"You remind me of someone I know," Carrie heard him tell the girl. Carrie felt a shiver of apprehension. What exactly did he mean, she wondered.

Before he left, she had purchased a bottle of vanilla, some spices, orange and grape nectar and some fly spray. He gave Livvie a long look again before he went out the door.

"Good day to you, Mrs. Johnson, and thank you very much. See you next month or so."

Later that night, Carrie told George about the man and how interested he seemed to be in Livvie. "He even asked when her birthday was."

"Did she tell him?" asked George.

"I called to her to come into the pantry before she could answer. Do you suppose that he knows the...real mother...and thinks that Livvie looks like her?"

"Did he say where he was from?"

"I asked him and he said he was from the Lisbon area."

"Well, maybe this was all a coincidence, and you're making too much of it. Maybe he just thought she was a pretty little girl and she reminded him of someone. You know how that goes." George was trying to reassure his wife so she wouldn't worry needlessly.

"You know, George, I've never told you this, but sometimes when I look at Livvie, I, too, think she reminds me of someone." They were both silent for awhile. "Do you suppose the mother is someone we know of or have seen before?"

In July, the Johnsons attended an open-air concert in Kindred. There was an improvised bandstand set up on the main street. Also, a Dr. Darrow from Fargo dazzled the audience with his sleight of hand tricks.

Livvie was interested in seeing all the band instruments played by the members of the Community Band. She said she would like to play one someday, perhaps the flute.

"Well, we'll see," said her father. "Maybe when you get into High School."

"I'd like her to take piano lessons, too. Do you think we could ever afford a piano?" Carrie asked her husband on the way home that evening.

"We'll see. Maybe we could find a good used one."

"Oh, that would be fun to take piano lessons," cried Livvie excitedly.

"I see here," George said, as he was reading the Kindred Tribune one evening, "that they approved the work on Highway #46. It's to be graded and graveled, starting west of here a few miles. Work will begin this summer yet." Putting the paper down, he said, "That will sure be nice to get a better road out here. They're going to do it right up to the Kindred Highway."

"My, that will be nice, won't it?" Carrie agreed.

In August, right before harvest, George suggested that they go over to Norman Church's ice cream social. It was held outdoors in the church park. It was a beautiful evening and the food was good, as always.

"Yah, these church ladies sure can cook, can't they?" remarked an acquaintance, sitting by them at one of the long tables that had been set up outdoors.

"Oh, there's Ole Braaten over there, just coming," remarked Carrie. "He's got several of the youngest children along." As he got closer, they hailed him and told him to come and sit by them.

"How are you getting along then?" Carrie asked Ole as he came and sat by them. He was carrying a plate for the youngest, Donnie, and the older ones could help themselves.

"Well, you know, it's been hard," he said sadly.

They all attended a program in the church later and on the way home, Carrie remarked to George, "I thought Ole looked awfully sad and lonely, didn't you?"

"Yah, I was thinking the same thing. It's only been two years now, hasn't it, since Mathilde died?"

Carrie had joined a Kindred homemaker's club and she was elated one evening when a friend called to tell her that their exhibit had won first prize at the Fair in Fargo. Their booth showed dolls dressed as a bride and groom and it had a miniature garden. They also had a pantry with home-canned vegetables and a miniature yard with chickens. They would be getting $25 for their efforts, her friend said.

"I've always been glad that I joined that club," Carrie told George later. "I've met so many nice women."

"I'm very proud of the way you've become so active in everything around here, in the church and community," he told her.

Beatrice Ulness called Carrie one afternoon in late October. She said that there was a new baby over at their neighbor's, Chris and Lillian Erickson. They had a little boy this time. "That makes four boys and two girls now."

"And how is Lillian doing?" asked Carrie. "I've been a little concerned about her. She told me she thought she was too old to be having another baby."

"Well, I was over to see her and she and the baby are doing fine," said Beatrice. "They named him Christian Marcellus."

"Oh, that's quite a long name, isn't it?"

"They're going to call him Marcellus."

She told George about the conversation later that afternoon. "See, I told you that you and Beatrice would become good telephone friends!" he teased.

"She also said that Carl's sister, Gladys, has found a fellow in Wyoming and is planning to get married next summer."

"Anything else?"

"I guess Luella has found a young man in Walcott. His name is Dahl. I think his first name is Phillip."

"What would you ladies do without the telephone?" he joked.

"Well, I think you're just as interested in what I find out every day!" she retorted.

He just chuckled and buried his head in the newspaper.

CHAPTER 26

The spring of '33 began on a promising note. There was just enough rainfall for a good start for the crops. George decided to haul the rest of his last year's crop of wheat to the elevator.

"I hope I can get more for it than last year. It was 19 cents a bushel the last time I sold some."

After George left the house, she told Livvie to run out and catch her father before he left for town. "Tell him to remember to pick up a new battery for the radio."

"All right, Ma, I'll tell him," said the young girl. "Then we can listen to Fibber McGee and Molly tomorrow night."

"And the Lux Radio Theater is on, too," Carrie reminded her.

A couple hours later, George came home from town and walked into the house, shaking his head. "The price wasn't what I'd hoped for but I felt I had to sell anyway," he told Carrie. He sampled a cookie from the cooling rack. "I sure hope that this year is better. It can't get much worse, can it?"

The next evening, the new battery was put into the big Atwood Kent radio and the three of them gathered around for an evening of pleasant listening. Later, George and Carrie tuned into President Roosevelt's "Fireside Chats," as they were called. Livvie lost interest then and she played quietly nearby with her paper dolls.

Franklin Roosevelt had just taken office a few weeks earlier after he soundly defeated Hoover. He had promised a "New Deal" to lead America out of the Depression. The country was in tough shape. Thousands of workers were unemployed; there were bread lines and many people had lost their homes.

Americans of all walks of life hung on his every word as they huddled around their radios, listening to their new president. Could he lead them out of the worst depression in the country's history?

Two weeks earlier, the President had declared a "bank holiday" where he closed all banks in the country. There had been a "run" on some banks a week before that and a panic situation had set in. Every bank would now have to be examined and those that were in good financial shape would be allowed to reopen.

"I never heard that the Kindred Bank had to close, did you?" asked Carrie.

"We were just talking about that in town today. I guess the reason that it didn't close was that it never received the telegram informing them of the President's order."

"My, isn't that something!" Carrie commented. "We were lucky here."

"Well, I have it on good authority that the Kindred Bank has been run exceptionally well and is on good financial ground."

One evening in late June, shortly before ten o'clock, the telephone started ringing and it kept up a steady, long ring. This meant that there was an emergency and everyone was to pick up the receiver. Carrie reached it first. When she put it to her ear, she heard the news that a church was on fire.

"George, there's some church on fire. Do you suppose it's ours?"

George grabbed the receiver and listened for more details. Finally he butted in and asked what was going on. He was told that the Norman Lutheran Church east of Kindred had been struck by lightening a short time ago and was on fire.

He hung up and related what he had heard to Carrie. He went into the bedroom and put on his pants and a shirt and said that he was thinking he would drive over there.

Freddie heard the commotion and came downstairs. After hearing about the fire, he said that he would go with George. The men left a short time later.

"Be careful now!" Carrie called after them. She never could forget that other fire many years ago that took the life of Fred so suddenly. Sitting down to wait, she turned on the radio and took out her handwork.

George and Freddie returned home about two o'clock in the morning. They found Carrie asleep in her chair. She awoke with a start. "Oh, you're finally home. Uff da, but you smell smoke!"

"Well, the church is no more," announced George. "It took only about two hours for it to go."

"It's a good thing we went to help, though," said Freddie. "There were a lot of men there, both from the congregation and many from town, too."

"We helped carry things out as fast as we could," said George, washing his hands and face at the kitchen sink. When he wiped himself on a nearby towel, he left black smudges from all the soot.

"We got all the pews out, and the chairs and tables and even the piano," said Freddie.

"Yah, and we even were able to save the pulpit and some of the windows."

"Wasn't it dangerous to be in there?" Carrie asked, hardly believing that they could have possibly saved all that.

"Well, it was burning real slow for quite some time. The chemical engines came out from Kindred but the steeple was too high and they couldn't get enough pressure to get the water on the fire."

"When the flames reached the belfry, then things started to get exciting!" exclaimed Freddie.

"Yah, Carl Simensen and Sophus Ottis had quite a close call. They had just finished taking a door down, to try and save it, and the huge bell, weighing about two tons, came crashing down only a few feet away from them!"

"That's when everyone was ordered to get away from the building. It didn't take long after that for the whole structure to go."

"It must be terrible to stand and watch as your house of worship goes up in flames," Carrie remarked.

"There were tears on the faces of many a grown man, I tell you!" George said, shaking his head as he recalled it.

"I wonder what they will do now?" Carrie wondered.

"Well, I'm sure they will make some decisions in the next few days."

"Daddy, what are we going to do for the Fourth of July?" Livvie asked a few days prior to the holiday.

"I was thinking that maybe we should drive over to Leonard to their celebration. What do you think about that, Carrie?" George asked his wife.

"That sounds like a great idea." She turned to her son. "Freddie, what are you going to do that day?"

"Maybe Oswald and I will think of something. We'll probably find some dance to go to in the evening.

The morning of the Fourth, George, Carrie and Livvie headed for Leonard. There was road construction the first few miles.

"Won't it be nice when this road gets all done," commented George, maneuvering around the gravel piles on the road. "Just a few more miles left and then it will be finished all the way to Kindred."

Freddie had been working with the road construction crew since early spring, and so had his friend, Oswald. The pay wasn't too great and the work was hard but Freddie was able to live at home. They were just happy to have found jobs in these tough times.

The parade had already started when George pulled into town and they had to drive for some time to find a parking space. They walked toward the downtown area and stood and watched as the parade went around for a second time. They purchased their dinner at a food stand and then George announced that he wanted to go and watch the tractor pull.

"Livvie and I will stay here. We'll meet you later," Carrie told him.

Carrie was looking for a bench so she could sit down awhile when she spotted a familiar figure coming toward her. She stopped in her tracks. It was the mystery lady! The woman looked at Carrie and then at Livvie. Carrie didn't know quite what to do. She was with a younger woman and when they got closer, Carrie could see that the other woman looked much like Livvie.

Carrie's heart started to beat heavily in her chest. She fumbled in her purse for a nickel and told Livvie to go and stand in line for an ice cream cone. When she looked up again, the older woman was right in front of her but the younger woman was gone.

Carrie couldn't avoid the woman. She sat down on a nearby bench and tried to get a hold of herself. The woman came and sat down beside her.

"So that's the child," she uttered to Carrie.

"Yes, that's her. Was that....the mother...with you?" Carrie hardly dared to ask.

The woman hesitated for a few moments and finally said, "Yes, that's the child's mother."

"Does she know that Livvie is here?"

"Oh, no! I sent her on an errand for me. I felt I needed to talk with you."

Carrie was sweating profusely and she felt weak. She was glad she had found a place to sit just then.

"How has it been going for you....and the child?" The woman asked kindly, looking at Carrie intently.

"Very well. She's a delightful child."

"And a very beautiful one."

"She looks very much like...her mother...don't you think?" Carrie asked.

"Yes, I believe she does."

Just then Livvie returned and stood in front of her mother, licking her ice cream. The woman looked closely at the child who was standing before her and Carrie could see tears welling in her eyes.

Carrie was getting very nervous, wondering when the younger woman would be returning.

"I...we... really should be going, I think," Carrie stammered.

"Mama, can I go and be with Maggie and Ruthie for awhile? They're just over there," Livvie said, wondering why her mother was acting so strange.

"I was thinking that you should go and find your father. I...don't...feel very well."

"Oh, Mama, we just got here. I want to be with my friends. Do you really feel sick?"

"Well, you go then, and I'll...just sit here for awhile."

"I'm sorry if this situation has made you upset. Have you told the child anything yet?"

"No, she doesn't know that she is adopted. We thought we'd wait until she's older to tell her. We really don't know if that's the right decision or not."

"Well, my..." she started to say. "I might as well tell you that the young woman who was with me is my niece. I guess that's all I can tell you now." She lowered her voice even more. "She never quite got over the fact that she was forced to give up her child, but she is engaged to be married now so I think that will help some."

"What if she sees Livvie. Will she be suspicious? I mean, won't she notice that the child looks like her?" Carrie looked around to see where

Livvie was.

"Oh, no, I don't think so. A person is always the last one to think that someone looks like them. I could tell right away, but then that's because I recognized you."

"Are you ever going to tell the...ah...mother...that you know where her child is?" asked Carrie.

"No, I won't do that. Her parents are so afraid what people will think if they know about what happened. When the child gets older," the woman went on, "and you tell her that she isn't yours, she will want to perhaps find out about her real mother."

"Yes, I've thought of that. What shall we tell her?"

The woman took a piece of paper from her handbag and wrote something on it. She handed it to Carrie. "Here, this is my telephone number but I won't tell you my name yet. When the child wants to know about her...real mother...you give me a call and we'll arrange something. I think my niece would want to know about her, even if the grandparents may not."

Carrie hesitated before she could bring herself to take the piece of paper. On it was information that would change Livvie's whole world, once she knew. She finally reached out for it and put it quickly in her purse.

The young woman, Livvie's real mother, was coming towards them now. Carrie was riveted to the spot. She wanted to flee but she just had to have a closer look at the woman who had borne her child.

"Here, Auntie. Here's your umbrella," she said, panting. "Were you getting too hot in the sun?"

The older woman rose and quickly asked Carrie, "What did you name the child?"

"Her name is...Livvie." Carrie could hardly get the words out. Her mouth was dry and her throat was tightening up.

The older woman nodded to Carrie as she prepared to leave. Carrie heard the younger woman ask her aunt who she had been visiting with. I wonder what she answered her, Carrie mused to herself. She was in a very agitated state and wished Livvie would come back so they could go and look for George. She just wanted to get to the car and go home. And she didn't want Livvie to come face to face with the two women anytime that day.

When George found her sometime later, he thought she looked flushed and upset. "What's the matter?" he asked his wife as he sat down beside her.

"I can't even talk about it yet. I wish we could go home but I suppose Livvie would be terribly disappointed. She found some of her friends from school and I don't know where they've gone." She started to tremble and George took her hand.

"What happened when I was gone?" he asked, growing more concerned by the minute.

"The mystery woman. She's here!" Carrie managed to say.

George looked at her. "And? Did you talk to her?"

She nodded her head. "And that's not all. Livvie's...real mother was with her."

George looked aghast. "What did she say? What did Livvie do?"

"I sent her off for some ice cream. The mystery woman came and sat down here by me. She had sent the younger woman to get something for her so she could talk to me."

Carrie found her hankie and started fanning herself. George thought that he needed to get his wife home. Just then Livvie and her friends came walking by.

"Livvie, I think that we need to get your mother home. She's not...ah...feeling well."

"Ohhh," groaned all three girls. "Does she have to go?" asked Maggie. "Could she stay and ride home with us, do you suppose?"

"I don't want to miss the fireworks!" wailed Livvie.

George looked at Carrie as he answered. "Well, I suppose she could do that if it's all right with your parents."

"I'll run and ask my mother. I know where she is."

Before anyone could say anything, the young girl had taken off toward the lemonade stand. About a minute later, she came running back, saying that that would be all right with her parents.

The girls all jumped up and down in their delight. "Well, you be a good girl then, Livvie, and we'll see you later," said George, as he began ushering Carrie in the general direction of their car.

Carrie was emotionally drained and very quiet on the way home. When she got into the house, she changed her clothes and lay down on the sofa. George made a pot of coffee and Carrie sat up again when he brought her a cup.

"Are you going to be all right now?" George asked, concern written on his face.

"I guess so. It was just such a shock! And I worried that maybe Livvie would find out.....before we want her to."

"Yah, this thing bothers me, too," he said, rising and running his hand through his hair. "When we do finally tell her that she's adopted, do you think she will want to get to know her.....real mother?"

"I don't know. I guess if it was me, I would be curious about her." Carrie rose now, too. "I really don't know what to expect. I'm dreading that time when we have to tell her."

A couple days later, Carrie had just finished wiping up the kitchen floor and she said to Livvie, "Uff da, with this wind blowing the dust around almost every day, it sure is hard to keep things clean!"

She glanced out the window just then and saw a car drive up and stop at the end of the sidewalk. She saw that there were two women in the vehicle and her heart began to beat fast for a few minutes.

"Oh, its Lena and Gladys," she said aloud, relief flooding over her. She quickly poured out the wash water and hung the rag up behind the pantry door. Taking her apron off, she went to open the screen door.

"Oh, Lena, it's so good to see you! And you, too, Gladys. My, what a pleasant surprise!" she said as they came into the kitchen. "I should have had you come in the front door. I just washed this floor. Be careful, it might still be slippery."

She ushered them into the parlor and offered them a seat. "What brings you by today? Have you been visiting over at Carl's?"

"Yah, we came over this morning for a short visit and thought we'd stop by here before we head back to Walcott," explained Lena. "Gladys has been here about a week now and wanted to see Carl and Beatrice."

"I hear you are getting married later this summer," Carrie commented to Gladys.

"Yes, in late August. I've come home to get all my things and head back to Wyoming for the wedding. Jesse, my fiancé, couldn't get enough time off to come here to be married."

"My, you'll be living so far away. You must really like it out West," Carrie remarked.

"It's all right. I liked my teaching job in Medicine Bow. Then I met Jesse. He's an oil driller for a company there."

Carrie made and served some coffee and cookies to the two women and they continued catching up on things.

"I sure miss you, Lena," Carrie told her. "How are you and Luella doing in Walcott?"

"I miss my home here but I guess we're doing all right. Luella is still helping Randolph at the store."

"Beatrice told me last week that Carl is going to be working for the Farmers Union Oil Company now," remarked Carrie.

"Yah, he thinks that will be a good job. That will be nice, with the baby coming and all."

"How is Beatrice feeling?" asked Carrie.

"She's feeling fine. She's due the last of the month so it could be anytime now," Lena answered.

"Will you be working after you get married, Gladys?" Carrie asked.

"Well, I don't think they want me once I get married. You know how they feel about married teachers!"

"Goodness! When are they going to get over that old-fashioned idea!" exclaimed Carrie.

The women laughed at this but shook their heads, knowing that it might be a while yet.

"When we were over at Carl's, Lillian Erickson came by and said that she wants to put on a bridal shower for Gladys, being none of us can make it out to the wedding. It's going to be the middle of August. You'll be getting an invitation," Lena told Carrie.

"Oh, that will be fun, won't it?" Carrie enthused.

Carrie walked the two women out to their car a short while later.

"Isn't this constant dust getting to be just awful?" Lena commented.

"It sure is. I wonder how long before we get a good rain. We've only seen a few drops here in the past three months!" Carrie informed them.

"Well, we'll see you at the shower, then," Lena said as she got into the car.

"I'm so tickled that you stopped by and I look forward to the shower. I miss you so much, Lena. Our little visits on the telephone, and all," she laughed.

She almost felt a tear forming as she watched the car leave the yard but she collected herself and headed for the garden to check on things there.

"Oh, my, its too dry to even grow a decent garden," she said aloud, sighing.

On the very last day of July, Carl called to tell them the news that Beatrice had delivered a baby boy the night before. Dr. Jelstrup had been called and had made it just in time.

"What are you naming him?" asked Carrie, excited about the blessed event.

"Donald Elroy," answered Carl, proudly. "He's a fine-looking little fellow."

"I can't wait to see him. I'll be over in a day of two with some chicken soup or something. Give Beatrice our congratulations."

When Carrie hung up the telephone, she ran outside to tell the news to George.

"Well, I suppose Carl will be busy passing out cigars now for awhile!"

"He'll probably take them with him when he delivers gas and fuel oil all over the country!"

Later that day, the Jewel Tea man stopped by. Carrie liked to buy things from him because then she earned points and she could get some pretty dishes and bowls when she had enough saved.

"So, Mrs. Johnson," he said, "how many points do you have saved up now then?"

"I'll get them and we'll see. Maybe I have enough for something free!"

After laying out her coupons and counting up the points, it was decided that if she bought two tins of coffee, she would be able to get a nice-sized bowl. Carrie purchased and paid for the coffee and was excited when the salesman returned from his car with a bowl for her. After he left, she washed it up and put it on the counter and admired it. I'll serve the salad in it tonight for supper, she thought.

"Have a good time tonight, dear," George called after Carrie and Livvie as they left the house to attend the bridal shower for Gladys Ulness. It was to be held at the home of Lillian Erickson, a close neighbor to the Ulness home. Carrie drove the car herself and stopped by to see if Beatrice had decided to go or not. It was only about two weeks since her baby, Donnie, was born.

"I'm going to try and go for a little while," Beatrice told Carrie when she came in the back door. "I'm pretty tired but Donnie is sleeping now and I think Carl can handle things until he wakes up hungry!"

She was ready in a few minutes and the three of them drove the short distance over to the Erickson's. There were many cars in the yard and ladies were streaming into the house.

"Oh, won't this be fun! I surely didn't want to miss it entirely," exclaimed Beatrice.

There was a short program and then a toy wagon that had been fixed up to look like an old covered wagon was wheeled in by some of the young girls, Livvie included. It was loaded with all the shower gifts that the ladies had brought. Everyone laughed when they saw it.

"We thought that being you were moving 'out West,' this would be a fitting thing to put all your gifts in!" exclaimed Lillian.

"How clever!" someone exclaimed and the others agreed.

It took quite sometime for the bride-to-be to open all the gifts, as there were about 70 ladies in attendance. Beatrice had walked home after staying for almost two hours. It was almost midnight when a delicious lunch was served by the hostesses and everyone was tired but reluctant to go home. It had been such an enjoyable evening for the women and a rare night out for many of them.

Gladys would be packing her things the next day and leaving by train for Wyoming. The small wedding would take place a few days after she arrived there. Even Lena would not be attending and she felt bad about that but it was just too far away.

George and Freddie finished the harvest earlier than usual. There wasn't much to combine. It had been too dry again. They hauled most of the wheat to town and sold it at a very depressed price.

"We need the cash so I almost had to sell it," remarked George that evening. Carrie took a good look at her husband. He seemed a little "down," she thought. He buried his face in the local newspaper for a time and then looked up.

"Shall we take in the doings at the Sons of Norway park this weekend then?" he asked Carrie.

"It sounds like it would be fun," Carrie answered.

"Yah, we need some fun after that depressing harvest," he said wryly.

On Saturday morning, shortly before noon, George, Carrie and Livvie headed for the park. There were literally hundreds of cars going in the same direction.

"Where are all these cars going to park?" Carrie wondered aloud.

There were men near the entrance of the park directing traffic. Some had to park near the site of the Norman Church, which recently had burned down. One could see that rebuilding of the church had already begun.

The event at the park was put on by the Kindred Commercial Club to celebrate the completion of the Highway 46 project, the upgrading and graveling which extended west past Leonard and ended at the Kindred Highway junction.

There was a kittenball game in the afternoon between Kindred and Walcott and a tug-of-war between the married men and the single men. The single men won. Freddie had taken part in this event.

In the evening, there was a musical program and a speaker. Music was provided by the Kindred band as well as the Sheldon and Enderlin bands. Refreshments were sold at various stands throughout the day.

"That was a fun day," exclaimed Carrie on the way home. "I ran into so many women I know but never seem to see very much anymore."

"I was talking to Mr. Trom and he estimated that there were about 1000 people there! Just think of that!"

"Oh, my! That's hard to believe."

Livvie was bouncing around in the back seat in her excitement. "I liked the games best," she said. "Ruthie and I ran in the sack race and almost won except for that dumb Bertram who tripped us!"

"Don't call anybody dumb, Livvie," Carrie mildly scolded her daughter.

"I think Freddie has a girlfriend," she tattled.

"And who might that be?" asked Carrie, smiling over at George.

"That snooty Larson girl!" replied Livvie. "I hope he doesn't marry her!"

"Well, I'm sure he hasn't found the one that he wants to marry yet. He's still too young for that," Carrie told her daughter.

Later that evening, in the privacy of their room, Carrie commented to George that she felt that their children were growing up too fast.

"Freddie could possibly be getting married in the next few years and Livvie is no longer a little girl anymore," she lamented. "Where has the time gone?"

"Well, now, my dear," George soothed his wife, "don't worry about that. Livvie is only eleven and I don't think Freddie will be getting married any time soon, even though he is almost twenty-two."

"I wish they could stay little for a long time." And, she thought to herself, I wish that I could have had more children. A few minutes later, when she was in bed, she turned to God in prayer and asked him to forgive her for not being satisfied with what she had. She thanked the Lord for their many blessings. She fell asleep counting all of them.

CHAPTER 27

One fine September morning, as Carrie was out in the backyard hanging up clothes, she heard the telephone ring. Livvie will get it, she told herself, but she hurried anyway to hang up the last item.

"Ma, telephone!" cried her daughter. "The operator says the call is long distance! Hurry!"

Carrie quickened her steps and her heart started beating faster. Has something happened? she wondered.

"I hope it isn't bad news," she said to Livvie as she came in the door.

She picked up the receiver with dread and heard Hilde's voice on the other end. Livvie watched her mother's face intently. Carrie motioned for her daughter to bring her a chair.

"Oh, no! How terrible!" she said several times. After the short conversation, she handed the receiver to Livvie for her to hang up.

"What's the matter, Mama?" she asked

"It's Mr. Daud. He died last night of a heart attack. I just can't believe it." Carrie instructed Livvie to go and get her father from the barn.

When George entered the house, he came to Carrie and took her hands in his. "What happened?"

"Mr. Daud died last night," she repeated. "A heart attack, the doctor said. Oh, I feel so bad about that." She started to sob. "He was such a wonderful man and will be missed by so many. Whatever will Mrs. Daud do now?"

Hilde called back later that evening, telling Carrie when the funeral would be.

"The funeral is Friday at the Canaan Moravian Church," Carrie told George after hanging up. "I sure would like to go."

"Well, we can do that," he said. "I know you certainly want to be there."

On Friday, shortly after noon, George and Carrie set out for Davenport. They were going to stop and pick up Amund as he had called, too, saying he would go with them.

"That certainly is a beautiful church," George remarked as they drew near the huge sandblasted red-brick structure. "I've never been by here before."

"This new church was built in about 1914, I think," Amund said.

"I was only in the old one when I worked on the farm," Carrie related. "I went with the Dauds a couple of times."

"I understand that Mr. Daud donated a good sum of money to help build this present building," Amund mentioned.

"Well, I surely could believe that!" exclaimed Carrie. "He was so generous and I know that they liked coming here."

The funeral service was well attended. In fact, the church was full to overflowing. Mr. Daud was liked and well respected far and wide. The Dauds' two sons were there as well as Eunice and her family. Carrie hadn't seen any of them for quite some years now.

The burial was in the cemetery right on the church grounds. She explained to George that the men and women are buried on separate sides and the children have their own section. "Families don't have their own plots, either," she continued. "When you die, you are laid in the next space available. No one is more important than anyone else. And see how the tombstones all are lying flat."

"It's very impressive," George remarked, looking around with interest.

After the casket was lowered into the ground, Carrie went up to the family. She embraced Mrs. Daud, as the older woman had done to her on several occasions. Mrs. Daud had her emotions in check and she thanked Carrie for coming. Hilde, however, sobbed into Carrie's shoulder and when Carrie stood back to look at her dear friend, she saw that the woman had truly aged and looked very stricken.

On the way home, Carrie remarked to George and Amund that she supposed that Hilde was really wondering what would happen to her now if Mrs. Daud should move. "The Dauds were her only real family, you know. Where would she go and what would she do?"

Several nights later, Carrie, unable to sleep, got up and went to the kitchen. "I'll have a nice cup of warm milk," she said aloud. She looked at the clock on the wall. It was almost midnight. As she was sitting and drinking the warm liquid, she heard Freddie come in the yard.

A few minutes later, he came into the house and was surprised to see his mother sitting there. "I saw a light on and was wondering who was up at this hour. Is anything wrong?"

As he came close to Carrie, she could smell liquor on his breath.

"Freddie, have you been drinking?"

He removed his hat and sat down opposite her. "I had a drink or two at the pool hall with the boys," he admitted.

"I wish we still had prohibition," Carrie said emphatically. The prohibition amendment had recently been repealed.

"Oh, Ma, a few drinks don't hurt anyone!"

"Maybe not, but it leads to excessive drinking in some cases. Freddie," she continued, taking his hand, "I don't want you to ever be one of these men who become drunkards and who hang around saloons and gamble and things like that."

"I won't do that, Ma," Freddie said patiently. "I just like a drink now and then. I won't let it become a habit." When she continued to hold his hand, he added, "I promise."

"You were always such a good boy and a real comfort to me when your father died. And now, you've grown into such a fine young man. I want so much for you." Her eyes pleaded with him and he could see tears forming. He patted her hand and leaned over and gave his mother a kiss on the cheek.

"Oh, I almost forgot!" Carrie said, jumping up. "A letter came for you today. It's from South Dakota, the postmark says."

Freddie took the letter and turned it over a few times before opening it. "Maybe it's from Grandpa Shutz." His grandfather had kept in touch with his grandson over the years and Freddie had driven down to Wilmot about a year and a half ago to see the old gentleman. After Mr. Shutz had left Davenport so many years ago, he had gone to work in a railroad depot in Wilmot, South Dakota, and had eventually remarried. He wrote to Carrie and Freddie on occasion.

Freddie slit open the letter and began to scan it. "It's from my aunt. It says that Grandpa passed away a few days ago." Here Freddie, with tears beginning to form in his eyes, looked up at his mother. "Oh, I knew that I should have gone down there again. I kept putting it off!"

"Well, just be glad that you did go down there when you did. He got to see you as a grown man and I'm sure that meant the world to him. He was such a kind man and so good to me," Carrie stated. When she took a good, hard look at her son, sitting across from her, she realized that he probably looked more like his grandfather than his real father.

Freddie turned back to the letter. "It says that the funeral is Thursday. That was yesterday!" He stood up. "I should have been there," he almost shouted.

"I know that you would have liked to have been there, had you known sooner, but you can't do anything about that now," Carrie tried to soothe her son. "Why don't you sit down and write a letter to the family tomorrow."

"Yah, I must do that. I think I'll go to bed now." He sounded weary. Carrie came up to him and gave him a hug. "I hope you can sleep now, after hearing this. I'll wake you for church in the morning. It's early services tomorrow."

Sunday afternoon, there was to be a baseball tournament down at Nels Jordheim's pasture, west of Walcott. Four teams would be participating: Walcott, Riverside, Barrie and Viking. Freddie was going to be playing on the Barrie Township team.

"Do you want to go down there for the games?" George asked Carrie on the way home from church.

"No, I think Livvie and I will go over to Carl and Beatrice's. Lena and Luella are planning to be there this afternoon."

"Well, maybe Carl would like to go with me to the games and then we can stop by there when we get home."

"We'll call over there and talk to him," Carrie suggested.

As it turned out, Carl came over and picked up George and they headed south to the Jordheim place. Carrie and Livvie drove over to the Ulness home about mid-afternoon. Beatrice was just ready to serve coffee to the women. Lillian Erickson had stopped over, too. She had one-year old Marc along with her and her two young daughters, Judith and Dorcas.

Livvie and the two Erickson girls ran back to the Erickson farm to play in their playhouse, which had been built for them by their grandfather. Livvie thought this was just the greatest thing. The little house had a porch on the front and flowers growing out of window boxes. Whenever she came home from playing there, she always asked her daddy to build her one just like it.

"If I build you one, then it wouldn't be so special when you go over to play in theirs!" he always answered by way of stalling. Livvie would get very frustrated with his answer.

It was late afternoon by the time George and Carl returned from the baseball games. When they walked up to the front door of the Ulness home, they could hear gales of laughter coming from the house. They looked at each other, wondering what they would be getting into.

The laughter subsided somewhat when they spotted the two men in the doorway of the parlor. "Do we dare to come in here? It sounded like a bunch of hens cackling from out there!" remarked Carl.

"Oh, Lena, you must tell the men what you just were telling us," said Carrie, wiping tears from her eyes from laughing so hard.

"You tell them, Luella," said Lena. George and Carl found chairs and were all ears.

"Well, we just heard about something that happened to Gladys and Jesse on their honeymoon. Actually, they didn't take a honeymoon right away because Jesse couldn't take time off from his job so they decided to take an extra day or so over the long Labor Day weekend to go to Texas to visit his mother. Gladys hadn't met her yet.

"Well, anyway," continued Luella, warming up to her subject, "they took off late on a Thursday after work and drove like crazy to get as far as possible. Jesse was a notoriously fast driver and their car looked very much like the one being driven by Clyde Barrow, the gangster and his girlfriend, Bonnie. You remember reading about them lately, don't you?" she looked at each of the men and they both nodded.

"Their fast driving with only quick stops for gas must have caught the attention of someone who tipped off the police that they were the suspected gangsters. Jesse was dressed very nicely, as always, and Gladys, a tall, good-looking blonde, resembled Bonnie, the gang moll."

The men were sitting forward in their seats, waiting in anticipation. "They didn't stop until late the next day, after driving all night. It was in a small town in northern Texas. They decided to stop at a motel and clean up a bit and then drive some more to get to the town where Jesse's mother lived."

Luella stopped to catch her breath. The women enjoyed hearing the tale all over again. "Jesse told the motel clerk that they wanted a room for only an hour. You can imagine what he was thinking about this time! He gave them the key and when they were out of sight, he must have called the police, because he, too, thought he was dealing with the famous gangsters here."

"Then what happened?" asked Carl, impatient for the ending.

"I'm getting to that," said his sister. "When they came out of their room, all showered and cleaned up, they were walking to their car when they noticed it was surrounded by a number of men in suits. Jesse walked up to one of them and asked, 'Are we having a church meetin' here?'" The women all laughed again at this.

"Two of the men came up to Jesse and acted like they were going to grab his arms. He backed away and demanded to know what was going on. They asked him his name and he answered, 'who wants to know?' One of the men told him that he better show some identification right away or he would be in deep trouble. Gladys told Jesse to answer the man. She was mighty scared by now. Jesse took out his wallet and a couple of the men scrutinized it. 'Can you prove that you really are this Jesse King?' they ask him. 'Well, it says right there, as plain as day, that that's me. This is my wife, Gladys.'"

"And then what?" Carl asked, just imaging the scene.

"The men in suits didn't like his smart answers but they asked if there was someone they could call to verify his identification. He gave them the name of his boss and they went into the motel to place a call. They took Jesse with them. After about an hour, they were finally satisfied that he was who he said he was. He asked for an apology to him and his wife which they grudgingly gave and then they were on their way once again."

Everyone had a good laugh over this incident.

"Tell them the rest, Luella," said Lillian.

"Well, the funny part about this is that Gladys didn't want any of us back home here to hear about the incident so she wasn't going to tell us, but the Minneapolis newspaper got wind of it and printed a story about it. Someone who used to live around here and knew the Ulness family, read it and sent the article back to his family here and they, in turn, sent it on to Lena in Walcott."

"Oh, no!" said Carl, laughing even harder this time. "Does Gladys know that we know?"

"Yah, I called her the other night and asked her about her trip to Texas and asked if anything unusual had happened," said Lena. "She figured then that we had heard about it but couldn't understand who would have told us. She was still pretty upset about it but said that maybe in a few years they would be able to laugh about it all."

"Well, that's one trip they'll never forget!" commented Carrie.

Livvie came back then and Lillian excused herself, saying that she had to hurry home and make supper for her family.

Beatrice told the rest of them to come to the dining-room table for a bite to eat. She had made apple salad, salmon sandwiches, hard-boiled eggs and cake.

As the Johnsons left later that evening, Carrie thanked Beatrice for the nice afternoon and the delicious supper. Carrie burst out laughing on the way home every time she thought about the honeymooners. That night in bed, she and George talked and laughed about it some more.

About a month after Mr. Daud's funeral, Carrie received a letter from Hilde. It was full of news. She said that things were really moving fast around there. Mrs. Daud had been busy with her lawyers day and night. She decided to split up the farm into smaller parcels and sell them off. She would be moving into Casselton with her daughter and would spend her time between there and Chicago and Cincinnati, where her two sons lived.

Mr. Thompson and his family were given the section that included the farmstead for his long years of faithful service. However, Hilde had said, he didn't want to farm anymore so he planned to sell it and retire. His two sons had long gone to the city. Mr. Daud had paid for them to attend college and one became an engineer and the other was in business of some sort.

Hilde was given enough money to retire in style so she was planning to buy a house in Davenport. 'Just think, I'll have a house of my own for once!' she wrote. 'When I get settled, you must come and see me.'

The last piece of news was that Mrs. Daud wanted Carrie to have the piano! They were to come up and get it at their earliest convenience.

"Can you believe it, George?" Carrie said when he came in for lunch.

"That's really very generous of her," he said.

"Well, she was the most generous person I ever knew. It's no use to argue with her if she's made up her mind," Carrie remarked. "Won't Livvie be excited when she comes home from school and hears that we will be getting a piano at last!"

"I wonder," said George, "if they will have trouble finding buyers for all that land that the Dauds' owned. It seems no one has any money to be buying land nowadays."

The following Sunday, Carrie, George and Livvie took a drive over to visit with Alice and Tollof and to see their new baby. Alice was Lena's daughter and she had married Tollof Grant a couple years earlier and now they farmed north of Horace.

"Did you say that this baby was adopted, Ma?" asked Livvie on the way there.

"Yes, she was. They got her in August sometime."

"Why did they adopt her?"

"Well, I guess they thought they couldn't have a baby of their own." answered Carrie, always disliking any conversations with her daughter about adoption.

They spent a couple of hours with the Grants and baby Janet, and, over coffee, the conversation turned, as it always did these days, to the dry weather and the poor crop outlook.

"Gee Moses!" remarked Tollof, shaking his head. "When are we ever going to get some rain?"

"I hope we get a good soaking before freeze up now so that next spring we'll have plenty of moisture," said George.

"I can't stand all this wind and blowing dirt," added Alice. "There's hardly a decent day to hang the clothes out on the line!"

"It sure was exciting to hear that Gilla and Hank are going to have another baby!" exclaimed Carrie, changing the subject to a more happy one."

"Yes, she's due sometime later this month," replied Alice.

Alice and Tollof had already heard the story of Gladys and Jesse being mistaken for gangsters but they all had a good laugh anyway, just thinking about it again.

Tollof chuckled and shook his head. "Jiminy crickets, but that must have been a little scary!"

When the Johnsons were on their way home again, Livvie had this to say.

"I guess maybe it isn't so bad to be adopted. The baby looked very happy and healthy, didn't she?"

"Yes, of course, she did, Livvie," said Carrie, looking over at her husband who was driving.

"Wouldn't her real mother feel bad about giving her up?"

"I'm sure she did, but sometimes things just work out best that way." Carrie wished her daughter would quit asking so many questions but she was determined to answer them the best she could.

"I sure wouldn't give up my baby if I had one, though," Livvie said.

"Well, if circumstances were such that you ...ah...couldn't take care of it, maybe you would have to."

"What would those circumstances be?" Livvie persisted.

"Well, for instance, if you weren't married," Carrie said patiently. She could see that George was squirming in his seat.

"Well, why would God send a baby to a girl if she wasn't married?"

"Oh, Livvie, your questions are getting too difficult for me to answer!" said Carrie, finally losing her patience.

"Well, I want to know!" the child kept on.

"Livvie, when you get older, these things will be explained to you. Not now!"

Livvie realized that she would get no further with her mother at this time so she let it rest.

One day, late that fall, Freddie announced that he was planning to look for a job in town. "Now that the fall work is all done, I think I'll check on that job opening at the bank. There's an opening with Standard Oil, too, driving their fuel truck. With that, he finished his breakfast, grabbed his hat and took off for the shed to get the car.

Carrie looked at George. "What do you think of that?"

"Well, there's not any money in farming anymore so I guess that would be good if he could find something else."

When Freddie returned at noon, he was all excited. "The bank job sounds promising," he said. "I think the fact that I'd had some business school might work in my favor. I'll hear sometime next week."

In that day's mail, there came a letter from Mrs. Daud herself. She wanted to confirm that she did, indeed, want Carrie to have the piano and she suggested that they come soon and get it.

"Maybe we better plan on going tomorrow," suggested George. "Can you help, Freddie?"

"Yah, I can do that. Let's go right away in the morning, can we?"

The next morning, after Livvie was dropped off at school, George, Freddie and Carrie all squeezed in the truck cab and off they went, up to the Daud farm.

"Shall we surprise Amund and Edith and stop for a cup of coffee?" suggested George.

"Oh, let's do that," said Carrie. "Won't they be surprised to see us!"

They found Edith at home, but of course Amund was at the garage so the men went up there to see him. He closed up for a short while so they could all have a little visit at the house together.

"Do you need any help with that piano?" he asked, as the Johnsons were again in their truck and ready to leave.

"I'm sure there are still some men left on the farm to help us," George assured his brother-in-law.

Excitement mounted in Carrie as they drew near to the farm. "I remember the very first time I came here," she recalled. "Peter had picked Amund and me up at the train depot and drove us out here in the buggy. Why, it looked like a little town that we were coming to!" she exclaimed. "I was almost speechless when I first saw it."

George pulled up close to the front door, as he figured they would be taking the big object out that way. Carrie jumped out of the truck and hurried up the porch steps. Hilde opened the door for them and the two old friends embraced.

"Come in, come in," Hilde commanded. "We didn't know when you were coming but, as you can see, there isn't too much left in the house. The movers came from Casselton just a couple days ago and loaded up a lot of things."

Mrs. Daud came downstairs and greeted the Johnsons and told them to come into the kitchen and they'd all have a cup of coffee before the work began. "I'll have Corky round up a few other big men to help with the piano."

"We can't thank you enough, Mrs. Daud, for your generous gift!" Carrie told the older woman. "Our Livvie was so excited! She wants to start lessons right away."

"Well, I was trying to think who could use a piano and you came to mind. I figured your girl would be at the right age for lessons by now."

Corky and two big, burley men came in the back door and Mrs. Daud told them to sit down and have some coffee and doughnuts.

"Still making doughnuts then, Hilde?" asked Carrie, helping herself to a second one.

"Oh, my, yes," she laughed. "I'm wondering what I'm going to do with myself with no one to cook and bake for."

"Maybe you can bake things for the cafe in town," suggested Carrie. "When are you moving there? Have you found a house yet?"

"Oh, I've been waiting to tell you!" exclaimed Hilde. "I bought a house just yesterday and guess what? It's the little house that you lived in with Fred!"

"Oh, my! If that doesn't beat all!" Carrie exclaimed. "That house should be just right for you, Hilde!"

"Yah, that's all I need. Mrs. Daud was kind enough to give me enough furniture to fill it up. I'm going to have the carpenters fix it up some before I move in there. I'm getting a whole new kitchen! They can start next week. I hope to be in by Christmas."

"Oh, I'm so excited for you, Hilde," said Carrie. "I'll have to come and see you."

"Well, if we eat any more of these doughnuts, we won't be able to lift that big piano," remarked George. "We better get moving."

The five men moved the piano out on the porch and then, after laying some planks between the top step and the truck bed, they easily slid the big piece of furniture into the vehicle.

"Well, we better be going then," George said.

"Oh, thank you again, Mrs. Daud," Carrie said, and gave her a big hug. "Come and see us some time." The two women wiped tears from their eyes, knowing in their hearts that they wouldn't be likely to see much of each other again.

"Good luck on your move, Hilde. Write me and tell me how it's going," called Carrie from the window of the truck cab as they moved away from the house.

They arrived back home just before noon. "Who is going to help us unload the piano?" asked Carrie, concerned.

"Well, I could call Carl to come over after supper and maybe one or two of the other neighbors."

"Oh, it would have been nice to have had it in the house before Livvie comes home from school," suggested Carrie.

George rubbed his chin and thought awhile. "Maybe I can get together some men this afternoon."

About lunchtime, Carrie heard George and Freddie come into the yard and she looked out and saw two cars following them. Six men in all came walking up to the house. The truck was parked around by the front door. She hurried and opened the door and held it open. It didn't take long before the piano was rolling along the floor and into the dining room where Carrie had cleared a space for it.

Of course she had to offer the men some coffee and she was glad that she had just made a batch of molasses cookies the day before. They ate up every cookie and when she put more on the plate, they were gone in no time, too!

Livvie came bursting into the house just then and ran into the dining room. She squealed in delight, threw her coat down and sat herself down upon the piano stool. She ran her fingers lightly over the keys almost reverently. The men, who had helped do the moving, stood in the doorway, watching the girl.

"That's all the thanks we need for our effort," chuckled Mr. Iverson.

"Yah, it looks like we've made someone mighty happy!" exclaimed Mr. Graff.

All the men put their wraps on and left, one by one, with both Carrie and George calling their thanks after them.

"When can I start lessons, Ma?" asked Livvie.

"We'll look into it soon. I heard that Mrs. Rustad in Kindred is taking on new students so maybe I'll give her a call tomorrow."

"Why not tonight," cried Livvie. "Please!"

"Well, I suppose I could do that," laughed Carrie.

After supper, Livvie was very helpful with the dishes, trying to hurry her mother along. Finally Carrie went to the telephone on the wall and rang central. The operator asked whom she wanted to call and Carrie told her and soon Mrs. Rustad was on the line. Livvie was jumping up and down all during the conversation.

When Carrie hung up, she turned to her daughter and said that she could start this Saturday.

"Oh, goodie!" exclaimed the excited girl. "What time?"

"Your lessons will be at 10 o'clock every Saturday morning."

"How much does she charge for the lessons?" asked George from his favorite chair in the parlor.

"Twenty-five cents a lesson," answered Carrie. "That's pretty reasonable, don't you think?"

"I think it is," he said.

All that evening, they could hear Livvie playing with the piano keys. Sometimes the sounds they heard were not friendly to the ears but they just looked over at each other and smiled indulgently.

CHAPTER 28

The winter of '33-'34 provided some snow cover but the farmers were skeptical that it would be of much help. Nevertheless, in the spring, they planted their crops with the usual optimism.

On a fine Sunday in early May, Carl and Beatrice had a gathering at their home of some of the Ulness family. George and Carrie were invited, too. The men went out to watch a baseball game in progress and Carrie and the other women got caught up on all the latest family news.

Lorraine, Lena's granddaughter, who had graduated from high school the spring before, was there. Her mother, Alma, who had been suffering from TB for many years, had just died in March. Lorraine was now working at the Kindred Post Office.

Carrie noticed a deep sadness in the young woman's eyes. And, no wonder, thought Carrie. First her father left home, and hasn't been heard from since, and then her little sister died quite suddenly. And now, her mother had died of a long illness. The girl was practically alone in this world.

Hank and Gilla were there with their new little daughter, Gretchen. Hannah and Louis came with their three young boys and their 5-year-old little girl, Esther Lily. She was such a cute little girl, with long, blonde curls cascading down her back. Livvie loved playing with her so the two soon paired up and asked their mothers if they could go over to the Erickson place.

"I bet they're hoping they can play in the playhouse!" laughed Lena.

Randolph and Nora were unable to come as Nora was expecting a baby sometime that month.

"All these babies!" exclaimed Carrie. "They're just coming left and right!"

Lena just beamed with pride. Luella was asked when she was going to be married and she said she thought it would be awhile yet.

While the women talked of babies and marriages, the men were on their favorite subjects—weather, crops, baseball and cars!

It was soon time to assemble all the food that everyone had brought and it was a huge spread, indeed!

"Gee, Moses!" exclaimed Tollof. "Look at all that food!"

"We won't starve today, will we?" joked Hank.

"No, these wives of ours can really put on a meal, can't they?" Louis added.

All the children were fed at the kitchen table and the adults gathered around the big table in the dining room. Some of the men went out on the porch and sat on the steps.

Everyone seemed to linger, not wanting the pleasant day to end, but several families had to go home and do the evening milking, including the Johnson family.

On the way home, Carrie commented on what a pleasant day it had been.

"I suppose you got caught up on all the latest gossip!" chuckled George.

"We surely did!" answered Carrie. "And I'm not going to tell you any of it," she laughed.

"Ma, can I have a big birthday party this year?" asked Livvie from the back seat. "I haven't had one since I was nine."

"Well, we'll see, Livvie," her mother said. "Maybe we could."

When they reached the house, Livvie ran right to the piano and started practicing her next week's lesson.

"We sure don't have to tell her to practice, do we?"

Livvie got to have a party for her 12th birthday on June 5. Ten young girls arrived at the house, dressed in their finest and bearing gaily-wrapped gifts. Livvie had planned a variety of games, such as pin-the-tail-on-the-donkey, button-button, hot potato, hide the thimble, drop the handkerchief, and several more that they didn't get around to playing.

Birthday cake was served with sandwiches and cherry nectar. Then the long awaited gift opening. They spun the bottle to see whose gift Livvie would open next. She received many wonderful items. Carrie listened to the girls all "oooh" and "aaah" over every one as they were opened in turn.

Livvie received an autograph book, a hand mirror, some perfume, several flowered handkerchiefs, a porcelain figurine, a small booklet and some talcum powder.

Before the girls left, she had them sign her new autograph book.

"Now you can bring this to Parochial School next week and have Peter sign it!" teased Katherine.

"Oh, she doesn't like him anymore, didn't you know?" said another girl.

"She likes Johnny now, don't you, Livvie?" said another.

Livvie was stealing glances at her mother, hoping that she wasn't hearing all this.

That evening at supper, she told her father and brother all about her wonderful party. "Thank you, Ma. It was so much fun."

"Well, I figured that maybe this is the last little birthday party that you will have. You'll soon be getting too old for them."

The conversation turned to Freddie's job at the bank and the bleak outlook regarding the crops. The rains hadn't come as hoped, and the incessant dust and dirt kept blowing.

"Did you see in today's paper about the terrific dust storms down in Kansas and Oklahoma?" asked Freddie.

"Yes, I did!" exclaimed Carrie. "There was a picture showing actual sand drifts covering the fence posts. Can you imagine that!"

The summer continued hot and dry, with some of the worst windstorms yet seen in the area. About two weeks before harvest, on a particularly hot and muggy day, the sky became very dark late in the afternoon. Carrie had an eerie feeling that something was about to happen.

Freddie came home from work and George came in from the barn and was washing up when they looked out to see sheets of white coming down. They ran to the back door and were amazed to see huge hailstones hitting the ground and bouncing about three feet back up again!

"Oh, no!" exclaimed George. "This is all we need on an already questionable crop!"

The deluge lasted about ten minutes and after it subsided, they all went outside and picked up the large hailstones.

"Ma, they look like eggs!" exclaimed Livvie.

Carrie picked up several and had to agree with her daughter. What will this do to the grain that's still in the fields, she wondered? She looked over at her husband. George and Freddie both looked grim.

"Let's go and have a look then," George said to his son. They got into the old truck and headed out to the nearest field.

Livvie gathered up an apron full of the "eggs" and carried them to the house and put them into a large bowl. Carrie put the supper back into the oven to keep warm until the men returned.

About a half-hour later, Carrie heard the truck come into the yard so she took out the food and set it on the table. The men came in and soberly took their places. Carrie looked at her husband to lead the table prayer. She could see that he didn't feel like talking right then so she started the prayer herself.

The food was passed in silence. Finally Livvie asked the inevitable question. "How bad is it, Pa?"

"It looks bad," he answered, looking at Carrie.

Were those tears forming in his eyes, she wondered? She waited for him to say more.

"The north quarter is almost totally wiped out," Freddie told her. The barley doesn't look much better. The corn looks pretty sickly, too."

Carrie shook her head. What could she say? Another year's work all for nothing, she thought.

"I'm glad you have a job, son," George said, looking at Freddie. "There'll be no money in farming again this year."

As Carrie and Livvie cleared away the supper dishes, she thought that she had never seen George so "down" before. He always was so optimistic about everything. He was usually cheering her up. How can I cheer him up now when things look so bleak, she wondered?

The family gathered around the radio and listened to some of their favorite programs, but Carrie could tell that George wasn't really listening. Soon he got up and went into the kitchen. When Carrie went in there later, he was sitting at the table, pencil and paper at hand and was bent on some figuring.

She stood behind him and put her hands on his shoulders. So tense they were! She began rubbing them gently. After awhile, he reached up and took one of her hands and led her to the chair beside him.

"Well, I guess we'll get by, with some extra scrimping, that is." He tried to keep his tone light but Carrie knew how he was hurting.

"Tell me what I can do," she said. "Shall we start selling cream and eggs, do you suppose?"

"It seems that everybody is doing that so we'd have to probably bring it to Fargo and that takes money, too, for gas."

Later that night, when husband and wife were in their bed, Carrie could sense that George was lying there awake, only pretending to be asleep.

"Dear," Carrie said gently, "I know you're not sleeping yet. Turn around and look at me. Let's talk about this."

George turned to her and she put her arm around him. "Are you really worried?" she asked.

George lifted himself up on his elbow and gazed down at her. "We'll be all right. The biggest thing in our favor is that everything is paid for. We won't lose our land or machinery." He sat up and swung his legs over the side of the bed.

"I'm afraid that won't be the case with some of our neighbors. They stand to lose everything and I feel so badly for them. They still owe on their land, you know. My father made sure that our farm was paid for in just a few years. We sold our farm down in Iowa and applied it all to this farm here. I'm grateful now for his foresight."

The next few days, Carrie tried to think of new ways for them to save a little. "Do you think that we should tell Livvie that we can't afford to have her take piano lessons anymore?" she asked George.

"On, no, we won't have to do that. Things aren't that bad, Carrie!" He smiled at his wife. "We got the piano for nothing so we sure can afford to keep sending her to lessons. That doesn't amount to very much each month."

"Well, I was just trying to think of different things we could do, you know, to save a little bit here and there"

George put his arms around her. "My dear wife, you are so thrifty already that if you skimped any more, we'd have no meals on the table," he teased her.

At the end of November, there came a nice rain and there was a fairly good snow cover that winter. Another good snow came the first part of

April. George couldn't start seeding until the end of April and finished about three weeks later because of intermittent rains.

Optimism was running high among the farmers. Maybe this was the end of the drought cycle.

"Maybe we should take a little trip over to Spring Grove to see your family," George said one day.

This caught Carrie completely off guard but it didn't take her long to start getting excited about the prospect. "Do you think we can afford it?" she asked.

"Yes, I think we can afford that. We really should go down there. It's been a long time since you've seen everybody."

Livvie was very excited when she was told. Freddie said he'd take care of things at home.

Three days later they were on the road. "How long will it take us to get there, Pa?" asked Livvie.

"Seeing as how we got such a nice, early start, I think we should be there by supper time."

"Oh, that would be great!" exclaimed Carrie, who was just as excited as Livvie.

After an uneventful trip, with no flat tires and only two stops for gas, they pulled into the Amundson yard about a half-hour before the evening meal. They were welcomed heartily and before they knew it, were seated down to a big meal of Carrie's favorites.

"Oh, Ma, I haven't tasted klubb since I left home!" exclaimed Carrie, taking a big portion.

"My mother used to make this, too, and I rather liked it," commented George.

"What's klubb, anyway?" asked Livvie, turning her nose up at it.

"Well, I don't think I'll even tell you what it's made of," laughed Carrie, "then you for sure won't eat it!"

"I'll tell you what klubb is, Livvie," said her grandmother. "It's a blood sausage made of blood, potatoes, flour and some spices. It's then cooked in boiling water for 2 to3 hours. I usually serve it hot, sliced, with butter and simmered in milk."

Livvie made a gagging noise and the grownups all laughed.

"You don't know what's good," Mr. Amundson told his granddaughter.

For dessert, Mrs. Amundson brought out a pie and set it on the table.

"Oh, Ma, is this your good Juneberry pie?" asked Carrie.

"Yah, Mattie and I went and picked some berries last week. They aren't very easy to find, but Olaf told us he'd seen some bushes that looked like Juneberries over by the old Bemer place, in the woods."

After supper, Olaf and Mattie came over. Their daughter, Agnes, who was now 18 years old, came along. Their other daughter, Manda, was married and living over near Austin. Their only son, Burt, was living at home and helping Olaf with the farming.

It wasn't long before Sylvia and her husband, Rudy, came driving into the yard, too. Their children, Johnny and Esther, were both living and working in Decorah.

"My, all your family is pretty spread out, isn't it," remarked George.

"Yah, it isn't like the old days, when family stayed close to home," Mrs. Amundson replied, shaking her head slowly back and forth.

"And then we have Rosina and her husband living over at LaCrosse," Mr. Amundson chimed in.

At the mention of Rosina, Carrie's mother jumped up and went to the buffet and retrieved a picture and handed it to Carrie. "Did you get their latest family photo? We just got it the other day."

"No" said Carrie, examining the picture closely. "My, but doesn't Arlene look just like her father! Let's see, how old is she now, about ten?"

"Yah, and Ivonne is almost eight," replied Mrs. Amundson. "I think she looks like you, Carrie."

George took a closer look and said, "I believe you're right."

Livvie and her cousin, Agnes, had gone for a walk and the grown-ups were busy catching up on the past few years.

"What is Agnes going to do now that she's done with high school?" Carrie asked Mattie.

"She'd like to go into nurses training. She'll probably go to LaCrosse for that. Burt is engaged and will be getting married in the fall."

"Oh, I hadn't heard that," remarked Carrie. "How about Manda?"

"She'll probably be getting married soon, too. She has a steady fellow."

"Our family sure grew up fast, didn't it?" remarked Sylvia.

"Where did the time go, anyway?" laughed Carrie.

"How about Freddie?" asked Mattie. "He's getting about the marrying age, too, isn't he?"

"Well, he'll be twenty four in November already!" answered Carrie. "He doesn't have a special girl, yet, though."

"And Livvie," said Mattie. "She must be about twelve then."

"She just turned thirteen last month," said Carrie.

"She certainly is a very pretty girl," commented Sylvia.

"Does she know about…ah…the…adoption yet?" asked Carrie's mother.

"No. We thought we'd tell her when she's a little older."

"Well, I hope you don't have an experience like someone we know in town did with their son, who was adopted," said Sylvia.

"What happened?" asked Carrie, her heartbeat quickening. George's ears perked up, too, at this statement. He had been visiting with the men in the other corner of the room.

"He found out accidentally, from some kids at school, and when he confronted his parents about it, he was very angry because they hadn't told him earlier. He left home shortly after to try to find his real parents. They haven't heard from him since."

"How old was he?" asked Carrie, beginning to be filled with dread.

"He was going on fifteen," Sylvia said. "Too young to be out on his own. It's been several months now since he ran away."

"Well, we certainly have agonized about this situation. It's hard to know just what to do," said Carrie.

"Perhaps he'll soon be back," said Mrs. Amundson. "He'll find out just how nice he had it at home and that his parents really loved him."

"I should hope so," said Sylvia. "His mother is really broken up about it. She's a close friend of mine and it's been tough on them."

When the young girls came back from their walk, their grandmother started making coffee and setting the table with cake and cookies. It was about midnight when everyone left for their homes.

"It was so good to see you again," Sylvia said to Carrie and George. "Can you come for supper at our house tomorrow night? You, too, Olaf and Mattie."

After several days of visiting, talking and eating too much, the Johnson family left for home. On the way, Carrie remarked that it would have been fun to have gone up to see her dear, old friend, Pauline, up near Hudson.

"Well, that would extend our trip quite a bit," George told her. "Maybe next time."

As the family was heading for home, George observed that the fields along the way didn't look very good. "Just like back home," he said. "Too dry."

When they arrived in their farmyard, Freddie was out in the barn, doing the evening chores.

"You're not going to like the news I have for you, Pa."

"What is it?" asked George.

I was checking the field of wheat to the south here," he gestured, "and its showing signs of rust.

"Oh, no! Not that, too." George helped to unload the car and carry things into the house. He changed his clothes and accompanied Freddie out to have a look.

"You're right. It's rust! What else can go wrong with our crops," he wondered, and shook his head slowly. "This will really affect the yield. What with the drought and now this problem, we won't have much to combine here."

A month later, it was harvest time but, as George had predicted, there wasn't much to harvest. The wheat yield was very poor and the barley looked so bad that they just cut some of it with the mower and used it for hay. Some of it, they just plowed under.

"I sure was hoping to buy a new truck this year," George told Carrie one evening, "but I guess we'll get along with the old clunker for another year or two, anyway."

That fall, Livvie returned to school and she also started "reading for the minister," as it was called. She and the rest of the 8th and 9th graders from their church met once a week at the church for instruction from the Pastor. Unfortunately, the Gol minister, Rev. E. Ballestad, their long-time and beloved pastor, resigned in November of that year. Pastor Johnson from Kindred Lutheran came out and served the congregation until a new pastor could be called.

"Just think," said Carrie to Livvie one day, "this will be your last year in the Barrie School. Then you'll be going to high school in town. Time sure flies!"

The next few months flew by fast, too, and in May of the next year, it was Livvie's eighth grade graduation. The ceremony was held in the Walcott School, with several country schools in the surrounding townships taking part.

Livvie asked if she could have a new dress for the special occasion, so Carrie sent for one from the Sears catalog. Livvie had mostly been wearing dresses that Carrie sewed for her and she had even started doing some sewing herself.

Livvie was so excited the day that the package came in the mail. She tried the dress on right away and modeled it for her parents. It was a short-sleeved, pale yellow chiffon with a black velvet belt.

On the night of the ceremony, George beamed with pride as his daughter walked across the stage to receive her certificate. "She sure looks grown up, doesn't she?" he remarked to Carrie.

Carrie was thinking ahead, to the time when Livvie would graduate from high school. "Then we have to tell her our secret," Carrie mentioned to George later that evening, in the privacy of their own room. What will happen then, she wondered?

The rest of that summer, the summer of '36, turned out to be the hottest and driest any one could ever remember.

After a week straight of temperatures up way over 100, Carrie remarked that she didn't think she could take much more of it.

"It's so hot and miserable during the day and then it's too hot to sleep during the night. I'm just getting exhausted," she told Beatrice on the phone one day.

"Donnie's really been fussy, too, and Carl hasn't been feeling good lately. The doctor is coming out in the morning to check him over."

That night, the Johnson family actually took their mattresses out on the porch and slept there.

"That's the best night's sleep I've had in about two weeks," Carrie remarked.

At noon the next day, Carrie called over to the Ulness home and inquired after Carl. Beatrice was close to tears, Carrie could tell.

"The doctor says he has rheumatic fever and he'll have to stay in bed for many weeks," Beatrice told her.

"Oh, no! Let me know if there's anything I can do. If you need things from town, call us and we can get them for you."

When George came in to eat, Carrie told him of her conversation with her friend.

"That's too bad," George said. "That means Carl will be out of work for a long time then. What will they do for money, I wonder?"

"And here I complain about the heat!" exclaimed Carrie. "I should be ashamed of myself!"

"Well, this heat does take a toll on everybody. I think everyone is very edgy and fretful and just plain worn out! How much longer can it last, anyway?"

It lasted all summer and into the fall. The wheat that was harvested that year only brought ten bushels to the acre. "That's the worst wheat yield I've ever had!" George told his family one evening.

"More and more farmers are going under," Freddie commented. "There will be a rash of auction sales this fall and next spring, mark my words!"

"I'm sure at the bank there you realize just how tight things have become for many people," George remarked.

"Yes, and how desperate! I'm actually worried about what some people may actually do in this crisis."

One Sunday afternoon, George and Carrie went to Davenport to visit Hilde. She loved having them come but they didn't make it often enough to suit her. Carrie always thought it felt a little funny, coming into this house which she and Fred shared for those few years. Hilde had it fixed up real nice, however, and it looked entirely different now.

"I'm sure glad that hot summer is over, aren't you?" Hilde exclaimed. "I have a hard time with heat. I'll never know how I stood it all those years in that hot kitchen out at the farm!"

"What do you hear from Mrs. Daud?" Carrie asked her.

"I hear quite regularly. She likes writing letters, as you know. She's still in Casselton but will go to Chicago for Christmas and then on to Cincinnati."

"How about Corky? Do you hear anything about him?"

"I see him now and then. He helps out at the pool hall and also does some cleaning jobs around town. I have him over for a meal once in awhile."

"We felt bad to hear the hotel has closed here in town," said George.

"Yah, now we don't have any hotel at all. And to think that we once had two of them!"

"I'm afraid we'll see more and more businesses closing in the next year or two. These small towns just can't survive with the farmers all going broke," George commented.

"Yah, isn't it just terrible what is happening all over the country," remarked Hilde.

"Have you heard how things are going out on the farm? Who took over after Mr. Thompson left?"

"Well, he sold it to some business men from Fargo and they hired a manager to run things for them," Hilde told them. "The big house out there sits empty."

After a good visit, Carrie said that they better leave. "We want to stop by and see Amund and Edith for a little bit, too."

CHAPTER 29

In the mid to late thirties, there was much excitement about the possibility of getting electricity in the rural areas of America.

"It's sure taking awhile, though," George said to Carrie one evening as he put down the newspaper. "It was two years ago that Roosevelt created the Rural Electrification Association."

"Well, things like that take time," Carrie said. "I hope, though, that it won't be too much longer."

"It says here in the Tribune that work on constructing the lines should finally begin in the spring," George was reading.

The previous fall, there had been a meeting in Kindred to form a temporary REA organization. Max Strehlow was named chairman of the project.

"If anyone can get the job done, he can," George had said.

At that meeting, George was chosen as a committee member from his township to go around and secure signatures of those who would be using the electric energy. His job was finished and now everyone had to just wait.

"So where is this electric energy going to come from?" asked Carrie.

"It will be supplied by the Valley City Municipal Power Plant."

"That's a long way for it to come," she commented.

In January, a local member-owned cooperative was formed and named Cass County Electric Cooperative, Inc. Its headquarters would be in Kindred. Other counties would probably join the organization and many of the small towns would also be included. Kindred would not be serviced by this co-op as it already had its own power.

The only requirement to belong to this co-op was a $5 membership fee. The government was loaning money to the co-op in the form of a 20-year loan.

By mid-April, George had his crop planted and on the 24th of that month, a hard wind with rain and snow encompassed the area for about three days. The roads were so bad that there was no mail delivery for a time.

"I sure hope that this means an end to the drought," he told Carrie, as he had told her many times before.

In June, Livvie was confirmed with six other young people. The newly installed pastor, O.E. Engebretson, conducted the service.

"Another milestone in our daughter's life," mused George.

Freddie came home from work one day and announced, "I have a big date for the dance in town tomorrow night!"

"Who is the girl?" asked Carrie.

"You know her."

"Well, who is she?" asked Livvie, getting impatient.

"One of the Stevenson twins," he answered.

"Which one?" asked Carrie, getting rather impatient herself with this game Freddie was playing.

"The prettiest one!"

Livvie put her hands on her hips. "Freddie! They look exactly alike. Don't tell us then!" She pretended to walk away.

"Yes, they're identical but I tell Lenora that she's the prettiest."

"How can you tell them apart?" asked Livvie.

"Wouldn't you like to know, little sis!"

Livvie did walk away this time. When Freddie went outside, she returned to the kitchen to help her mother again.

"Isn't Freddie being a jerk?" she said.

"Oh, he just likes to have fun with us," Carrie said.

"Ma, can I go to the dance, too? I'm confirmed now and you always said that I had to wait to do those things until after I'm confirmed."

"Oh, Livvie, I don't want you to start going out just quite yet. You're still my little girl."

"Mother! I'm not a little girl anymore. I'd like to just go with a group of my friends and see what goes on. I wouldn't be going with a boy or anything like that."

"I don't think so, Livvie. Maybe next year."

"Ma, I'm fifteen now. Don't you think that I could start dating this summer?"

"We'll have to discuss this with your father later," Carrie said with finality.

Livvie wasn't allowed to go to the dance but neither were her closest friends either, so she didn't make too much of a fuss about it.

"It's going to be different raising a daughter this age, isn't it?" George mentioned to Carrie. "It will be hard not to be too strict, but I'm not ready for her to go out with boys yet."

On Sunday, the day after the dance, Freddie had to answer all Livvie's questions as the family sat around the dinner table.

"Did you have a good time? What did she wear? Do you like her?"

"Hey, all these questions!" he laughed. "Yes, I had a good time and yes, I like her and I think I'm going to marry her some day!"

"What?" cried Livvie. "How do you know that already?"

"I'm just teasing, Squirt."

"Don't call me 'Squirt,' you jerk!"

"Hey, no name calling in this house," their father reminded them.

"So did Oswald have a date, too?" asked Carrie, to change the subject.

"Not to begin with but he ended up taking Glenda Braaten home."

"Oh, really?" said Carrie.

"Yah, it was kind of funny," Freddie related. "Quite a few young fellows were hanging around her and Avery Anderson thought that he had the upper hand where she was concerned and then Ozzie steps in and makes his move. Before anyone knew what was happening, she was in his car and the other fellows wondered what happened."

Carrie and George laughed at this. They could just picture it.

"How come you never took Glenda out?" Livvie asked her brother. "She's so pretty, I think."

"Oh, she's pretty, all right. Lots of the guys think so, but I guess I just prefer blondes," Freddie answered in a teasing tone.

"How about Glenda's sister, Mildred?" Livvie persisted. "She's a real cute one, too."

"How come you're trying to pair me up with the Braaten sisters?" Freddie asked Livvie.

"Well, I like them and we know them," she reasoned.

"Just leave my love life to me, Sis!"

One evening, as Carrie sat mending on some work clothes, and George was settled in his favorite chair with the paper, he started reading aloud to her. "It says here, 'work will start within 30 days,'" referring to the electric line construction. " 'The actual time of getting started seems long but there has been a tremendous amount of preliminary work such as: securing the necessary number of energy users, mapping the entire route, preparing for the bids, securing easements, sighing up memberships.'"

"There sure is a lot involved in this electricity business, isn't there?"

"Fifteen hundred customers have signed up so far. Think of all those buildings that need wiring," George said.

"When are we going to get our wiring done?"

"Well, I've talked to Joe and he'll get here as soon as he can. He has a large crew working for him but it all takes a lot of time, you know."

"I heard in town today," he went on, "that the new co-op will be housed in the old Farmers and Merchants Bank building."

"Is that right? Well, that will be a good place for it," Carrie remarked. "By the way, I got a letter from Lena today. She's out in Wyoming now, staying with Gladys. She says she'll be staying the winter there."

"So where is it that Luella and her new husband ended up?"

"They moved out to Colorado. He found work there, but Lena doesn't say just what it is he's doing."

"I've heard of several people moving to Colorado. Perhaps there's some public works project that they're able to work on," George said.

In the August 26th issue of the Tribune, it stated that work had finally started on the REA lines.

"It's about time!" exclaimed Carrie.

"Your mother is really getting impatient to get hooked up so she can get some of those new appliances that we've been hearing so much about."

"You should see the big stack of poles alongside the railroad tracks in town," said Freddie. "I guess they come from Florida. Milt and I walked over there at noon today. There's crates of cross arms, brackets, and insulators. We saw the hole-drilling machine, too. You should just see it!"

"Maybe we'll have to take a drive into town tonight, Carrie, and see for ourselves," chuckled George.

George continued reading the article. "It says here that the foreman for the contracting company says the line will be up in 80 days. 'Work will be carried on day and night with three shifts of men at work.'"

"Just think of that!" said Carrie, shaking her head.

"The editor says here, 'the countryside is teeming with men and trucks, drills and wire-stringing crews.'" George put the paper down. "This is really something, isn't it?"

"Which appliances shall we buy first, Pa?" asked Livvie excitedly.

"Well, I guess we all have a wish list. Your mother wants a number of things for the kitchen. I want to get a water pump. What do you want?" he asked his daughter.

"Being I have to do the ironing most of the time, I'd like an iron."

"Yes, that would be nice," chimed in Carrie. "There are so many things we could buy if we had the money. I want a refrigerator and a kitchen range, someday."

"How about an electric radio?" asked Freddie.

"Our battery one works just fine for now. Eventually I can imagine that we'll have all these things. They will become so common as time goes by. You know," George continued reflectively, "this rural electrification will really change the way things are done around this area."

"Yes, and I hope it comes soon!" exclaimed Carrie. "Why don't we take a drive into town, George. Livvie, do you want to come along?"

Freddie's romance continued hot and heavy into the fall and at Thanksgiving time, he and Lenora announced that they were engaged.

"Oh, my!" exclaimed Carrie when she found out. "When will you get married?"

"Lenora wants a Valentine's Day wedding. What do you think of that?"

"So soon?" asked Carrie.

"Well, it's not soon enough for me but I guess I'll just have to wait another three months!"

Later that night, George said to Carrie, "Well, what do you think of that news then? Your first child, getting married."

"It came kind of sudden, but I do like Lenora a lot. She's a very lovely young woman and, after all, Freddie is twenty-six years old now!"

At Christmas time that year, Carrie and Livvie were delighted to open their gifts from George to find each had received an electrical appliance. Carrie received a toaster and Livvie got her iron.

When work on the lines was delayed in January due to inclement weather, both the women of the household became very impatient. They were ready to try out their new things.

After some stormy weather in early February, the 14th turned out to be a nice, sunny day. The wedding for Freddie and Lenora was held in the Kindred Lutheran Church at 4 o'clock in the afternoon. The bride's twin sister was her only attendant. Oswald stood up for Freddie. The flowers and decorations were all in red. A reception was held in the church basement and then the couple headed for Fargo to spend a couple days.

Joe Owen and his crew had finally been out to the Johnson farm and did all the necessary wiring in the house and outbuildings. Up until this time, they had had their own lighting plant and the house had been wired for that earlier. They needed to purchase a conversion kit to make the needed changes. Joe installed plug-ins in each room for any electric appliance they may decide to purchase. George had him wire his barn and two sheds, and even put up a yard light.

Freddie and Lenora had purchased a small house in Kindred and moved in right away. George and Carrie and Livvie came to see them after they had settled in. Carrie brought supper along.

"Oh, this is so nice of you, Mrs. Johnson, to bring us a meal all prepared!" Lenora planned to continue working at the Evingson's Store and had returned to work that day.

"So, Freddie," Carrie said, as they were eating the meal she had prepared, "Is Oswald still going with the Braaten girl?"

"As far as I know, he is."

"Maybe he'll be next to get married."

"Well, he told me that he was going to see how it worked out for me first," Freddie joked. He took his wife's hand and gave it a squeeze. "I'll have to tell him it's working out just fine." His new wife beamed up at him.

In June, Livvie had her long-awaited 16th birthday. "Now I can go to dances and date and all those things!" she announced to her parents.

George and Carrie just looked at each other wordlessly. "Yes, now you are quite the young lady," her father told her. She was wearing her auburn hair in a grown-up style and she looked very mature. "A very pretty young lady, I might add," he said. "I'll have to beat the young men back with a stick. They'll all be coming here in droves!"

"Oh Pa!" she exclaimed, rolling her eyes, "They'll do no such thing."

The very next Sunday, though, the first one came calling. His name was Charles Berg and he lived on a farm west of Kindred. It was someone that Livvie's parents hardly knew.

"So, you're from the farm, are you?" George grilled him. "And how old are you?"

"I'll be a senior in the fall, sir," he answered, nervously.

Livvie rescued him by saying that they were going to go out for a ride in Charles' car.

"Be back in an hour," George told them.

Livvie rolled her eyes again and looked up sweetly at Charles.

After they left the yard, George said, "Whew, this is going to be hard, having our daughter dating now."

"Just relax, dear," said Carrie. "Things will work out just fine." At least this is what she prayed for every night. She had prayed for Freddie and he found a nice young woman and seemed very happy. Now, for Livvie. And what about our secret, she wondered to herself. It will soon be time to tell her.

Carrie received a letter from Lena telling her that Luella and her husband, Phil, had just had a baby boy and named him Wayne. Gladys and Jesse had just adopted a little girl, named Sharon. She told George this news that evening.

"And when I called Beatrice this afternoon to tell her that I had heard from Lena, she told me the good news that she and Carl are going to have another baby, in November. Isn't that great?"

"Yah, that sure is. How do they like living in town, now?"

"Oh, Beatrice likes it just fine."

"I wonder who will be buying the big house by the river?"

"I guess they don't know yet."

Freddie and Lenora drove out later that afternoon and while Carrie was fixing supper for all of them, Freddie gave his wife a knowing look and told his mother to have a chair. "We have some news."

George's ears perked up and he came and sat down beside his wife.

"Oswald and Glenda are planning to get married in October," he announced.

While Carrie was happy to hear that, this wasn't the news that she was hoping to hear. When Freddie saw her crestfallen face, he laughed.

"Oh, and by the way, Lennie and I are going to have a baby!"

Carrie jumped up and exclaimed, "Oh, you teaser! I was hoping it was something like that!" She gave each of them a hug.

"When will it be?" she remembered to ask a few minutes later.

"The doctor says it will come about the middle of January."

"Oh, how exciting!" exclaimed Carrie, her face just glowing with joy.

"Are you feeling all right?" she asked her daughter-in-law.

"I'm just fine. I'm planning to work a couple more months."

One day at the end of summer, a man came out and installed the meter on their house for the expected electrical current.

"It shouldn't be much longer now!" he promised.

Harvest that year wasn't anything to brag about, but it was better than it had been in quite some years. George was optimistic about the future

"If the crop is good again next year, then I'll buy that new truck I've been needing."

In November, there was an electric appliance demonstration staged at the Kindred Auditorium. It was sponsored by the Cass County Electric Co-op and six different companies had displays, including three local dealers. George and Carrie attended and they found it to be helpful and interesting. It was explained how to best install and use the new appliances, especially the various motors. A Miss Miller gave a talk on lighting and also on cooking with electricity.

At noon the Kindred School band played a twenty-minute concert and in the afternoon, the Glee Club from the school sang several numbers. Livvie was a member of the latter group.

On the way home, Carrie said she thought that it had been a very informative day. George had to agree.

"Now, if only they'll get the juice flowing so we can try it all out!" he exclaimed.

The next week, they received a call from the electric co-op telling them that that evening at 9 o'clock, the power would be turned on in their area.

Carrie was so excited, and when Livvie came home from school, she couldn't wait to tell her.

"It's finally come!" exclaimed the young girl. "Will our rooms be much brighter now than with our old lights?" she asked.

"Father says it will be a lot brighter. He'll have to disconnect our own light plant now this evening."

After supper, George went down in the cellar where they kept their battery-powered light plant and began to disconnect the wires. He quickly installed the conversion kit as Livvie held a kerosene lamp so he could see.

"Now we wait," he announced, as he settled himself in his chair in the parlor. They kept the kerosene lamp burning.

"That sure doesn't give off much light, does it?" remarked Carrie. "This is all we had in the old days, though."

The clock chimed once at 8:30. Excitement was mounting. Livvie got up every few minutes and walked the floor. They kept an eye on the clock.

"Do you think it's really going to happen right at 9 o'clock, Pa?" she asked.

"Well, they said it would."

At a minute to nine, Carrie and Livvie got up and each went and stood by a different light switch. Carrie had her hand on the one in the parlor and Livvie had gone into the kitchen. George went and stood by the kitchen window. He wanted to see the yard light come on.

The clock rang out nine times. The three of them waited breathlessly. Finally George said, "Now!"

The two women flipped a switch each and instantly the rooms were filled with bright light.

"Oh, my!" was all Carrie could say. Livvie squealed with delight. George, looking out the window into the back yard, said, "Well, will you look at that!"

They all ran from room to room, flipping on switches and then they'd look out into the yard. It was an exciting night, indeed!

Carrie put two slices of thinly sliced bread into the toaster and waited. Livvie plugged in her iron and could feel it warming up almost instantly.

"Oh, I can hardly wait to iron tomorrow," she laughed. "You never thought you'd hear me say that, did you, Ma?"

Carrie laughed, too. "Come and see the toast. Let's get some jam and we'll have ourselves a snack!"

CHAPTER 30

Almost every day, the rural people found new uses for their electricity. One day, shortly before Christmas, George came home from town with a string of Christmas tree lights.

"Oh, can we put up our tree tonight and try these new lights?" asked Livvie excitedly.

"Maybe we'll do it on Sunday," said her mother. "Can you wait that long?"

Livvie took the lights out of their box and plugged them in the nearest plug-in. "Oh, look! They're bubbling!" she cried in delight.

Carrie had a suspicion that George was going to be giving her some appliance for Christmas but she wasn't sure just what. On Christmas Eve morning, she found out. A delivery truck pulled up to their back door and two men got out. It was Mr. Muller and a helper from the hardware store. George came hurrying from the barn.

He ran up to the house and told Carrie to go in the parlor and wait. Livvie watched as the three men struggled with a big object.

"Oh!" exclaimed Livvie and clamped her hand over her mouth.

"What is it, Livvie?" asked Carrie. "I can't wait!"

"You'll see," her daughter teased. "It's big and it's white."

"All right, Carrie. You can come into the kitchen now," called George.

There in the middle of the floor stood a refrigerator!

"Oh, my!" Carrie was speechless. Tears formed in her eyes. She looked at George and he was delighted at her response.

"Merry Christmas, dear."

"Won't that be wonderful? Oh, thank you! Will it fit in the spot where the old icebox is?"

"You bet," answered George confidently. "I measured."

The men moved the old one out and placed the new one in the exact same spot. It fit just perfectly. "Not an inch to spare," remarked Mr. Muller dryly.

Carrie admired her new appliance all day long. And just the week before, George had installed a water pump which pumped water up into her kitchen sink. All she had to do is turn on the faucet!

"Next, we'll get an electric water heater and then you can have hot, running water."

"We are sure getting modern, aren't we?" she laughed.

In January, right on schedule, Freddie and Lenora's baby arrived. It was a little girl and she was born in a hospital in Fargo. It would be two weeks before mother and baby could come home, so Carrie didn't know how she would be able to wait that long to see her first grandchild.

She passed the time by sewing some baby garments and diapers. The day after Freddie brought his new little family home, George, Carrie and Livvie drove to town to pay them a visit. Carrie brought a kettle of chicken soup and loaves of homemade bread for their supper.

As she cradled little Sandra Kay in her arms, tears began to roll down her cheek.

"Why, Ma, I thought you'd be happy about the baby," Freddie teased.

"It's just been so long since I've held a tiny infant in my arms."

George and Livvie took their turns holding her, too. Carrie opened her bundle of newly sewn baby things and gave them to Lenora.

"Oh, these will be just wonderful!" exclaimed her daughter-in-law. "Thank you so much! And thank you for the supper. You don't know how welcome that is!"

"Oh, yes, I think I do," laughed Carrie. "I remember how tired I was after the two boys were born."

"How about me?" queried Livvie.

Carrie hesitated and looked at George for a moment. "And you, too, of course."

After they left Freddie's, Carrie suggested that they stop in for a quick visit at Carl and Beatrice's and see their new baby. Carrie had seen him only once since he was born.

Beatrice was thrilled to see them. Carl was still at work. Donnie was quick to show off his new brother, who was sleeping in the bassinet.

"This is baby James," the 5-year-old told the visitors.

"What a beautiful baby!" Carrie exclaimed, meaning it sincerely. Beatrice beamed proudly.

A few days later, as George and Carrie were sitting in the parlor listening to the radio and reading the newspaper, Livvie came in and plunked herself down on the sofa. She was carrying a photo album.

"How come I don't look like either one of you?" she asked.

Carrie felt her heart stop for a few seconds. Is this it, Lord? I'm not ready for this yet. I thought we had another year before we would have to tell her. She looked over at George. He just cleared his throat and waited, not knowing what to say.

"What's the matter?" Livvie asked, looking from one parent to the other. When no one said anything, she asked, "Why are you acting so strange?"

Then all of a sudden, a realization hit her and she jumped up and stood before them. "I'm adopted, aren't I?" When they still didn't respond, she persisted. "I am, aren't I?"

She covered her face and began to cry softly. Carrie went to her and led her back to the sofa and put her arms around her.

"Livvie, we were always planning to tell you. We were waiting until you graduated and then we were going to do it. You don't know how hard this has been, keeping this a secret from you. There were so many times when we just didn't know what to do. When is the right time to tell a child that she is adopted?"

Livvie tried to stop crying and she looked up at her mother. "But you're the only mother I've ever known!"

Carrie hugged her again and now they were both crying. George stood and started pacing back and forth, running his hand through his hair.

"Do you want to hear all about it now, Livvie, or do you want to wait until you're not so upset?" Carrie asked.

"Tell me now," she answered, wiping at her eyes with a handkerchief that George had handed her.

Her parents explained, in length, how it had all come about. Livvie seemed to be handling it quite well. Then, feeling totally exhausted, the young girl excused herself and said she was going up to bed.

"I think I'll do the same," Carrie told her husband. He joined her and they talked quietly for some time before they fell into a troubled sleep.

The next morning, a Sunday, they talked some more before going down for breakfast.

"Well, it's almost a relief, isn't it?" remarked George. "How we've been dreading this task."

"Yes, I'm almost glad it's over but I wonder how she is going to take it. I imagine it is the shock of a lifetime."

They went downstairs quietly, and before long, Livvie joined them. She looked like she had also had a troubled night.

"How are you this morning, dear?" asked Carrie.

"I'm all right, I guess. I don't even know how I'm supposed to feel about all this."

"No, of course you wouldn't," said her mother, kindly.

"Does everyone else know? All my friends?"

"I don't know if your friends know. It depends on if their parents told them."

"Shall I...mention it to them?" Livvie asked, looking suddenly very young and vulnerable.

"Oh, Livvie, you don't have to, unless you want to. It would serve no good purpose, though.

"No, perhaps not," the girl agreed.

Livvie didn't talk very much about it for the next few weeks. Then, after school one day, she asked the question that Carrie knew would be coming next.

"Do you know what my...other mother's name is?"

"No, I don't know her name or much about her at all."

"Will I ever be able to find out who she is?"

After some hesitation, Carrie answered. "Yes, there is a way we can find out, if you really want to do that."

"How can we find out?" persisted Livvie.

"I can contact the...ah...lady who brought you to us, I think."

"Do you think that my...mother...would want to meet me?"

"I'm sure she would, but we would have to talk to this lady first. She was an aunt of...the young girl."

"When can we do it?" Livvie wondered.

"Well, I guess now is as good a time as ever. I'll try to reach this lady I told you about and then we'll see what develops."

The next morning, after George had taken Livvie into town for school, Carrie went to her bedroom. In the top drawer of her dresser, under the flowered paper lining, she found the folded piece of paper that she had put there so many years ago. How long had it been since that day when the two women had met unexpectedly in Leonard, she pondered.

The woman had asked her not to look at the note until it was time. Now was the time, so, with trembling fingers, Carrie slowly unfolded the old piece of paper. She stared down at the telephone number before her.

She went to the telephone and dialed central. She told the operator the number she sought. Then she waited. She had to pull up a chair to sit on, as her knees were growing weaker by the minute.

"Hello," said a voice on the other end of the line.

After the greeting was repeated, Carrie finally found her voice.

"This is Mrs. George Johnson." She paused for a moment. "From Kindred."

"Ah, yes," said woman. "So it is time."

"Yes, we told her. Now she wants to meet her real mother."

"I knew this day would be soon coming. I knew she would be eighteen soon and that you would possibly be telling her then."

"It came about a little sooner than we expected, but now it's over. Where do we go from here?"

"I will talk to my niece this afternoon and get back to you. I'll call you tomorrow morning. Is that all right?"

"Yes. That will be fine." Carrie hung up and continued to sit there. George came in just then and she told him what she had just done.

He sighed and sat by the table. Carrie got up and poured two cups of coffee. Her hands were trembling, she noticed.

"This will be a very ...difficult time for Livvie," Carrie said.

George just nodded his head in agreement.

"She's going to call here tomorrow." She told George the name of the mystery woman, which had finally been revealed. "Have you ever heard that name before?"

"Well, the last name is familiar, but there probably are many of them out that way. I think my mother knew someone by that name once upon a time."

The next morning, Carrie was nervous, waiting for the telephone to ring. When it finally did, she jumped and her heart started beating faster. It was the call she'd been waiting for.

When Livvie returned from school that afternoon, Carrie told her that she had talked to the aunt of her real mother.

"She asked if we could meet her on Saturday afternoon. We're to park outside the Leonard bank at 2 o'clock and she will then take us out to the farm where....your mother lives."

For the remainder of that week, Livvie was unusually quiet and subdued. Carrie asked her if she was nervous about the upcoming meeting.

"Yes, I guess I am," she replied. "I won't know what to say to her."

"She'll be very nervous, too, I'm sure," Carrie assured her.

On Saturday, shortly after dinner, George, Carrie and Livvie started for the town of Leonard. It was a nice spring day and the roads were good for travelling. No one spoke much, as they each were thinking their own thoughts.

They arrived in town early so they found a place in front of the bank and sat and waited. About twenty minutes later, they saw a big, black car drive by and turn around and come back. It parked across the street. A woman got out and walked over to the Johnson's car. George rolled down his window and the woman peered in at them. Her eyes rested on Livvie. The young girl stared back.

"Well, then, I guess we can go. You can follow my car."

George nodded and started the engine and waited for the black auto to start out. They followed for quite some time, changing directions now and then. The black car slowed down by a grove of trees and turned in. George followed. They came into a nicely kept farmyard and parked in front of a big, square white house.

The Johnson family was reluctant to get out of the car. The woman came over and tapped on the window and indicated for them to follow. They all arrived at the porch steps and the woman turned and smiled at them.

"I'm sure everyone is very nervous, especially Livvie here. I know my niece is also very apprehensive about today. Just try to relax and everything will be all right"

The front door opened and a young woman nodded at all of them and held the door for them to enter. When Livvie slipped by her, she had an intake of breath as their eyes met. The young woman smiled.

Mrs. Kintyre, the aunt, led them all into the parlor and told them to have a seat. Carrie and Livvie took the sofa and George found a chair nearby. The young woman and her aunt sat across from them. There was an uncomfortable silence for a few moments.

Mrs. Kintyre cleared her throat and began. "Livvie, my dear girl, I know that this is an extremely difficult day for you, as it is for my niece here. In fact, I think that we should leave the two of you alone here for awhile. My niece wants to tell you everything and I'm sure you have many questions."

Livvie looked at Carrie for a moment with pleading in her eyes. Then she straightened in her chair. "All right," she answered.

Mrs. Kintyre rose and Carrie and George followed suit. They left the room and went into the kitchen and the older woman indicated that they should take a seat by the table. She went to the stove and poured three cups of coffee.

Carrie was so nervous, wondering what Livvie was going through, that she could hardly hold her cup still. George noticed and reached out and covered her hand with his.

The older woman sighed. "This is a day that we knew would come eventually, but now that it's here, it does seem a little strange." She smiled reassuringly.

"My niece…her name is Meredith, by the way…has been waiting for this day for many years. She didn't want to give up her baby, but…her parents insisted, to save the family from scandal, you see."

Carrie nodded, understanding the situation.

"Her husband knows about Livvie," Mrs. Kintyre went on. "He knew before they were married. However, Merrie's parents…we call her

Merrie...don't know about this meeting and would be appalled if they knew that their daughter was meeting the child she gave up."

Taking a sip of her coffee, the older woman sighed again. "You see, Merrie's father is my brother and he's a very stubborn and harsh man. I took pity on the girl when she found herself to be in....ah...trouble...and I tried to help her the best I could."

Carrie, despite the lump in her throat, said, "I thank you for that and for arranging this meeting today. I think that this is something Livvie needed to do, once she found out she was adopted. I guess if it were me," she continued, "I would have to know who my real mother was."

After about an hour, Livvie and Merrie came into the kitchen and joined the others. They both looked like they had been crying. Merrie refilled the coffee cups and served chocolate cake to go with it.

As Carrie looked back and forth between Livvie and Merrie, she could see a definite resemblance there. But those eyes. They belonged to someone else, Carrie thought.

George was the first to suggest that it was time to leave. He stood up and Mrs. Kintyre said that she would be leaving, also, so they could follow her back to the main road.

"That would be kind of you," he said. "I think I got kind of confused on the way here."

On the way home, Livvie was very quiet and Carrie didn't press her for details. She went to her room upon entering the house. She came down when called for supper, however, but was quiet throughout the meal.

As she and Carrie were doing the dishes, Livvie started telling her mother what had transpired.

"She was only seventeen when she had me, Ma," she began. That's about my age now! She said that my....father....was a young man who told her that he loved her and she thought she was in love with him. Then, he abruptly left the area and she never heard from him again. He didn't even know... about me." Livvie's eyes began to fill with tears.

"Her father was furious when he found out about her condition and he made her hide in the house from all outsiders. When I was born, Mrs. Kintyre took over. Merrie was sent to Fargo to attend school and she found work there and never came home more than once a year. She hated her father so much! He's still living but she rarely sees him. Her mother doesn't dare do anything that goes against her husband's wishes."

"Oh, how awful!" Carrie exclaimed.

"She has two small children, now. A boy and a girl. They were with their father this afternoon. I hope to meet them someday."

During the weeks and months that followed, Livvie was never the same happy-go-lucky girl that she had been. She was given to a certain moodiness at times. She turned seventeen in June and started her senior year of school that fall. She often stayed overnight at Freddie and Lenora's and watched the baby if the young couple had something going on.

Carrie, too, took many trips into town to see her little granddaughter.

"Ozzie and Glenda just had a baby girl this week," Freddie told Carrie one day late in November. "I tease him that he copies everything I do," chuckled Freddie. "First I get married and then he gets married. Then we have a baby girl and then he has a baby girl."

Carrie laughed. "What did they name her?"

"I believe it was Marilyn or something like that. He called us last night and he was pretty excited!"

"Where is it they're living now?"

"They live on a farm near Dwight, North Dakota. That's down by Wahpeton. Maybe some Sunday, before it gets to be a lot of snow, we'll take a drive down there."

"I think I'm going to look for a part time job over Christmas vacation," Livvie announced at the beginning of December. "And then maybe I can work Saturdays the rest of the school year. Lenora told me there was an opening at the Larson's store."

By the next week, she had the job and began working on a Saturday morning. That evening, George and Carrie drove in to buy the weekly groceries and they stopped in to see her. She admitted to being very tired. It had been a long first day! They waited until she got off work and they took her across the street to the drug store for some ice cream.

"Stan Murphy came in the store this evening," Livvie told her parents. He asked if he could give me a ride home but I told him you were already on your way in for me. He asked if he could come over tomorrow afternoon."

"Who's this Stan Murphy?" asked George, warily.

"He's the boy I met at Luther League over at St. John's Church last week. I told you about him." Turning to her mother, she added, I really like him and he's so nice."

George made a mental note to find out all about him come Sunday. They finished their ice cream and left for home.

On Sunday afternoon at exactly two o'clock, a car drove in the yard. Livvie had been watching out the window for the past half-hour. Now she went and sat down on the piano bench and started playing. When a knock sounded at the front door, Carrie went to answer it and she ushered in a very nervous young man.

"Livvie," she called, "your company is here."

Livvie introduced him to her parents and then George sat down in the living room with the young people.

"So, where do you live, Stan?" he asked.

"We live on a farm north of Warren, sir," he answered.

"And how old are you?"

"I'm soon twenty, sir." Anticipating the next question, he said, "I farm with my father and brothers. We own a section up there."

Seemingly satisfied for now, George excused himself and went into the kitchen and then out to the barn.

Stan seemed to relax and Livvie just laughed. "I think you passed the first test!"

Young Stan Murphy became a regular visitor at the Johnson home and George accepted him as a suitable boyfriend for Livvie. On some of his visits, he would find himself engaged in interesting conversations with Livvie's father on subjects ranging from farming to the war in Europe.

On May 25, 1940, Livvie graduated from high school with 26 other young people. A week later, she turned eighteen. She received a gift from her real mother.

"Oh, isn't this beautiful!" exclaimed Livvie.

The package had come in the mail the very morning of her birthday. It was a gold locket and on the back it was engraved," To Livvie, from M." It opened up and there was a place for two pictures. She put it on and wore it all the time. She couldn't tell anyone who it was really from. Some assumed it was from her mother, Carrie.

The crops that year were the best in many years and the prices were going up. George felt confident enough to go out and buy the new truck he had been waiting to get for so long. Actually, it wasn't a brand new one; it was a 1936 Chevy and in pretty good shape.

He came home with it one day and drove up to the back door and honked the horn. When Carrie came out to see what all the noise was about, he motioned for her to get in and he took her for a little spin.

"You're acting like a child with a new toy, George," she laughed, as he returned her to the yard a few minutes later. "Dinner will be ready in about ten minutes."

That evening, George was huddled by the radio, listening to a news commentator talk about the war overseas. He turned to Carrie with a grim look on his face. "Things don't sound too good, do they?"

"You don't think the United States will get involved in it, do you?"

"I don't know. Perhaps we'll have to."

German troops had rumbled into Poland the year before, and France and Britain immediately declared war on the invading nation. Then, this past spring, Norway and The Netherlands were the target.

In September, the United States' new draft law came into effect. The country was also busy building up its arsenal of airplanes and warships. The US was supplying war materials to Britain and Russia.

"I thought that after the last war we had, there wouldn't be any more," mentioned Carrie. "I don't remember much about that war, except that I was relieved when none of my brothers had to go."

"I was worried about getting drafted back then but my father wasn't well and I had to keep the farm going so I was spared."

George leaned back in his favorite chair and reflected for a long moment. "You know," he began, "we have it pretty good now, don't we? There were some tough years with the Depression and the drought and all, but we survived."

He rose and started pacing. "When we first got married, Carrie, I wanted to give you everything. And then times got so bad, we hardly had money for anything."

Carrie put down her sewing and looked at her husband. "I have always been so proud of the way you handled all that; the disappointing crops year after year, the low prices, the drought. You always kept your faith and your good humor."

"Well, I guess I can tell you now that I wasn't as strong as you think I was. There were many times when I went out in the barn to think and I would end up crying in frustration," George admitted.

"Then I'd pray my heart out and a calmness and peace would come over me. I could then return to the house with renewed faith and hope."

"Oh, George, dear," cried Carrie, "I didn't know. Why didn't you tell me?"

She rose and went to put her arms around her husband. He patted her back comfortingly.

"Well, like I said, we have it pretty good now," he said.

"Yes, we do," Carrie agreed. "Freddie is doing well and we have a beautiful grandchild and another on the way," reflected Carrie. "And it turned out all right with Livvie. Telling her about the adoption and all. She really took it quite well, don't you think?"

George nodded. "I was a little worried about her at first, but she's handling it just fine now. It couldn't have been easy for her, being so young and meeting her real mother and everything."

"I've always wondered if she has ever asked her real mother who her....real father is," Carrie remarked.

George shook his head back and forth slowly. "She'll probably never find out that."

A short time later, husband and wife climbed the stairs to their bedroom. As they knelt beside their bed for their evening prayers, they had many things for which they were thankful. Their love for each other and their God was uppermost.

CHAPTER 31

Livvie worked full time now at the Larson's Store in town. She continued to see the Murphy boy and the romance seemed to be getting serious. Freddie kept teasing her, asking when she was getting married.

Livvie's real mother made an effort to keep in contact with her daughter on occasion since their initial meeting a few years earlier. That summer, Livvie had met her half-brother and half-sister. The young children had not been told yet their true relation to Livvie. They thought she was just a family friend.

Just before Christmas, Stan surprised Livvie with a marriage proposal and a ring. When they hurried to tell George and Carrie, Livvie remarked that she wondered why he hadn't waited until Christmas.

"I bought the ring yesterday and I couldn't wait a whole week!" he told her.

Livvie's parents were a little taken aback by the announcement but were nevertheless happy for the young couple.

"But Livvie's so young," Carrie said to George later, when they were alone in their room.

"Yes, she is, but she's always been mature beyond her age. They'll be all right, dear," George assured his wife.

Livvie wanted a spring wedding so May 1 was chosen for the big day. They were married in the Gol Church on a beautiful Saturday afternoon. Livvie's real mother, Merrie, slipped in the door at the last minute and Livvie was standing with her father, ready to walk down the aisle.

"Oh!" Livvie exclaimed as she turned to see who the latecomer was.

Merrie approached the radiant bride and embraced her quickly. "Best wishes for much happiness, my dear," she murmured. Then she found her way up into the balcony to watch as her daughter got married.

A reception was held out at the Johnson farm following the ceremony. About 60 friends and neighbors were invited. Livvie was watching to see if her real mother would come. As the afternoon wore on and the guests began to leave, it was apparent that Merrie had decided against coming. She did, however, leave a gift at the church for the young couple.

Livvie and Stan opened their gifts that evening with the immediate family gathered about. When she opened the gift from her real mother, tears sprang to her eyes.

"Oh, how beautiful!" she exclaimed. She held up a large, lace bedspread. "I bet that she made this herself," announced Livvie. "I've seen some of her work at her house."

As Carrie held the lovely piece of work in her hands, she said, "I can only imagine the love that went into this gift."

"We'll put this on our bed and sleep under it every night," Livvie said, looking at her new husband.

He looked at her tenderly, knowing all about the circumstances of her adoption.

After a short honeymoon up in Winnipeg, the couple settled into their home on the Murphy farm. There was a small house next to the big house that had once been used by the hired men. After much painting and decorating, it looked very homey, indeed. Carrie had driven up several times to help her daughter get settled in.

One Saturday afternoon, George and Freddie drove the truck into the Murphy yard, bringing the piano for Livvie. She was very excited to get it and, although they really didn't have room for the big piece of furniture, the dining table was pushed over and room was found. Livvie sat down immediately and began to play a song from memory.

Carrie had received a letter early in the summer from Lena Ulness, saying that she was coming to North Dakota to spend some time with each of her children. She and Hannah came over to visit Carrie one afternoon.

"It's so nice to see you again!" Carrie told the older woman as they embraced. "I've missed you so much."

"Yah, it's good to be back here again. We drove over to our old house before coming here. It seems strange to have someone else living there now, but I had to sell it. Carl and Beatrice didn't want it. It's a big place and lots of work to keep it up."

"How long do you plan to stay up here?" George asked her when he came into the house to join the ladies for coffee.

"Well, I'll be going to Randolph's next, over in Walcott, and stay about a month. Then I'll go over to Alice and Tollof's for awhile, and then to Carl's and to Gilla's. I'll be at Carl's when Beatrice has her baby. I thought I could help out with the boys while she's in the hospital."

"Why, that will be nice for them," said Carrie.

"Then I'll be going back to Colorado for the winter. It's not so cold there, you know."

"Lena, have you ever heard anything at all from Alfred?" asked Carrie as they were finishing their lunch.

Lena shook her head sadly and tears formed in her eyes. "No, not a thing."

"Do you suppose something......bad...happened to him? Surely he wouldn't go this long without ever getting in contact with you."

"I wish I knew, I wish I knew," Lena answered, shaking her head back and forth sadly. "I've prayed about him so much, you just don't know."

Carrie was sorry now that she had brought this up. She changed the subject and was soon showing the women some pictures of Livvie's wedding.

"Oh, my!" said Lena. "Livvie certainly turned out to be a beautiful young woman, didn't she?"

"Well, we think so, of course. And we think a lot of Stan. He's such a fine, young man."

Carrie went on to tell Lena about Livvie's real mother and the circumstances surrounding that.

"Did you ever figure out how this aunt of hers found out that you and George were wanting a baby?"

"Well, yes, we think we did," Carrie began to explain. "It turns out that George's mother knew this Mrs. Kintyre many years ago and she had run into her at some doings, over by where her daughter lives, and they got to talking. She must have mentioned that George and I had married and that we were wanting a baby very badly. One thing led to another."

"Isn't that something!" exclaimed Hannah.

"It all ended well then, didn't it," remarked Lena.

"Yes, Livvie handled it pretty good and now she's happily married."

"Do you think she'll ever know who her real father is?" asked Hannah.

"I don't suppose she will ever know that," Carrie said. "Unless her mother chooses to reveal that to her someday."

"I guess it would serve no purpose," said Lena. "Especially if he's left the area completely."

On the third of July, Freddie and Lenora's second baby was born. It was a boy this time. George and Carrie drove to Fargo to the hospital to visit mother and baby.

Freddie was there and was all smiles. "We thought we'd name him Lawrence Frederick. How does that sound, Ma?"

"That would be a very nice name, I think," she answered her son, looking at him with understanding. He was naming his son after his own real father, who had died so many years ago.

When they were allowed in to see Lenora, Carrie said to her, "You were so big that I thought you were going to have twins!"

"Well, the doctor thinks that I was carrying twins, at first, but then I lost one early in the pregnancy," Lenora said sadly.

Freddie, always the optimist, said, "Well, let's be happy for the fine baby we do have!" He took his wife's hand and she smiled up at him.

"Yes, we have two wonderful children now."

The warm, lazy summer of '41 shifted into fall with ease. George harvested an average crop, the corn being especially good. They heard from Livvie every week, sometimes by postcard and other times by a long-distance phone call.

The first week in October, she called George and Carrie and invited them to come for Sunday dinner. She sounded excited and a little mysterious.

When the day came, they attended church first and then headed north to Livvie and Stan's. As they entered the small home, the aroma of oven-fried chicken met them. Livvie had always been an adequate cook but she had really blossomed after her marriage. She served three kinds of vegetables from her own garden and a delicious apple pie for dessert.

"This pie is very good, Livvie," praised her father.

"The apples are from the old apple tree in back of the big house. The recipe is from Stan's mother."

"You always were good at rolling out crusts, Livvie, even as a child," Carrie remarked. "Some women never get the hang of it."

"You were a good teacher, Ma," said Livvie.

"Did we tell you that Beatrice had her baby a couple weeks ago?" Carrie told her daughter.

"No. What did she have?"

"They had a girl this time. Carl was very excited!"

"I'm sure he was! What did they name her?"

"Elaine JoAnn," Carrie said. "Beatrice said that she named her after an old school chum, someone she roomed with at teacher's college."

"Oh, that's a nice thing to do," Livvie remarked.

She then looked at her husband and said, "I think it's time we told them, don't you think?"

Stan lifted his coffee cup and raised it in Livvie's direction. "We have some wonderful news to share with you." He cleared his throat. "You are going to be grandparents again!"

"Oh, Livvie!" exclaimed Carrie, looking at her daughter. "How wonderful!"

"Yes, isn't it? We're so excited. We couldn't wait any longer to tell you."

"When is this going to happen?" asked George.

"About the middle of May, the doctor said," answered Livvie.

When the discussion of babies subsided, Livvie looked at her husband again. "We have some more news, too. Stan and his father and brothers have bought some land west of here and we may be moving onto it."

"How far away?" asked Carrie, with dread creeping into her voice.

"Oh, not very far away," laughed Livvie. "We'll go for a ride after we get the dinner dishes done and you can see for yourself."

Livvie wouldn't say any more on the subject as the two women hurried through the dishes. Stan brought their car around and the four of them hopped in. Stan headed north a couple miles and then west, on the road leading to the old Daud farm. They pulled into the yard and Carrie could see that much had changed since she had worked there.

The big, old barn had been torn down and some of the outbuildings, the large bunkhouse included. The towering elevator still stood, however, like a sentinel on the prairie.

"My, how this has changed," Carrie remarked. She thought that they had just stopped here to see the old place before going on.

When they didn't move, George looked at Stan questionably. Stan and Livvie both burst out laughing.

"This is it!" Livvie blurted out.

"What do you mean, 'this is it,'" Carrie remarked dryly.

"We've bought these two quarters here," Stan explained, "and Livvie and I may move here."

"You mean, live in the big, old house?" asked Carrie.

"No," answered Livvie. "That's too big for us and it's in major disrepair."

"Well, then what? Are you going to build a new house?" asked George.

"Not right away. We thought we'd live in the Thompson house for a time, while the big house is torn down," Stan explained to them. "We'll save the lumber from that and build a new, smaller house someday"

"Not too far in the future, I hope," said Livvie, looking at her husband.

"Well, this is certainly a surprise!" commented Carrie.

"Lots of surprises today," laughed George. "Do you have any more up your sleeve?"

"I don't think so," chuckled Stan. Little did he know that the biggest surprise for Carrie was yet to come.

"Ma, do you want to go have a look in the big house?" asked Livvie.

"Sure, that would be fun."

Stan said to George, "Let's have a look around the place, shall we?"

So as the men took off towards the few remaining buildings, Carrie and her daughter climbed the once-familiar steps to the front porch. Carrie paused here and remembered fondly the day when the wicker settee was delivered.

"We spent many hours on this porch, I tell you!" Carrie said. "Pauline and I and Manny, too, and several others."

Livvie opened the front door, which was unlocked, and led the way into the front parlor. There was nothing left but some empty wood crates. Carrie walked into the dining hall. It looked much bigger than she remembered, now that it stood empty, also. Next she went into the kitchen. The two, black kitchen ranges remained, standing side by side, like guardians of an era past.

"I can almost smell Hilde's doughnuts!" She explored every cupboard and walked into the pantry. An old coffee bean crate was all that was left.

"Do you want to go upstairs?" asked Livvie.

"No, I don't think that is necessary." Sighing, she said, "Isn't it too bad that this magnificent, old house has been left to just get run down."

She walked again into the front parlor. "This was always my favorite room. The big piano was here and there were two big fern plants by the bay window. She looked into the hall to the stairway. Pointing, she said, "That was always kept so polished and gleaming. I remember walking down that stairway in my wedding dress to meet my first husband."

Livvie didn't interrupt her mother's nostalgia. "The minister stood in front of the fireplace there."

"And Hilde was your maid of honor, wasn't she?"

"Yes. Dear, old Hilde." Carrie sighed again. "We should stop in and see her today on our way home." She walked to the window and stood looking out.

"Ma, I have something else to tell you. I got a letter from my real mother...Merrie...the other day. She finally told me who my real father is."

Carrie turned to look at her daughter and waited.

Livvie took a letter from her pocket. As she unfolded it she said, "He was some Canadian with a strange name. Here it is. Alphonse Kastet," she read.

That name jolted Carrie to the core. She could only stare speechless at her daughter. Livvie went on. "She says that he was a farm hand who went from farm to farm in this area."

Livvie looked up and saw her mother's strange expression. "Ma, are you all right?"

"I...I just need to sit down someplace. I don't feel so good all of a sudden."

Livvie led her to an empty crate and knelt down beside her. Carrie looked into her daughter's eyes. *Those eyes! That's where I've seen those eyes before! I always knew there was something about them that seemed so familiar.*

Instinctively, Livvie asked, "Mother, did you know him?"

Carrie didn't know just how to answer her daughter. She paused a little too long.

"You did, didn't you? Was he here? Did he work on this farm?"

"Yes, he...ah...worked here for a short time while I was here."

"What was he like?" the young woman asked earnestly. "Did you know him very well?"

"I...guess I didn't know him...as well as I thought I did," Carrie faltered.

"Uncle Amund knew him too, then?" Livvie pressed.

"Yes, he worked with him."

"I wonder where he is now and if he would like to know about me," Livvie mused.

Carrie stood and went to her daughter. "Livvie, my dear, from what I know of your...ah...real father...I don't think that he would be very happy to hear from you."

"How do you know that?"

"Well, he...ah...wasn't the type of man who would want to know that he had a child from a past...indiscretion."

"Indiscretion? Is that what I was?" wailed Livvie

"To him, yes, you probably would be."

"How can you say that if you hardly knew him?"

"I don't know, Livvie, I just have a feeling about him, that that's the type of man he is." Carrie paused. "He was considered a ladies' man back then."

Livvie broke down in sobs. Carrie tried to comfort her. "I'm just telling you the truth, Livvie. Maybe I should have tried to shield you from it, but then you would have had false hope about him."

"I'm sorry, Ma. I'm kind of emotional these days and then when this letter came, I just thought maybe I could get to know him someday."

"I don't think you should count on it, dear. Let it rest for now."

Livvie wiped her tears and composed herself just as the men came in the back door.

"Is supper ready?" George called, jokingly. He and Stan walked into the parlor, laughing, and found the two women. They both stopped short.

"Is something the matter?" asked Stan, looking at his wife anxiously.

"Ah, no, we were just talking... about things...in the past."

"Yes, it's too bad about the house being in such bad shape," said George, thinking that the women were lamenting the condition of the house. "I guess it was too much house for anyone to move into and keep up."

"Actually the Thompson's house is in better condition than this one is," remarked Stan. "I think we'll be very comfortable in there for a few years. Till our own house gets ready." He came and took his wife's hand.

"We thought we'd build it on the same spot as this house, facing the east like this."

"That will be very nice," remarked Carrie, recovering her composure.

"Do you want to walk around outside at all, dear?" George asked Carrie.

"No. Actually I'd really like to be going home. I...I'm feeling very tired all of a sudden."

"All right," said Stan. "We'll take you back to our place and you can get your car."

When they were in the Murphy yard, Livvie asked, "Are you sure you don't want to come in for a cup of coffee before you go?"

"No," Carrie answered quickly. "I think we should leave for home right away."

A few minutes later, as they were heading south on the Kindred road, George said, "All right, what's the matter? Something's wrong, I can tell."

"Oh, George, I never can fool you, can I?" Carrie half smiled.

"What were you two talking about in the house?"

"Livvie has found out who her real father is."

George was silent. Carrie went on. "And it's someone I...ah...used to know. He worked on the farm when I was there."

It was some time before George could say anything. "Why did that upset you? Who is this man?"

Instead of answering, Carrie looked down at her hands and twisted her wedding ring absentmindedly.

"Carrie?" George said, rather sharply. "Are you going to tell me? If you know something about the...real father...of my daughter, I'd like to know about it."

"He worked on the farm for a short time one summer. I think it was the second summer I was there. He was very handsome. I was attracted to him. He seemed to like me, too." Here she paused for quite sometime.

"And?" asked George, urging her to go on.

"He...we... went on a buggy ride one Sunday afternoon."

George looked at is wife, almost dreading what he was going to hear next.

"He tried to take advantage of me but I pushed him away. He tore my dress and when we got back to the farm, Mrs. Daud saw me come into the house. She wanted to know what happened. I told her and the next morning, Mr. Kastet was gone."

George let out a sigh, relieved to hear that nothing compromising had happened to Carrie.

"So, his name was Kastet."

"Yes, Alphonse Kastet. He was from somewhere in Canada."

"Where did he go after he left the Daud farm?"

"I don't know, but some years later, he evidently worked on a farm west of here someplace. There he met Livvie's... mother."

"And then he disappeared."

"Yes, the scoundrel!" Carrie said this with loathing in her voice. "Amund said that he was known around the farm there as a cad and a ladies' man. He had tried to warn me. I learned my lesson, but it almost had a tragic ending."

When George and Carrie arrived home, Carrie went right up to their room and changed into something more comfortable and then, feeling very tired, she lay down on their bed.

About a half-hour later, she awoke with a start and realized that she had fallen asleep when she only meant to rest for a few minutes. She hurried downstairs and found George sitting in his chair with the Sunday paper.

"I'm sorry. I guess I fell asleep."

"That's nothing to be sorry about."

"I just felt...so worn out, after this afternoon. Too many surprises."

"Yes, this day was full of surprises, that's for sure."

"Remember that I always remarked that Livvie's eyes reminded me of someone?"

George just looked at her. "Don't tell me. I can guess. They are his eyes."

"Yes! The moment she said his name, I thought of that, and then I knew."

Carrie was deep in thought for awhile. "You know, it seems awfully strange to think that my daughter's real father is the very man that I almost got involved with. Why, I could have married him and then I would have been Livvie's...real mother!"

George came and sat by his wife on the sofa. He took her hand. It was trembling. "Why, you are really shook by all this, aren't you?"

"I guess I am. The more I think about it, the more it's sinking in!"

"Well, there's nothing to be done about it now. Let's just let it rest."

"You are so good for me, George Johnson!" Carrie turned and gave him a warm embrace.

Carrie rose. "I'll fix us a little bit of supper. How about some egg-salad sandwiches and an apple?"

"Sounds good to me."

"He called me his Bonanza Belle." Carrie blurted this out as the two of them were finishing their light meal.

"Who? What?" George was puzzled as to her meaning.

"Alphonse. He called me his Bonanza Belle."

"And I guess that was a very fitting name," George teased.

"Why do you say that?" she asked.

"Well, he most certainly meant it as a compliment."

"I don't know. Sometimes it didn't sound as if he meant it in a complimentary way."

Several days later, Freddie called to tell his mother some news. "Remember, Ma, I told you that Ozzie and his wife always copy everything we do? Well, they just had a baby and guess what! It was a boy, too!"

"Oh, how nice for them." She laughed at her son's attempt to pretend that he was miffed. He really was delighted for his best friend.

"Have they picked out a name yet?"

"Yah, they have. They named him Orlan Rodney."

"Well, I've never heard that name before but I think it's nice," Carrie said.

That year at Thanksgiving, Carrie had all her loved ones gathered around her table. Freddie and Lenora were there with their two little ones. The new baby was sleeping peacefully and little Sandra was sitting in Livvie's old high chair, banging her spoon loudly. Amund and Edith were there, too, with their grown children.

Livvie and Stan were telling about their move over to the old Thompson house on the Daud farm.

"We don't want to put too much work into fixing it up as it's only temporary but it does really need some painting."

"Now Livvie," warned Carrie, "you get out of the house when the men start painting. That smell won't be good for you in your condition."

"I'll do that gladly, Ma!" laughed Livvie.

"You know, things have really come full circle, haven't they?" mused Carrie, as they were all enjoying their coffee. "I started out on that farm and now my daughter will be living on it."

"Yes, and now Livvie will be the Bonanza Belle!" George winked at Carrie.

As November came to a close, George took the calendar down from the wall one evening after supper. He flipped to the new month that would be starting the next day. "December 1941," he remarked. "Soon the end of another year. I wonder what the next year will bring?"

"Only God knows," sighed Carrie.

"I guess that's for the best."